Jackie Kabler was born in  her childhood in Ireland. She w_____nd then a television news _____ars, spending nearly a decade on GMTV followed by stints with ITN and BBC News. During that time, she covered major stories around the world including the Kosovo crisis, the impeachment of President Clinton, the Asian tsunami, famine in Ethiopia, the Soham murders and the disappearance of Madeleine McCann. Jackie now divides her time between crime writing and her job as a presenter on shopping channel QVC. She has a degree in zoology, runs long distances for fun and lives in Gloucestershire with her husband.

www.jackiekabler.com

 twitter.com/jackiekabler
 instagram.com/officialjackiekabler

Also by Jackie Kabler

THE VANISHING OF CLASS 3B

JACKIE KABLER

One More Chapter
a division of HarperCollins*Publishers*
1 London Bridge Street
London SE1 9GF
www.harpercollins.co.uk
HarperCollins*Publishers*
Macken House, 39/40 Mayor Street Upper,
Dublin 1, D01 C9W8
This paperback edition 2023
2
First published in Great Britain by
HarperCollins*Publishers* 2023
Copyright © Jackie Kabler 2023
Jackie Kabler asserts the moral right to
be identified as the author of this work
A catalogue record of this book is available from the British Library

ISBN: 978-0-00-854455-3

Printed and bound in the UK using 100% Renewable Electricity
by CPI Group (UK) Ltd

Chapter One

REYNOLD

Day 1: Friday, 9.45 a.m.

It's sunny the day the children vanish. It's been sunny for a week, one of those warm, dry spells you don't really expect in early April in the Cotswolds. The minibus is black, a sixteen-seater Mercedes with reclining leather seats, tinted windows and air conditioning; far too fancy, some might say, to take a group of over-excited seven- and eight-year-olds on a school day trip. *Some* might say, elsewhere, but nobody would say it here, because this is Littleford Primary, and here they do things differently. This bus hasn't been hired for the day, for a start; the school recently bought it, brand new, at a cost of over £70,000. Fundraising isn't an issue at Littleford. Not *every* parent is wealthy, but those with cash to spare are more than generous, and Reynold Lyon, who's leaning against the playground wall, pretending to be engrossed in a phone call, is probably the wealthiest and most generous of them all. Even today, off work and doing the school run, he's dressed head to toe in designer sportswear, classic black aviators hiding his tired eyes. His most recent donation of £30,000 paid for nearly half of the new minibus, but unfortunately even the fanciest of buses isn't immune from mechanical problems.

'Damn. There's a bloody red warning light!'

Year 2 teacher Erica Lindsay had spluttered the words and then immediately clapped her hand over her mouth, looking around guiltily to check if any of the children were within earshot. This had been forty-five minutes ago, Erica hopping into the driver's seat to start the engine while the three other staff members accompanying Class 3B on their day out attempted to round up their charges.

'What? Are you serious?'

Her teaching assistant, Dominic Moore, scurried over, peered at the dashboard and groaned.

'I'm no expert, but that's the coolant warning. That might mean a leak. How the hell did that happen?'

He swore softly under his breath, like Erica, glancing around as he did so. Reynold, who'd been listening with mild amusement, glad of the distraction, smiled to himself. He didn't mind swearing at all, but there was a little cluster of other parents in the playground waiting to wave their offspring goodbye, and he, like the teachers, knew not all of them would be as tolerant. He wondered, briefly, if he should go and offer to help, to see if he could work out what the problem with the bus was, and then immediately decided against it. He might have three expensive motors parked in the driveway of his home just down the road, but he really didn't have a clue about engines. He had people to worry about that

2

sort of thing for him. He had people to worry about almost everything for him.

Almost.

'Right. It'll need to go into the garage for a check, and we don't have time. Plan B,' he heard Dominic say decisively.

And so it is that three-quarters of an hour later, Reynold's seven-year-old twins, Luca and Lola, and their classmates, who've been burning off their excess energy rampaging around the playground, are finally climbing not into the black Mercedes but into a rather battered-looking white Ford Transit bus, complete with rusting wheel arches and an air-freshener in the shape of an Arsenal jersey swinging gently from the rear-view mirror. The replacement bus has been hired at short notice from village taxi driver Arnie – everyone knows Arnie, although nobody seems to know his last name – who drove it into the school playground a few minutes ago with a beep of his horn and a wide grin, clambering out of the driver's seat and greeting the stressed-looking teachers with a deep bow.

'Emergency bus ready to depart,' he said, handing over the keys.

'You're a life-saver, Arnie,' Erica replied, and Arnie dipped his head modestly, waved at the children and ambled off.

Reynold, still standing apart from the other parents, and still speaking animatedly to nobody on his phone, watches now as the children scramble for seats inside the bus, their delighted faces clearly showing *they* couldn't care less what vehicle they're being driven in, as long as it gets them to their destination. Lola, who's nabbed a window seat, taps urgently on the glass, trying to get his attention, and he smiles and blows her a kiss.

'Bye, baby,' he mouths, and she grins and waves. Reynold waits until he sees Luca safely seated too, in the row behind his sister, then glances over at the little knot of other adults swarming around the open side door of the bus. He knows them all of course, some better than others, but he's not in the mood for small talk right now, hence the ongoing fake phone call. He's the only dad here today; the others are all mums and a couple of female nannies, and he's been trying not to look over at them, trying not to catch her eye, but he can't help himself. He can't go over and speak to her, not when there are so many people here. But he needs... *something*. A look? A nod? *Something* so he knows everything is OK.

He stares at her from behind his dark glasses, still holding the silent phone to his ear, willing her to turn around. And moments later, as if she can read his thoughts, she does. Her head swivels, and she looks straight at him, for a second, two, three. She's wearing sunglasses too, so he can't see her expression, and his chest tightens. But then, almost imperceptibly, she nods, and a ghost of a smile plays across her lips. Reynold feels a wave of relief. He nods back, and she looks at him for another moment then turns away, resuming the conversation she's having with one of the other mothers.

He takes a deep breath.

Good. All is well, he thinks.

The teachers are climbing onto the bus, Erica Lindsay in the driving seat, and now the doors are being slammed shut, and the children are whooping and waving, and the adults in the playground are waving too.

'Have fun!' calls one.

'Behave yourselves!' shouts another. 'See you this evening!'

Reynold smiles again as Lola presses her nose to the window, squashing it against the glass and eyeing him comically. He gives her a thumbs-up sign as the bus begins to move slowly towards the school gates, then glances at the Rolex on his wrist. The trip had been due to commence at nine, but it's now nine forty-five, and he needs to get home, a little knot of anxiety twisting in his stomach as he thinks about how much he has to do today. He raises a hand vaguely in the direction of the group of mums and nannies, already beginning to disperse, then follows the bus out of the playground, stopping to watch as it comes momentarily to a halt to let a red Post Office van pass. Then its right indicator flashes, and the old white minibus with its precious cargo turns onto the winding street that leads through the centre of the village. Moments later, it disappears around a bend in the road.

Chapter Two

REYNOLD

Day 1: Friday, 9.50 a.m.

Reynold walks briskly down the street, phone tucked back into his pocket, the morning sun already warm on his face. He's lived in Littleford for three years now, but even in his current state of mind the picture-postcard beauty of the place still amazes him. Honey-coloured Cotswold stone houses, thatched roofs, mullioned windows, and even a gently babbling river with a bridge; when Reynold and his wife, Petra, decided they wanted to leave London for a quieter life in the Cotswolds before the twins started school, the house search had begun and very quickly ended right here.

'It's like something out of a fairy tale,' Petra had whispered, as the estate agent walked them through the gates of the £2.5 million house they now call home. 'And this house! It's perfect, Reynold.'

He had to agree. It was spectacular, all of it, and they made an offer on the property that same day. Littleford is small and quiet, but it's just six miles north of the pretty, bustling market town of Cirencester, and London is a mere two-hour drive away, the location perfect for their needs. While most of the ivy and wisteria-covered cottages date back to the sixteenth or seventeenth centuries, The Granary is only ten years old, a stunning, architect-designed three-storey home built around the shell of a former grain storage barn. Set a little back from the road at the southern end of the High Street, the house has a sweeping driveway lined with silver birch trees, a beautifully tended garden with a home gym and a swimming pool, and an interior like a glossy magazine spread come to life. Reynold's plan is to head straight to his study on the top floor but, as he closes the front door behind him and walks quickly across the flagstone-floored hall, he abruptly changes course, deciding to have a coffee first. He hasn't been sleeping well for the past week or so, and he needs the caffeine. In the kitchen, which looks out onto the terrace, he makes himself a double espresso and drinks it slowly, standing at the French windows and watching blue tits pecking at the bird feeder hanging from the old beech tree. It was Luca who insisted they start putting seed out, and Reynold quickly became glad he'd followed his animal-loving son's orders, finding it strangely therapeutic to stand and watch the birds coming and going. There are normally a couple of squirrels scampering around too, but the only creature on the lawn today is Brandon, the young local handyman who also helps out with a spot of gardening. He's an annoyingly handsome lad, and a bit of a DIY genius – Reynold's talents don't really stretch to using paint brushes or hammers – but today he's doing his bit to keep the outside space in perfect manicured order, kneeling on the grass next to a flower bed, a blue trug beside him. As Reynold watches, he turns, raises a hand and smiles, flashing even white teeth. Reynold waves back, then downs the last of his coffee and heads for his office.

A day off is never really a day off for him; today, if he can force himself to concentrate, he'll be working on the format for a new television game show. His main job for the past five years has been hosting the award-winning Netflix chat show *Wednesday With…*, an hour-long programme on which he interviews politicians, celebrities, or anyone else who's made the news that week. Reynold is fifty-five now, and this show is the biggest of his career to date, although he's been a household name on TV in the UK for years. But he's not just a front man; Reynold's also devised some of British television's biggest game shows, selling the formats to production companies and seeing a very nice return for his efforts. And this new one… he's got a feeling about it. There's nothing else out there quite like it, and he needs to focus today, needs to get it absolutely right before he starts thinking about pitching it. Friday is always his day for locking himself away in his office; Monday to Wednesday he's in London, planning and filming the show; Thursday is de-brief and re-group day; and he tries to keep Saturday and Sunday as family time. His wife, Petra, is twenty years his junior and a model, taking on fewer jobs now that's she's a mum but still in demand; she tends to work most Fridays, knowing that Reynold will be at home to do the school runs. They decided from the beginning to do parenthood without any full-time help; Reynold sometimes looks at his life with awe, astounded that in his fifties he's a father, a husband, happy. Happy *most* of the time anyway.

Now, though, as he sits down at his desk and turns his laptop on, he feels a twinge of guilt. More than a twinge; a wave, that crashes over him, making him feel nauseous.

If Petra knew…

He swallows hard, thinking back to the looks that were exchanged in the playground earlier as the children boarded the bus.

If only I could go back in time, change things…

He shakes his head, trying to banish the thoughts. It's too late now. What's done is done.

I'm sorry, Petra, he thinks. *I'm so, so sorry.*

There's a photo of her on his desk, one of his favourites from a campaign she fronted for a high-end jewellery range a few years back. She looks beautiful, auburn hair piled high on her head, her green eyes a perfect match to the emerald earrings she's wearing, her skin milky white against the chartreuse velvet of her dress. He looks at the picture sadly for a moment, then his gaze moves to the framed photograph next to it, a shot of the twins he took himself in the garden just after Christmas, when they'd all built a snowman together. Luca is standing, looping his arm around its shoulders, while Lola kneels beside it, both of them beaming, cheeks pink from the cold and the excitement. He runs a finger gently across the glass and feels a lump in his throat. He's only just dropped them off at school, and he misses them already.

'OK, stop it. You have things to do. Forget everything else for now,' he says out loud.

He stares at the photo for a few moments longer, then resolutely opens his laptop and gets to work.

Chapter Three

LITTLEFORD PRIMARY SCHOOL

Day 1: Friday, 12.05 p.m.

'I'm *so* annoyed about the bus. It's virtually brand new. I mean, *honestly*…'

Headteacher Olivia Chamberlain glares out of her office window at the offending vehicle, then turns back to school business manager Richard Cunningham who's hovering anxiously next to her desk.

'I know,' he says. 'And the garage is chock-a-block until Wednesday at the earliest, I'm afraid. Although I suppose we don't need it until after half-term now, do we? It'll probably be something minor anyway, considering the thing's barely been driven. And it's still under warranty of course, so it won't cost us anything to fix. I agree, most annoying though.'

Olivia sighs.

'Oh well. These things happen. At least the trip didn't have to be postponed. Thank goodness for Arnie. And for Dominic too, organising an alternative so quickly. All's well that ends well, I suppose.'

'Indeed. Right – better get on. Do you need a coffee or anything?'

'No, thank you. I'm fine.'

Richard bobs his head and scuttles out of the room, closing the door gently behind him. Olivia sighs again and checks her watch. The replacement bus had left the school just forty-five minutes late, but shortly after its departure Dominic had texted to say they'd hit traffic on the A429, which would further delay their arrival at the Cotswold Wilderness Park near Stratford-upon-Avon, which they'd originally been due to reach by around 10 a.m.

Won't be there until 11.30 earliest now. So unlikely to be back at school before 5.30, maybe a few minutes later as might hit traffic again on way back. Best to warn parents?

It's just after midday now, and Olivia knows she'd better not put it off any longer, especially on a Friday when people are bound to have plans. There are just ten children on the Class 3B trip; the year groups are divided into A and B streams for things like outings, and the kids were given a choice: science museum or wildlife park. There were more takers for science, so today it's a smaller than usual group, and as Luca and Lola Lyon are twins, that means just nine sets of parents to warn that the bus will be returning somewhat later than scheduled.

They'll probably have figured that out anyway, seeing as most of them were here when it left late, Olivia thinks, gratefully.

Littleford Primary is small, but it's mighty, she always says; she's been headteacher for twelve years now, and the school has only ever received an 'outstanding' rating from Ofsted, the government department which inspects educational establishments across the country once every four years or so. She's very proud of this; she intends it to continue, and while little blips like the one they're experiencing today aren't ideal, it's not the end of the world, she decides now.

She reaches for her phone, then notices a light dusting of rust-coloured powder on it, pollen fallen from the vase of flamboyant white lilies that's sitting on her desk. She opens her drawer, pulls out a tissue and carefully wipes it away.

Beautiful, but messy. A bit like the children, she thinks, with a wry smile, as she tosses the tissue into the wastepaper basket. Fresh flowers on her desk are one of her little indulgences. They make her office smell wonderful, like a florist shop, so different from the musty carpet and dusty book smell she still remembers so vividly from her visits to her own headteacher's office all those years ago. She admires the lilies for a moment, the graceful curve of their petals and their red-orange anthers, then turns back to her phone, scrolling down her list of message groups.

Class 3B. There it is.

She picks up her reading glasses, pops them on and begins to compose her apology.

Chapter Four

CLARE

Day 1: Friday, 4.50 p.m.

I n her small terraced home on a side road off the northern end of the High Street, Clare Tustain is banging around in her kitchen, throwing cutlery into drawers and slamming cupboard doors. After school drop-off, which of course left her running late thanks to the bloody bus debacle, she'd raced off to her job at a pet boarding kennels just outside Cirencester. She'd somehow managed to get there just fifteen minutes after her official start time, but it had been hard work trying to catch up. A dozen dog kennels plus the cattery to clean out, and then the exercising, and then her boss had asked her to sit on reception for an hour too, during which time she'd had to deal with *two* irate callers, both trying to book their dogs in for the Easter holidays and refusing to accept that they were already fully booked and, in fact, had been for at least two months.

'It's Good Friday *next* week, for goodness' sake,' she'd hissed at the phone as she ended the second call. What was wrong with people? Then she'd arrived home, still feeling stressed and flustered, to find that Nick had left a sink full of dirty breakfast dishes for her to deal with yet *again*, not even bothering to run water into the cereal bowls to stop the porridge congealing into cement-like lumps.

Fine, you have to get to work too, but would it kill you just to turn the buggering tap on? she thinks bitterly, as she finally finishes washing up and putting everything away, wishing for the millionth time that they could afford a dishwasher. Her hands are already raw from the disinfectants she uses at work; sometimes it's just too much to have to plunge them into hot water yet again as soon as she gets home. But as she reaches for the tub of lavender-scented hand cream that sits next to the sink and slathers some onto her sore, dry skin, she feels a little shiver of hope.

Maybe, one day soon…

Because things might be about to change. Her luck, her *life*. It's something she's been fantasising about for so long, and now…

Maybe. If we can just be brave enough…

She stands there daydreaming for a few moments, a smile playing on her lips, then sighs. There are things to do first. Things to organise. But right now, she needs to get the house tidied up before she has to head back to school. She checks the time. Nearly five. The head, Mrs Chamberlain, had messaged earlier to say that due to their later than expected departure, the class would be unlikely to return for pick-up before five-thirty.

OK. Half an hour to get this place shipshape, she thinks, as she heads into the living room, scooping up a pair of discarded pyjama bottoms from the hall floor as she goes. As she starts plumping cushions and picking toast crumbs from the carpet – why Nick insists on eating his breakfast on the sofa when there's a perfectly good table *and* a television in the kitchen, she's never understood – she wonders if they can stretch to fish and chips from the chippie down the road tonight. Then, she thinks about Reynold Lyon, and the vast sum of money he handed over to fund the stupid broken-down school bus.

Thousands. Just like that. What must it be like to have so much spare cash you can donate thousands to a school fundraiser, and not even think about it? When we have to think twice about whether we can afford a takeaway once a month?

Clare sighs again. She hates feeling like this; hates feeling bitter and frustrated and envious. She's just tired, that's all. She actually thinks Reynold's OK; she doesn't know him that well, but he's always friendly enough, and pretty down-to-earth considering how rich and famous and *foxy* he is. He and his wife, *the model*, do all the school runs themselves; they don't, as far as she knows, employ a nanny at all, and that's major brownie points, in her humble opinion. Some of the wealthier Littleford parents rely so heavily on nannies she sometimes wonders if their kids even recognise them when they come home in the evening. The Beckfords, for example. Eldon Beckford's a TV chef; he and his wife, Amy, run a chain of posh Caribbean restaurants, and their poor children have been practically raised by nannies from birth. Amy, amazingly, *was* in the gaggle of parents seeing the kids off on their trip this morning, but it was a rare sighting. She's usually *far* too busy and important to take her own son to school.

As she runs the vacuum cleaner around, picking up more of Nick's crumbs, Clare thinks about Reynold again, and wonders if *he* eats toast in the living room and leaves it for someone else to clean up. She bets he doesn't. He looked hot in the playground today, with that perfectly coiffed grey hair and those eyes the colour of chocolate mousse. So different to her Nick, with his shaggy brown hair – more mouse than mousse – and his scruffy plaid shirts.

Oh, stop it, you mean bitch.

She turns the vacuum cleaner off and shoves it into the cupboard under the stairs, feeling a little pang of guilt and shame. Nick does his best. And he loves her, and Stanley. Stanley, who was so excited to be heading off with his class this morning, the biggest smile on his cheeky little face as he climbed onto the minibus. Her beautiful, happy little boy. Clare feels a bit sick suddenly, as she often has recently when she thinks about Nick and Stanley.

Can I really do this? she whispers. *It's going to break Nick's heart…*

She swallows hard. She hasn't got time to think about it now. She checks the time again, then grabs her keys from the hall table and rushes out of the house.

Chapter Five

LITTLEFORD PRIMARY SCHOOL

Day 1: Friday, 5.58 p.m.

Olivia Chamberlain is pacing up and down her office, peering anxiously out of the window each time she passes it. There's now a little group of parents huddled together near the gate, but as for Arnie's rickety old minibus…

'Where the *heck* are you?' she mutters.

She stops pacing and stabs at her phone for the umpteenth time, once more dialling the numbers of each of the four staff members who are with Class 3B: Erica Lindsay, Dominic Moore, Cally Norman, Oscar Jones. Every number goes straight to voicemail. She's been trying to reach them since just after five, attempting to establish how far away they are and when precisely they expect to be back, but it's now two minutes to six and she hasn't been able to get hold of any of them.

Arnie and his old banger, she thinks crossly, her brow creased in a frown. *I bet that's broken down now, hasn't it? Somewhere between here and Stratford, with no phone signal. Dammit!*

Olivia glances out of the window again, pushing a strand of long grey-blonde hair off her forehead. Some of the parents are chatting, but others are looking towards the school building, as if expecting someone to appear with an explanation as to why they're still waiting. She groans. It had to happen sometime, she supposes; there are numerous educational day trips during the school year, and to date every outing has run like clockwork, discounting the occasional case of travel sickness and one visit to A&E, when a Year 2 boy tripped and cut his head on the sharp corner of a display cabinet at a museum two winters ago. She wonders now if the trouble with the Mercedes this morning was some sort of omen. Maybe she should have just postponed the trip until after Easter, instead of sending the children off in the rusty old Ford. But they would have been *so* disappointed, and Arnie's vehicles, while not always the prettiest to look at, are usually fairly reliable…

She sighs. She's alone in the building now; class finished for the week nearly three hours ago, and all the other staff and children have long gone. Richard hung around for a while, finishing off some admin and then sticking his head round her door at five o'clock to see if she wanted him to wait.

'I don't mind, but I do have a skittles match at the pub this evening and I wanted to go home and grab something to eat first,' he'd said hopefully, and she'd shooed him away.

'Go! They'll be back soon; I won't be here much longer myself. Enjoy your weekend,' she'd said, and he'd grinned, thanked her and headed off, wobbling out of the gate on his slightly-too-small red bicycle two minutes later. Now she wishes she'd asked him to hang on after all; she could have palmed this little job off on *him*. She's not relishing going out to tell the parents that their Friday evening plans are to be delayed even more than first thought, and she's rather keen to get home herself, a Waitrose curry and half a bottle of wine waiting in the fridge and a costume drama box set to finish. It's been a long week, and she's tired, and she really could have done without this this evening.

She checks the time again. Ten past six. She feels a prickle of unease. The Cotswold Wilderness Park closes at 4.30 p.m. this week – she's double-checked; the gates will have been closed an hour and a half ago. It's less than an hour's drive, maybe just over an hour at a push on a Friday evening, which was presumably why Dominic's text earlier had told her he expected they'd be back at 5.30 or just after. They really should be here by now, should have been back a *while* ago, and they should certainly be contactable. Assuming they've broken down in a poor signal area, then – because why else would none of them be answering their phones? – surely the first thing they'd have done would be to flag somebody down to ask them to call for help, or to knock on the door of the nearest house and ask to use the telephone? And then to call her, at the school, to let her know what's happening? They're four competent, experienced, trustworthy members of staff. So why has she heard *nothing*? She thinks about the route between here and the animal park. She's driven it many, many times herself – one of her best friends lives not far from Stratford. Has she ever hit an area of no or low mobile phone signal? She thinks about this for a minute.

No. I chatted to my mother on my hands-free for the entire journey up there a month or so ago, didn't I? It's fine. The signal on that road is fine, all the way. Good, even...

So it can't be that, after all. But why else would none of them be answering their mobiles? It's not as if she can even try calling the children. The younger ones – and Class 3B, all seven- and eight-year-olds, fall into that category – are not permitted to have phones at Littleford, and even the older children who *are* allowed to carry a phone for emergencies must have them switched off during school hours.

Oh... oh no!

A horrible thought occurs to her, and she shudders, as if someone's slowly caressing her body with an icy finger.

An accident. Have they had an accident? Come off the road somewhere? Is that what's happened? Maybe a wheel came off that old bus, or the engine blew up... Maybe they skidded into a ditch, or a field. Maybe they're out of sight of the other traffic, so nobody's even come to help them yet. Maybe they're all unconscious. Maybe... Oh God. Oh, GOD. Maybe... maybe some of them are DEAD...

Olivia gasps, her heart beginning to thud, her hand reaching for the edge of her desk for support. She gulps in some air, forcing herself to breathe deeply and slowly.

No. No, it can't be that, can it? Arnie wouldn't let the children go off in a dangerous vehicle. And Erica is such a careful driver...

'Get a grip, woman. It's only just after six. They're not *that* late. Not yet,' she tells herself out loud in her best, firm headteacher voice. She looks around her office, trying to ground herself: the gallery of children's artwork on the wall opposite her desk, the neat pile of paperwork in her in-tray, the embroidered cushions on the two comfortable chairs used by parents and other guests. Everything as it should be. Except...

not quite. Because this is *weird*. If they're OK, if they're just stuck in traffic and still on their way back, they'd be getting her calls, wouldn't they? Or at least some of them would be. They can't *all* have dead batteries. No, something's wrong. Something is *wrong*, she knows it.

TAP! TAP! TAP!

She jumps violently and whirls round. There's a face pressed against the glass of her office window, a young woman with a white-blonde bob and a pair of oversized black spectacles.

TAP! TAP!

It's Clare Tustain, mother of seven-year-old Stanley, spotting her now and peering in at her, one hand raised as she raps the window with her knuckles.

'Mrs Chamberlain? How much longer are the kids gonna be?' she shouts. 'We're getting fed up waiting out here!'

Olivia takes a step forward and forces a smile.

'I'll come out,' she mouths.

Clare frowns, then seems to understand and nods, backing away from the glass. Olivia casts one more despondent glance towards the school gate, hoping desperately to see the minibus miraculously appearing, but it doesn't, of course, and clearly she can't put this off any longer. She's going to have to tell the parents she currently has absolutely *no* idea where their children are, and this is *not* going to be fun. She takes a deep breath and heads for the door.

Chapter Six

LITTLEFORD PRIMARY SCHOOL

Day 1: Friday, 6.15 p.m.

'What on earth do you mean, you don't know where they are? How can you not know where they are?'

Reynold Lyon sounds exasperated, and Olivia doesn't blame him.

'Well, I've been calling them for over an hour, since around five, and I can't get hold of any of the staff on the bus. I'm sure everything's fine – it's probably just Friday night traffic – but I'm not quite sure why none of them are answering their phones...'

Her voice tails off as there's an outburst of questions and exclamations from the little group of parents.

'What? *None* of them?'

'This is ridiculous! We have dinner plans!'

'Have they had an accident or something? Have you called the police?'

The clamour stops as Clare Tustain's strident voice rings out above the rest.

'Well, have you?' she asks.

Olivia swallows.

'No. Not yet. I was hoping… but you're right, Mrs Tustain. I'm getting a little anxious too. I mean, they're only about forty-five minutes late so far. But the fact I can't reach any of them… it's starting to concern me. Maybe we *should*…'

She can feel a muscle in her face twitch as all the parents start talking at once again. Some of them are pulling out their phones, tapping, scrolling.

'The Live Traffic app says the road between here and Stratford is clear,' says one man. 'It can't be heavy traffic that's delaying them.'

'And nothing about any accidents on the police Twitter feeds,' says another.

'Well, it's probably just a breakdown then. Hang on – did the bus have a tracker?' asks Reynold. 'I mean, I know the new one has, obviously. But what about Arnie's old jalopy?'

'I–I don't know,' says Olivia hopelessly. The TV presenter is right – the Mercedes has a built-in tracker, enabling her to know, via an app on her phone, precisely where it is when it's away from school premises; she can view a record of exactly where it's been, what time it arrived there, even what speed it's been doing on the way. The technology, when it was explained to her, simultaneously astounded and deeply reassured Olivia. But now, of course, this wonderful high-tech vehicle is sitting here in its parking space at the side of the school, and the children and staff are God knows where in a creaky old bus which, according to Richard who'd popped out to the playground when it had arrived, still proudly boasts a *tape deck*.

There's no way it's going to have a tracker, is there?

'I'm ringing Arnie,' says one of the mothers, a frantic look on her face. The group falls silent, all heads turning to watch as she holds her phone to her ear. Her hand is trembling slightly, Olivia notes, and her own stomach begins to churn as the woman fills the taxi firm boss in on what's going on, stammering in her haste to make him understand.

'It doesn't? Oh, Christ, Arnie… OK. Yes, yes, I'm sure it is.'

She nods, listening, then says, 'Really? Oh, that's so good of you, thank you. Call us back as soon as you can, OK?'

The woman – it's Rosie Duggan, mother of seven-year-old Harper – ends the call and looks around, biting her lower lip.

'No tracker,' she says, her voice shaky. 'But Arnie says the bus might look a bit knackered but it's just been serviced and is running perfectly. He was quite indignant about us suggesting it might have broken down. Which is something, I suppose. Anyway, he's actually on a job on the A429 right now, and he has another driver just leaving Stratford. They're going to check the route for us, see if they can see them parked up anywhere. But he's also confirmed what we already know – traffic is pretty light this evening and there are no reports of any accidents. So he's as confused as we are.'

There's a moment of silence, then another mother says tentatively, 'Maybe one of the kids has been sick? They might have stopped at a garage or something to clean up?'

Olivia looks at her, her mind racing.

'That *could* have happened. But… well, one of the staff would have called me. They *know* they have to keep the school updated if there's any sort of problem or delay. Why are none of them picking up their phones?'

'Right.'

It's Clare Tustain again, a decisive look on her face.

'OK, well this has gone on long enough. We can't wait for Arnie. Mrs Chamberlain, I think you need to call the police. *Now.*'

Chapter Seven

Day 1: Friday, 7.05 p.m.

'Well, an entire bus load of kids and teachers can't just disappear, can it? They must be somewhere!'

Detective Superintendent Sadie Stewart knows she's sounding unprofessionally grumpy, and she takes a deep breath. The nearest police station to the school in question, Cirencester, had escalated the call to her in Cheltenham, and that wouldn't have happened if there wasn't genuine concern.

'OK,' she says, in a calmer voice. 'Where are we with this at the moment?'

Detective Chief Inspector Daniel Sharma gives her a quick summary: it's now an hour and a half after the bus's scheduled return time, and apparently the headteacher and parents awaiting the children's arrival home have gone into panic mode.

'It doesn't sound *that* late, on the face of it,' Daniel says, rubbing a hand across his neat goatee beard and frowning. 'But

26

it is a bit unusual. There's been no contact with the bus since this morning, when one of the teachers messaged to say they'd be back a bit later than planned because they had a late start and then hit traffic. Nothing since, no message to say they've diverted anywhere or anything like that. And it's Friday evening, isn't it? They need to get the kids back home so everyone can start their weekend. Traffic is light on the route, there have been no reports of any accidents, and the strangest thing is that now none of the staff are answering their phones, even though the signal is strong all the way. Two local taxi drivers have just driven the length of the route the bus would have taken and they've seen no sign of them either. They're not parked in a layby or anything like that. Fourteen people in total. That's ten kids from the school's Class 3B, and four adults. What do you think, boss?'

Sadie stares at him, thinking.

'No tracker on the vehicle?'

Daniel shakes his head.

'Nope. The school bus broke down this morning so they had to find a replacement at short notice, an old model. ANPR then?'

Sadie nods.

'Please. Actually, let's do it on the way. We'll get down there.'

She stands up abruptly, and Daniel, who's been perching on the edge of her desk, leaps off, bending to scoop up the jacket he dropped on the floor when he came into her office a few minutes ago. He makes the call as they head downstairs and out into the car park, Sadie leading the way, a knot forming in her stomach.

Only an hour and a half late, she thinks. *But still…*

She's learned, during her years in the force, to trust her gut, her sixth sense. And although her logical mind is telling her there's probably nothing to worry about here, her body is telling her otherwise.

OK, so there are lots of possibilities. But maybe none of them are good, she thinks, listening to Daniel giving the details of the missing bus to the person on the other end of the phone, and the knot in her stomach tightens as she manoeuvres the car out of its space and heads out of town. It's a half-hour drive to Littleford normally, but once she's on the dual carriageway she puts the blue lights and siren on, Daniel still on hold on the phone in the passenger seat. She sees, out of the corner of her eye, his free hand reaching out to the dashboard to steady himself as she puts her foot down, and despite her rising anxiety she allows herself a little smile. She loves driving with blues and twos – she enjoys the speed, the feeling of control, the way the powerful car responds to her touch. Just over twenty-two minutes later they've reached the outskirts of the village, a picturesque little place with a river flowing lazily past quaint stone cottages and ivy-covered pubs; as she slows down for the last half a mile, Daniel finally ends his call and turns to her.

'OK, so the ANPR cameras picked up the bus several times this morning, on the A429, the fastest route to the Cotswold Wilderness Park. And it was picked up again just before four-thirty, heading in the other direction, so presumably on its way back to Littleford. It would have been bang on schedule at that point. But… well, this is where it gets a bit strange' – he frowns, looking at the notebook resting on his thigh, the page covered in what looks, to Sadie, like a totally illegible scrawl, written at seventy-plus miles an hour – 'the sightings stop shortly after that. There's nothing further down the road at all. Which means, I assume…'

Sadie sees the turning for Littleford High Street up ahead and hits the brakes.

'That the bus took a diversion off the A-road somewhere not far from Stratford? Why would it do that?' she says, as she flicks the indicator on and turns right.

Daniel shrugs.

'I don't know. And that would have been, what? Three hours ago now? Where is it? Where did it go? Why no contact from anyone on it? I don't like this, boss.'

The knot is still there in Sadie's stomach, and now her mouth suddenly feels dry, her mind beginning to race. She had a conversation about ANPR, and its use as a crime-fighting tool, with her young nephew, Teddy, only last weekend; at just nine years of age, he's already decided he wants to be a police officer, and regularly bombards Aunt Sadie with questions, this time about Automatic Number Plate Recognition technology and how it all works. She'd carefully explained that there are around 13,000 cameras dotted throughout the country and even mounted on some police vehicles, constantly capturing and analysing vehicle number plates. She'd told him the cameras are used in the private sector too, in car parks for example, but that it's the police ANPR cameras, located on main roads and motorways, which are so useful in her job.

'We can cross-check the ANPR data against our own, on the Police National Computer, and that helps us track down people of interest,' she'd explained, as he stared up at her with his big brown eyes, taking it all in. 'People who might have committed crimes, I mean. It's very clever, and very helpful.'

Teddy's mum, Sadie's younger sister, had bustled in at that point, telling them that tea was ready, so she'd left it there, not wanting to overload him with too much information, and leaving out the fact that the ANPR system, good as it is, has its limitations, the biggest being that few rural roads have any cameras at all. A savvy criminal can make a pretty undetectable getaway by avoiding main thoroughfares, and in the Cotswolds there are so many little backroads, meandering through rolling countryside and tiny villages... but why would this bus leave the main road?

'There it is. The school. On your right,' says Daniel suddenly, and she nods, spotting the handsome gabled building and slowing the car. She turns in through the gate, passing a huddle of people who all turn to look at the police car with tight, fearful expressions.

Ten kids. This isn't good, she thinks. *They must have had some sort of accident, mustn't they? But why no report of one? Where are they? And now it's almost dark, which won't help one tiny bit...*

She switches the engine off and turns to Daniel.

'Right, I want background checks on all the teachers on that bus, just in case. And we need to get some cars out there. We need to comb those side roads near the last known sighting. If they've had an accident, it must be a bad one if none of the staff are contactable. I'm just finding it hard to understand why nothing's been reported yet, unless they've done some sort of spectacular dive into a lake or something. There aren't any big bodies of water in that area though, are there?'

He shakes his head.

'Don't think so. We probably need to put out a full county alert, see if anyone's seen them anywhere at all in the past few hours. I'll do that now… Uh-oh. Incoming…'

He nods at Sadie's window, and she turns to see an elegant-looking woman peering in at her.

'Any news?' she mouths.

'Here we go…' says Daniel quietly, and Sadie gives him a wry smile and climbs out of the car.

'Is there? Any news?' says the woman again. 'Sorry – good evening, officers. I'm Olivia Chamberlain, headteacher. We're getting extremely concerned now. I've lost count of the number of times I've tried to call my staff, and all their phones are still going straight to voicemail. Some of the parents are about to get in their cars to go and start looking themselves, but we just thought we'd wait for you to arrive first. I mean, it's nearly eight o'clock now, so something is clearly very wrong…'

She's talking so quickly her words are garbled, and now her voice cracks, and she stops speaking and swallows hard.

'Sorry,' she whispers. 'I'm just *so* worried…'

'I totally understand, and I'm sure everything's going to be fine, but you were right to call us. We're getting officers out there as we speak to search the area along the route.'

Sadie gestures at Daniel, who's still sitting in the car, chatting animatedly on the phone.

'And I'll need to get some more details from you about those on board. But it's probably best if you leave this to us, for now. I can totally understand the children's parents are very concerned, but I'd prefer it if they stayed here, or went home, maybe, just until—'

'What's going on? Has anyone got any information yet, for goodness' sake?'

A loud, shrill female voice makes Sadie turn sharply. A blonde woman wearing large black-framed glasses is standing right behind her, flanked by a dozen or so other men and women. Even in the gathering gloom of the playground, she can see that some of them look terrified, and she feels her chest tighten.

'I'm so sorry, no news yet, but I'm sure we'll track them down soon,' she says, in what she hopes is a reassuring tone. 'Ms…?'

'Tustain. Clare Tustain. Mrs,' says the woman tartly. 'My son, Stanley, is on the bus. This is getting ridiculous. I can't understand why nobody knows where they are.'

'It is, rather,' says a man. 'Ridiculous, I mean.'

The voice sounds familiar, and Sadie turns to look at the speaker. His face is familiar too – he's tall and extremely attractive, probably mid-fifties, with neat silver-grey hair swept back from a tanned forehead – but she can't place him.

Is he on TV, maybe? An actor?

She's not sure, and now he's being interrupted by another man, who's pushing through from the back of the group.

'Seriously, we need to get them home as soon as possible,' he says in a voice high-pitched with worry. 'My wife's at home going out of her mind. Sorry – Ben Townsend. My daughter's on the bus and my wife is distraught. If anything bad's happened… What's your best guess, officer? Do you think they've just broken down somewhere, or… well, I'm trying not to think the worst but…'

There's a cacophony of voices then, everyone suddenly

talking at once. The headteacher raises a hand in the air and says something Sadie can't hear above the commotion, clearly trying to quieten the parents like she would a class of noisy children, but it's not working, and she turns to Sadie with an expression of despair.

'Please,' she says. 'Please find them. Something is really wrong here. I just know it is.'

Sadie nods.

She's right, she thinks. *I feel it too. Something is seriously wrong. But what? Where the hell is Class 3B?*

Chapter Eight

BEN

Day 1: Friday, 8.10 p.m.

B en Townsend watches the police car move slowly out of the playground with a sense of rising panic. How is he going to tell his wife that now the police have been called in, and nobody seems to have any idea where the children are? Monique has been in a state of high anxiety all day; she was wandering aimlessly around the kitchen when he left for work this morning, fretting about how their daughter, Willow, was going to cope with a school day trip. She would cope just *fine*, as she always did, Ben had assured her, but it was no use. Monique was what he believed was known as a 'helicopter parent', always hovering and worrying. Actually, worrying was an understatement. His wife tended to work herself up into frenzies, which definitely made home life rather... *fraught*, at times. By the time he got back this afternoon – he always tried to finish early on a Friday – she was wandering aimlessly around the living room instead, constantly checking her watch and getting in a complete tizzy about the predicted slightly later return time of the school bus. In the end, in an effort to calm her down, he'd told her he'd just go down to Littleford Primary and wait, and made her pour herself a large glass of wine. He'd been greatly relieved when she agreed, but the relief had been short-lived, the continued non-appearance of the bus meaning he'd had to text her several times since to tell her the children were still yet to arrive, and he'd received increasingly hysterical replies.

'Christ, Clare,' he says now, turning to Clare Tustain. There's a chill in the air, the pleasant warmth of the afternoon melting away with the daylight, the sky above the playground soot-black and starless.

'She's worse than usual today. It's going to tip her over the edge if they don't get back soon. What in buggery's happened to them?'

Clare has just opened her mouth to reply when raised voices behind them make them both look round. It's Reynold Lyon, and that TV chef mate of his, Eldon Beckford. Ben doesn't know either of them very well, only that Monique turns into a simpering mess whenever they encounter them at school functions, but he knows *who* they are, of course. Everyone does.

'Well, if she thinks I'm going to go home and wait like a good little boy while my son is God knows where, she can think again,' Eldon is saying loudly. His voice is deep, normally with a pleasant sing-song Bajan accent, but now he sounds enraged, and when Reynold places a hand on his arm, he shrugs it off with an irritated jerk.

'Eldon… it does make sense…' he says, but Eldon shakes his head.

'Fine, you stay here. But I'm getting in the car and I'm going to look for them,' he growls. 'Anybody with me?'

'I'll come,' says one of other dads. Ben looks at Clare and hesitates. He's not panicking, not yet, but he wants to go too, to do something, to do *anything*. To do anything rather than go home to Monique right now, if he's being honest. The police officer, however, had been quite clear in her instructions before she left.

'Please,' she had said, 'go home. I need to know where you all are, for when we track down the bus. I'm quite sure everyone will be fine and that there's a rational explanation for why we're currently unable to get hold of them, but just in case… if half of you are haring around on country roads and in and out of mobile phone signal, it's just going to complicate things. Mrs Chamberlain has given me all the information I need, so I now have all your numbers, and I promise, I *promise*, you'll be informed as soon as we have any news, OK?'

'What do you think?' Ben says now.

Clare shivers. She's wearing a thin khaki jacket, not really warm enough for the time of year, and she pulls the zip up to the neck and rubs her hands together.

'I think we should do what the cop said,' she says. 'Go home, Ben. I'm sure they'll be fine. We'll be laughing about this tomorrow. They'll be back within the hour, I bet.'

There's a beep from her pocket, and she reaches into it and pulls out her phone, squinting at the screen.

'Nick. He's just got home from work and he's wondering

where we are. I'm going to run, Ben. Go and sort Monique out. It'll be OK. I'll see you soon.'

She reaches out and touches him gently on the arm, and he nods and gives her a small smile, then watches as she turns and walks briskly away, heading for the gate. Ben loiters for a minute longer, listening to the handful of other parents still bickering about whether they should go home as requested or form their own search party, and the entreaties of Olivia Chamberlain, who's attempting to get them all out of her playground, then makes up his mind and heads for his car.

When he pulls up outside their house ten minutes later, Monique is flinging the front door open before he's even switched his headlights off. She's quite drunk – he sees that immediately; her eyes have a glassy look and she's clearly spilled something down her blouse. His heart sinks.

'Darling…' he begins, but she's grabbing his arm and pushing him aside, peering behind him into the dark driveway and then, realising he's alone, staggering backwards and shrieking, 'Where is she? What's happened? Oh God, oh God, I knew it, I knew it…'

Ben closes the front door, sighing inwardly. Yes, he's worried too; of course he is. But there's going to be a simple explanation for all this, he's sure of it, and histrionics aren't going to help.

'It's OK. Everything's fine, silly. Don't worry…'

He takes his wife's hand and, still muttering soothingly, leads her into the lounge. But even as he tries to calmly explain what's happening, the thoughts that are always accompanied by a swirl of guilt deep in his stomach come creeping back into his head.

I'm so tired of this.

But I won't have to put up with it much longer, not if everything works out.

Nearly there now.

So. Nearly. There.

Chapter Nine

COTSWOLDS POLICE HEADQUARTERS

Day 2: Saturday, 4.57 a.m.

'So, in summary, we're looking for a 2009 white Ford Transit sixteen-seater, ten children and four adults. Nothing on the ANPR cameras since shortly after 4.30 p.m. yesterday. It's now' – DCI Daniel Sharma glances at the big clock on the back wall of the incident room – 'nearly 5 a.m. Zero contact from anyone on board since around ten o'clock yesterday morning when the Year 2 TA – that's teaching assistant, for the benefit of the child-free, by the way – the TA, Dominic Moore, sent a text to the headteacher to tell her they might be a bit late back. All the phones are still going straight to voicemail, so presumably somewhere without signal or switched off. We're trying to get a handle on exactly *when* they lost signal, and where they were at the time, but there's more than one service provider involved and at this time of night, or morning, or whatever it is… it'll be later today before we get any useful information.'

He runs a hand over his beard, looking around the room at the small group of assembled officers. Concern for the whereabouts of the bus has grown rapidly in the past few hours, all thoughts of sleep abandoned, and just after midnight DSU Stewart made the decision to call in a few bodies to be on standby at police HQ, just in case. The main work is still being carried out on the ground, numerous cars driving around the winding country roads all night, beginning in the area close to where the bus was last picked up on camera and then gradually widening the search. Stratford is actually in the Warwickshire police area, so they've been assisting too overnight, searching inside their county border. But so far, nothing. Daniel, who'd merely been puzzled by it all when the call first came in, is now starting to feel agitated and jittery, unable to sit or stand still for more than a few minutes. He tries to keep emotions out of the job, but he has two small children himself, and the very idea that they might be taken on a day trip and then simply not come home…

'This is really starting to piss me off now.'

His thoughts are interrupted by Sadie, who's been standing to his left as he gives his quick briefing. He turns to look at her.

'I mean, they must be *somewhere*,' she says. 'They can't have gone *that* far without pinging another camera. Why on earth can nobody find them? It's been *hours*. More than *twelve* hours now since the last sighting, for God's sake. And if it was an accident and they've come off the road, surely there'd be some visible evidence, even at night? Skid marks, broken fences, damaged vegetation; a sixteen-seater minibus isn't exactly small, is it? It's going to leave some trace. I can't get my head round it.'

'Same. It's just really, really strange. Do we know how the parents are holding up? They must be going out of their minds by now.'

'We've had several calls to the desk downstairs, demanding information,' says one of the detective sergeants. 'Apparently a few of the parents ignored your request and headed out to do their own search, boss. Not sure if they're still out there, but I guess we can't blame them. The others have been sitting at home all night, waiting. They're all in a class WhatsApp group so they're staying in touch with each other on that. It's been reiterated that as soon as we have anything to tell them, we'll be in touch, but I suppose we can understand how worried they must be.'

'Of course,' says Sadie. 'Thanks for the update, Anna. It must be a parent's worst nightmare. And with every hour that goes by... And you know what? There's something else that's occurred to me.... Just hang on a sec...'

She tucks a stray strand of dark hair behind her ear with a tut of irritation. The neat chignon she usually sports is looking considerably less perfect than usual, Daniel thinks, noticing too the dark shadows under her almost cat-like green eyes. It's been a long night; he knows he's not looking his best either, and now he's feeling a little queasy too, the greasy pepperoni pizza they called out for a few hours ago sitting heavily in his stomach. Sadie had nibbled on a single slice and then dropped it into the bin, saying she wasn't hungry, and he knows her well enough by now to recognise this as a sign that she's on edge, choosing instead to drink mug after mug of the strong black tea she prefers to coffee. Sadie doesn't have children of her own, but he can tell she still totally gets it. It's one of the things that makes her such a good copper – empathy. She understands it. The fear. The horror that something unspeakable might have happened.

Ten children. Ten, he keeps thinking.

Now he steps back out of Sadie's way as she moves towards the whiteboard they've begun to make notes on and stands there, staring at the list of names and frowning. He gives her a moment, taking the chance to pick up the coffee mug on the windowsill next to him and swallow a large gulp of the cooling over-brewed drink. The blinds are still open, and rain is drumming against the window, the car park three storeys below a sickly yellow in the light of the streetlamp directly opposite. He wonders if Class 3B is outside in the rain, or indoors somewhere safe and warm, then tells himself there's no point in speculating, and turns back to the room, with its stained green carpet and overbright strip lighting.

'What is it, boss?' he asks.

'These parents,' Sadie says. She's still staring at the names he wrote on the board earlier, basic details obtained from the headteacher at Littleford Primary. There are seventeen adults listed, eight couples and one single parent – two of the children are siblings; twins in fact – but they don't have much detail about any of these people yet. Daniel's hoping they won't need to, hoping that any minute now there'll be a call to say the bus has been found and everyone on it is fine, and they can all sigh with relief and go home to bed. He's pretty sure that's not going to happen though. He's starting to get a very bad feeling about this case.

'I mean, some of them are just… well, *ordinary*, for want of a better word,' Sadie is saying. She must have shrugged her dark-grey suit jacket off while he was looking out the window, and the pink blouse she's wearing looks crumpled, one half of the collar standing up, the other lying flat. He resists the urge to reach out a hand and smooth it down, and instead says, 'Yes, but not all. I noticed a couple of familiar names there. It's probably not that much of a surprise, not in that part of the Cotswolds, I guess. It's a wealthy community, in and around Littleford – some really big houses.'

She nods and turns to the room to make sure everyone else is listening, then taps the board with a slender forefinger.

'We've got Reynold Lyon, for a start. I thought I recognised his face at the school earlier, although I couldn't place him at the time. He's a TV presenter of course. Married to the model Petra Sanderson, well known in her own right. They're parents to the twins on the bus.'

She pauses, looking down the list of names, then taps the board again.

'Then there's Eldon Beckford. He's a famous chef. I think he's got a Michelin star or two, and he pops up on some of the TV cooking shows, doesn't he?'

'He was a judge on the last series of *Great British Menu*,' says a young detective constable, and Sadie nods.

'So, another high-profile guy. Married to Amy, who works with him at their restaurants, the head said. And then' – she runs her finger down the list – 'we have Spike Greer. Ex-footballer.'

'Played for Chelsea. Bit of a legend. I was quite excited to see his name. I didn't even know he lived around here,' says Daniel.

Sadie gives him a sideways glance and raises an eyebrow.

'Well, I'm very happy for you. Anyway, football isn't my thing but he's probably not strapped for cash, is he? Even in retirement.'

'I very much doubt it,' Daniel says. 'He's a regular pundit for the BBC, and that probably pays a decent whack.'

She nods.

'Do you get where I'm going with this? Please tell me it's not just me? *Three* sets of high-profile, wealthy parents?'

It's Daniel's turn to raise an eyebrow.

'Kidnap?'

It hadn't even occurred to him until now. A phone suddenly starts ringing at one of the desks, and he spins around, but Anna has already jumped up from her seat. He turns back to Sadie.

'Really? Do you think it could be?'

'I don't know,' she says. 'But it has to be a possibility, right? Especially if accident or breakdown is ruled out, as now seems increasingly likely? Although I'm confused about how they might have done it – an entire bus load of people? I just don't—'

'Boss!'

Anna is standing at a desk to their right, still clutching the phone.

'There's news. They've found it. The bus. Just in the last few minutes.'

There's a whoop from somebody, and a murmur of excitement runs around the room, but Anna is shaking her head, and Sadie holds up a hand.

'Anna, what is it? They've found the bus? Do you mean *just* the bus? Is it empty, then?'

Anna hesitates.

'Not quite,' she says.

Chapter Ten

ELDON

Day 2: Saturday, 5.20 a.m.

'I can't bear this much longer. Where *are* they, Eldon?'

Amy Beckford is huddled under a cream cashmere blanket on one of the big leather sofas in the lounge, her long, dark hair pulled back into a messy bun, her eyes bloodshot. She looks drained, wrung-out, but her hands are in constant motion, her fingers twisting and smoothing the fine wool of the blanket. Twist, smooth, twist, smooth. Eldon watches her for a few moments, not knowing what to say, then sinks down beside her.

'I don't know,' he whispers. 'I just don't know.'

He reaches for her right hand, and she lets him take it in his and squeeze it, before slipping it from his grasp and resuming her blanket twisting, tears running down her face.

'My baby,' she moans softly.

Eldon sinks his head into his hands. Their *actual* baby, two-year-old River, is, thankfully, sound asleep upstairs. It's eight-year-old Noah who's absent, their firstborn, their smiley, cheeky little scamp.

My mini-me, Eldon thinks, and a wave of nausea sweeps over him. For a moment he thinks he might actually throw up, right there on the hand-woven Turkish rug that Amy paid a fortune to ship in from Istanbul. He takes a deep breath, then another.

I'm just tired, that's all, he thinks. *Tired. And scared. So. Bloody. Scared.*

He's not even sure what time it is; he's lost track. Sometime after five, he assumes. He only got home a few minutes ago, after driving round the back roads in the dark for endless tortuous hours, seeing little of any interest other than police car after police car doing the same thing. No white minibus, no children. Reynold, who he's known for several years, had come with him in the end, despite his initial protests, and Eugene Pearson had come too. He doesn't know Eugene very well, but he's father to a sweet seven-year-old called Wanda, who he remembers clearly from Noah's last birthday party. They'd hired a bouncy castle for the back garden, and Wanda had somehow managed to bounce right off it, crashing onto the lawn with a sickening thud. As the head of every adult present had turned, all simultaneously imagining broken bones, ambulances and a ruined afternoon, Wanda had lain absolutely still for approximately three seconds and then abruptly sat up, smiled widely, announced that 'That was just like *flying*!', leapt to her feet and rejoined her friends. She's an only child, and tonight Eugene had been beside himself, sitting in the back of Eldon's Range Rover alternately wringing his hands and feverishly tapping the map on his phone, making increasingly panic-stricken suggestions about where they should look next.

'It doesn't make any *sense*,' he kept saying desperately, his voice cracking with emotion. 'They can't just *disappear*, for Christ's sake…'

In the passenger seat, in contrast, Reynold had been quiet and tense, repeatedly muttering that maybe this wasn't a good idea after all, and that they should go home and let the police do their job. Eldon had shaken his head, agreeing with Eugene that they must, they *had* to, carry on searching, but as the first pink streaks of dawn appeared, the blackness of the night sky softening to grey, he finally capitulated.

'We're all exhausted,' he said. 'We can go out again later, if we have to. And the police are all over it – at least we know that. It can't be much longer. They'll find them.'

He'd spoken the words calmly, soothingly almost, but as he turned the car round and headed back to Littleford, his stomach had rolled and his throat had ached, the fear that had been bubbling away just under the surface for the past few hours threatening to overwhelm him. As soon as he'd dropped Eugene off at his modest semi just outside the village and said goodbye to Reynold at the end of The Granary's driveway, he'd driven the few hundred yards to his own home at breakneck speed, tyres spinning on the gravel as he pulled up outside the front door. Then he'd sat there for a full five minutes, choking back tears and staring at the house, the thought that Noah wasn't inside it, safe in his bed, almost unbearable. Eldon loves this place, this home he and Amy have made for their two boys; The Post House dates back to 1600, one of the oldest buildings in the village, the enormous wooden beams in its sitting room taken from the ruins of a nearby abbey when Henry VIII ordered the dissolution of the monasteries in the 1500s. The house has an extraordinary sense of history, and yet at the same time works perfectly for his very modern family, the vast designer kitchen in what was once the telephone exchange for the village perfect for testing all his new recipes, the bedrooms looking out onto a beautiful courtyard garden.

How can we go on living here though, if something's happened to Noah?

The thought was horrific, and suddenly Eldon hadn't been able to sit still any longer, clambering from the car on unsteady legs, his hands trembling as he fumbled with his keys. Amy had called him a dozen or more times during the hours he'd been away, twice with a clearly unsettled River crying pitifully in the background, but he hadn't heard from her in over an hour by the time he let himself into the house, and he'd been wondering if she'd finally fallen asleep. She hadn't, of course; he'd found her exactly where she is now, frightened and shivery in her blanket nest, sobbing and picking up her phone every couple of minutes as yet another message popped up on the Class 3B parents' WhatsApp group. He normally kept his notifications switched off – he left that sort of thing to Amy – but she'd thrust the phone at him when he'd arrived home.

'It hasn't stopped, all night,' she said, her voice thick with tears. 'Everyone's just sitting up, waiting. What the hell's going on, Eldon? Why on earth can't the police find them?'

He'd scrolled quickly through the string of messages, pausing to read a handful of them properly.

PETRA SANDERSON: Just called the police station. Still nothing. I feel sick.

TASHA GREER: I called too. They told me dozens of officers are out searching. I'm so scared. Gresham hates being away from home at night, I can't bear it. What are we going to do? I can't get my head round it. Ben – are you online? How's Monique?

BEN TOWNSEND: I'm here. She's in a bad way, Tasha. Not coping very well. Trying my best to keep her calm.

CLARE TUSTAIN: Sorry to hear that, Ben. I feel sick too. But I don't think there's any point in calling the police, to be honest. When there's news, they'll tell us. That copper promised. If you can believe a cop's promise, of course…

Now, Eldon lifts his head from his hands and looks at his wife, but her eyes are closed, her breathing fast and shallow. She's not asleep though, her fingers still working at the blanket, and he wonders if he should try to have the conversation he now knows he needs to have with her, then immediately decides against it.

Let her rest, just for a few minutes.

He desperately wants to talk to her, though. He's not quite sure what's been going on with her lately; she's been a little distant with him for months now, but even more so in the past few days – they threw a party last weekend, and he drank too much, probably made a fool of himself being too loud, too over the top, as he often is when he's drunk. He doesn't remember, not really; the champagne and the rum were flowing, the music pumping, and the last few hours of the night are just a blur, but it's what he assumes, from the way Amy behaved the next morning – not meeting his eye, pulling away when he tried to slip an arm round her. She didn't say anything; she rarely does, preferring to cool off quietly for a few days after an argument, things gradually returning to normal without discussion. But now he *wants* a discussion. He wants to tell her how frightened he is, about more than just Noah being missing. And he wants to make a plan, just in case. The police are involved in this now, and if they're going to have to sit down with a police officer at some point, and be asked questions, even simple questions about their son, they need to make sure neither of them is going to fall apart. They never talk about it, *never*, not these days. But now he thinks they have to. He *knows* they have to.

He leans back slowly and sits there, staring blankly into space, his eyes stinging with tiredness, the thoughts tumbling over each other in his mind. Around him, the house is silent, no sound yet from River upstairs, even though it's daylight outside now; he can see it through the gap in the heavy velvet curtains at the window. But the room is dim, just two small lamps on, and Amy *is* asleep now, he realises suddenly, her hands finally still and curled in her lap, her cheeks streaked with tears. A feeling of utter exhaustion sweeps over him, and he wonders if he might let himself sleep too, just for a few minutes. Sleep, and forget, briefly. But just as his eyelids close, he hears a beep and at once he's upright in his seat, reaching for Amy's phone. As he reads the message, his stomach twists with fear.

> **OLIVIA CHAMBERLAIN**: Good morning, all. I hope everyone's bearing up? I need to let you know I've just had a message from the police. Please don't be too alarmed, but would it be possible for everyone to convene at the school at 7.30 a.m.? There's news.

Chapter Eleven

LOWER LOCKTON

Day 2: Saturday, 6.45 a.m.

The ambulance pulls away slowly, the driver manoeuvring it carefully along the narrow road, and Sadie watches until it's out of sight, then turns to Daniel.

'Right – we've got a few minutes before we need to head to the school. Let's just go and see if they've found anything else.'

He nods, and they make their way back across the field, following the tyre tracks towards the thicket of trees where the minibus is just visible, a flash of white metal amongst the leaves. They're half a mile outside the village of Lower Lockton, about forty minutes from Cheltenham and just inside the Gloucestershire county border. They're now assuming that they guessed correctly; that the bus must indeed have turned off the A429 not long after leaving the Cotswold Wilderness Park yesterday afternoon, and then wiggled its way along tiny back roads, but as for why, they still have no idea. They have no idea either about why it did what it clearly did next: drove through a gate, crossed a field, and parked deep within an area of woodland. The field has, technically, a public right of way across it – there's a stile, as well as the gate – but it's obviously little used, the grass overgrown to almost waist height, and full of nettles. The early morning dog walker who spotted the bus and its horrifying contents ('Always, *always* a dog walker!' Daniel said, when they'd been told) had still been there when they arrived at the scene, and had told them that locals prefer the adjoining field, which also leads into the woods, but is much easier to walk through.

'The farmer who owns this one doesn't use it – hasn't done for a year or more now – so he doesn't bother to keep it mowed,' he said. 'Should do really, as it's a public right of way, but hey ho…'

He was a slender, shaven-headed man in his forties, still a little pale from the shock of his discovery. He was, he'd said, in the habit of taking his Yorkshire terrier out before dawn most days, in order to be at his job in an Evesham bakery by 6 a.m., and he definitely hadn't expected to come across what he did on this quiet Saturday morning.

'To be honest, it was lucky I saw it. The bus, I mean. That bit of the wood where it's parked, well, you can't really see it from the main pathway – it's way off to the side. The only reason I ended up coming over into this field and spotting it through the trees was because Peanut here' – he gestured towards the small dog sniffing at a patch of grass a couple of feet away – 'he saw a rabbit or something and went tearing off, and I had to go after him. He's a right little bugger – he'll chase anything that moves. Rabbits, cars, tennis balls, runners, for my sins… anyway, that's when I saw it. Gave me a right fright when I looked inside, but as I said, it was lucky I did, really. Not many people come here. It's a bit out of the way, you know? I'm here most mornings and often I see nobody at all. It could have been there for days.'

They've taken the man's details and let him head off to work, and now Sadie and Daniel watch as the half dozen officers who've so far made it to the scene weave their way carefully between the trees. The sun is already glittering on the dew on the long grass in the field, but in here it's damp and cool, the air tangy with the scent of decomposing leaves. There'll be a proper search when the SOCOs – the scene of crime officers – arrive, but so far, there seems to be nothing else to report, other than the two things which were immediately obvious as soon as the bus was located. First, the small pile of mobile phones sitting neatly on the driver's seat. And second, the body. Except that it wasn't, as the dog walker first thought, and reported to the police, a *dead* body. It had been easy to see why the poor man thought it was though; the woman had been so badly beaten she was unconscious and motionless, slumped on the floor of the bus between the two rows of seats, her blood spattered across the windows. The first officers to arrive quickly established that this woman is Erica Lindsay, the thirty-nine-year-old Year 2 teacher who was, according to the passenger list Sadie was given by the headteacher, driving the bus. Her ID was in her handbag, which had been lying on the floor beside her, her wallet and phone – switched off – also still inside. The three mobile phones on the driver's seat, all also switched off, belong, Sadie assumes, to the other three staff members on board. Erica, still unconscious and clearly very seriously injured, is now on her way to hospital. But of the remaining adults, and the ten children, there is no sign whatsoever, not on the bus or anywhere in the immediate vicinity.

'So… not a breakdown or an accident, clearly. An abduction of some sort, then, as you suggested?'

Daniel turns to Sadie, and she hesitates for a moment, then nods.

'Maybe. I mean, something terrible has obviously happened here. We can't assume anything for now, but… the way the bus has been left so deep in the trees – it's clearly an attempt to hide it. But who knows what happened after that?'

He nods.

'I bet you've got some initial thoughts though. I know what you're like. Go on, hit me.'

She gives him a half-smile. He knows her too well, because of course she does have some 'initial thoughts', although there are still big questions to which she has no idea of the answers.

'Right, well…'

She gestures towards the field, and they make their way carefully out of the wood, stepping over tree roots, then walk along the path of flattened grass, mud sucking at their shoes, until they're back at the gate.

'My thinking is this,' Sadie says. 'And of course, this is just one theory, from initial impressions, and I could have it entirely wrong. First, I'm very much hoping none of the others are hurt; if they are, it didn't happen here. The only blood is around the victim inside the bus, and my guess is that's just hers. There's no sign of anyone else in the vicinity, so all the others are, therefore, now in some other location and, hopefully, still alive and well.'

She holds her hands in the air, crossing both middle fingers over her index fingers, a silver signet ring glinting on her left hand.

'So – and yes, I am, for now, going with some sort of abduction theory – how did it happen? OK, I have no idea what made them turn off the main road in the first place. Did somebody force their way onto the bus at some point, maybe? Someone armed with a weapon? Someone with local knowledge, who knew about this wood? Maybe they got on board and hid while the bus was parked at the wildlife place – we need to check CCTV. Then – more speculation, obviously – did whoever forced them to drive here make them all turn off their phones and leave them on the bus, so we can't use them to trace them?'

She pauses, looking around.

'Then... you see that small layby?'

She points to the left of the gate, where there's a pull-in area big enough for about three cars, and Daniel nods.

'I want that secured too, as soon as the SOCOs get here,' Sadie says. 'It rained last night, but I can still see tyre tracks from more than one car. Did this unknown somebody march everyone from the bus across the field and out here into a few waiting cars? Except poor Erica Lindsay, for some reason? The grass has been flattened by feet as well as bus tyres. It would all have been over in a matter of minutes, wouldn't it?'

Daniel stares down the road, a frown wrinkling his smooth olive-skinned brow, clearly envisaging the scene.

'Yes, it would,' he says slowly. 'It would need a few accomplices, of course. But if it was multiple vehicles, each with adults and a few kids – well, nobody would bat an eyelid, would they? On the roads I mean. That would look completely normal. Sounds like a decent theory to me, boss.'

Sadie nods. She's starting to feel a little sick; a combination of a long night with no sleep, and an increasing sense of helplessness.

'This is a very quiet road,' she says. 'I know it's early, but even so I don't think a single car's passed by in the last twenty minutes. If that's what happened, and they worked quickly, then it's quite possible there are no witnesses at all. And we have no idea how many vehicles, or what they look like... and all this happened yesterday afternoon, Daniel. They could be anywhere by now. *Anywhere.*'

He shakes his head, and she can see her own growing despondency reflected in his dark eyes.

'Why leave one teacher behind, though? Why beat her up so badly?' he says, turning to look back towards the treeline, his frown deepening.

'I mean, if she recovers, she'll be able to tell us what happened. That's a risk, if it really is a kidnap, isn't it?'

Sadie nods, following his gaze.

'It is. Maybe they thought she *was* dead. She's not far off, from what I gathered from the paramedic. But she'd *better* wake up, and soon. We need her.'

She sighs. She's desperate for a hot, strong tea, a warm bath and a cosy bed, but she knows none of those things are forthcoming any time soon, and the next task on her list is already filling her with a low-level sense of dread. She turns to Daniel.

'Look, I could have this all wrong. If it *is* a kidnap, it must have been planned well in advance. Someone knew where that class of children was going to be yesterday, which implies some sort of inside knowledge, and that's something we need to look at very seriously. But it could be something else. If we don't get contact from anyone soon, a demand for money from those wealthy parents maybe, well…'

She shrugs, then taps her watch.

'And speaking of the parents, we need to go and brief them. I'm not looking forward to this one tiny bit, I don't mind telling you.'

'OK. Let's get it over with then,' he says. Then he adds, 'What else could it be? What else could have happened here?'

She shakes her head.

'I have absolutely no idea.'

Chapter Twelve

REYNOLD

Day 2: Saturday, 7.57 a.m.

'Oh, Reynold. My babies. My *babies*.'

Petra turns to Reynold, and he sees the anguish in her green eyes. Her face is pale and puffy after a night of crying, and as he reaches for her hand he sees a trace of blood on her index finger, the nail bitten to the quick. It's an old habit he thought she'd conquered – normally, despite being so hands-on with the twins, her nails are always perfectly manicured in case of a short-notice modelling job – and he raises the finger to his lips and kisses it gently.

'It'll be OK, darling. It will. It has to be,' he whispers into her hair. A little sob escapes her, and Reynold blinks as the mischievous faces of Luca and Lola flash into his mind; the memory of the last time he saw them, waving at him from the old white minibus, makes him suddenly feel nauseous. He and Petra are sitting in the assembly hall at Littleford Primary with all the other Class 3B parents, and the police have just told them the latest news about the search for the bus and its occupants. Around them, others are crying too, but some have begun standing up and shouting questions, mini-explosions of fear and anger going off all around the room.

'What are you actually *doing* to find them, then?' yells one father, his face red with fury. 'What if it's some sort of child sex traffickers? Christ, if they hurt one hair of my son's head…'

'The adults have gone too – hardly going to traffic two blokes and a woman if they're *child* sex traffickers, are they?' mutters another father.

'Maybe… maybe they took *them* to help look after the kids? That would be some comfort, at least…' says a mother, her voice an anguished whisper. The woman sitting to her left has buried her face in her hands, her shoulders shaking with the ferocity of her weeping.

'Shit. What if they've been taken by some sort of sadistic paedophile who's going to torture 'em to death?'

Petra gives a horrified gasp and bursts into tears again, and Reynold turns to see who just spoke and glares at him. It's Spike Greer, the ex-footballer. Reynold knows him – they generally get on well – so he catches the man's eye with a gesture of his hand and shakes his head.

'Not helpful, mate,' he says quietly, but Spike doesn't respond, immediately turning back to the Detective Superintendent who's standing on the dais at the front of the room, and saying angrily, 'I mean, how the *fuck* can there be no trace of 'em? They've obviously been attacked by some nutter – what if that poor cow Mrs Lindsay dies? And there are ten kids and three adults still missin'. What if they're all dyin' somewhere too? *Thirteen* people. How can you find no trace of thirteen fuckin' people? They can't just disappear. Jesus *Christ*.'

He thumps the wall beside him, and his wife Tasha puts a hand on his arm, clearly trying to quieten him, but he shrugs her off with a furious, 'I mean, for *fuck's* sake…'

Reynold's eyes flit around the room, his gaze resting on each distraught face in turn, and he wonders idly why he himself feels so weirdly calm. True, he still feels a bit sick, his insides in turmoil. But other than that, it's as if he's watching some sort of television crime drama; as if what's happening here isn't quite real.

Maybe it's all the years of live TV, he thinks, as he rubs Petra's back soothingly. *Keep calm and carry on, no matter how chaotic everything is just behind the camera…*

Sitting in front of them, Ben Townsend is practically having to pin his wife, Monique, to her seat; she seems to be in a very bad way, crying and trembling so much she looks as if she might slide off her chair into a crumpled heap on the carpet at any moment. Next to them, the woman with short blonde hair – Clare, Reynold remembers – exchanges glances with Ben and gives Monique a quick squeeze on the arm, before turning to slip an arm around her own partner, who's sitting stock-still and white-faced to her left, looking as if he's in deep shock. Across the room, Eldon and Amy Beckford are standing against the wall, Amy visibly shivering. Reynold tries to catch her eye, but she's staring straight ahead, her eyes red. Eldon's jaw is so rigid he's grimacing.

'Look, I totally understand how frightening and upsetting all this is,' the detective is saying now. She's a slender, dark-haired woman who Reynold guesses is in her early forties, and she looks exhausted, dark circles under her eyes.

'It's very early days, but all I can say for now is that other than poor Mrs Lindsay, there's currently nothing to suggest that any harm's come to anyone else who was on the bus. And by the way, although none of them are here yet, the teachers' families are all being contacted and will be kept fully informed too. We have a forensics team at the scene right now, and if there's anything to find, you can be assured they'll find it, and find it fast. In the meantime...'

'In the meantime WHAT?'

It's Spike again, so furious now he's bright red from the top of his shaven skull to where his pudgy neck vanishes into a straining designer polo top. Spittle flies out of his mouth as he bellows at the police officer.

'In the meantime WHAT?' he thunders again. 'You need to be searchin' every buildin', every inch of land, looking at every bit of CCTV. We need this in all the papers, on every news programme – why isn't it on the news yet? What the buggerin' hell are you actually *doin'*?'

The policewoman holds up a placatory hand. 'I promise you, this is our biggest priority right now by a million miles, OK? Every officer we can get our hands on is being brought in as we speak. But as for the press, well... if this *is* a kidnap situation, as we fear it may be, we're still working on our strategy for involving them.'

She pauses and rubs a hand across her forehead.

'We're hoping to just wait a few more hours to see if any contact is made; trust me, depending on what's happened here, this story making the news may *not* be helpful at such an early stage. But of course, we don't really know *what's* going on, not yet. Until we get more information, we have to keep an open mind, and things may well develop very rapidly over the next few hours, which is what I'm hoping. We want to get your children home to you safe and well as much as you want them back, I can assure you of that, but at the moment the timescale for that is out of our hands. What I *can* promise right now, though, is that we'll keep you fully updated, and we'll be appointing a number of family liaison officers as soon as possible. Obviously, with so many people involved, this is... well, it's a big job... a *huge* job, but...'

'Detective Superintendent!'

There's a sudden shout, and the police officer's voice tails off. Over by the row of windows which run across the width of the room, the headteacher is gesturing towards the playground and the road beyond.

'What you just said about possibly holding off on involving the press – I'm afraid you might be too late,' she says. 'I could be wrong, but I think a TV news van's just pulled up.'

Chapter Thirteen

COTSWOLDS POLICE HEADQUARTERS

Day 2: Saturday, 1.01 p.m.

'First, this lunchtime, the Cotswold village in shock after the bizarre disappearance of ten children and three teachers from a bus which had taken them on a school day trip. The bus was found abandoned in an area of woodland near Lower Lockton early this morning. On board, just one teacher, badly beaten and unconscious. The whereabouts of the remaining occupants of the bus are currently unknown, and police…'

The voice of the ITV one o'clock news presenter is abruptly silenced as DCI Daniel Sharma grabs the TV remote control and hits the mute button.

'That *damn* dogwalker,' he says. 'OK, it had to come out eventually, but we could have done with a few more hours. If this *is* a kidnap, having it splashed all over the press before they've even had a chance to make contact could put those kids in even more danger.'

Sadie sighs.

'It is what it is. We had no choice.'

When the TV news vans had turned up at the school (the first one, a Sky News vehicle, had been quickly followed by two more, from ITV and the BBC), apparently alerted to the story by the man who'd found Erica and the bus, she really *had* been given no choice. Despite what she'd just said to the assembled group of parents about involving the press, Spike Greer had immediately stalked out and filled in the reporters on *exactly* what was going on, including his considered opinion that the *useless* police weren't doing enough to find the children. Sadie, springing into damage limitation mode, had then felt forced into giving a brief statement too, and had, rather against her better judgement, promised a full press conference as soon as possible.

She and Daniel had headed home shortly after that, to grab a shower, some food and a couple of hours of restless sleep. Now they're back at police HQ, trying to coordinate a search operation but really, Sadie thinks, they're playing a waiting game: waiting for forensics from the bus site, waiting for some sort of contact (from whom, she still has no idea), and waiting for Erica Lindsay to wake up and tell them what the *hell* happened to her, and where everyone else has gone. She'd spoken briefly to the woman's husband earlier; his grief and fear had been heartbreaking, and she'd had to step outside the incident room for a few minutes to compose herself after she ended the call. She's still feeling a little shaky now, but she's trying her hardest to focus. Emotional responses have their place in policing – *she's* always believed that anyway – but today is *not* the day for them.

'This will be world news by this evening. Not just national news. You just wait and see,' she says to Daniel now. 'It's already blowing up on social media. Those reporters couldn't believe their luck, could they? You saw their faces when Greer told them whose kids were among the missing. This is probably the biggest news story of the year so far. Look at that. *Shit.*'

On the silenced TV screen, the faces of some of the children are now being shown. There are the blond-haired, green-eyed twins, Luca and Lola Lyon, holding hands with their famous parents, the photo clearly taken at a film premiere or some similar event. Next, eight-year-old Gresham Greer, standing on a football pitch with Spike, a wide grin on his freckled face, and then Noah Beckford, perched on a kitchen worktop between his restaurateur parents, the *OK!* magazine logo plastered across the top of the photo.

Sadie turns to look at their own collection of pictures, some provided by the school and the parents, others easily found online, now neatly lined up on the board on the wall, notes written under each one. It's the offspring of the famous parents who are getting all the airtime right now, but there are, of course, six other children here too. Eight-year-old Oliver MacDonald-Cook, son of Brett and Jon, a Scottish couple who only moved to Littleford a year ago. Harper Duggan, daughter of single mother Rosie. Luke Carr, son of Vanessa and Alex, and Wanda Pearson, daughter of Eugene and Polly. Sadie doesn't know much yet about any of these parents, but she has a feeling that in the days to come, she'll get to know them very well indeed. Then there's Stanley Tustain, son of Clare and Nick, and Willow Townsend, daughter of Ben and Monique. She remembers Clare because she's loud and voluble and stands out in a crowd, and she remembers Monique too, from this morning; while everyone in the room had been understandably distressed, she was the mother who had seemed to be on the verge of complete hysteria, wailing and shaking, and having to be almost forcibly restrained in her chair by her husband.

Sadie's eyes flit from photo to photo, then settle on the next row, where Daniel has pinned pictures of the four adults. Erica Lindsay, of course. Then, there's the Year 2 TA, Dominic Moore, an athletic-looking man in his twenties with very short dark-brown hair and a trendy beard. The quartet is completed by the school's Year 3 teacher, Cally Norman, and Oscar Jones, who teaches Year 1, both also in their twenties. The head, Olivia Chamberlain, had described all four as extremely competent, trustworthy and utterly reliable, traits which, she'd told Sadie as she'd left the school earlier, were bringing her some shred of comfort at such a terrible time.

'If they're all still together, those children will be all right, I know it,' she said. 'Cally, Oscar, Dominic – they're all superb staff members. They'll fight for those children with their lives.'

Her eyes had filled with tears, and she'd hastily thanked Sadie for everything the police were doing then turned away, scuttling off down the corridor, her shoulders hunched under her pale-green mohair cardigan. Now, Sadie looks at the four faces intently. She hopes that the headteacher is right, but she's sceptical by nature, and right now she can't rule anything or anyone out.

'What do you think, Daniel? Going back to the kidnap theory for now, in the absence of anything better, well, if this was all planned well in advance, which it must have been, then somebody connected with the school *must* have had some involvement, otherwise how would the kidnappers know where that bus was going to be and who'd be on it? We're going to have to look at everyone, and I mean *everyone*. All the parents, *now*. And all the adults on board that bus, even Erica, unlikely as that may sound. Maybe she was somehow involved, and got cold feet or something so needed to be dealt with. What do you think?'

Daniel, who's sitting on the edge of a nearby desk, sipping from a large takeaway coffee cup, shrugs.

'I know we have to consider them, and yes, even Erica. But it's not my gut feeling? You?'

She shakes her head.

'We can't entirely rule them out though.'

The preliminary background checks she'd requested on the members of staff have thrown up no red flags so far; none have a criminal record, and a quick look at their bank accounts shows no sign of debt or any financial irregularities. Plus, the headteacher had referred to their glowing references from previous employments. There's certainly nothing obvious there to worry Sadie. But still…

'No, we can't rule them out,' agrees Daniel. 'But, as someone said earlier, if we're still thinking abduction as the most likely scenario, maybe the younger three *were* taken so they could look after the kids? And maybe whoever took them beat up Erica as a warning – this is what will happen to you too, if you don't come quietly?'

'Yeah, maybe. The phones thing supports that theory too, I suppose.'

Information is still trickling in very slowly, but one thing they do know now is that the staff mobile phones were switched off at around 4.30 p.m. yesterday, all within about thirty seconds of each other.

Daniel nods.

'It definitely has the feel of "Hand over your phones, *now!*" I just can't imagine what else it could be. But we *could* be totally wrong. I'll be interested to see what they get from the real school minibus though.'

It was something that had struck Sadie as soon as she'd seen the shiny black Mercedes bus parked outside the school. The head had told her it had flashed a warning light just before the trip was due to start, hence the last-minute replacement. Today, this seems deeply suspicious. Had the bus been tampered with? It has a tracker, so would have been easy to trace if *it* went missing. Did whoever is behind this gamble on the fact that a short-notice alternative from a local rental company might be a little harder to find?

She's waiting impatiently to hear back about that; waiting too for the CCTV footage from the Cotswold Wilderness Park, and for images from any other cameras the bus might have passed before it left the main road and ended up in the wood. It's all on its way, but the waiting is making the knot in her stomach bigger with each passing minute. In the meantime, the search area is widening rapidly as the day progresses, local officers redeploying from other cases and many more being drafted in from surrounding counties, all facing a seemingly impossible task.

'We can only assume some sort of vehicle or vehicles were used to take them away from the bus dump site,' Sadie had said in her briefing for the search teams earlier. 'But as we have no intelligence on that, all we can do is keep our eyes peeled. I'm thinking abandoned buildings, barns, caravans, disused properties – somewhere a group might have been taken to lay low for a while. When we hold the press conference, I'll ask the public to search their own outbuildings, sheds, all the usual too. And of course, there's always the chance the group's been split up. Look carefully at every child you see... anyone who might look distressed. We'll get you more information as soon as we get it ourselves. That's all I've got for now. I'm sorry, guys. Good luck.'

She's not holding her breath for a result any time soon. There've been so many hours between the bus going off radar yesterday afternoon and being found this morning. *Too* many hours.

'Have the families of the missing teaching staff all been spoken to now, by the way?' she asks Daniel.

He nods.

'I think so. Erica has no kids, but her husband's by her bedside as you know. The other three are all currently single, but we've already made contact with Dominic Moore's parents. They wanted to drive straight down here – they live in the Lake District – but they've been persuaded to stay put for now. They're elderly and the dad is quite poorly, and there's not much they can do here anyway. And it turns out that both Cally Norman's and Oscar Jones's parents are deceased, but the head's given us next of kin details from their employment files, so that's in hand too as far as I know.'

'Good. Thanks, Daniel.'

She turns back to the wall, her eyes moving slowly across the rows of photographs again, taking in the bright eyes, the smiling faces, trying to commit them to memory. They're her responsibility now. It's up to her to find them, to bring them home safely. But how?

They could be out of the country by now. They could all be dead at the bottom of a lake somewhere—

'Boss!'

She's so lost in dark thoughts that she jumps. It's Daniel, standing at a desk halfway down the room now, clutching a phone in his hand and gesturing at her wildly.

'Sorry – miles away. What is it? Please tell me it's good news?'

She moves quickly towards him, weaving her way between the desks with their towering piles of paperwork, and hears him say, 'Hang on, Anna. I'll put you on speaker.'

'Thanks. Can you hear me OK?'

It's Anna Turner, Sadie realises, the detective sergeant who's been waiting at Erica Lindsay's bedside at the hospital.

'Anna! What news?' she says urgently.

There's a pause, then Anna says, 'It's not good, I'm afraid. Erica Lindsay died ten minutes ago.'

'Shit.'

Sadie's eyes meet Daniel's, and he shakes his head sadly.

'Bugger,' he whispers.

Sadie feels a rush of despair. *Dead.* The poor, poor woman. And as for this investigation, she'd been hoping, so very much, that Erica might be able to point her in the right direction, and now… She swallows a lump in her throat, suddenly afraid she might cry, then realises Anna is still speaking.

'… she briefly regained consciousness, and I was able to talk to her, just for a minute,' she's saying. 'She wasn't making much sense, to be honest. It was just mumbling, just nonsense. But she did say two words, several times.'

'What words?' asks Daniel, and his eyes flit to Sadie's again.

'Masked. Man,' says Anna. 'She said "masked man".'

Chapter Fourteen

LITTLEFORD

Day 2: Saturday, 4.55 p.m.

'I can't believe she's dead. Erica Lindsay is *dead*. Good God.'

Nick Tustain looks at his wife with anguished eyes, then sinks his head into his hands and lets out a long shuddering groan. Clare, who'd been standing next to the window when the call came in from their newly appointed family liaison officer, too fearful and on edge to sit down for more than a minute, suddenly feels as if her legs might give way, and staggers to the nearest armchair, dropping into it like a rock flung from a bridge.

'Jesus,' she says softly.

For some reason, she hadn't expected this. At first, what's happening seemed like a bad dream, a little hazy around the edges, horrible while it's going on but something that would soon be over, with everything and everyone OK again. But now someone is dead. Actually *dead*. Clare looks at her husband again, his head still buried in his hands, fingers clawing at his scalp, and she realises that he's crying. She knows she should get up out of her chair and go to him, try and comfort him, but she can't move, her heart suddenly beating so fast she can feel it kicking against the wall of her chest, her palms slick with sweat.

Stanley. My darling.

She looks around the living room, at the tatty tan sofa, bought second-hand from a charity furniture shop, at the frayed, faded rug in front of the three-bar electric fire, and then at the photograph of her son on the mantelpiece above it. Stanley, wearing his school uniform, smiling back at her. Stanley, the best thing she's ever done. Possibly the *only* good thing she's ever done. She had hoped, so desperately, that her life might be about to change for the better. That one day, very soon, she might be able to give this little boy, the light of her life, the sort of future she so badly wants him to have. The sort of future he deserves. And now…

She looks at Nick again, his sobs louder now, his shoulders shaking, and his obvious pain is almost unbearable. But she *still* can't seem to move, her limbs leaden, her body frozen. It's almost, she thinks, as if the fear and the guilt and the shame that have been building, threatening to overwhelm her, have suddenly become a physical presence, dark and heavy, weighing her down, pinning her to her chair. She can feel hot tears running down her own cheeks now, but she can't even summon the energy to wipe them away, her hands limp in her lap.

Is it all over? Can it really work out the way I wanted it to, now? she thinks.

She has no idea, no clue. And so she sits, and she waits, for whatever's going to happen next.

At the Townsends', Ben is sitting slumped in an armchair too, trying to process the horrific news.

Erica Lindsay, dead? Murdered? Is this real?

Apparently, it is. She died this morning, and the police, clearly sticking to their vow to keep the families fully informed, had called half an hour ago, telling him that her family had been told but asking if he could refrain from speaking about the tragedy to the press, who are now roaming the village, or indeed to anyone else outside their immediate group. Stunned, he'd muttered that of course, he wouldn't say a word, and now he's just sitting, still in shock. He'd liked Erica a lot; she'd taught Willow, taught all the kids, last year, and she'd been fantastic, even when Monique had demanded meetings with her *three* times in the first term because she didn't think Willow was coming on well enough with her reading. Mrs Lindsay, clearly very used to dealing with neurotic parents, had been calm and reassuring, repeatedly telling her that the little girl was actually *ahead* of many of the others in her class, and definitely *not* struggling. To Ben's great astonishment, because his wife doesn't often back down about *anything* when it comes to their daughter, after the third meeting Monique had quietly acquiesced.

'*Finally*, a teacher who understands my concerns,' she'd pronounced. 'She's going to keep a close eye on Willow, but I think everything's going quite well now. Isn't that wonderful?'

It truly had been, and Ben looks across the room now, to where his wife is curled up in the big armchair by the fire, her eyes closed, and wonders how on earth he's going to tell her that the only teacher she's ever really liked and trusted is now lying dead in a hospital mortuary. And what does this mean for Willow? For *all* the children? His stomach lurches, and he hopes Monique stays asleep for a bit longer. He can't face talking to her right now. He needs to process this; he needs to *think*.

How can everything have gone so wrong, in just one day? All the scheming, all the secret planning…

'I could have saved her. Why didn't I save her?'

He jumps. Across the room, Monique, eyes still closed, is muttering under her breath.

What did she just say?

She'd opened a bottle of red wine this morning when they'd got back from the school after the police briefing; she'd opened a second at lunchtime, when they'd seen Willow's photograph pop up with all the others on the lunchtime news. He'd refused to join her, telling her that one of them needed to keep a clear head, and that drinking herself into a stupor wasn't going to help anything, but she'd ignored him as usual. She'd finally passed out in her armchair an hour ago, and now she's mumbling again, the words slurred. He stands up slowly and walks over to her, trying to work out what she's saying.

'Should have taken her off. Off the bus…' she whispers.

Her eyelids flutter, and she moans softly. Ben stares at her, waiting, but there are a few seconds of silence and then his wife starts to snore gently.

It's OK. She's just regretting letting Willow go on the day trip, that's all, he thinks, and a brief sense of relief is immediately replaced by a fresh surge of grief.

Willow. My little angel. We'll get you home safe, I promise. Everything's going to be fine, just as I planned. Stay strong, baby.

But even as the silent words sound loud and fierce inside his head, the doubts start to creep back, and he sinks into his chair, his legs suddenly weak. He's scared, he realises. He's never been this scared in his life. He buries his head in his hands, and he starts to cry.

At The Granary, Reynold and Petra are sitting at the small bistro-style table in the conservatory, cooling coffee mugs in hand, both of them silent, lost in thought. The normally cheerful room feels grey and sad and far, far too quiet, and Reynold, who often craves the peace and tranquillity of his village home when he's caught up in the madness of the studio and London, suddenly feels an ache somewhere deep in his gut. He turns to look out into the garden, at the climbing rope hanging from the oak tree and at a lone blackbird pecking desultorily at something in the grass. The faces of his children flash before his eyes again. He feels light-headed, and he knows he needs to sleep; he hasn't slept at all for... *how long?*

He glances at his Rolex. He's been awake since just after six yesterday morning, and now it's almost five in the evening. *Thirty-five hours.* Yes, he needs to sleep, but it's been impossible. He knows he's not alone; messages have been pinging in from the Class 3B WhatsApp group all day, even more frequently in the past hour; the other parents are all exhausted, all terrified.

POLLY PEARSON: I'm so tired. But how can we go to bed with this going on? Are they going to start killing the others too? I can't breathe.

VANESSA CARR: Me neither. Poor Mrs Lindsay. I feel sick to my stomach. I'm so frightened. What are we going to do?

ROSIE DUGGAN: I don't think I'll ever sleep again. This is like a nightmare. I can't believe someone's KILLED her. Have you had any press at your doors? I know we're not supposed to speak to them but would it help, maybe? Let whoever's got the kids see how devastated we all are?

TASHA GREER: Don't. We need to listen to the police on this one. And don't look at social media either. All the armchair detectives are already spewing their nonsense on there about some of us not having enough security for our high-profile kids and loads of other shit. Lay low, for now anyway, that's my advice. And yes, it's horrific. Love to you all.

Reynold nods as he reads the last message. *She's right*, he thinks, but he's not surprised some of the less media-savvy are thinking of the press as friends, especially when they're all so sleep-deprived. The police have even advised them not to share too much about what's going on with their own friends and relatives. All the families are being bombarded with calls and messages from all over the world; most of them have now set their email accounts to auto-respond and recorded new voicemail messages, promising to update aunts and old school friends and even grandparents as soon as they have any news. Others have simply opted out altogether, unplugging landlines and leaving email inboxes to overflow.

It's just too much, isn't it? someone said on the group earlier, and there'd been a flurry of replies, all agreeing. It's lovely that so many people care, but even the thought of a well-meaning grandmother arriving on the doorstep is too much for most of them right now. The police have advised no visitors, just until they know what's going on, and Reynold for one is more than happy to oblige.

'Why is it taking so long, Reynold?'

Petra speaks suddenly, making him jump.

'I don't know,' he whispers.

'So *long*,' she repeats. 'Why haven't we heard anything? If they've been kidnapped, and this is about money, why hasn't there been a ransom demand? Isn't that what kidnappers do? Why is there just… silence?'

She bangs a fist on the table, and tears fill her bloodshot eyes. She still looks beautiful to Reynold – she always does – but as he reaches out a hand to stroke the soft skin of her forearm, he finds himself thinking idly that her modelling agent wouldn't recognise her right now, her hair greasy and straggly, her face drained of colour.

'I don't know,' he says quietly. 'We don't know *what* this is yet, but…'

'What if it's *not* just a kidnap?' She interrupts him, her voice louder now, shrill with fear. 'Someone killed Mrs Lindsay.

What if they're going to start killing them all, one by one? Oh God, Reynold, I can't bear this, I can't—'

She stands up abruptly, her hip bashing the table as she does so. Her mug tips over, a dark pool of coffee spilling across the polished metal surface, but she doesn't seem to notice.

'I'm calling Amy Beckford,' she says.

There's a frenzied look in her eyes, and Reynold feels a sudden chill, as if someone's just opened a window on a frosty morning.

'We need to join forces. We need to get more people out there searching,' she says, and she's on the move now, pacing up and down the shiny tiled floor, head moving left and right, looking for something.

'The police are doing their best, I'm sure they are, but we need more manpower, more boots on the ground, Reynold. We have money – I don't care how much it costs... Oh shit, where's my phone? Where's my damn phone? Did I leave it in the bathroom? I need to speak to Amy. Between us we can—'

'No!'

She stops talking, head whipping round to look at him in surprise, and Reynold, who's standing up now too, realises he's said the word rather more loudly than he intended to.

'Sorry – I mean, yes, that's a good idea. But no, don't call Amy, not right now. I spoke to Eldon when you were in the loo and he said he's finally managed to persuade her to lie down and rest. Leave it for now, babe, OK? Everyone's shattered. And the family liaison officer said they're going to hold a big press conference as soon as possible, didn't he? The whole country will be looking for them after that.'

He's lying to her – he hasn't spoken to Eldon today at all –

but he just can't handle her speaking to *anyone* right now. He needs it to be just them, getting through this together.

'Please, Petra. Come here. I love you. It's going to be OK.'

He holds out his arms, and she hesitates for a moment, her eyes still wide with dread. Then she lets out a little sob and staggers towards him, burying her head in his chest.

Amy Beckford is not resting, of course. River has been needy and clingy all day and, having had to fire their most recent live-in nanny three weeks ago after discovering she'd sold private family photos to one of the sleazier celebrity magazines, it's Amy who's been having to deal with him; the little boy is restless and clearly missing the presence of his beloved big brother.

She's just taken the child upstairs to give him a bath, and Eldon is scrolling through the latest WhatsApp group messages, feeling sick again. He agrees with everyone else – what's happened is horrendous. Erica Lindsay was a truly nice person, and an excellent teacher. The Year 3 teacher, Cally Norman, is excellent too though – a pretty, blonde, bubbly girl in her late twenties, old enough to have an air of authority and the respect of her pupils, but still young enough to identify closely with her charges. She joined the school almost exactly a year ago and immediately impressed Noah with her '*sick* trainers', an observation made when they'd bumped into her at the farmers' market in Cirencester one Saturday morning not long after she arrived. Eldon knows Erica's teaching assistant, Dominic Moore, a little too, and always finds him to be a good bloke. And although he hasn't actually met the other staff member who's missing, Year 1 teacher Oscar Jones, who only joined at the start of the new school year last September, he's heard good things about him too, again from Noah, who's been wildly impressed with the man's football skills in the playground.

At the thought of Noah, Eldon's hands begin to shake, and he puts the phone down on the arm of the sofa and breathes deeply, trying to quell the rising terror. It's little things that keep worming their way into his mind, like the fact that yesterday was sunny and warm, but it rained overnight, the temperature several degrees cooler than recently.

'Did they bring coats? Did they have jumpers with them? What was he wearing? Were they in uniform? Will he be cold, Amy?' he'd said to his wife in a moment of high anxiety earlier.

She'd turned to him with an anguished expression, River whimpering on the carpet next to her, little hands gripping her knees, wanting to be picked up yet again, and she'd replied sharply, 'You were around before I took him to school. You should *know* what he was wearing, Eldon. They never wear uniforms on a day out. He was wearing jeans and a sweatshirt, and yes of course he had a coat with him. They always have to bring one. Even I know that, even if it *is* the nannies who normally sort the kids' clothes. And how should I know if he'll be cold? I don't know where he is, Eldon. I don't *know* where he is, OK?'

She'd practically screamed the last few words at him, and River had looked up at them both with startled eyes and started screaming too, bringing their discussion to a halt.

Now, despite the atmosphere between them still being somewhat icy, Eldon suddenly feels as if he can't be alone for another second. He can't bear this, any of it. He can't bear Noah not being here, and he can't bear having to be in this sort of close contact with the police. Sweat breaks out on his brow every time the phone rings. He gets up and walks swiftly upstairs, following the sound of splashing water and – to his relief – little giggles from a clearly less grumpy River, to the children's bathroom on the second floor. The door is ajar, and he stands there for a moment, watching his youngest son happily zooming a small plastic boat through the bubbles in the big claw-footed bath. Amy is kneeling on the floor, gently shampooing the child's hair.

'Darling. Amy,' he says softly, and her shoulders stiffen, but she doesn't respond.

'Amy,' he repeats. 'We need to talk. We can't put it off any longer, OK?'

She takes a few seconds to reply.

'Talk about what?' she says, and he can hear the tightness in her voice, the unwillingness to go there.

He pauses, but she doesn't turn around, and he knows she doesn't want to look at him, doesn't want any part of this. He's going to have to force her into it, and it's not going to be easy. It's going to be dreadful.

'Amy. Come on,' he says quietly.

'Talk about *what*?' she says, and the last word is a vicious hiss.

'You *know* what,' he says.

Chapter Fifteen

COTSWOLDS POLICE HEADQUARTERS

Day 3: Sunday, 7.10 a.m.

'Right – let's see where we are. Gather round, please.'

Detective Superintendent Sadie Stewart swigs the last of her drink and strides to the front of the room, hoping she looks and sounds more energetic than she feels. She managed a few hours of broken sleep last night; it was one of those nights, though, when she desperately wished she wasn't single, had ached for arms to hold her, for someone to whisper in her ear and tell her it was all going to be OK, that she was doing a great job. Instead, she dozed under her duvet alone, waking with a pounding headache and a stomach that began churning with nervous energy within seconds of her eyes flickering open.

Now she's back at police HQ, bracing herself for another long day. Her head is, thankfully, slightly clearer than it was when she woke up, after two strong teas, two paracetamol and a sugary pastry from the tray someone ordered in to keep the early shift going. She nods at DCI Sharma, who's standing on the other side of the whiteboard.

'OK, Daniel?' she says. He nods and gives her a small smile, but he looks shattered too, she notes. They all do, but there's no time for weariness or rest, not today, maybe not for many days to come. This thing is escalating by the hour; now, they have not just the abduction of thirteen people – for abduction is surely what it must be – but also a murder investigation on their hands.

'First, how are the families bearing up?' she asks, as the other officers in the room pull chairs closer and perch on desks, and then fall silent, waiting to hear the latest news.

It's a little milder out there today, at least, Sadie thinks.

There's still a chill in the air but even at this early hour, the sun is shining in through the windows, dust motes dancing in the air around them.

Are the children somewhere where they can see the sunshine? she wonders, and she squeezes her eyes shut for a second then rubs her forehead as if trying to erase the thought, imagining how it would feel if her beloved nephew was among the missing; if Teddy hadn't come home last night.

Daniel clears his throat.

'The families aren't great, as you can imagine. Erica's husband's in an appalling state, obviously. They don't – *didn't* – have children; it was just the two of them, and they were married for fifteen years. He says he has no idea how he's going to live without her.'

He pauses, looking stricken, then takes a breath and says, 'Olivia Chamberlain, our headteacher, says everyone at the school is absolutely heartbroken. And the families are all extremely upset too. Erica was a very popular teacher. But it's also made them even more frightened. They're terrified this shows a level of violence which could lead to more deaths. We have some very, very scared parents on our hands.'

Sadie nods.

'Completely understandable,' she says. 'I know the FLOs are doing a sterling job of trying to reassure them, but it's not easy. And by the way, just so everyone is clear on this, we have *not* revealed to the families that Erica referred to a "masked man" in her final words. No point in causing further distress. We're simply telling them today that we do have more reason now to believe this was an abduction and the children and staff are being kept somewhere against their will. We're saying that because of this theory, we're expecting contact very soon, and telling them to sit tight. The waiting is agony though, isn't it?'

The 'masked man' revelation means that the National Crime Agency's anti-kidnap and extortion unit have now been informed about the case. Their specialist support will, Sadie knows, doubtless prove invaluable in the coming days, but as there's still been no contact from any abductors, there isn't much they can do at the moment. Her team is also now working in collaboration with a regional Major Crime Investigation Team made up of senior officers from adjoining police forces, and their discussions overnight have raised all sorts of dreadful possibilities.

'The best guess right now is that this is most likely to be a classic kidnap for ransom, given the high profile and financial status of many of the parents,' she tells the team now. 'But obviously there are other potential scenarios: unlikely, but *maybe* one of the parents is a member of an organised crime group, and this is some sort of vendetta kidnap; or it *could* be a terrorist or political thing – maybe the abductors are about to demand weapons, or the release of prisoners, something like that. Again, unlikely. But all we can do now is wait.'

'It's just been such a long time,' Daniel says. He's taken his jacket off, and he's wearing a pale-blue shirt that looks crisp and fresh and perfectly ironed. Sadie glances down at her own green dress, which she threw on straight from the tumble dryer this morning. She feels like a crumpled mess.

'I mean, it's been more than thirty-six hours since they were taken. What are they waiting *for*? Surely the longer they have to keep thirteen people hidden and captive, the riskier it gets for them?'

'You would have thought so, yes,' agrees Sadie. 'They must have a damn good hiding place. And there *must* be more than one abductor involved. Again, that suggests this was well planned, and involved insider knowledge. It wasn't a spur-of-the-moment decision to hijack a bus full of kids and abduct them. There's absolutely no way. I want to look closely at Olivia Chamberlain and *every* staff member at that school, just in case. And whoever's looking into the backgrounds of the parents needs to be doing it with a fine-tooth comb, to see if there's anything that might have triggered this. In the meantime, we carry on looking for them. Have the searches turned up *anything* yet?'

Daniel shakes his head.

'Nothing,' he says.

He turns to the room.

'As you all know, the search area has been gradually

widening, beginning in the immediate vicinity of the bus site, in and around Lower Lockton. We've searched everywhere – barns, abandoned farm buildings, an airport hangar that's rarely used, a derelict manor house... the list goes on. We've asked local councils to check any empty properties and put out appeals to landlords to check their vacant flats and houses. Our colleagues all over the country are keeping their eyes peeled too of course. This is one of the biggest police searches ever carried out in the UK, and that's official. The calls from the press are becoming relentless, as you can imagine – we *are* planning to hold a presser later today but we've already released a couple of statements, and asked hoteliers and B&B owners to keep an eye out, bearing in mind that the group may have been split up. I mean, the whole country's looking for them, really. There are reports coming in from all over the place from people who've been out searching local woodlands and remote beaches coming back with a kid's shoe or whatever and wondering if it might be from one of our missing children.'

He sighs.

'Again, nothing relevant so far. And of course the story's now properly global, even more so since the news of Erica's death was released. We're being bombarded with so-called sightings from all over the place. Scotland, Paris, Berlin – we even had one from Washington DC an hour ago. There are hundreds more popping up online too. It's impossible to check them all out, and unfortunately so far none are convincing enough to get us excited.'

Sadie nods. The fact that the story has rapidly started to grip not just the UK, but the entire world, trending on social media and leading news bulletins across seven continents, has come as no surprise.

It's got everything, hasn't it? she thinks. *Missing children, celebrity parents, a murder, the brain-bending mystery of how so many people can seemingly vanish into the ether…*

'Could they have been taken abroad?' she asks.

Her gut feeling is that she doesn't really think so – *far* too risky – but she asks the question anyway.

Daniel shakes his head.

'Highly unlikely, I'd say. Obviously, there's no sign of any of them on any passenger lists at any of the air or ferry ports – that would be too easy. We're still going through CCTV footage – and from the nearest railway stations too – and that's a huge job, but so far no sign of any of them. Yes, with fake passports and IDs and some sort of disguise it's *possible* they were smuggled out of the country. But thirteen of them? Even if they were all split up and whisked off in different directions, it's so dicey, isn't it? I just feel the kidnappers will want them all in one place. Much easier to control, and the need to involve fewer people.'

Sadie nods.

'I agree. I feel the most likely scenario is they went to ground fast, not long after they were taken from the bus. They'd have known this would be a massive story very quickly. Which means, as you say, it would just be too dangerous to try and take that many kids and adults too far away. But where *are* they?'

For a few moments nobody speaks, the only sound the blaring of a car horn on the road outside drifting in through the open window. Then Sadie says, 'OK, a few other things. It appears that the school bus, the one the kids were supposed to have been taken out in on Friday, *was* tampered with, as suspected. Its parking place at the side of the school building is actually a blind spot for the building's CCTV cameras, something the head apparently wasn't aware of. She's appropriately mortified now, as you can imagine.'

'For Christ's sake,' mutters one of the assembled detectives, and there are groans from several others.

'I know,' Sadie says. 'The CCTV footage we do have shows nobody in the school grounds who shouldn't have been there over the twenty-four hours or so in the run-up to this, but the position of the bus means someone could easily have hopped over the rear wall to get to it with nobody noticing, especially if they did it at night. Don't ask me exactly what was tampered with, I forget. Car engines are not my forte. But whatever it was it caused a red warning light to come on. They probably assumed the staff wouldn't take the kids out in it if there was something obviously wrong, and would find a replacement. They'd know by looking at it that the bus was brand-new with a high-tech tracker and so on and would have been too easy to find once it went off radar, buying themselves more time, therefore.'

'They still took a risk though, didn't they?'

Daniel is frowning.

'I mean, the school could have just decided to cancel the trip. Or the local minibus might not have been available to hire?'

'True,' says Sadie. 'I suppose there's an element of chance in anything like this though. If there's a local taxi firm just down the road and they have minibuses, there's a decent chance the school will look there first before abandoning a trip and disappointing the kids. Obviously a gamble that paid off.'

'I suppose so. And I suppose even if they'd rented a new bus and it *did* turn out to have a tracker, they could still have gone ahead. They'd just have to move everyone out of there even faster.'

Daniel turns to the board behind him, and taps a photo of a red-faced white-haired man wearing a shabby-looking tweed jacket.

'That's Arnie Garrett by the way, the guy they rented the replacement bus from. Very well known locally, a good bloke by all accounts. No record. We've talked to him, and he seems as shocked and upset as everyone else. Nothing there to raise any suspicion that he might be involved in any way.'

'And nothing of any use from forensics either,' says Sadie. 'Wow. This is a depressing briefing, isn't it?'

She rubs her eyes, feeling exhaustion sweeping over her. More than exhaustion; there's despair there too, bubbling up and trying to get a grip on her, but she refuses to acknowledge it.

Focus, woman, she thinks.

'Nothing much from the bus site, other than a lot of Erica Lindsay's blood. No DNA from whoever attacked her. We know he was masked, so probably gloved too, but they haven't even found fibres of any use. There are dozens of footprints going through the field to the road, but they're all messed up, and there *were* some tyre tracks in the layby, but all of a very common type and of course it's impossible to know if they were made by vehicles related to this case or not. So…'

She shrugs.

'And as for footage from cameras along the bus route,' says Daniel, 'nothing of any use there either. The bus does pass a few CCTV cameras on the streets as it heads out onto the A429 but we can't see anything untoward going on inside it; we're assuming that whatever happened must have happened *after* it passed that last ANPR camera – somebody flagged it down, pretended they had some sort of emergency and needed help, and boarded it that way, maybe? We just don't know, and—'

'We've got something!'

Daniel stops speaking abruptly as there's a yell from the back of the room. An officer whose name has temporarily escaped Sadie is scurrying towards them waving a piece of paper.

'What? What is it?' she says.

'I'm sorry to interrupt. I didn't realise you were in a briefing,' says the officer. He's slightly out of breath, as if he's just run up a flight of stairs, and there's a bead of sweat on his forehead. 'But this is important, we think. I could have emailed it but I wanted to show you in person.'

'That's fine. Show me,' says Sadie, and the man holds out the sheet of paper, jabbing at it with a finger, as a ripple of excited whispers runs around the room, and several officers rise to their feet.

'This is a still from the CCTV footage from the Cotswold Wilderness Park,' says the newcomer. 'We started off looking at the car park, but we didn't see anything suspicious there, nobody hanging around near the bus or anything like that. And then when it came to home time, all four staff members and all ten kids got on looking quite happy and off it went. But we thought we'd have a look at pictures from some of the other cameras around the park, just in case.'

He wipes his forehead with the back of his hand.

'And thank Christ we did. This still is from a camera outside the café, where they stopped for half an hour at one o'clock to eat their lunch. It was a nice warm day, as you'll remember, so they sat at the picnic tables out front. You can see them all here...'

He points, and Sadie looks at the three tables he's indicating, the children and adults sitting with paper cups and food plates in front of them. She can't see anything out of the ordinary, and feels a surge of impatience.

'OK. And?' she says.

'Here, behind this bush,' says the man. 'There's someone there. Someone watching them.'

Sadie leans closer, and beside her Daniel does the same, their heads almost touching. She looks at the figure, clearly hidden from the view of those enjoying their lunch but easily seen from the elevated position of the CCTV camera, and a jolt of adrenalin shoots through her. She looks up at the officer who's holding the picture, who nods.

'They stand there for the full half an hour,' he says. 'And then leave when the kids finish lunch. We've spotted them again at a couple of other points around the park too. They always made sure they weren't seen by the school group, by the look of it. Kept their distance. But the other images aren't as clear as this one. Can you see who that is, boss?'

Sadie nods slowly and turns to meet Daniel's eye.

'Woweeee,' he says. 'What the *hell* is she doing there?'

'That's what I'd like to know,' says Sadie.

Because of *course* she recognises the lurking figure, just as Daniel does. It's one of the parents. One of the bloody *parents*. The woman who was in such a state at the briefing they held at the school yesterday morning. The woman who was crying so much her husband was practically having to hold her upright. Sadie glances at the faces on the board, the photos of the ten missing children, but she's already learned them by heart, and she knows that the woman is the mother of eight-year-old Willow Townsend, a beautiful little girl with her black hair in two topknots high on her head.

She looks at the CCTV image again. None of the parents went on the school trip. Or so she'd *thought*. So what on earth was Monique Townsend doing hiding in a bush at the Cotswold Wilderness Park on Friday afternoon, just hours before three adults and ten children vanished into thin air?

'Bring her in. *Now*,' she says.

Chapter Sixteen

COTSWOLDS POLICE HEADQUARTERS

Day 3: Sunday, 6.15 p.m.

'Are you OK, Mrs Townsend? Are you sure you're happy to begin?'

Sadie studies the tear-stained face of the woman sitting opposite her in the interview room. Monique Townsend looks awful. She's neatly dressed in well-pressed jeans and a navy blazer, but her face is puffy and swollen from crying and she seems to be in a state of high anxiety, the fingers of her right hand frantically twisting the wedding ring on her left, her eyes repeatedly darting from Sadie to the table to the door, as if she's desperate to flee the room. When she was brought in an hour ago, the desk sergeant reported a faint smell of alcohol about her person, but the duty solicitor – Monique's husband Ben accompanied her to the station, and insisted she have legal representation – has since established that she had two small glasses of wine with lunch, and is now completely sober and happy to be interviewed. Even so, looking at the state of the woman, Sadie feels the need to check. Her daughter is missing, of course, which *could* partially account for her appearance and the odd way she's behaving. But she seems so nervous.

'Yes, I'm fine,' says Monique abruptly. 'Can we just get this over with?'

'Of course,' Sadie replies.

There's a little bubble of excitement deep in her stomach – *Does this woman know her trip to the wildlife park is about to be exposed?* – but she keeps her tone calm and measured.

'And just to confirm, this is a voluntary interview, and you are free to leave at any time,' she continues. 'However, we will be recording this conversation and anything you say can potentially be used against you in any subsequent criminal proceedings. Do you understand?'

Monique sniffs loudly, glancing at her solicitor. Sadie knows her; it's Katy Lloyd, a tall, broad-shouldered woman in her mid-fifties.

Katy nods, and Monique hesitates for a moment then says, 'Yes. I understand.'

Sadie nods too, and turns to Daniel, who's sitting on her left. Immediately, he launches into the preliminaries, starting the recording and giving the names of the people in the room and the reason for the interview, and Sadie lets her mind wander, just for a few moments. It's been a challenging day, to say the least. The Sunday newspaper headlines, for a start. The story, unsurprisingly, was on every front page, each splash more lurid than the last. 'THE VANISHING OF CLASS 3B!' screamed the *Daily Mail*, and Daniel had raised an eyebrow.

'Makes it sound supernatural,' he muttered. 'As if aliens came down and took them or something.'

'It's starting to feel a bit like they actually might have,' Sadie had replied.

Then, there was the press conference, which ended just half an hour ago. It had, unsurprisingly, been packed, reporters jostling for position shoulder to shoulder in a ground floor room which, in retrospect, was rather too small, and brandishing an intimidating number of TV cameras and microphones. Outside, a long row of satellite trucks transmitted the proceedings around the world. Sadie had watched a few snippets from the previous night's foreign news shows earlier, and the coverage had been even more frenzied than she'd thought it would be. The fact that, on day three, the investigation still has so few leads seems to be adding fuel to what is now, clearly, a global fire that shows no sign of going out, and Sadie had felt her hands trembling as she took her seat.

She'd opened by telling the assembled journalists the same thing the families had been told: that the police now had reason to believe that the missing children and adults were being held in some unknown location against their will.

'We have still had no contact with any abductor and therefore no confirmation of this, however, and until we do we're going to carry on looking for them,' Sadie said. 'Unfortunately, despite what is now the biggest search in British policing history, there's still been no trace of them. There've been hundreds of alleged sightings, both here in the UK and abroad, and we thank the public for these, but again, as yet none have come to anything. As such, we're appealing once more for anyone who sees, or thinks they see, any of the missing adults or children to get in touch with us immediately, and for the public to continue to be vigilant. We would also like anyone who saw anything suspicious in or around the village of Lower Lockton on Friday afternoon or early evening to come forward. However, as this is also now a murder investigation, we would urge extreme caution. If you *do* see anything suspicious, please do not approach but call 999—'

She'd been interrupted at this point by a flurry of questions, everyone wanting to know the same thing, neatly summed up by Aidan Summers, a well-known tabloid newspaper reporter.

'What is this "reason to believe" they're being held against their will? And why no contact from any kidnappers?' he said, sounding exasperated. 'I mean, is this terrorists or what? Is it normal to wait three days to issue a ransom demand?'

Sadie had simply told the sea of increasingly hostile faces that she was unable to release any more information at this stage and that the police, like everyone else, still didn't know exactly what was going on.

'I promise you, as soon as we get more clarification, we'll keep the press and the public in the loop as far as it's safe to do so,' she said. 'Our absolute priority is no further loss of life, and getting these children and adults home safely and as quickly as possible.'

'Can we speak to any of the families?' someone else shouted from the back of the room, and Sadie shook her head.

'Not right now,' she said. 'As you can imagine, this is an extremely difficult time for them all, and they're struggling. We would ask that you continue to respect their privacy. As the case develops, this may change, of course, and we'll let you know immediately if any family members are happy to appear on camera or give press interviews. We, and they, thank you for your understanding.'

She had ended the press conference with a huge sense of relief. So far, it seemed that most of the journalists *were* behaving reasonably well, much to her surprise – there'd been a few reports of the press hanging around trying to doorstep some of the parents over the weekend, but when asked to leave, they'd obliged, and it also seemed that the families were respecting her request for them to resist speaking to the press, at least for now.

'Even Spike Greer,' Daniel had said. 'Amazing footballer, but I thought he might become a bit of a liability after what happened at the briefing at the school. Seemingly not anymore. I think Erica's death has spooked them all. None of them want to risk saying the wrong thing now in case one of the kids is next.'

'Boss?'

Sadie, lost in thought, suddenly realises Daniel is ready for her to start the interview and nods, glancing down at her notes and dragging herself back to the task in hand.

'Sorry. Right. Mrs Townsend… Can I call you Monique?'

Across the table, Monique sniffs again and says, 'Sure.'

'OK. I'd like to start by showing you some photographs, Monique. These are stills taken from CCTV footage which was captured at the Cotswold Wilderness Park on Friday afternoon.'

She slides three pictures across the table, watching the woman's face closely. Monique's eyes widen, and then she swallows hard twice, as if she has something stuck in her throat.

'I… I…' she begins, then stops talking again, her eyes lowered.

'Is this you?' asks Sadie.

She taps the clear image of Monique, the one taken from the CCTV footage of the seating area outside the café. Monique swallows again, and nods.

'Yes,' she whispers.

'And this? And this? These are pictures of you too, aren't they? At other locations around the park.'

Sadie points to the other two photographs, and again Monique nods.

'Yes, that's me,' she says, without looking up.

'So would you like to explain why you were there? And apparently trying to stay out of sight of the children and teachers? Just hours before they all disappeared? And could you also explain why you didn't think this little outing of yours was worth a mention?'

Monique turns to her solicitor, an alarmed look on her face, and Katy nods reassuringly.

'Go on,' she says.

Monique glances down at the photos again, then takes a deep breath and looks back at Sadie.

'OK. I know this looks bad,' she says. 'And yes, I should have told you before, but I just felt so… well, so *stupid*.'

She inhales and exhales again, as if trying to calm herself. Sadie says nothing, waiting.

'I'm… well, I'm a bit of a worrier,' says Monique, and gives an embarrassed laugh. 'Actually, that's probably a gross understatement. My husband, Ben, says I'm obsessive when it comes to Willow. I suffered from ghastly anxiety all the way through my pregnancy and I thought it would go away once I'd delivered this beautiful, healthy little girl but… well, it just didn't. If anything, it got worse. I worry *all* the time. When she was a baby and a toddler I worried she wasn't hitting all her milestones. When she went to nursery – Ben insisted; *I* would have kept her at home – I was so worried she'd be crying all day without me that I started to drive down there a few times a day and peer in the windows. How *ridiculous* is that? Standing outside with my nose pressed against the glass, watching her. The staff made me stop in the end; I think they thought I was completely mad. And Willow was fine, *totally* fine, by the way. It was *me* who had the separation anxiety, not her. And then when she went to school, I worried she wasn't learning to read quickly enough, and that she wasn't making friends easily, and… oh, endless, endless things. And the silly thing is, I *know* it's all in my head. I know she's OK – *better* than OK. She's amazing. And I've been to the doctor, and I've been given anti-anxiety medication and I've had therapy and… well, everything. But nothing seems to work. I've just never been able to get on top of it, and it's *exhausting*. It's *horrible*.'

She sinks her head into her hands and groans, and Sadie feels an unexpected pang of sympathy.

Monique is clearly not a well woman. But still…

'It all sounds very difficult for you, and I'm sorry to hear that,' she says. 'But… Friday. Talk to me about that. Because, unfortunately, Monique, it does seem at this point that you were one of the last known people to see Class 3B before they vanished. So you can understand my concern, can't you?'

Monique raises her head, tears streaking her cheeks, and nods.

'Yes, I do understand,' she says. 'But I promise you, I know nothing, *nothing* about what's happened to the children. I'm utterly devastated – I'm barely *functioning*... Look, I know those pictures make me look suspicious. I can see that. I'm an idiot. I didn't even think about CCTV. But then, I didn't know they were all going to go missing...'

She lets out a sob, and Katy frowns, looking at her with a concerned expression.

'Monique, are you sure you're all right to continue?' the solicitor asks.

Monique nods, wiping her eyes with the backs of her hands.

'Yes... yes,' she says. 'I'm sorry. OK, so, Friday – it was just something I *needed* to do. I'm generally OK now when she's at school. I know she's safe and happy. But on the odd occasion when they go on trips, I totally freak out. I mean, last time I spent the entire day walking in circles round the living room and nearly driving myself mad, so this time, well... I couldn't help myself. It wasn't like they were going far, so I thought I'd just drive up there and have a peek, you know? Willow can be a bit of a fussy eater, so I just wanted to make sure she was eating her lunch, and that she was enjoying herself. And she was. She looked fine; *everything* looked fine. So I just hung around for a bit, and then I came home again. That's it, I swear. I have *no* idea what happened after that, *none*. God, I wish I did...'

She sounds distraught, and her eyes fill with tears again. Katy reaches down to the large black leather handbag she propped against the leg of the table when she entered the room earlier and pulls out a tissue.

'Here,' she says, and then turns to Sadie and Daniel.

'Are you both happy?' she asks. 'I think you have your explanation of what Mrs Townsend was doing there?'

'Just a few more questions,' says Sadie, as she thinks, *This woman has serious issues. Whatever help she's been getting, it's clearly not working…*

'What time did you get home, Monique?'

Monique is silent for a few seconds.

'Umm… I think I left around two?' she says. 'I wanted to get back before Ben got home. He's an architect, and he usually finishes early on a Friday. I didn't want him to know— I mean, I didn't want him to realise what I'd been doing…'

Her voice tails off. Sadie stares at her for a moment, then turns to Daniel with a questioning look.

He nods.

'That tallies,' he says. 'We have you on CCTV getting into your vehicle in the car park just after 2 p.m., Mrs Townsend. And you were picked up on an ANPR camera just outside Littleford village shortly after three. So it does appear you drove straight home. But what did you mean when you said you wanted to get home before your husband did, because you didn't want him to know what you'd been doing?'

So you picked up on that too, thinks Sadie.

'*Did* you know the people on that bus were about to go missing?' says Daniel. 'Were you passing information on to someone else, maybe? Do you know where they are now, Mrs Townsend?'

'NO! NO!'

Suddenly Monique is on her feet, standing up so quickly that her chair topples over, clattering backwards onto the floor.

Looking startled, Katy puts a hand on her arm, but Monique shakes her off with a violent shrug.

'Don't touch me!' she screams. Then she turns to Sadie and Daniel, her eyes wide.

'How could you even *think* that?' she shouts. 'I *told* you about my problems. I told you why I was there. How can you *accuse* me—?'

There's a manic edge to her voice, and Sadie holds up a hand, but Daniel is on his feet now too.

'Mrs Townsend. Monique. We need you to calm down, OK? We're simply asking you a few questions. Nobody's accusing you of anything. We're just trying to establish the facts. We're very, very concerned about Willow, and about all the other missing children and adults—'

'Well, you're asking the wrong person,' snaps Monique. She's still breathing heavily, anger flashing in her eyes. 'And I'm done with this conversation.'

She turns to Katy.

'They said I could stop this interview at any time, didn't they? Well, I want to stop now, please. I'm going home.'

Chapter Seventeen

LITTLEFORD

Day 4: Monday, 10.15 a.m.

Ben Townsend closes the bedroom door quietly and creeps across the landing and down the stairs, carefully skipping the creaky third tread from the bottom. He makes a mental note to call Brandon, the local handyman, to ask him if he can pop in later and have a look at it, then wonders why he's even thinking about it. It might cheer Monique up to have the guy in the house – she, like most of the women in Littleford, seems to be rather taken with him. But what does a dodgy step matter, at the moment? Ben has a hollow feeling in his stomach that's nothing to do with the fact that it's after ten and he still hasn't eaten breakfast. He's been up since five, a combination of fear and anxiety – and, if he's honest, suspicion too – making him too tense and jumpy to stay in bed, even though he's never felt this shattered in his life. But Monique – he's just checked, for the sixth time – is still asleep, curled into a tight little ball under the duvet. She got stuck into the wine again last night after they got back from the police station, and although he tried to persuade her to go and have a nice hot bath instead, to try to find some other way of switching off from the horrors of the weekend even for just a few minutes, she angrily refused.

'They accused me, Ben. *Me*. They accused *me* of knowing something about where the children are. How dare they? This is destroying me, it's destroying all of us, and they drag *me* in for questioning? I need a drink, OK?'

He'd left her to it. He simply hadn't had the energy to argue with her anymore. But all night, the thoughts have been racing through his head, and now he sits at the kitchen table, watching rain drum against the window, and goes over it all yet again.

She followed them to the Cotswold Wilderness Park. She was there. OK, so it's not entirely out of character behaviour, but even so… and then on Saturday, what exactly did she say, when she was muttering in her sleep? 'I could have saved her… I should have taken her off the bus…'

Ben can feel his heart rate speeding up.

Does she know something about what's happened? he thinks. *Could she possibly? But she'd never hurt Willow, would she? Never, ever…*

He groans, leaning forwards onto the table and resting his forehead on the smooth wood. He feels like he may actually be going mad. Monique is his *wife*. She *loves* their daughter, loves her almost too much. Yes, their marriage, their relationship, has been slowly deteriorating over the past few years, there's no doubt about that; he's tried so hard to help her, but she has so many issues, her behaviour sometimes is *so* extreme. Most of the time, he's not sure if he even loves her at all anymore. But there's no way she can be involved in any of this, just no way, surely? And the police let her go, didn't they? They told her she was being released subject to possible further investigation, something like that. But they let her go, and they wouldn't have done that if they really thought she knew anything about where the kids are, would they?

No. Of course they wouldn't.

Ben stands up, walks to the kettle and switches it on, then stands staring through the rain-streaked window. In the back garden, Willow's red and green swing sways gently back and forth in the breeze, and he squeezes his eyes tightly shut and imagines, just for a moment, that she's out there playing, hidden from his view, and that any minute now the back door will burst open and she'll run in laughing, her hair damp and her cheeks flushed. Then he opens his eyes again, feeling sick. Where is she, his little girl? What's happened to them all? Is this his punishment, for what he's done, and for what he's been planning to do? Because Monique may have a lot going on, but he's hardly a saint, is he? Far from it. So is this karma? Is this all his fault? Or... The thought hits him like a punch to the gut.

Shit. Oh shit, shit, shit. Could Monique possibly know? Has she found out somehow? Could she have got involved with making the kids disappear to get her revenge?

Ben's stomach contracts, and he slaps a hand over his mouth. He just makes it to the kitchen sink before he throws up.

'Sit there and watch your show. Good boy.'

Eldon Beckford tucks a blanket around his two-year-old and points at the TV, and the little boy snuggles back against the sofa cushions and sticks his thumb in his mouth, eyes already fixed on the screen. Eldon breathes a small sigh of relief. The television programme – something about a girl whose best friend is a duck – will keep River occupied for at least fifteen minutes, he hopes. The child is still unsettled and clingy, clearly missing his brother and picking up on the anguish of his parents, even though they're trying hard to act as normally as possible around him. But right now he seems happy enough, and Eldon is crossing his fingers he stays that way, for a while at least. He's not going to work today, of course. None of the parents are; they're all a mess, mentally *and* physically. Eldon hadn't even had to make a decision about it; his restaurant management team contacted him as soon as the news broke over the weekend, telling him not to worry about anything, that they could run everything until this was all over. And so now, unusually for a Monday morning, he's alone in the house with his youngest son. The family liaison officer is yet to arrive, they currently have no nanny, and Amy has gone out for a drive, making River a hasty breakfast of porridge with banana before telling Eldon she felt as though the walls were closing in on her and that she needed to escape for a while.

'If I stay in this house much longer I'm going to go crazy,' she told him. 'I can't bear it. How much longer, Eldon? What's going on? Maybe if I go out, there'll be some news when I come back. This silence, this *nothing*… it's driving me insane…'

Tears had filled her eyes, and Eldon had reached for her,

wanting to comfort her, but she'd brushed past him, muttering something about being back soon and making sure River had his milk. She'd been up since the early hours; he'd heard her wandering the house, sobbing, but he knew it was pointless trying to get her to come back to bed. He'd lain there, wide awake, listening, his own pain and dread making it impossible to sleep, until the darkness felt like it might smother him, at which point he'd pushed the duvet back and gone to find her. He'd found her in Noah's bedroom, kneeling on the floor by his bed clutching the teddy bear he'd had since he was four months old, and crying softly. She'd let Eldon hold her briefly then, and he'd cried too, whispering into her hair.

'It's going to be OK, baby. He'll be home soon. Our family will be back together again and this is going to feel like some hideous nightmare. I promise you.'

He'd hoped to comfort her, even a little, but she'd pulled away from him, wiping her eyes and giving him a strange look. She'd told him she was going to check on River, but she hadn't come back to bed, and he'd tried to sleep again but failed, his head buzzing. What had that look *meant*? Amy definitely wasn't herself, but she hadn't been even before the children vanished. He'd *thought* her increased coolness towards him in the past week had been to do with last weekend's party, but if it was just that, surely she'd have put it behind them now in the light of the current horrors? Was something else going on?

Now, Eldon's still thinking about it, as he sits listlessly in the armchair by the window, one eye on River, one on the driveway, waiting for Amy's car to reappear. He understands her need for some time alone, for some headspace, but this is the second time she's been out for a drive on her own in the past couple of days; she went out on Saturday evening too, after she finished bathing River and putting him to bed. Eldon had been so desperate to talk to her, but she'd simply refused, telling him it could wait, that she couldn't handle any more stress, that her head might actually explode.

'I'm not joking,' she said. 'I can't, Eldon. Not now. Please.'

He'd felt a surge of alarm, an irrational desire to barricade the bathroom door and not let her out until they'd had the conversation, and for a few seconds he'd stood stock still, staring at her, willing her to change her mind. Then he'd seen her expression of dread and nodded.

'OK. Not tonight. But soon, Amy. This is too important. You know it is. We *need* to discuss this.'

She'd grabbed her jacket and car keys and practically run from the house, and she hadn't reappeared for more than two hours, looking pale and red-eyed but definitely a little calmer. And so now he sits by the window, and he waits, again.

This is what life has been reduced to now, isn't it? he thinks. *Waiting. Waiting for news about the kids. Waiting for something horrific to happen. Waiting for a miracle.*

And waiting to talk to his wife. Because he has to now, *today*, whether she likes it or not. It's time to get their stories straight.

———

Clare Tustain turns her car engine off and reaches for her phone, tapping the screen to check her messages. Nothing. She feels ill, her temples throbbing with a headache no number of painkillers seems able to fix. Nick was still in bed when she went out this morning; he'd spent most of the night down in the living room, telling her he needed to stay up in case there was any news.

'What if they find the kids in the night, Clare? There was that big press conference; the whole damn world is talking about this now. So what if whoever's taken them decides there's been too much publicity and it's all too risky, and they just dump them by the side of the road somewhere? One of us needs to be awake, just in case. Imagine if a message came through and we missed it because we were asleep?'

She'd been too sad, too scared, too full of guilt, too bone-achingly tired to argue with him. She'd slept badly though, and at five-thirty she'd crawled out of bed and gone downstairs, telling Nick that she'd take over on message-watch now and that he needed to go and rest. He'd reluctantly agreed, and minutes later she'd heard soft snores emanating from their room. After forcing down a strong coffee and a slice of toast, she'd gone out in the car, and now she's home and wondering what to do next. Slowly, she opens the driver's door, but for some reason she can't move, doesn't *want* to go back inside. She's not sure she can stand another day of just *sitting* in the house, waiting.

This is torture, she thinks, and suddenly she feels completely overwhelmed, as if her entire world is slowly dissolving. Everything that seemed to be just within her grasp a few days ago – is any of it still possible, now? Clare looks at the front door of her home, and thinks about Stanley, her darling boy, who's not there, and about Nick who is, and about the pain he's in, and about how he'll react when he finds out what she's done. Slowly, she leans forward until her cheek touches the cool curve of the steering wheel, and she starts to cry.

In his office upstairs at The Granary, Reynold Lyon is working on his new game show idea. He knows the fact he's working today would look odd, if the police or indeed any of the other parents knew about it; Petra told him as much half an hour ago, when she stalked into the room, hair all mussed up and still in her white silk dressing gown, and gaped at him with an astonished expression.

'You're... you're working? Now? *Today*? With the children still missing and our whole world falling apart? What is *wrong* with you?'

'I need the distraction, Petra,' he'd said quietly. 'I'm sorry. If the police want us all to stay at home until there's a development, fine. I can do that. But I can't just *sit*. I'll stop when the family liaison guy gets here, but I'm going out of my mind, OK? I'm as devastated as you are, but sitting around crying isn't going to help. If I can get this finished, it could be big, sweetheart. And when we get the twins back – and yes, I said *when*, because that's absolutely what I believe will happen – that's only going to benefit them too, isn't it? So, please just let me do this. I'm here, just upstairs, OK? And I don't think it will be too much longer, you know. We'll hear something any minute now, I'm sure of it. This will all be over really soon.'

She'd stared at him for a long moment, then shaken her head and given a resigned shrug.

'Whatever. Fine,' she'd said. 'But sometimes, Reynold, I just don't understand you.'

She'd glanced down at the phone which she now seemed to have permanently clutched in her hand, obviously checking for any new messages, then looked at him again and sighed.

'And Brandon's just arrived,' she'd said. 'He's come to fix that broken cupboard door and do a few bits outside. I don't know if we should have cancelled him, after what the police said about not having visitors, but it's too late now. We had a chat about what's been going on, and he actually had tears in his eyes, the poor love. He's so fond of the twins, and he knew Erica Lindsay too, of course, because he's done so much work down at the school. He said he was really sorry, and if there's anything he can do... Anyway, you'll just have to ignore the noise.'

She'd left the room then, leaving him to it. Now, taking a quick screen break, Reynold glances out of the window next to his desk. The hammering and drilling from downstairs has stopped, and Brandon's now at the far end of the garden, doing something with a long tool – a hoe? Reynold has no idea, but the guy seems to be wielding it expertly. Reynold's in pretty good shape himself for fifty-five, but even from here he can see the muscles bulging in the younger man's arms as he works.

He's... what? Twenty-four, twenty-five? he thinks, and wonders if Petra's watching him too. It's one of the few problems with having a wife who's twenty years younger than he is; sometimes, he worries about things like this. Petra adores him, he knows that, and he's never had the slightest reason to doubt her fidelity, but even so... should he really have hired such a fit bloke? Should he have used Eric, the seventy-year-old who's been a village handyman for decades, instead? It was just that Brandon came highly recommended, working as he did for several of the other Littleford Primary School parents. And to be fair, he *is* an excellent all-rounder. He's a nice guy too, always happy to stop what he's doing to have a chat. And, as Petra had said, he's so good with the kids. Luca, in particular, loves to hang out with him when he's working outside, passing him tools and following him around the garden, the two of them chatting incessantly about birds and worms and God knows what else. If only the man wasn't so damned attractive...

Oh, for God's sake. You have more important things to worry about right now. Get a grip, Reynold tells himself.

He rubs his eyes and turns back to his screen. He needs to focus, just for another hour or so. Needs to get this *finished*. Needs to stop thinking about Luca and Lola, and everything that's going on, just for a short while. At the thought of his children, he feels a quivering in his stomach. He complains about the noise and mess and chaos they create all the time, but he loves them to their very bones, and the big, bright, beautiful house feels dark and lifeless without them, their absence causing him to physically ache.

'It's an actual pain. How is that possible? Actual real *pain*,' he'd said to Petra last night, and she'd nodded.

'I feel it too. It's the worst pain I've ever had, and I gave *birth* to them,' she replied, and she clasped her hands over her stomach and began to sob again, rocking slowly back and forth like she did when the twins were babies and she'd cradle one in the crook of each arm and sing quietly to them in her melodic, low voice to soothe them to sleep.

Every time her phone beeps with a message he feels sick; he's turned his notifications off now, unable to bear it. But all they've had in the past twelve hours or so have been updates about Monique Townsend's shock arrest and subsequent release, and he's not even sure now that it *was* an arrest, not as such. It sounds more as if she was just asked to go into the police station voluntarily, for questioning, after they somehow discovered that she had, for some bizarre reason, followed the school bus to the wildlife park on Friday to check on her daughter. The group had been in uproar about it overnight, of course, even though her poor husband, Ben, had tried to play it down, telling them it was all part of an anxiety disorder Monique suffered from and that she absolutely, one hundred per cent, had *nothing* to do with any of this and had no idea where the children were.

'But why not tell anyone before now? Why not say she was there on Friday afternoon? Why wait until the police came looking for *her*? It's so... so freaking *weird*!' Petra had spluttered. 'I mean, she's always been a bit odd, but this?'

'Well, the police have let her go now,' Reynold had replied evenly. 'And they wouldn't have done that if they thought there was anything more to it, would they? I agree, it's very strange behaviour. But people *can* be strange, we know that. There's no point in the group falling out over it, is there? We need to stick together right now.'

'God, Reynold. Why are you always so *reasonable*?' she'd retorted. 'It's your precious job, isn't it? Always taking the middle ground, always being impartial. This isn't a frigging chat show, this is our *lives*. Our *kids'* lives…'

It had threatened to erupt into a full-blown row, but Reynold had defused the situation by pulling his wife into his arms and holding her tense, stiff body tightly, whispering into her ear, telling her that everything was going to be OK, he knew it was, and when was he ever wrong? Even as the words left his lips, though, he'd felt a stab of guilt so sharp his knees had felt weak.

I'm so sorry, Petra, he'd thought, and at the same time he'd felt her soften, her anger and frustration melting away, and seconds later she had wrapped her arms around him too. They'd held each other for a long time, their tears mingling, damp cheeks pressed together, and Reynold had tried to force what he's done, the thing she doesn't know he's done, out of his head, for what's the point in obsessing about it? It's too late, and one day soon he might have to deal with the repercussions. But for now, all he can do is take it one day, one *hour* at a time…

Shit.

His mind is wandering again. He takes a deep breath and starts to read the proposal on his screen. It's two pages long, and he forces himself to go through it slowly and carefully, checking every detail, imagining what it will look like on TV. It works; he knows it does. It's good, maybe *really* good. The biggest, the *best* game show for years. When he gets to the end he goes back to the beginning again, reading it once more, changing a word here and there, polishing, perfecting. And then he reads it one final time and, despite himself, he feels a frisson of excitement.

It's ready, he thinks. *I've done it. This is IT.*

He hits 'save' and closes the document, and he's just about to switch his computer off when he hears a sound that makes him whirl around in his chair, his heart leaping into his throat.

A scream.

Petra, screaming.

He jumps to his feet and runs, taking the stairs two at a time, and she's still screaming, but now it's his name he hears, over and over again.

'REYNOLD! REY-NOLD!'

Her shrieks are coming from the kitchen, and he thunders into the room, gasping, bracing himself for an intruder, or maybe a police officer bearing terrible news, because surely something horrific must have just happened for her to sound this terrified, but it's just Petra, standing there alone, and he stops dead, breathing heavily.

'What—! What the—?'

A movement outside catches his eye, and he spins around, but it's only Brandon, sprinting down the garden towards the house, clearly also wondering what on earth is going on. Then he notices that Petra's gripping her phone in her hand, display facing outwards towards him. There's a horrified expression on her face, and when she speaks her voice is thin and shaky.

'There's a message. Look. *Look.*'

He looks. It's a text, from an unknown number.

All of the adults and children taken from the Littleford School bus trip on Friday are safe and well.
We will tell you what we want from you very shortly.
There will be no engagement or discussion.

Await further instructions.

And underneath, a second message.

PS. One of you has a secret.
We know what it is.
And if you want to keep it a secret, it's time to PAY.

Chapter Eighteen

COTSWOLDS POLICE HEADQUARTERS

Day 4: Monday, 11.50 a.m.

'A *wait further instructions*? Christ. Haven't we already waited long enough?'

DCI Daniel Sharma sits down heavily in the nearest chair, and groans. Perched on the desk opposite, DSU Sadie Stewart shakes her head slowly.

'I feel ill,' she says.

Ever since the frantic calls from the parents began coming in, her stomach has been churning, her mouth dry, anxiety building like an ever-tightening fist around her throat. She takes a sip of water from the bottle next to her. All nine families have received the same two text messages which, some ninety minutes later, it has already been established were sent from the same unknown and now untraceable number – presumably a burner phone immediately destroyed by the kidnappers.

'All the teaching staff on that bus had every parent's

number in their mobiles,' Daniel had pointed out earlier. 'They must have made one of them hand theirs over before the phones were switched off and dumped. Unless they got the numbers ahead of time somehow, which is possible I suppose.'

Sadie nods, reading out the transcript of the messages again.

'"All of the adults and children taken from the Littleford School bus trip on Friday are safe and well. We will tell you what we want from you very shortly. There will be no engagement or discussion. Await further instructions. PS, one of you has a secret. We know what it is. And if you want to keep it a secret, it's time to pay." *No engagement or discussion?* They're clearly not planning on giving us any opportunity to negotiate, are they? Just another wretched waiting game. But at least we know now. Absolutely, *definitely* a hostage situation.'

She's spent the past twenty minutes scanning the most recent surveys of UK kidnappings, trying again to work out what might be behind this one. Most – some forty per cent, it seems – are criminal or gang related and around twenty per cent domestic, with smaller percentages sexually or politically motivated. Only six per cent are traditional ransom kidnappings, and the specialist team has confirmed that the kidnap of a big group like this, including both children and adults, is pretty much unprecedented anywhere in the world.

'And *who*? That's the other big question,' Daniel replies. 'Male perpetrators, most likely. It says here' – he waves his own copy of the report Sadie's been reading – 'that only around seven per cent of kidnappers are female. Fits in with the "masked man" thing, at least. But, this bit about a secret? What's that all about?'

'I don't know. That's really bugging me. It says *one* of them has a secret, so why take *all* the kids, *and* the teachers? That's pretty drastic. We need to talk to the parents urgently, and see if anyone will confess to anything. If we can find out what this mysterious secret is, it might lead us to whoever's behind this. I know nothing obvious has come up on any of the background checks so far, but we need to find out what the hell this is all about. Immediately.'

'It must be a heck of a dirty little secret, eh?' says Daniel.

Sadie nods.

'And you know what else?' she says. 'We can't rule out one of the parents somehow being *involved*. In the actual kidnap, I mean. I'm not entirely happy with Monique Townsend's "overanxious mother" story, for a start. We need to keep a close eye on her. On all of them, in fact. But we need to be careful, and diplomatic. They've all lost their children, and maybe it's someone else connected to the school or the families who's been passing on information. I just have no idea…'

She pauses, suddenly feeling a little overwhelmed, and Daniel nods and sighs, leaning back in his chair and lifting his hands to massage his temples.

He's feeling it too. So many unknowns. So little to go on. It's horrible, she thinks.

'What a mess,' she says.

They stare at each other for a few seconds, and Sadie can see in the droop of his shoulders and the weary look in his bloodshot eyes that he's struggling with this as much as she is. Then, abruptly, he stands up.

'Yes, it's a mess. But come on, there's no point in just sitting here. We might have to wait until these bastards decide to get in touch again, but there are still things we can do. I'll go and get us some coffees – yes, tea for you, I know – and then let's have a closer look at the parents, OK?'

Five minutes later, mugs in hand, they're sitting close together, Daniel's laptop open in front of them, at the desk nearest the whiteboard. Over the past few hours, somebody has added photos of every parent to those of the missing children, so they're now all in little family groups, lined up across the board. Other members of the now huge team are still working on the deep dive into the pasts of all these adults, as well as into everyone else connected with the school, and as yet nothing of concern has been raised.

But have we missed something? Sadie wonders, as she puts her mug down on the desk. There are so many people to investigate, and she trusts her colleagues, but right now she wants to look *herself* at everything that's available on the Police National Computer; a full picture of each individual's prior contact with the police and the legal system – arrests, convictions, cautions, reprimands, warnings, penalty notices. Is there anything here, among the parents' records, that could have triggered such a major crime?

'Right,' she says. 'Let's go. First, Eugene and Polly Pearson. Parents to Wanda.'

She looks at the photo of seven-year-old Wanda, blonde hair tucked behind her ears, cheeky smile and almond-shaped blue eyes, and her throat tightens again. Daniel taps his laptop screen.

'Nothing. Neither parent known to the police.'

'OK. Spike and Tasha Greer.'

She looks at the next set of photos, at eight-year-old

Gresham grinning in his football kit, and at his shaven-headed ex-footballer dad and petite, pretty mum.

'Hang on… OK. Nothing on the mother. But a few hits on Spike – his real name is Graham, by the way. Two drunk and disorderly arrests back in his Chelsea days. One allegation of assault from a West Ham player. I think I remember that. I mean, he was never out of the papers in his heyday, was he? But he was never actually charged with anything. And nothing at all for the past ten years. Marriage and parenthood has obviously been good for him.'

'Hmm,' says Sadie, thinking about how aggressive the man's behaviour was at the school on Saturday morning.

'He's still a bit fiery though, isn't he? Although that doesn't mean he's got anything to do with this, of course. And his past is well documented by the look of it, so not exactly a secret. Unless there's something else we don't know about yet. Anyway, next?'

'Vanessa and Alex Carr. Son Luke. Nothing on them either. Then we have Rosie Duggan. She's a lone parent, daughter Harper. No criminal record herself, but she did make allegations of harassment and stalking five years ago. She said she'd been in an abusive relationship which she'd managed to escape but then he wouldn't leave her alone. The guy was given a restraining order and that seemed to do the trick. Nothing since then. Maybe we should talk to him, though? He wasn't Harper's father, by the way.'

'Who's her father, then?' Sadie asks.

'Unknown,' replies Daniel. 'A one-night stand, apparently.'

'OK. Well, having an abusive ex-partner doesn't sound like

blackmail fodder to me. But let's bring in the ex anyway, see what he's got to say for himself.'

Sadie scribbles a note on her pad.

'Next?'

'Brett and Jon MacDonald-Cook. Moved down from Scotland a year ago. Brett is a chef and got a new job at Barns House – you know, that fancy hotel near Cirencester? Jon's a stay-at-home dad. Their son is Oliver, aged eight. They adopted him when he was three months old. His mother was a Glasgow drug addict who subsequently overdosed and passed away. Neither of the dads has a record of any sort.'

Sadie thinks for a moment, staring at the photo of Oliver, a thoughtful-looking boy wearing round tortoiseshell-framed glasses.

'Maybe speak to Police Scotland? Again, it all sounds above board – just another adoption, no secret there. But what if there's some animosity from the birth mother's family, if she had one? Maybe they wanted her son to stay in Glasgow? Maybe they didn't like the idea of him having gay dads, who knows? They might want some compensation, in the form of a kidnap ransom? Unlikely, I know – I mean, again it begs the question, why take the entire class and their teachers too? But no stone unturned and all that...?'

'I agree,' says Daniel. 'Anything at all out of the ordinary, we need to look at it. So, who's next? Eldon and Amy Beckford, our TV chef and restaurateur and his wife. Son Noah, and they have a younger boy as well. Nothing on Eldon. Amy though...'

He pauses, turning over a page.

'Oh. Nothing much. She was arrested for shoplifting in

Harrods – we're talking nine years ago. But she was pregnant at the time, and apparently suffering from morning sickness that lasted all day. She was caught with a silk scarf in her handbag but claimed she'd been looking at it and suddenly felt terribly ill, so she'd just shoved it in her bag without thinking as she rushed off to find the toilets. She was released without charge.'

'Sounds plausible enough,' says Sadie. She's never been pregnant herself, but she remembers when her sister was expecting Teddy, and how urgent that rush to the bathroom often was.

Daniel nods. 'Yep. I suppose someone *could* use that against Amy Beckford though, if they were desperate? Now that she's so well known, and would probably be mortified to be labelled a thief, even if it really was unintentional?'

He hesitates, and Sadie shakes her head.

'It's a stretch. A mass kidnap, for something as minor as that? I can't see it,' she says.

'Suppose not. So, Clare and Nick Tustain, and their son Stanley. She's the slightly gobby one. She works at some sort of dog or pet boarding kennels; he's in IT. Nothing on them either. Boring, this lot, aren't they?'

He raises an eyebrow, and Sadie manages a small smile.

'Being law-abiding is *not* boring,' she says, and he winks at her.

'Our job would be very dull if everyone was, though,' he replies. 'OK, Ben and Monique Townsend. We know Monique of course. He's an architect; she's a stay-at-home mum. But again, no record for either.'

Sadie frowns and gives a little grunt.

'Fine. Just one more then?'

'Yep,' he says. 'Aaaaand finally: our TV chat show star Reynold Lyon and his model wife Petra Sanderson. Parents to twins Luca and Lola. Amazingly, again both squeaky clean. I'm not sure why I'm so surprised at that, actually. I suppose you expect these showbiz types to have had a few wild nights in their time, don't you? Maybe a bit of a coke habit or something. But no, not a sausage. And that, boss, is that. Not a whole lot to go on, is there? A few small bones, but no nice big skeletons.'

Sadie sighs, feeling a wave of despondency.

'No. So does that mean one of them has been up to something we don't know about? Something serious enough to make someone take an entire bus load of people hostage?'

'Maybe. But what?' says Daniel.

'Absolutely no idea,' she replies. 'Maybe something new will emerge if we keep looking, and keep asking questions. Or maybe the kidnappers will give us a clue, eh? Maybe they'll tell us what this is all about in their next message.'

'Maybe. Miracles do happen, now and again. OK, back in a mo. I need to pee,' Daniel says.

'Way too much information, Dan.'

She smiles and watches him as he crosses the room, then stands up and lifts her hands over her head, swaying gently from side to side, trying to ease the tension in her back. Then she stands and stares at the board, eyes moving slowly from family group to family group.

Is one of you behind this? she asks the faces, silently. *Or are you all really just victims? And which one of you has the secret?*

What have you done? And why is everyone being punished for it, not just you?

The adult faces look back, saying nothing, and Sadie looks again at the children, at their bright eyes and their gap-toothed smiles, and feels tears prick her eyelids. Why is this case making her so emotional?

They're just so goddamned SMALL. So young, to be going through this, she thinks, as her gaze moves across the board. Little Stanley Tustain, with his cheeky grin. Luke Carr, a dusting of freckles across his nose. And the twins, Luca and Lola Lyon, with their striking green eyes, clearly inherited from their stunning mother. Sadie reaches out and runs her fingers over the last two photos, then pulls her hand back again quickly, hoping nobody in the room has noticed.

At least you two have each other, wherever you are, she thinks. *At least, I hope to God you do. I hope you're all together, keeping each other warm. Keeping each other's spirits up. I hope your teachers are looking after you, and each other too. We'll find you soon, though. We will, I promise. We'll get you home. Stay strong, OK?*

And then she turns away abruptly, trying very hard to ignore the voice that's whispering to her from somewhere deep inside, and saying something she really, really doesn't want to hear.

Don't make promises you can't keep.

Chapter Nineteen

LITTLEFORD

Day 4: Monday, 2.05 p.m.

'**B**ut it says *ONE of you has a secret*! *One* of us! I just don't understand, Reynold. Has somebody in the group done something terrible, do you think? But why take *all* our children?'

Petra is stomping up and down the kitchen, phone still clutched in her hand. Every minute or so it beeps; another message, another expression of bewilderment, another few lines of wild speculation. She's got dressed since the texts arrived, the silk dressing gown swapped for a pair of faded jeans and a pale-blue denim shirt. She's even brushed her hair and put on a bit of makeup, a hint of lip gloss and a slick of mascara, and Reynold can see that although she's deeply confused and still in a high state of anxiety, there's hope in her eyes now, and a little less distress in her voice.

'*All of the adults and children taken from the Littleford School bus trip on Friday are safe and well.*'

She's been reading the words out loud to him over and over for hours, obsessing over what they might mean.

'*Safe and well.* They wouldn't say that, if they'd hurt them, would they?' she said the first time. 'They *wouldn't.* I know they hurt poor Mrs Lindsay – they *killed* her – but… children are different, aren't they? And the fact they've made a point of saying they're all OK – they *must* be, mustn't they? This is good news, Reynold. It is. Isn't it?'

'Of course it is. It's great news,' he'd replied. 'It means this might be nearly over. They'll ask for money next, or whatever it is they want. And then hopefully we can sort it out, and get the kids home.'

She'd nodded, not asking any more questions, seemingly not caring about the mechanics, just focussing on the prospect of Luca and Lola being released and coming home. He'd wondered if he should voice a note of caution, urge her not to get *too* excited, warn her that things could still go wrong, but he didn't have the heart. Except now she's asking about that cryptic line about someone having a secret, and Reynold can feel his heart beginning to race.

'I don't know,' he says. 'But it's not us, is it? We don't have any awful secrets. At least, *I* haven't. Not sure about what you got up to though, back in your wild youth?'

He smiles at her, trying to lighten the mood for a moment, and she stops pacing and, to his surprise, smiles back.

'Nothing!' she says. 'Unless you count the many crimes against fashion I committed. Some of the outfits I had to wear in those early catwalk shows… God!'

She sighs, and her smile fades.

'Oh, bugger it, there's no point in trying to guess, is there?

Everyone's doing that on the WhatsApp group, and nobody seems to have a clue what secret they're referring to, or if they do they're not saying. Look, I'm going out for a walk, just for half an hour. There don't seem to be any people from the press hanging around in the village today, and I need to get my head together. And it's such a beautiful day out there – have you seen that sunshine? I think it's an omen. We're getting them back, Reynold, I know we are.'

Her eyes are suddenly shiny with tears, and she blinks them away.

'I assume you're going back up to your office? Marc's gone for now, by the way. He said to call if we need anything. And you call *me* if you hear *anything*, OK?'

'Of course I will. See you in a bit. I love you.'

'Love you too.'

She blows him a kiss and leaves the room, and a minute later Reynold hears the front door closing. Alone, at last. He's glad that Marc Hackett, their family liaison officer, has left too. The young, muscular man with bleached blond hair and a friendly smile is perfectly nice and has been very helpful in keeping them abreast of everything that's been going on with the investigation, but his presence is making Reynold even more anxious, for some reason. Especially now.

He stares into space for a few moments, then turns his head to look out into the garden as a movement catches his eye. It's one of the resident squirrels, grey tail bobbing as it scampers across the lawn before running straight up the trunk of the beech tree, startling a magpie which squawks and flaps away. Petra is right; overhead, the sky is the blue of a Santorini sea, and Brandon, who's still out there pruning something down by the pool now, has taken his T-shirt off, his torso lean and tanned. When he'd heard Petra screaming earlier and raced from the garden into the kitchen, she'd blurted out the news about the messages to the startled-looking young man before Reynold had had the chance to gently shoo him away.

'I'm not sure you should have done that,' he told his wife. 'I don't think the police would be too happy about us telling the hired help that the kidnappers have made contact.'

'You can't call people "the hired help", Reynold,' she'd snapped. 'And he's a *friend*. I need *someone* outside the family to talk to, and he's been great. He's worried about us; everyone is.'

Now Reynold turns away from the window and walks slowly upstairs to his office. Brandon had looked shocked at the content of the messages, and he's not surprised. He's pretty shocked himself. He wasn't expecting *this*. Wasn't expecting this at all. This is a plot twist, if ever he saw one.

One of you has a secret.
We know what it is.
And if you want to keep it a secret, it's time to PAY.

Is this message aimed at him? Is it possible? There's already an accusatory feeling in the WhatsApp group, people telling each other that *somebody* must know what it's referring to. And Reynold has a horrible feeling he might, but he hasn't admitted that, of course. He could be wrong – after all, he's not the only one in Littleford who lived it up a little, back in the day. He certainly had some wild nights out and slept with a lot of women – of course he did. Sometimes, more than one woman at a time. But he was young, and easy on the eye, and on television, and that's what life was like back then. He *definitely* broke a few hearts. But he didn't do anything *terrible*. Nothing *illegal*. Others may well have done much, much worse. And then Petra came along and, well, everything changed. *He* changed. He fell in love, properly, probably for the first time. He's a family man now, a father. He's finally grown up and settled down. Except…

Reynold sits down heavily at his desk and sinks his head into his hands.

Except… there *is* something. Something more recent. He's done something, something bad. He doesn't even know why he got involved, and he's tried to get out of it, more than once, but for some reason it hasn't been that easy. But surely nobody could have found out about *that*? Could they?

Christ. Reynold groans. Only one other person is supposed to know about what's been going on, and he finds it almost impossible to believe that she'd have told anyone. But what if she has? Or is she wondering too, panicking about the message in the same way he is?

Because if this comes out…

He feels his palms growing clammy, and a bead of sweat runs down his forehead. He knows he should just be thinking about his children right now. They're the ones who've been spirited away, and the thought that they might be scared or unhappy is gut-wrenching. But if everyone finds out what he's done, it won't just be his own family it will devastate. The ripples will spread far and wide…

And, Jesus, the newspapers. The press will have a field day.

Reynold swallows hard and makes up his mind. He's going

to have to talk to her, somehow. And as soon as possible. But how can he do that without raising suspicion? Call a meeting of all the parents, maybe? He leans back in his chair and starts to formulate a plan.

'Monique – seriously? Is that a good idea?'

Ben holds out both hands beseechingly, but his wife brushes past him.

'It might not be a good idea, but it's the only one I've got right now. The stress is *killing* me,' she says, as she leaves the room.

Ben watches her go and feels misery welling in his chest. When the messages came through, he stared at them with a mixture of relief and sheer terror for a full minute, then ran to the bedroom. He shook Monique awake, repeating the news over and over again, knowing from bitter experience that when she was in that sort of state – groggy and hungover – it took a while for anything to penetrate. When she finally understood what he was saying she'd immediately crawled out of bed and staggered into the en suite bathroom, from where he'd then heard vomiting – twice – followed by the sound of the shower being turned on. He'd gone down to the kitchen to get some coffee on the go, and when she appeared twenty minutes later she'd looked shamefaced, wrapping her arms around his neck for a minute, her hair damp against his cheek, before dropping into a chair.

'I'm sorry, Ben,' she'd whispered. 'I drank too much last night. I wasn't in a good place. But this is a positive development, isn't it? I don't know what this secret thing is all about. I can't even think about getting my head round that right now. But if the kids are OK, that's enough for now, isn't it? And maybe the police will leave me alone after this, now they've got something else to focus on?'

He hadn't replied, still half wondering if his wife might somehow be involved in all this, and if, therefore, she really does know what *he's* been up to, but not daring to ask her, especially as she'd seemed relatively calm for the first time in days. And so he'd stayed silent, and she'd accepted the mug he'd handed her and sat there, sipping slowly and tapping on her phone as the WhatsApp group began to light up. Now, a few hours later, she's just left the kitchen clutching a bottle of Pinot Grigio and a glass, insisting that another drink is the only way she's going to get through the day.

'It's not even three o'clock!' he calls after her, but he gets no reply and moments later hears the living room door slam.

This is a nightmare.

Ben sits down at the kitchen table. His mouth is so dry his lips feel as if they're cracking. He's been trying not to think about it too much while he's been around his wife, but now he's starting to sweat, his breath coming in little gasps as the full realisation begins to hit him, the words of the text message neon-bright in his mind's eye.

One of you has a secret.
We know what it is.
And if you want to keep it a secret, it's time to PAY.

This is about him, isn't it? It is; he knows it is. Somebody knows. But who, and how? And *does* Monique know? Is she putting on a big act? *Is* she behind this kidnap somehow, or helping whoever is? And what will happen next? How much money will these people want? He has some savings, and the house is worth a decent whack, but what if they want hundreds of thousands? What if they want *millions*? What then? And if he can't pay, does that mean everyone will find out? And why is the room suddenly so *hot*?

Ben stands up, rushes to the back door and stumbles out into the garden. His chest feels tight, little black dots dancing in front of his eyes, and he sinks to his knees on the hard granite surface of the patio and forces himself to breathe slowly. In, out. In out.

Calm. He has to stay calm. He can't fall apart, not now. He was so close, so *effing* close to everything he ever wanted. But maybe it's not all over. Maybe this can still work out. Maybe the message *isn't* aimed at him.

Ben takes another slow, shaky breath. Should he confront Monique, maybe? Ask her straight out if she knows what he's so scared she knows? Maybe. Not yet though. There's somebody else he needs to speak to first. Today, ideally.

Maybe Monique's drinking is a good thing, he thinks. *Maybe I can sneak out later. She'll probably be unconscious again in a couple of hours.*

And in the meantime, he can sit down at his desk and go through his accounts. Check the finances, see how much he can raise, if it comes to it. Ben swallows hard, clambers to his feet and heads back into the house.

'Clare! Breathe. Breathe, OK? I think you're having a panic attack. You're OK. Everything's OK.'

Clare Tustain twists her head to look at her husband, who's crouching next to her chair, and tries to follow his instructions.

Breathe, breathe.

He's right, she thinks. She *is* having a panic attack. It's been years since this happened: the chest pain, the trembling, the tingling in her hands, the ringing in her ears, the light-headedness, the absolute conviction that this is it, that she's having a heart attack, that she's actually going to die, right here, right now, in her own shabby living room. She'd had them regularly, back then. And now she's having another one, and she knows exactly what's triggered it.

The message. The damn message.

It can only be aimed at her. She never thought this would happen, never. She had nightmares about it, at the start, nightmares in which everyone found out what she'd done, nightmares in which her life slowly fell apart as a baying crowd howled with derision. But nobody ever *did* find out, and so she gradually started to relax, to think that maybe she – or more accurately, *they*, because of course she's not alone in this, is she? – had somehow, miraculously, got away with it. Years have passed now, and big things were about to happen – great things, she hoped. Everything had been planned so carefully, for so long. And now... how has it gone so horribly wrong? Because somebody, somehow, *knows*. It's just that she can't work out *how* anyone can know. Because only one other person in the world knows, and there's no way, absolutely no way—

'Clare? Are you feeling better?'

Nick. He's still squatting by her chair, concern etched on his pale face, and she looks at him, at his crumpled, checked shirt and his tousled hair and feels a surge of guilt so agonising it makes her gasp. Instantly, he reaches for her, cupping her face in his hands.

'Babe, you're OK. It's all going to be OK. This is *good*. I don't understand the thing about someone having a secret, but the kids haven't been harmed, I'm sure of it. We just have to hang on. We can do it, we *can*.'

She nods, still struggling to get her breathing under control.

Yes, just hang on, she thinks. *Wait for the next message. See what happens. And I need to make a phone call, now, as soon as I can. Is it too risky to call? But I have to. I can't do this on my own anymore...*

She straightens up in her chair, her husband's hands sliding from her face.

'I'm hanging on,' she says. 'You're right. We can do this. We have to, don't we?'

———————

'So that's sorted, then. That's our story. No deviation, no more details. That's all we can remember, OK?'

Eldon Beckford clasps his wife's hands tightly in his, and she nods. She's stopped crying, finally, but her mascara has run, black rivulets streaking her cheeks. He lifts a finger to wipe it off, but she pulls away.

'I'll wash my face in a minute,' she says. 'I need to check on River.'

The little boy is, thankfully, having a nap upstairs in his bedroom, and although there's no sound other than an occasional snuffle coming from the baby monitor on the mantelpiece, Eldon nods and Amy leaves the room, walking slowly, almost painfully, as if there's a great weight clinging to her shoulders. She was still out on her drive when the messages arrived, and once Eldon had read them, fear twisting his stomach, he'd called her, terrified that she'd see them popping up on her phone while behind the wheel and lose control of the car.

He should have known better. Amy is, by a million miles, the most careful driver he's ever known, even now, with all this going on. But he could hear the dread in her voice, as she said, 'Don't tell me. I'll be home in two minutes. Two minutes, OK?'

He'd scooped up a protesting River from his spot on the sofa and rushed out into the driveway, ready to greet her when she pulled in about ninety seconds later. He'd watched as, with shaking hands, she'd reached into her handbag and pulled out her phone, and as she read the messages he'd seen an unidentifiable look cross her face, a strange combination of confusion and terror and then, weirdly, acceptance; a little nod, as if this is what she's been expecting all along.

He'd stared at her for a few moments, and then he'd shifted his wriggling, whimpering son to his other hip and said quietly, 'We need to talk. Now.'

'Yes,' she whispered.

And so they'd settled River down for a nap and, finally, they'd talked. At first she'd seemed distracted, eyes repeatedly flitting to her phone, until he begged her to turn it off, just for a few minutes.

'This is important. This is so *fucking* important, Amy,' he'd said and, because he rarely swears, that seemed to shock her into focussing properly on what he was saying, and soon she was sobbing, and telling him she understood, and that yes, of course, she'd do anything he thought they should do.

'So we're both on the same page? You've got it? Do you want to go through it one more time?' he'd asked, and she'd shaken her head.

'I've got it,' she said. 'But… Eldon, there's something else I need to…'

She paused, pushing a stray lock of hair back from her forehead.

'Something else you need to talk about? What is it?'

Suddenly, she had a haunted look on her face, and he felt a chill run through him.

'Amy? Talk to me?'

She squeezed her eyes shut, as if thinking hard, then opened them again, meeting his questioning gaze and then looking away.

'Oh… it's nothing. It doesn't matter. It's just… I'm glad we had this chat. I'm sorry I've been avoiding it. I know you've been wanting to talk about this for days but I just couldn't face it, you know? I miss Noah so much. I just want him home. That's all that matters now.'

They'd hugged then, and she'd cried like a child in his arms. Now, he sinks back onto the sofa, his limbs feeling floppy with relief. If the message *is* aimed at them, then at least if it does come out, and the police come to question them, they've talked about it now and they'll have identical stories. But it might not come to that. If these people want money to stay quiet, they can *have* money. He'll sell the restaurants, sell everything, if he has to. That's the joy of being a chef; he can start again, any time. They can take his property, and his money, but they can't take his skill, his talent. But will it be that easy? Do blackmailers ever really go away? Will paying them, if that's what they demand, just encourage them to come back for more somewhere down the line? Eldon groans. He can't think about that, not now.

One day at a time. That's all I can do. That's the price you pay, isn't it, for doing what we did? However happy and successful you may be – and we have been both happy and successful, most of the time anyway – there's always that tiny niggle eating away at you. That little, persistent voice that whispers to you in the early hours, telling you that one day, you could lose everything. And now here we are. It's happened, hasn't it? But… it might be OK. And after all, as long as we get Noah back, what else really matters?

Eldon glances at the handsome Patek Philippe watch on his left wrist. He'll sell that too, if he needs to. It can all go, every last bit of it, if it means their secret is safe and their family is reunited. He doesn't care about anything else.

It's still only mid-afternoon. Will the kidnappers send their demands today, in another message? Or will they keep them all on tenterhooks for another interminable night? Eldon shakes his head slowly, and a strange sense of calm descends on him. All he can do now is wait, and suddenly that seems like a nice, restful thing to do. The calm, maybe, before the most destructive, violent storm of his life. Eldon closes his eyes, and in seconds, he's drifted off to sleep.

Chapter Twenty

LUCA

Day 4: Monday, 4.02 p.m.

Luca Lyon shifts on his air bed, trying to get comfortable. The bed deflated a little in the night, and it's not as bouncy as it was before. He'll ask Miss Norman if she can pump it up for him later, when he's finished playing Pokémon. He frowns, concentrating on the games console that's resting on his knees. It's one of those small handheld ones that works with batteries; it's nowhere near as good as the one he has at home, linked up to the flatscreen TV in his bedroom, but it's better than nothing. There are four of them, these little consoles, and they have to share, but it's his turn now and for the next hour he plans to sit here and play. Then, when he has to hand it over to Noah Beckford, he might read a book, or just have a nap. He didn't sleep very well last night; his sister Lola, who's currently on the other side of the room, plaiting Harper Duggan's hair, was crying again, and he kept having to get out of bed to go and slip his arm round her.

'Sssh, we'll be going home soon. Miss Norman said so. Don't cry, Lola,' he'd whispered, even though he'd felt like crying himself too. He didn't though. His dad once told him boys shouldn't; he'd said crying was for girls, and Luca has never seen his dad shed as much as a single tear in his whole life, even when he has people telling him really sad stories on his television show. Luca isn't entirely sure his dad's right about the crying thing though; when he told Noah about it, Noah said it was rubbish, that everyone's equal and can do what they like, including crying. Even so, Luca's determined not to cry here, in front of his sister and all the others. They'll be on their way home soon anyway, and everything will go back to normal, and in the meantime there are games to play and books to read and chocolate to eat, so it's not so bad, is it?

The room isn't very nice though. It's underground – he's pretty sure about that. They had to wear blindfolds to get here; it was all part of the game that started when the bus drove into the wood, and somebody wearing a mask told them they were all going on an exciting adventure, a little extra bit of the day trip that had been kept as a big surprise. They'd all been a bit scared at first; the person looked like a baddie from a film, with just eyes showing, and they were carrying some sort of pretend gun, and even Miss Norman and Mr Jones and Mr Moore and Mrs Lindsay had looked frightened. But then the masked person had taken the adults aside and spoken quietly to them, and they'd all told the children everything was fine, and that they needed to do what they were told, because they were going on a special little journey. They'd all felt excited then, helping to tie each other's blindfolds and whispering to each other and trying to guess where they were going as they were led across the field and into some cars. They hadn't even been sure who was leading them, because none of the adults spoke, which made it even more scary and exciting. It was nearly evening, so they couldn't be going to a theme park or anything like that, they thought; maybe they were going for burgers and chips, or to see a film? There were shrieks of laughter as they were bundled into cars, all falling on top of each other and fumbling for the seat belts, and then off they went. They didn't drive for too long – Luca's good at guessing time, and he thinks it was about twenty minutes – and then they were outside again, walking on grass, and then inside, on a hard floor, their footsteps echoing as if the room was really big, and then going down some steep steps, still whispering and giggling and holding each other's hands.

Then they'd heard a door slam behind them. There'd been silence for a few seconds, and then Mr Moore had said he thought it would be OK if they all took their blindfolds off. When they did, though, Luca had been bitterly disappointed. They all had. It was just a big, long room with no windows, and nothing exciting in it at all. There were a few lightbulbs dangling from the ceiling, and air beds lined up along the walls, each with a pillow and a sleeping bag. To the left was a sort of kitchen, except it didn't have a cooker, just a sink and a little fridge and an old-looking table with a few chairs around it. In the middle of the room there were three big squishy bean bags, and a rug on the floor, and a box of books and some board games and the games consoles. There were a few other toys too: Lego, and a couple of remote-control cars, and two teddy bears.

'This is *cringe*,' Gresham Greer had said loudly, as they'd all stared. 'What sort of surprise is this? Who wants to sit in a mouldy old room and play with that load of crap?'

'Yeah, not me,' Wanda Pearson had replied, and she'd turned to Mr Jones and said, 'Can we go home instead? We're having pizza tonight!'

Mr Jones had looked at Miss Norman and Mr Moore, and for a few moments none of them had said anything, just *looked* at each other. Mrs Lindsay wasn't there; even now, Luca still isn't sure why not. He thinks she probably just decided to go home instead, lucky Mrs Lindsay. When they asked where she was, the adults all just looked at each other with kind of miserable faces, so he thinks they must miss her. She's nice, Mrs Lindsay. Anyway, then Mr Jones told them that, actually, part of the adventure was that they were all going to be staying *here* for the night, a bit like camping, except indoors. He said that, in fact, it might be for *more* than one night, maybe a few nights, and that it was like a big game, and that all our families were going to be trying to guess where we were, and didn't that sound like fun? He didn't look like he was having fun though, and nor did Miss Norman or Mr Moore. Their faces were all funny, all serious and worried-looking, and they kept muttering to each other, sort of under their breath. But then Willow Townsend started to cry, and the teachers all started smiling and saying 'Come on, no tears!' and telling them it was going to be a laugh and that everyone should pick a bed and think about it like a great big sleepover. They'd all cheered up then, and run across the room and flung themselves on the air beds, and then they'd played some games and then Mr Moore had found some sandwiches and cans of Coke in the fridge and they'd been allowed to eat them in bed.

There were pyjamas in some big bags in the corner, so they have a pair each now, because of course nobody brought any luggage with them because then it wouldn't have been a surprise, would it? There are some clean day clothes in the bag too, but not enough for all of them to change all their clothes every single day; it's just for when something gets really dirty, apparently. Luca's changed his T-shirt, but he's been wearing the same pants since Friday now, the ones his mum left out for him to wear on the day of the school trip. That seems like such a long time ago now, a squillion years, but Luca has counted and he's pretty sure it's just been three sleeps, which means today is Monday. It's hard to know the difference between day and night though, with no windows.

Luca shifts on his bed, and hears a little hiss of air. Yep, definitely deflating. It was fun for the first night; they all stayed up late chatting and sneaking into each other's beds, until Miss Norman got cross and said they really, *really* needed to try and get some sleep. But it's not so much fun now. There's only one toilet, through a little door near the kitchen, and one small hand basin, and while at first it was good not being made to have a shower, to his own surprise Luca kind of wants one now. There's a little pile of towels and flannels, and Miss Norman gave them one each and told them they must fill the basin with water and wipe themselves down from head to toe every morning, but it's not the same as having a proper shower. Luca can't wash his hair for a start, and he feels sticky and smelly, and the toilet is getting really rank, with thirteen of them using it all day.

The others are all getting stinky too. Some are worse than others. He's pretty sure Stanley Tustain wet the bed on the second night; he saw Miss Norman taking him aside and giving him some clean clothes from the bag, but there aren't any clean sleeping bags so he's just had to carry on sleeping in his. It's two beds away from Luca's, but he still gets a whiff of it every now and again and it's pretty yucky. He hasn't said anything to Stanley though; that would be mean, and Stanley doesn't seem very happy at the moment so teasing him about wetting the bed would make him even sadder. Luca's seen him crying twice, although he tries to hide it by lying face down on one of the bean bags and pretending to be resting. He probably misses his mum. Luca understands that; he misses his mum too, and his dad, misses them terribly. He misses his house and his garden and chatting to Brandon about the birds, and he misses *feeding* the birds, and he misses television and his bike and he even misses school a bit, and Mrs Chamberlain, and... He misses everything and everyone, really, but he's pretending he's fine, because he's a big boy now and this will soon be over, won't it? They've all been asking the adults when the game will end, because surely after three whole sleeps their parents *must* have been able to guess where they are by now, mustn't they?

'I think we only drove for twenty minutes,' Luca confided in Mr Moore on the second day. 'So we can't be *that* far away from Littleford, can we? My dad's really clever – I wish he'd hurry up and guess where we are so we can all go home.'

Mr Moore had looked at him with a sad face, and then smiled and told him he was sure it wouldn't be long now.

'The game will take as long as it takes, I'm afraid,' he said. 'We just have to be patient.'

His smile didn't look like a real one, though, and Luca

thinks now that Mr Moore's a bit fed up with being here too, just like he is. Concentrating on the games and books helps – a little bit anyway – if he does start to feel a bit wobbly. He wishes he could at least *speak* to his mum, but that's a no too; none of the kids have phones with them – it's not allowed – and Mr Jones told them all the adults managed to leave their phones on the bus in the excitement of the game.

'And even if we did have them, there's no signal in this room anyway,' he said. 'So we'll just have to manage without phones for a few days. We can do that, can't we?'

Lola has started *begging* to go home though; lots of the kids have, and they're all starting to tell each other what a *stupid* game this is, and how they're never playing it again. They've asked if they can go outside too – they're *so* fed up of being indoors, in this dimly lit place – but Miss Norman keeps telling them the weather's really, really bad outside, torrential rain and thunderstorms, and that it's much safer to stay indoors, and that she hates being cooped up inside too, but that they all just need to put up with it for a little bit longer. Luca's not sure if teachers are allowed to lie, but he's also not sure if that's quite true, because it was such a lovely day on Friday when they were at the wilderness park, all warm and sunny, so could it really be that bad now, just a few days later? And how does Miss Norman know what the weather's like outside anyway, when there are no windows?

He's starting to feel not sure about a lot of things now. The adults are all acting like everything's OK, but when they speak just to each other, quietly on the other side of the room, they don't *look* OK. They look like his dad looks when he's got a really big interview coming up on the telly, and he's really,

really busy, and his face is all scrunched up and he keeps sighing and biting his lip. Luca thinks he actually saw Miss Norman crying this morning too. There was certainly water on her cheek, and Luca's pretty sure it was tears, although maybe she'd just washed her face in the tiny little basin and hadn't dried it properly. He also thinks – just *thinks*, because he hasn't gone up the stairs (they're not allowed to, that's one of the rules) – but he *thinks* the door to this room might be locked, and that even the teachers can't open it. There's another person who comes once or twice a day, tapping a couple of times on the door every time to alert them, and brings food and drinks and towels and toilet paper. It's all cold, the food: crisps and bread and fruit and cheese and tomatoes and sweets and cereal bars and milk and fizzy drinks, which is fine but Luca would really love something hot now, something his mum has made, something that doesn't come out of a plastic packet. One of the adults goes up the steps and takes the stuff, and sometimes there's a little bit of conversation, and then the door closes again and a couple of times Luca thinks he's heard what sounds like a bolt closing, like the one they have on the shed in the garden at home, but bigger and heavier. He's not sure though.

He's also not sure if the person who comes is a man or a woman, so he's just started calling them *The Visitor*, and it's caught on – everyone says *The Visitor* now. He really wants to know who The Visitor is, but it's dark on the stairs, and when they talk, they talk *really* quietly, so he can't tell from the voice, either. Sometimes the conversation sounds angry, even in whispers, and he wonders what they're angry about. He thinks maybe the person who comes is the masked person from the bus, although it *could* be somebody else. He's not even totally sure if it's the same person who comes every time; it's hard to tell. He thinks about the masked person a lot, though, because the more he thinks about it, the more he thinks he might have *known* them. He couldn't see their face, of course, but there was something a little bit familiar about them. Luca just can't think what it was. Just… *something*. Has he met them before? They didn't speak much, and so again, Luca's not sure if it was a man or a woman, because their hair was all covered up with a black hat and they wore a big bulky jacket and a mask across their face, just their eyes showing. And when they did speak, it was in a really strange way, like they were putting on a voice. They sounded a bit like Noah's dad when he tries to do silly accents, something that makes Luca and Noah cry with laughter because Noah's dad is a fantastic cook – he makes the best burgers Luca's ever tasted – but he is really, *really* bad at accents.

But there was just something about them, this person. It's as if Luca can hear a tiny bell ringing far, far away, and if he concentrates on it really, really hard he'll be able to hear it properly. It's something to do, isn't it? Thinking. Thinking hard. Trying to work out what's going on here, because Luca's starting to really worry about that now. Worry that it's not really a game at all. It doesn't feel like a game, not anymore, because surely his parents – *any* of their parents – wouldn't be happy about a game that means they have to stay away from home for this long? When they can't even speak on the phone? With no showers, and just cold food to eat? It's almost like they've all been put in prison, like the ones he's seen on TV in the documentaries his dad watches. But they can't be in prison, can they? None of them have done anything wrong. So what else? What *else*…?

'Luca! Time's up. Did you enjoy that? Ready to hand it over?'

He looks up, startled.

It's Miss Norman, smiling at him and holding out her hand for the games console. Luca smiles back and gives it to her.

'Yes, thank you, Miss Norman,' he says, and she stands there for a moment, looking at him, and he notices that her eyes are red, and thinks again about the fact that she's almost definitely been crying. He doesn't like that. The thought of an adult crying makes him feel all wiggly in his tummy.

'You're such a good boy,' she says quietly. 'And your sister too. You're both so good.'

Her voice goes a bit funny as she says the last few words, as if her throat is sore, and she turns away quickly. Luca watches her go, then remembers he was going to ask her to pump up his bed for him. There's a pump over on the shelf in the kitchen, and he could try and do it himself, but he might be told off. He stands up, ready to run after her to ask, but she's crouching down over by the bean bags, handing the games console to Noah who's lounging on one of them, looking bored, and his face lights up with a big grin. And now Miss Norman is picking up some Lego, and now she's smiling too and joining in with Stanley and Willow and Wanda and Lola who are building some sort of big tower. Luca decides to wait. There's no hurry. The bed will be OK until later. He'll read a book in a bit. But for now, he's going to *think*. Think about the masked person on the bus, and about the person who comes to the door with the food. Think about reasons why the door might be locked. And think about how *brilliant* it will be to go home when this school trip is over, and about the massive hugs he'll give his mum and dad, and about what he'll have for dinner. Yes, he'll do that for a while. He settles himself back on his pillow and closes his eyes.

Chapter Twenty-One

COTSWOLDS POLICE HEADQUARTERS

Day 5: Tuesday, 7 a.m.

Detective Superintendent Sadie Stewart claps her hands loudly, and the room falls silent.

'Sorry, guys. I would have yelled like I usually do but I've been talking so much since Friday night that I'm in danger of losing my voice,' she says.

She clears her throat, then takes a sip from the tumbler of hot water and honey that's sitting on the desk beside her, trying to assemble her thoughts into some sort of logical order. She feels so tired that she could fall asleep right here, standing next to the whiteboard ahead of yet another briefing.

'We've got a bell at home that my wife used to get my attention when she was pregnant; she was confined to bed for the final few weeks when she was expecting our eldest,' says Detective Inspector Daniel Sharma, with a grin. 'I could bring that in for you, boss, if you like? Save your tonsils?'

There's a ripple of subdued laughter, and Sadie rolls her eyes.

'That won't be necessary, Daniel. But thanks for the kind offer. And if you could do most of the talking this morning, I'd appreciate it. We have another long day ahead, and of course we could have our second contact from the hostage takers at any moment, so we'll try to keep this as succinct as possible, everyone. So. First, in light of the messages received yesterday morning, we've been looking again at the backgrounds of all the parents involved, to see if there's anything there that might have triggered this mass abduction and what we expect to be an imminent ransom demand. Sadly, initial enquiries didn't give us much to go on – they actually seem to be a relatively clean-living, law-abiding bunch. We have no idea as yet what this "secret" is that the message referred to, and none of them have offered us any answers so far. We need to push them on it. But there were a couple of other red flags – Daniel?'

He nods and taps the picture of Rosie Duggan on the board.

'Harper's mum, Rosie. She has an abusive ex-boyfriend, who didn't take kindly to her leaving him. It was five years ago, and she had a restraining order on him which there's no sign he's breached, but we thought it wise to check him out anyway, in case he's after revenge. Turns out he moved to Wales three years ago, and is currently in Cardiff prison, eighteen months into a four-year sentence for assaulting a man in a nightclub. So I think we can safely rule him out of this one.'

'OK. The other one we wanted to check urgently was the MacDonald-Cooks. Any joy there?'

'Yep, that's our single-sex couple, for those not familiar.'

Daniel points to the photos of Brett and Jon MacDonald-Cook.

'Dads to young Oliver. His birth mother was a Glasgow woman who died from an overdose when he was a baby. This was a long shot, but we just wondered if she could have had any family who might have had an issue with the boy being adopted by two men, or who didn't like him being moved out of Scotland. It doesn't really fit with the message about a secret, but we still thought it was worth looking at, in case they might have felt they deserved some sort of compensation or something. Again, no joy I'm afraid. We've checked with Police Scotland in Glasgow and the birth mother had no known relatives. She was in her mid-thirties and had been on the streets for several years, apparently. There was an attempt to find her next of kin when she passed away, but nobody came forward. Very sad, really. So again, we think we can rule out any connection with our current case.'

There's silence in the room for a few moments. Sadie, feeling even more weary now, reaches for her drink and takes another sip, then says, 'OK, so we move on. We continue to look elsewhere for the motive. Right, a couple of other things. First, we've requested a news blackout. We've told the press there's been a major development, but that for the safety of our thirteen abductees, we're requesting that they stop running anything on this story, at least for the next couple of days, after which we hope we'll be able to give them some good news. We can't stop people talking and speculating about it on social media, of course, but all the major news outlets, both here and abroad, have agreed to comply with the blackout, which is great. Gives us some breathing space.'

There are appreciative nods and murmurs of 'Well done!' and 'Good job!' from around the room.

'Yes, it's a relief,' Sadie says. 'The anti-kidnap team have given us their take on the messages received, by the way. As we already know, in general the UK's position on payment of ransoms for hostages is very clear: if the hostage takers are a terrorist group, there are no payments and no concessions, the thinking being that paying only encourages further kidnappings. But they don't think this feels like a terrorist kidnapping; the children and teachers aren't the right sort of hostages, and they say this feels more personal, with that comment about one of them having a secret. So, their advice is just to wait, and see what these people want.'

'It's so frustrating, isn't it?' says Daniel. 'Very often at this stage in a kidnap situation we'd know who the hostage takers were, and we could bring in trained negotiators. Or we'd know where the victims are being held, and we could send in armed officers. But this one is so different. They're giving us *nothing*. No ID and no location. No opportunity for negotiation *or* rescue.'

'It's a unique and extremely difficult situation,' agrees Sadie. 'The only thing we can do while we wait is to carry on searching, but it's like looking for a polar bear in a snowstorm. We have no idea how far they travelled on Friday evening, or in what direction; the fact that pretty much the whole world is now looking for them and we haven't had a single verifiable sighting just confirms my gut feeling that they're somewhere very secure and very well hidden, and honestly, in my view, somewhere not too far away from the bus site. And even searching has to be done with extreme caution now. We don't want to stumble on their hiding place and panic them into hurting or – heaven forbid – *killing* any of the abductees before we have a chance to free them.'

Daniel sighs.

'It's crazy. Thirteen people! Three adults too. Kids are one thing, but those adults will be doing their best to attract attention or escape, won't they? And clearly, they've managed neither so far, so yes, wherever they're being held must be *very* secure. God, I hope they're still alive, boss. The adults too, I mean. They may well have met the same fate as Erica Lindsay by now, who knows.'

'Don't. Let's stay positive. The message did say all the children *and* adults are safe and well, remember,' Sadie says, but her stomach lurches. 'Right, so we carry on doing what we can. FLOs, you'll be speaking to all the families today about the content of the message and particularly that reference to a secret. Anything that seems even slightly suspicious, let me know immediately. If we can pin down a good motive for this hostage situation, it could be a great help. We'll also be speaking again to Olivia Chamberlain, the headteacher, to see if she's heard any gossip. The school's the heart of the village, and people love to talk, so you never know. And remember, we still haven't ruled out someone close to the school being involved in all this. Keep your eyes and ears open, OK?'

Again, nods from around the room.

'Good,' says Sadie. 'Thanks, guys, Let's do this.'

Chapter Twenty-Two

COTSWOLDS POLICE HEADQUARTERS

Day 5: Tuesday, 1.10 p.m.

'OK. Thanks, Mel.'

Daniel puts his phone down and shakes his head at Sadie, who's sitting at the desk opposite, nibbling disconsolately on a cheese and pickle sandwich.

'That was Mel. She's just left Vanessa and Luke Carr. Nothing.'

Sadie doesn't answer, just furrows her brow and pushes her plate aside with a sigh. Daniel knows how she feels; he doesn't have much of an appetite either. All morning, the family liaison officers have been talking to the parents of the missing children, but so far none have admitted to having any idea what the secret might be.

'So that's the Carrs, the Pearsons, Rosie Duggan and the MacDonald-Cooks all done. Nikki is with Spike and Tasha Greer now, so I'm expecting a call from her next— Oh, hang on…'

His phone has started ringing, and he grabs it.

'Ms Lemon,' he says. 'Any news?'

He listens, as the FLO – who's actually a family friend – fills him in on her chat with the ex-footballer and his wife.

'Ahh, thanks Nik,' he says, when she's finished. 'See you soon, OK? We'll have to get you round for dinner when this is all over – the kids would love to see you. Bye for now. Take care.'

Sadie is looking at him quizzically.

'Inviting attractive young FLOs round for dinner?' she says, and Daniel rolls his eyes.

'She's a *friend*,' he replies. 'Of my *wife's*. And mine, I suppose. Anyway, she's just left the Greers. Apparently, Spike went into a tailspin when the message arrived. He's convinced it's aimed at him. He told Nikki that although he was only ever arrested three times back in his bad-boy days, as we already know, there's one other thing he did nobody ever knew about. Quite a juicy little thing too.'

'Oh? Do tell.'

Sadie leans forward, hand cupping her chin, a sudden spark in her eyes.

'Well, apparently he had a brief affair with Mattie Tyler's wife, about fifteen years ago. Mattie played for Chelsea at the same time Spike did. The couple split up a year later, after she admitted numerous flings with all sorts of people, but the thing about her and Spike never came out. He's told Nikki he's felt guilty about it ever since, even though he and Mattie weren't close even back then, and he hasn't seen him for years. He's confessed all to Tasha now, but she's not that bothered because it was well before she came on the scene, and Nikki's told him she doesn't think it's significant enough to merit a mass child kidnapping, even if Mattie *has* found out about it. He moved to Miami a few years back and is happily married to a millionaire businesswoman of some sort, so it's unlikely he's short of cash. What do you think?'

Sadie's face falls.

'Aww, damn. I got excited there for a minute. A brief affair, fifteen years ago? And a couple who aren't even together anymore? It would be a massive overreaction, wouldn't it? If Mattie Tyler *did* find out about it, I mean. And if it's someone else who's found out, and thinks they can make some money out of it… I still can't see it, Dan. It doesn't feel right. I just feel like there's something bigger behind this.'

Daniel nods. His instinct is telling him the same thing. He picks up his notepad, checking his list.

'Oh. Meera called in from the school earlier too, while you were off getting that delicious-looking sandwich,' he says, and Sadie grimaces.

'Without giving too much away, she had a good chat with Olivia Townsend, trying to find out if any of the parents have anything to hide, but our headteacher hasn't heard anything juicy on the grapevine about any of them at all, apparently. Meera said she seemed very upset though. She was in tears by the end of their conversation. She seems to be taking it all very badly.'

'Well, it happened on her watch, didn't it?' Sadie says. 'The children were left in the care of the school for the day and ten of them didn't come home. It can't be easy for her. Unless she's upset for a different reason…?'

She drums her fingers on the top of the desk, then shrugs.

'Still no evidence to suggest she's involved though,' she says. 'So, back to the parents. Who's left?'

'The Beckfords, the Townsends, the Tustains and the Lyon-Sandersons,' Daniel replies.

'Right. I'm starting to wonder if it's a waste of time though,' Sadie says. She reaches for her plate again, and looks at the sandwich with an unenthusiastic expression.

'Oh? Why do you say that?'

'Well, if one of them does have a secret big enough to make someone take thirteen people hostage to punish them, are they really going to tell us about it? Even to save their kids? If they were going to spill, they'd have done it by now. But not a word, from any of them – if you discount Spike revealing he humped a long-ago team-mate's wife. I don't think we're going to get any joy, to be honest. I wish the bloody kidnappers weren't being so vague.'

Daniel nods.

'They're clearly not stupid. Being more specific about who this is aimed at would probably reveal the perpetrators' identity. The vagueness is likely all part of the plan to stay hidden and not allow any negotiation. Shit, this isn't easy, is it?'

'Longest five days of my life, Dan,' says Sadie. 'And I don't even care about whose bloody secret it is. Those *kids* are innocent. We've got to get them back. And we will. I just don't know how.'

Chapter Twenty-Three

CALLY

Day 5: Tuesday, 2.35 p.m.

'Miss! Miss Norman! Is The Visitor coming soon? I'm starving!'

Cally Norman opens her eyes with a start to see the face of Gresham Greer peering at her from about six inches away.

'Blimey, Gresham. I can practically see your tonsils,' she says sleepily, reluctantly raising herself into a sitting position and gently pushing the little boy backwards away from her.

He grins.

'You were asleep! It's only afternoon. But there's no food for snacks. I'm *starving*. Do you know when they're coming?'

'I'm sure it won't be long, Gresham,' she says. 'Why don't you see if you can beat your own record on the car thingy in the meantime? Three full loops, wasn't it?'

He beams.

'Yes! OK. Will you come and watch?'

'I will. Just give me a minute to wake up.'

He nods and scampers off, heading for the obstacle course some of the children have set up in one corner of the room, using books, towers of soft drinks cans and various other random items to create a hazardous circuit around which to steer the two remote-controlled cars. The ingenuity of these children never ceases to amaze Cally; it's been astonishing, the way they seem to have adapted so quickly to life in one room, finding endless ways to amuse themselves. Yes, there've been tears and fights and countless pleas to go home, but most of the time they seem to accept her assurances, and those of her colleagues, that they won't be here for much longer, that this elaborate 'game' is nearly over. That stupid story about a game was all they'd been able to think of to tell the kids, when they arrived here and the door was locked behind them.

It's Tuesday today, isn't it? Cally thinks. *Friday seems such a long time ago…*

She leans back on her pillow again. She feels exhausted, spending more and more hours of the day dozing on her bed. They'd decided to take shifts, the three of them, so that there would always be someone watching the children during waking hours, and trying to keep them occupied. Right now, it's Oscar's turn – Mr Jones, as the children still politely call him – and he's sitting at the battered old table in the kitchen area, supervising a makeshift crafting session. Stanley Tustain, Willow Townsend and Lola Lyon are trying to make snakes – *or worms, maybe?* – out of the cardboard tubes from toilet rolls, a pile of crisp and sweet wrappers and some coloured pens, although without any glue Cally's not really sure how they're managing it. The task seems to be eliciting great amusement though, with peals of laughter regularly ringing across the room, and the sound makes her smile. She's become incredibly fond of Lola Lyon, in particular, over the past few days; the little girl is kind and determined and brave, and despite the occasional tearful wobble, she's become one of the most positive little role models in this damn hell hole. Her twin brother, Luca, is a little star too. In fact, all these children are quite extraordinary, and when, in the long, dark hours of last night, Cally had wondered – and not for the first time –what this experience might really be doing to them, and how it might affect them in the future, she had suddenly found it hard to breathe, her skin breaking into a cold sweat. She'd stumbled out of bed and crept across to where Dominic was sleeping, grabbing his hand, and he'd woken with a yelp.

'Help me. I'm struggling,' was all she'd had to say, and he'd immediately pulled her down onto his sagging air bed and wrapped his arms around her, murmuring that it was all going to be over soon, his fingers running gently up and down her arm in the way she loved until she fell asleep, her head on his chest.

They're dating, Cally and Dominic. They have been for months, but few people know that; romantic relationships between staff members are very much frowned upon at Littleford Primary School. Oscar knows, and Cally has told her younger brother, but other than that, the fact that the Year 3 teacher and the Year 2 TA are an item is a closely guarded secret. Cally is twenty-six, nearly five years into her teaching career; Dominic is a little older, twenty-eight, and working as a TA for some extra cash while he does a postgraduate degree in Neuroscience and Education, working shifts at the school around his lectures at the

University of Bristol. He'd originally been a psychologist, now wanting to specialise in the emerging field of educational neuroscience, and Cally loves the way he's just going for it, following his dreams. He inspires her to try to follow hers, too. Her past hasn't been so great; her mother died when Cally was just eighteen, and life was far from easy even before that, and shitty, to say the least, for a long time afterwards. But the future... When this is all over, Cally dreams of bright, happy days, and the carefree life she's determined to live.

I'm going to do it for you, Mum, she often whispers out loud, when she's all alone. *All of it's for you.*

But for now, she's locked in a dingy underground room, and she just has to get through this, and out the other side, somehow. Her stomach growls, and she realises that, like Gresham, she's hungry too. Never mind. The Visitor – the name coined by the children for the shadowy figure who delivers their daily food boxes – should be here soon.

Distraction, Cally, she tells herself.

She turns to see Dominic sitting on a beanbag, a book on his knees and a little gang of children around him, and he smiles at her and waves a hand.

'Want to come and listen to a story, Miss Norman?' he calls.

'Not just now, Mr Moore,' she replies. 'I have a car race to watch.'

'Fair enough.'

He winks at her, and Cally rolls her eyes, then looks across to where Gresham is whooping and cheering as his car hurtles past him. All around the room, the children are smiling and keeping busy. Cally feels constantly scared and anxious, but they're not. They're making the most of the situation. It's what kids do.

They don't know, though, do they? she thinks. *They don't know how bad this could get...*

She swallows hard, then forces a smile onto her face, clambers off her bed and goes over to join Gresham.

Chapter Twenty-Four

REYNOLD

Day 5: Tuesday, 2.55 p.m.

Reynold Lyon is sitting at his computer, giving his new game show proposal one final read-through, when the family liaison officer arrives. Petra's gone out for a walk, and when the doorbell rings Reynold is briefly tempted to ignore it. He slept badly last night; barely slept at all, in fact, his brain whirring, trying to work out what to do about the message from the hostage takers. He still desperately wants to have a certain conversation, but how to do it? He just doesn't know what to do for the best, and so he hasn't done *anything*, yet, which is unlike him. He's normally so decisive, but this... this is different. This could be life changing. He considered carefully his original idea – that of calling a meeting of all the Class 3B parents to discuss the latest development – but now he's worried that too many questions will be asked about what the message could mean. It's been bad enough on the WhatsApp group, and in person it would be even trickier.

Awkward questions are exactly what he wants to avoid right now. So he's holding fire, waiting to see what happens next, and trying to distract himself, as usual, by focussing on work. The ringing doorbell is an irritant, but when it rings for the third time he groans and stomps downstairs. It has to be the police, he realises, and it won't look good if they know he's at home and ignoring them. He's right – standing on the doorstep is their now all-too-familiar FLO.

'Marc. Do come in.'

Reynold tries to supress his annoyance at the intrusion.

'Thanks, Reynold.'

Marc's grin is as friendly as ever.

'This won't take long. Just following up on the contact we had yesterday, and its rather cryptic nature, in case anything's occurred to anyone in the meantime? We're desperate to shed some light on it. I mean, we're hoping for another message very soon, which might clarify things, but in the meantime… Anyway, how are you today? How's Petra?'

'She's OK. Just getting through it minute by minute, you know?' Reynold replies. 'She's out, actually. She's gone for a quick walk; you know how the fresh air helps clear her head. Look, if you want to chat, let's go up to my office. In fact, you go on up – you remember where it is, don't you? – and I'll make us some coffee. Black, right?'

Marc nods.

'Perfect. Cheers, Reynold.'

Marc turns away and bounds up the stairs, and Reynold walks quickly to the kitchen. His heart rate has speeded up and he feels a little shaky, his palms clammy. He needed to get away from Marc just for a minute to calm himself, because he knows he needs this to be convincing; he needs Marc to leave here with no suspicion, with no inkling whatsoever that he's now realised the message is very likely to have been meant for *him*.

Just keep it simple, he tells himself, as he makes the coffee and, with steadier hands now, carries the two mugs across the hallway and up the stairs. *You have no idea what the message refers to. You've racked your brains but you can't think of anything you've ever done that would cause someone to threaten you like this. You're as in the dark as he is…*

He pushes open the door to his office.

'Here we go. Two coffees, freshly brewed. It's good stuff too, a dark roast from Nicaragua…' he says cheerfully, and then his words tail off.

'Marc? What are you doing?'

His tone is sharper than he intended, and Marc whips around and stares at him, a strange look on his face. The man is standing next to Reynold's desk, and when Reynold opened the door he'd been leaning over the computer, clearly studying what was on the screen. Reynold's stomach flips.

My show proposal. Shit. I didn't close the document down when the doorbell rang, did I?

'Mate, that's a highly confidential document,' he begins, but Marc is holding up a hand as if to silence him, and now he takes a few steps towards Reynold and reaches for the coffee mugs, taking both and putting them down on a side table.

'I think it's better if you don't say anything, Reynold,' he says, and his normally smiling face looks very serious, his brow furrowed, his eyes fixed on Reynold's as if he's trying to keep him in view – as if he expects Reynold to bolt for the door at any moment.

'I'm not sure what you mean…' says Reynold, but Marc holds up a hand again.

'I think you do,' he says. 'I've *seen* it, Reynold. I've *seen* that document on your computer. And I think we need to go to the station, right now. Because I think you have some questions to answer about this kidnap situation, don't you?'

Chapter Twenty-Five

COTSWOLDS POLICE HEADQUARTERS

Day 5: Tuesday, 4.15 p.m.

'Mr Lyon. Thank you for coming in.'

Pulling out the chair next to Daniel, Sadie sits down opposite Reynold Lyon, and studies the man curiously. He is, without doubt, extremely good-looking: that perfectly groomed thatch of hair, those deep-brown eyes, that body clearly honed to perfection by hours in the gym. But right now, he looks furious.

'Well, I wasn't really given much choice,' he snaps. 'But I must say, I'm extremely unhappy about this. Aren't we going through enough, with everything that's going on, without you dragging me in here like some sort of criminal? I have no idea what Marc's concerns are, but I am *absolutely*—'

'Mr Lyon, please,' Sadie interrupts him. 'This is simply some routine questions, after your family liaison officer saw something of concern on your computer. Something that rang an alarm bell for him. And having seen a screenshot, it's ringing alarm bells for me too. I'm sure we can clear this up quickly, but for now I'm afraid we've had to seize your computer and your laptop for further investigation—'

'This is absolutely preposterous!' Reynold explodes. 'I need those devices for work, and there's a lot of highly confidential information on them. You simply *can't* just—'

He's standing up now, practically spitting the words across the table at her and, abruptly, Daniel stands up too.

'MR LYON,' he says, loudly and firmly. 'SIT DOWN. Please. This sort of behaviour won't get us anywhere, and we're wasting time now in an investigation where we just don't have any time to waste. Have you forgotten that thirteen people are still in a hostage situation, including your own two children?'

Reynold glares at him, and at Sadie, then takes a deep breath and sits down.

'Sorry,' he says. 'I'm under a lot of stress – we all are. But this is just ridiculous. Go on, ask your questions if you must.'

'Thank you,' says Sadie. She glances at Daniel, who looks back at her, and she knows they're both thinking the same thing: *Why so angry, Mr Lyon? Something to hide?*

The man had declined legal representation, and so it's just the three of them in the small, stuffy room, empty apart from the table and chairs they're using and a water cooler in the corner, a tower of cardboard cups leaning drunkenly against it. Sadie clears her throat.

'Right. So, Mr Lyon, can you describe to me in your own words what your FLO Marc Hackett saw on the computer screen in your office, please? I believe it's a proposal for some sort of new television game show?'

Reynold sighs dramatically.

'Yes, it is. A top-secret proposal, which hasn't even been pitched yet. I swear, if this is leaked anywhere…'

'It won't be leaked, Mr Lyon. Can you please answer the question?' Sadie says sharply. The man is beginning to irritate her.

'Fine. Yes, it's an idea for a new game show. A large group of people – probably six families, both parents and kids – are taken to the middle of nowhere, somewhere really remote like a forest or a mountain valley, and dropped off. They'll have no cash, no phones, nothing, and they'll have no idea where they are – they might be in Scotland, they might be in Cornwall, they'll have to work that out for themselves. Then they have to find their way back to a certain point to win a massive cash prize, against the clock. Meanwhile, a group of what I'm calling "blockers" in helicopters will be following them around, putting obstacles in their way and trying to stop them getting to their destination. I'd like the blockers to be led by Krystal Bell, if possible – I can just see her jumping in and out of a helicopter in a tight catsuit, can't you? A bit like Anneka Rice did in *Challenge Anneka*, back in the day?'

He looks at Daniel as he says this, a sudden spark of excitement in his eyes, and Sadie feels her distaste for him growing. She knows who Krystal Bell is – she's a blonde tennis-player-turned-TV-presenter, who always seems to have her head firmly screwed on – and Sadie finds herself hoping that the woman would tell Reynold exactly where to stick his 'tight catsuit' fantasy, should she ever actually be offered the job.

Daniel has clearly decided to ignore the reference entirely.

'So, how do you plan to get these people to their drop-off point without them knowing where they are?' he says casually.

Reynold rubs his hands together and smiles. *He seems to be rather enjoying himself now,* Sadie thinks.

'They'll all be put on coach, with completely blacked-out windows, and music playing constantly to obscure any noise coming from outside. Then they'll be driven around for hours – maybe just round in circles if they're going to be dropped off close by, or maybe to the other end of the country. Then the doors will open and out they go. And of course there'll be the children there for the parents to take care of too, so that's an extra hindrance. They'll have to be very clever to work around all the obstructions laid by the blockers to get back to the prize point.'

He leans back in his chair, a small smile on his face.

A SMUG smile, Sadie thinks. She glances at Daniel again, and she knows that, as before, they're thinking along exactly the same lines.

Surely Reynold Lyon knows what he's just said? How is he saying it so calmly, explaining it so openly?

'I see,' Daniel says. 'So a group of adults and children. On a bus. Taken to somewhere remote, possibly a forest. No phones. Is this ringing any bells for you, by any chance, Mr Lyon?'

There's a moment's hesitation from Reynold, as he frowns at Daniel.

Then he says, 'No— I mean, well… yes, I suppose when you say it like that… but… Oh, my God! I just didn't realise… Look, this is a *game show* idea. You can't possibly think…?'

'Well, it bears a striking similarity to the current situation. I think we can all see that, can't we, Mr Lyon?' says Sadie. Across the table from her, Reynold Lyon is now slowly turning red in the face, the flush obvious even under his tan.

'NO!' he says, loudly. 'It's purely an unfortunate coincidence. A *really* unfortunate coincidence. I mean, yes, I can see why you might think— You'll think this is weird, but it never even *struck* me until right now… but I can *assure* you—'

'Trying it out, were you?' asks Daniel. 'A little trial run? Where did you have them dropped off, Mr Lyon? WHERE ARE THEY?'

He says the last few words so loudly that Sadie jumps. Reynold, who's still protesting, snaps his mouth shut, shocked into silence for a few moments, then he groans and sinks his face into his hands.

'I swear… I promise you… This is just a crazy, awful fluke,' he mutters, then lifts his head to look at them again.

'My *children* were on that bus. I love them more than life itself. God, I know this looks bad, and I can't believe I didn't see it before. But do you really think if I was doing some sort of secret pilot for a new show, I'd put my own children at risk? I would *never*, ever… Please, you have to believe me!'

Sadie waits for a few moments, watching him, noting the look of anguish in his eyes.

But is that for real, or is he just a very good actor? she thinks.

'It's a *very* big coincidence,' Daniel says coldly.

'I know. I know. I totally see your point of view, I do,' says Reynold, and his voice is little more than a hoarse whisper. 'I actually can't believe it didn't occur to me, but it really didn't. It's just a game show idea, but I thought it was a good one, and I think the network would have gone for it, but now it seems, well… Oh, Christ, I don't know how to convince you, but I swear on my children's lives, I have nothing to do with what's happened. *Nothing*. I just want them back…'

His voice cracks, and he sinks his face into his hands again.

'Can we take a break, please?' he whispers.

———

'It's this lot. This little group here.'

Sadie has been standing at the board for twenty minutes, thinking, and now she turns to see where Daniel is and beckons him over.

'Daniel, look. What do you think?'

She points. She's moved some of the pictures into a little cluster, eight photos now separated from the rest: Reynold Lyon and his wife Petra, Eldon and Amy Beckford, Clare and Nick Tustain and Ben and Monique Townsend.

'These four couples. They're making me uneasy,' she says.

Daniel nods slowly.

'Yeah. Me too,' he says.

It's nearly seven o'clock now, and a short while ago Reynold Lyon was released, pending further investigation. Sadie is still far from happy about the distinct similarities between the TV presenter's game show idea and the kidnap of Class 3B, but an initial look at the man's computer and laptop by the digital forensics team found nothing else suspicious. To her surprise, Reynold had cooperated fully with that, freely handing over his passwords, and so with no real evidence linking him to the kidnapping she didn't really have much choice but to allow him to go home. She's tempted to question his wife, Petra, too, but their FLO Marc Hackett told her earlier that the woman had practically collapsed when she arrived home to find that her husband had been taken to the police station, and is still in a 'frankly dreadful state' as he put it, so Sadie's decided to leave it for today, at least.

As for the others… Her eyes run across the row of faces. Monique Townsend and her peculiar behaviour is still bothering her too.

The fact that she was there, at the wildlife park, hiding in the bushes… I can't get over that, she thinks.

Again, she's got no real concerns about the husband, Ben, but she's lumping them together just in case. And then there are the other two couples, who didn't ring any alarm bells until today, but now…

Sadie thinks back to the conversations she had earlier with the two FLOs who've been assigned to the Tustains and the Beckfords. When asked if she'd had any thoughts about what 'one of you has a secret' might refer to, Clare Tustain apparently went 'as white as a white cat in a bag of flour', according to her FLO Gavin, a straight-talking Yorkshireman with the bluest eyes Sadie's ever seen. She thinks he might wear coloured contact lenses.

'She looked like she might pass out, for a minute,' Gavin had said. 'Then she pulled herself together and told me she was just feeling light-headed because she'd been too anxious to eat today. Came across as a bit dodgy to me. Not sure about the husband... She does most of the talking. Under t' thumb if ever I saw it, that lad.'

It was, apparently, a strangely similar scenario at the Beckford home. When Maria, their FLO, reported back, she said that both Eldon and Amy had seemed twitchy and on edge all day.

'It was weird,' she told Sadie. 'It was as if they couldn't look me in the eye, but they kept giving each other these sidelong glances. Amy looked quite agitated. I just felt they weren't telling me the truth at all when I asked them if that message meant anything to them. You know when you just *know*?'

And so the Tustains and the Beckfords are now there on the board with the Lyons and Townsends.

'What if they're all in something together? I mean, in *what* exactly I don't know. Not yet. But could that be why *all* the kids were taken, not just one? Maybe something else to ask the head, Mrs Chamberlain, as an outsider – does she know if those four couples are close? I think Reynold and Petra know the restaurant couple, the Beckfords, quite well, but what about the others—?'

'SHIT! Boss, quick!'

Sadie's question to Daniel is interrupted by a yell from the other side of the room, and they both turn round abruptly, to see a young detective constable waving a mobile phone in the air.

'The next message,' he says, as the room falls silent. 'It's just arrived with all the Class 3B parents.'

Daniel and Sadie are already at his desk, a sudden surge of adrenalin making Sadie feel breathless.

'Go on – tell us!' she says.

The man looks down at his phone.

'It says: *£5 million. By Friday. Deposit instructions to follow. Pay = the hostages will be released unharmed and your secret stays safe forever. Don't pay = justice will be meted out.*'

Chapter Twenty-Six

LUCA

Day 5: Tuesday, 7.03 p.m.

Luca Lyon is flipping through the pages of a book about British birds. He likes this book; there are lots of birds in it that he sees in his own garden at home, and that makes him feel happy. He's been trying to find as many things as possible to make him feel happy here, but it's been getting harder and harder. He turns another page, then puts the book down and scratches his head with all ten fingers. His hair feels dirty. *He* feels dirty. He stops scratching and studies his fingernails. There are lines of black under them, even though he washes his hands every time he uses the toilet, the way his mum taught him. The adults have been *trying* to keep this room clean – there's a sweeping brush and some cloths, and they're always wiping or brushing something, but it doesn't seem to make much difference. It's as if dust oozes out of the walls or something, and a fine layer of it lies over everything. He's starting to miss home desperately now, after *four* sleeps away.

He can't stop thinking about his mum, and how good her hugs are, and about his lovely big, clean bed that feels the same in the morning as it does when he gets into it at night. His blow-up bed was fun at first but he's getting really bored of it now, and the annoying way it slowly loses air as he sleeps. When he wakes up he can feel the cold, hard ground underneath him. Mr Jones told him it must have a leak, and they tried looking for it, but they couldn't find it, and anyway, they don't have anything to fix a leak with, not in here.

Luca picks up his book again and spends a few seconds studying a photograph of a bird called a green woodpecker. It's very pretty: dark-green wings, a yellow bottom and a red streak across the top of its head. He definitely hasn't seen one of those in the garden, and he vows to keep an eye out for one when he gets home. Because this evening, he's suddenly got a good feeling about that. Something has changed – there's a different *feel* in the room. In the *bunker*. They call it The Bunker now, and he likes the word, likes the way it sounds a bit rude but actually isn't.

'You stupid bunker,' he said to Noah Beckford last night, and they both howled with laughter. They learned about bunkers when Miss Norman said the room reminded her of one and told them a story about some wars when people built underground rooms to protect themselves from bombs that were being dropped from aeroplanes. In some countries they still use them now, to hide from big storms and tornadoes. Now they've all started calling this room The Bunker, and The Bunker definitely feels different tonight, although Luca can't quite figure out why.

The Visitor who comes to the door – the person Luca still

thinks might be the same person as the one who boarded the school bus wearing a mask – came again earlier, tapping twice as usual, and afterwards the teachers all huddled together and had a long conversation in whispers, and when they parted they all looked a little bit happier, although Miss Norman looked a bit scared. But then she came over to Luca – Lola was there too, sitting on his bed with him – and she told them she knew they were all getting more and more bored and fed up, but that she thought the game really was nearly over now, and they just needed to hold on a little while longer.

'Maybe just three or four more sleeps,' she said. 'And then, fingers crossed, we can all get out of here. That would be good, wouldn't it?'

Three or four more sleeps seems like an awfully long time to Luca, and at first the thought of it made him feel worse, not better. But actually, it's nearly time for bed now, isn't it? And that will be one sleep done, and then just a few more, and then home, home, HOME.

'We can do it, Lola. Mum and Dad say you can do anything if you put your mind to it, so we just need to put our minds to it,' he'd said to his sister earlier, and she had nodded fiercely.

'Of course we can,' she'd replied. 'Does it mean someone's nearly worked out where we are? In the game? Do you think it's *our* dad? What will he win? I hope it's a puppy!'

Luca had told her he didn't know – the teachers didn't seem to know what the prize was either, when he'd asked them – but he'd said he hoped it was a puppy too. He's gone back to thinking that this *is* just a weird game now, because trying to think about what else it might be was making his brain hurt, and anyway it won't matter soon because they'll all be going home. He's going to tell his mum he never wants to go on a school trip again though, not if they're going to be like this. This is the worst school trip *ever*.

At least they've had *nice* teachers with them. A few of them were chatting about that this afternoon, and they're all so glad they've ended up sharing The Bunker with these three, and not some of the others.

'Imagine if Mrs Chamberlain had come with us,' Willow Townsend had said. 'I mean, she's nice, but she's *soooo* strict. I bet she'd have made us do schoolwork all day every day instead of reading and playing games. It would have been *horrible*.'

'Ugh, yes,' agreed Stanley Tustain. The two of them were sharing a beanbag, legs thrown across each other. They've always got on well, but they've become *really* good friends since they've been in here, so much so that some of the other girls have started teasing Willow that Stanley's her boyfriend.

'And imagine if Mr Flannigan had come, with his stinky cigarette breath,' he'd said.

'EWWWWW!' they had all chorused, so loudly that Miss Norman had crossed The Bunker from where she'd been sitting at the kitchen table with Mr Jones to see what they were talking about.

When they told her, she'd said, 'Now, now, let's all be kind please. No personal comments,' but Luca saw a tiny smile twitching at the corner of her mouth as she walked away. It's been the closest thing to having a mum with them, having her here. She gives cuddles – really good, *big* cuddles – when someone is sad or worried about something, which has been happening quite a lot during the past few days in The Bunker.

And Luca thinks she has what *his* mum calls a 'soft spot' for him and Lola too. She checks on all the children, all day long, and at night too. But he's noticed she checks on him and his sister a bit more often than she does some of the others. He thinks it might be because they're twins, which he knows makes them a bit special. Or maybe it's just because both of their parents are quite famous, which, for some reason he doesn't really understand, sometimes makes adults more interested in him and Lola too. Although they're not the only kids in Littleford with famous parents, of course. Noah's dad is on telly all the time on the cooking shows, and Gresham Greer's dad was a footballer for Chelsea.

Luca doesn't think he wants to be famous. It looks like a lot of hassle to him. He wants to be a vet, or work in a zoo maybe, he's decided. Or maybe somewhere like Birdland, where his mum took him and Lola for an afternoon out a few months ago. He loved it there, wandering around the big woods and gardens, laughing at the antics of the parrots and macaws and watching the king penguins lumbering around their enclosure. There's a 'penguin cam' on the Birdland website, and Luca often logs on and sits there watching for ages, fascinated by the huge birds with their sleek feathers and the bright yellow-orange splashes on their chests and the sides of their heads.

He sighs. He hopes, very, very much, that Miss Norman is right about it just being three or four more sleeps. Maybe he'll lie down extra early tonight, just to make it go quicker. He sighs again, and goes back to his book.

Chapter Twenty-Seven

LITTLEFORD

Day 5: Tuesday, 8.45 p.m.

£5 million. By Friday. Deposit instructions to follow.
Pay = the hostages will be released unharmed and your
secret stays safe forever.
Don't pay = justice will be meted out.

Reynold reads the message for the tenth time. He's sweating profusely, he realises, his shirt sticking to his back, his hair damp where it's touching his forehead.

As if the farce at the police station earlier wasn't enough…

'I mean, how utterly *ridiculous*,' he'd raged, as he explained to Petra why he'd been pulled in for questioning. He hadn't even shared his show proposal with *her*, not until today, but when he did her distress seemed to subside rapidly, to be replaced by astonishment.

'Well, I'm afraid I can *totally* see where they're coming

from,' she said. 'You're sending a load of adults and kids off on a *bus*, Reynold. And dumping them in the middle of nowhere. Come on, even you can see the similarity, surely?'

'It's not a bus. It's a *coach*,' he'd insisted. 'It's nothing like the school minibus. It would be huge, with a toilet and a kitchenette and bunks… you know, a sleeper bus, the kind bands go on tour in—'

'Oh, it's the same bloody thing,' Petra had spat. 'I can't believe you could be that stupid. How on earth did it not occur to you? I despair, honestly.'

She'd stalked off upstairs then, and he'd thumped the kitchen wall in fury and then instantly regretted it, sinking into a chair and nursing his now extremely painful and, no doubt soon to look badly bruised, fist. Petra's right, of course. He *has* been an idiot, and of *course* he can see the similarity between the show proposal and what's happened to the school bus, now that it's been pointed out to him. He's glad Marc has left for the day, though. The FLO dropped him back home earlier, but he didn't stay long; Reynold had barely spoken to him on the drive back, still furious about what he can't help seeing as a massive invasion of his privacy, even though he knows the man was only doing his job. But the thought of being accused of somehow being involved in the abduction of all those people… *Him?* Reynold Lyon? Seriously?

Now, as he reads the latest message again, he's desperately hoping it might take the police's attention away from him, for a while at least. Because although his game show proposal may have nothing to do with what's happened, the other thing he's done almost definitely *does*. But… £5 million? Five *million*? The police have already been in touch to tell them they should not, under any circumstances, hand over any cash. But Petra, who came running downstairs again as soon as the ransom demand arrived, clearly disagrees, her green eyes flashing like those of a furious cat.

'I don't care what they say. Just work out how we can raise it, OK? We *have* to. Speak to Eldon, speak to whoever you need to speak to, but just do it. I want our children back, Reynold. And I don't even care whose secret shenanigans these vermin are referring to anymore. If we have to pay for someone else's wrongdoing, fine. I just want the twins home.'

Reynold agrees, of course. What choice does he have, if he wants to protect himself, wants to protect his entire family, from what he's done being revealed to the world? And yet, even if others can somehow be persuaded to contribute too, how on earth can they get £5 million together in the next three days? It's impossible. Reynold and Petra have savings and investments, of course they do, but everything is tied up in stocks and shares and bonds and property. They don't have easy access to anywhere *near* that amount of money.

Even though he's sitting down, Reynold suddenly feels rather faint. He closes his eyes and takes a few long, slow breaths, grateful that Petra has gone to have a bath. He needs to do something, and quickly, but what? He takes another breath, opens his eyes and reaches for his phone. He'll think about this for a few minutes, he decides. He'll think about the best way to take the next step, and then he'll make the phone call.

In his living room, Ben Townsend is also staring at his phone, mildly surprised by how much the hand holding it is shaking. Then he realises his entire body is trembling, his legs feeling so weak he thinks he might fall over, so he sits down on the sofa and continues staring at the phone. The door of the room is open, and from upstairs he can hear intermittent wails and sobs, punctuated by short silences which, he assumes, are when Monique is swallowing another mouthful of Rioja.

When the message arrived earlier she immediately flew into a frenzy, shrieking unintelligibly about 'secrets' and 'justice' and finally flinging a cushion at him and shouting, 'The police are useless. It's up to us to sort this out. But how are we going to raise that sort of money, Ben? *How?* We can't, can we? So what happens now? What happens to our beautiful baby girl *now*?'

Then she'd marched to the wine rack, grabbed a screw-top bottle, picked up a glass that had been drying on the draining board next to the sink and disappeared upstairs. Ben, who hadn't said a word during her entire tirade, has now lost track of how long he's been sitting here, rigid with indecision and fear. He's not sure what's going on anymore. Monique's reaction just now… She *can't* be involved, can she? Would she really have reacted like that if she knew where the kids were? He can't see it, unless she's a far better actor than he ever realised, which means she probably *doesn't* know that this is about him, and what he's done. And now, despite what the police have told them, for his secret to stay a secret he's going to have to pay, isn't he? If the money – this *insane* amount of money – isn't raised, somehow, by somebody, in the next few days, it's all going to come out. Everyone is going to know. But how can he ask the other parents to pay too, without telling them why?

Does it even matter anymore? he thinks, as he stares dully into space. *Aren't the children, and getting them home safely, the only things that are really important now?*

He and Monique are over anyway, aren't they? They've been over for a long time, if he's really honest; he's stayed far, far longer than he ever should have. So, what has he got to lose? He taps a number into his phone and holds it to his ear.

'Don't cry, babe. It'll be OK. I promise.'

In their bedroom at The Post House, Eldon strokes his wife's hair as she sobs violently, her face pressed into his shoulder. He's trying to keep it together, but he feels like bursting into tears himself. Since the latest message arrived, he's been trying to keep a lid on an almost overwhelming feeling of near-hysteria; Amy, on the other hand, took one look at the words on the screen of her phone, gasped in horror and began to cry.

'It's… it's me. It's *me*. They're coming after me. It wasn't supposed to happen. I didn't want this… I'm so sorry,' she'd whimpered, and he'd looked at her, puzzled.

'It's *both* of us, not just you,' he said. 'You know that. We're in this together, Amy. You can't blame yourself. Why are you saying that?'

'I… I just… Oh, nothing. I'm just so sorry, Eldon. I'm so sorry this is such a mess.'

'You have nothing to be sorry for, my darling. Yes, it's a

mess. But we can get out of it, OK? We just have to stick to our story. It's going to be all right, you have to believe that.'

Even as he said the words, though, he knew it wasn't just his wife he was trying to convince. Would it be all right, really? That was a couple of hours ago and, despite Eldon's best efforts to calm Amy down, she's still in a highly agitated state, unable to stop crying for more than a few minutes at a time, and repeating the same feverish request over and over again. She's doing it again now, pulling away from him to pace up and down the room, her face rigid with terror.

'Can we just pay them? Please, *please* Eldon. I don't care what we have to do. I know we don't have anything near £5 million in savings, but we have assets, don't we? Sell the restaurants, sell the house, if we have to. I'll live in a caravan, I couldn't care less. *Please.*'

'By Friday?' he replies, for the umpteenth time. 'Amy, I keep telling you. It's *impossible*, OK? Maybe we can *borrow* against the businesses, yes, when the banks open tomorrow. But £5 million? There'll be so many questions, you know that. They won't just hand over that sort of money overnight. They'll want business plans, projections, all sorts. And we can't tell them why we really want it, can we? And what do we say to the other families? I don't know what to do, Amy. Please, *please*, calm down and let me think... Shit. Who's that?'

In his trouser pocket, his mobile is ringing, and he fumbles for it, pulling it out and looking at the caller ID.

'It's Reynold,' he says. 'I'd better take this. Shhh, please, just for a minute.'

Amy abruptly stops walking and stares at him with an even

more frightened expression on her face, but he turns away, hitting the button to accept the call.

'Reynold, mate,' he says. 'How are you guys handling all this? Are you OK?'

Then he listens, nodding slowly.

'Fine,' he says. 'I think that's a good idea, actually. I think we all need to talk. In about an hour? Will you put a message on the group chat? Thanks, mate. See you shortly.'

He ends the call and turns back to his wife, who's still standing stock-still, eyes fixed on his face.

'What... what did he want?' she whispers.

'He's coming round,' Eldon replies. 'Everyone is, I think. All the parents. We need to get together and decide what to do. They'll all be here in an hour. So please, go and wash your face and pull yourself together. It's time to take control of this thing, Amy. If we don't, it's going to ruin us. One hour. Go.'

She stares at him for a few moments longer, and he braces himself, waiting for a fresh outburst. But then, to his surprise, she simply nods.

'OK,' she says quietly, and she turns and leaves the room, closing the door gently behind her.

Chapter Twenty-Eight

CLARE

Day 5: Tuesday, 9.30 p.m.

'We should have brought something. A bottle of wine, maybe,' mutters Nick, as he and Clare walk quickly down Littleford High Street, heading for Eldon Beckford's. It's a cool, dry evening, and as they pass the Royal Oak laughter and the sound of clinking glasses drifts from the open windows, normal people living their normal lives.

Clare gives her husband a sidelong glance.

'It's not a dinner party,' she says, trying to keep the irritation out of her voice. 'It's a meeting. We don't need to bring anything.'

He grunts and they march on, past the village shop, closed for the evening now, with its cheerful window display of yellow chicks and white bunnies grouped around a basket of chocolate eggs.

Easter Sunday is this weekend, Clare remembers. *Friday is Good Friday. Half-term break starts in two days' time.*

She'd forgotten all that. It doesn't seem important, not now. When the latest message had arrived, she'd been in the kitchen with Nick and had had to run from the room, gripped by a fear so sudden and extreme she'd thought she might lose control and blurt it all out; that she might, finally, tell him everything. She didn't, of course. Instead, she locked herself in the downstairs loo until she got a grip again, managing to mumble something about the stress giving her an upset stomach when Nick tapped on the door.

The police had been in touch within half an hour, their family liaison officer, Melissa, urging them not to do anything rash.

'We're still asking you all to sit tight, just for a little while longer,' she said. 'The search for the hostages' location is continuing day and night, and we're now thinking of possibly lifting the press blackout briefly to make a television appeal to the kidnappers. Please *don't* think about paying them any money. Paying a ransom isn't illegal, as such. But paying money to someone who may use it for purposes of terrorism or other criminal activity may make you guilty of an offence. And this person – or people – well, they're definitely criminals, right? They've murdered one person already – who knows what else they may be capable of? And of course, paying once might just make them come back for more, or it might mean you being targeted again in the future. Just keep the faith, OK?'

Clare and Nick had agreed. What else could they do? But when Reynold Lyon had popped up on the group chat, asking if all the parents could gather at the Beckfords's place as soon as possible to discuss their next move, and to please not tell the police, Clare had instantly told a wary Nick that they *must* go.

'I don't like going behind the police's back,' he'd whined. 'Surely they know what they're doing, and the best way to handle this? We could put the children in even more danger...'

'Nonsense.' Clare was already pulling on her denim jacket, desperate to get out of the house, to talk this through with someone else, to do *something*.

'We're just going to talk. Come on. Let's leave the car and walk. It'll do us good.'

And so now they're walking, heading down to the lower High Street, towards The Post House. At the thought of seeing him, and the conversation she knows they're going to somehow have to have this evening, Clare's stomach flips. When he'd called earlier, sounding strangely calm given the circumstances, she'd been horrified.

'Why are you calling me at home?' she'd hissed. She was in the kitchen and Nick, thankfully, had just gone upstairs to find his phone charger. But even so, she couldn't risk him overhearing.

'I can't talk to you, not now. Yes, I *know* we have to. But later, OK?'

She'd terminated the call seconds before Nick had re-entered the room. Now, she glances sideways at her husband again, noting the tight set of his jaw, the grim line of his mouth; she shivers, pulling the collar of her jacket up a little higher as they trudge on. She thinks again about how he will react when he finds out the truth, because he will now, she knows that. It's inevitable. She thinks about how much it will hurt him, and about Stanley, the innocent victim in all this, and she thinks her heart might break. She's not sure how much she loves Nick anymore, but she still cares about him, and he doesn't deserve this. But she can't fall apart, not now. So instead she vows to take this evening one step at a time.

Focus on the moment. Focus on the moment.

She repeats the words over and over in her head, in time with their footsteps, and she thinks about the last time they made this journey to The Post House. Was it really only just over a week ago? The Beckfords had thrown a party, a celebration of one of their restaurants winning an award of some sort, and they'd invited not only some of their fancy London friends but everyone they knew locally too, including all of Noah's friends' parents. Clare had been to the house a few times before, dropping off and collecting Stanley for playdates and parties, but the place still blew her away.

'The size of that fireplace! And those beams!' she'd whispered to Polly Pearson, who'd been as wide-eyed as she was. The party had been *incredible*. Champagne and cocktails on tap, and waiters in black shirts gliding through the crowd holding aloft trays with a seemingly endless supply of what they politely told guests were codfish fritters, stuffed plantain cups and a whole host of other Caribbean-style nibbles Clare can no longer remember the names of, but which tasted utterly divine. A well-known Ibiza club DJ – Clare had never heard of him, but she gathered from the shrieks of some of the younger partygoers that he was something of a big deal – played pumping music, and a state-of-the-art lighting system turned the entire vast living space into the coolest club Clare had ever been in. There were even two *fire-eaters* on the lawn, for God's sake, to entertain those who ventured out for a cigarette. She'd drunk far too much, and danced until her pretend-silk-but-really-polyester blouse was soaked through with sweat, but somehow, *somehow*, she'd managed to keep away from *him*, and he'd kept his distance too. It would have been so easy, on a night like that, to have let their guard down, to have sneaked off into a dark corner together to talk, but the fear of being seen, of being overheard, was too great. They were so close, so very close, to pulling this off. Or at least, they'd thought they were.

And now? How has it all gone so wrong, in just a few days? How? she thinks, and then looks, startled, at Nick, who's just said something to her in a sharp voice.

'What?' she says.

'I said, we're here,' he replies. 'You were about to walk straight past. Are you OK?'

She nods.

'I'm fine. Sorry, miles away,' she says.

As Nick raps on the door, though, Clare feels anything but fine. She doesn't think she's ever felt worse in her life, in fact. And she has a bad feeling about tonight. A *really* bad feeling. As if right now, she's teetering on the edge of a cliff, about to fall, and when she does, that will be it. *Game over.*

Chapter Twenty-Nine

THE BUNKER

Day 5: Tuesday, 9.35 p.m.

Outside The Bunker, The Visitor double-checks the lock, pockets the key and then pauses, listening to the muffled sounds of chatter and laughter drifting from the room behind the heavy wooden door, and smiling. It's the second visit of the day; earlier, The Visitor made the first drop-off, the standard box full of sandwiches, crisps and fruit, bought as usual from half a dozen different shops and petrol stations so as not to arouse suspicion. But tonight, on the way to somewhere else, The Visitor decided to return to surprise the hostages with a little extra: a couple of cartons of chocolate ice-cream cones, nestling inside an insulated bag, and a six-pack of cold beer for the adults. From the sudden burst of enthusiastic noise emanating from The Bunker, as the locked room is now apparently known, the treats have been well received.

Good, thinks The Visitor. It's been astonishing, really, how cheerful everyone down there has remained under the circumstances. The three teachers – or, more accurately, two teachers and a TA – have done a remarkable job of keeping all the children calm and relatively happy. When The Visitor has peered down the stairs, all sorts of things have been going on in that dingy room: remote controlled car races, storytime, even a Spanish lesson this morning, by the sound of it. OK, there've also been tears and plenty of begging to be allowed outside or to go home, The Visitor has been told. But that was to be expected, and overall it's been way, way smoother and easier than anyone ever dreamed possible. The age of the children has definitely been a plus; any older, and the ridiculous story the teachers came up with about the days spent in The Bunker being part of an elaborate game of hide and seek would never have worked. Yes, some of the children have questioned it, but on the whole, the story has been accepted, and that's been a huge relief. It's meant the children haven't been scared. Bored, frustrated, anxious, yes. But not *scared*. Not *frightened*. And now, finally, the end is in sight. Tonight will be the fifth night the group will be spending in The Bunker, but now the parents have received the ransom demand and will, The Visitor hopes, be getting the money together. Tomorrow, or the next day – exact timetable to be confirmed – another message will be sent, telling the families how to deposit the cash. And after they've done that, The Visitor will quietly unlock the door for the last time, and the thirteen people behind it will finally be free to leave.

The Visitor doesn't want to think about what will happen if the money *doesn't* arrive. That's for someone else to decide. If the money isn't paid, there'll have to be discussions. But they're all assuming it will be paid. How *much* to ask for was one of the biggest decisions; they argued a lot about that. At first, it was going to be a much smaller amount, a more realistic couple of million. But, right at the last minute, the decision was made to ask for more, a lot more. After all, this is a once-in-a-lifetime chance, isn't it? And it's all been risky, *so* risky. It could have gone wrong so many times. So they decided to go for it. Go *big*. Of course, £5 million is a lot of money to come up with at such short notice, even for the wealthiest. But if you get a *group* of people, they just might be able to raise it between them. That's the theory, anyway. And even if they can't raise it all, they should be able to get enough to make all this worthwhile, a group like that. There'll be some collateral damage, of course, innocent parties suffering needlessly, and that's a shame. But there's no avoiding that, and the hostages and the families will get over it. It's only a few days. A week, if all goes to plan. And then normal life can resume, can't it? The police won't find them, they're pretty sure of that. It would have happened by now, if it was going to. It's nearly over, and it's all going perfectly.

And so, for now, The Visitor feels little guilt, other than about the death of Erica Lindsay of course. That wasn't supposed to happen. The Visitor is keen to avoid any more bloodshed, and if the ransom money is paid, nobody else will get hurt. All thirteen people in The Bunker will come out of this physically unharmed and relatively unscathed. And the outcome, when all is revealed, will make everyone realise this *had* to happen. That it was all about punishment, and retribution. About making someone pay for what they did.

People will understand, thinks The Visitor. *They'll get why we did this. We had to. It was time.*

Because, despite what the most recent message to the parents said, this will *not* end with the handing over of the money and the release of the hostages. The secret referred to in the messages will *not* be kept. That was a lie.

We're going to ruin your life anyway, The Visitor whispers, checking the lock one final time and heading along the dark corridor that leads back to the outside world.

You have no idea what's about to hit you. None. And I can't. Bloody. Wait.

Chapter Thirty

ELDON

Day 5: Tuesday, 10.01 p.m.

'Where the hell is Reynold? He's the one who wanted this get-together, and he's the only one not here yet!'

Eldon marches into the kitchen, where Amy is taking glasses out of one of the cupboards and lining them up on the counter. She turns to look at him and shrugs.

'I'm sure he'll be here in a minute. And Ben and Monique have only just arrived too, remember. I wondered if they'd come at all, given the state Monique's been in. And especially after the police pulled her in. But she seems OK tonight. I think she's been drinking already though. Can you chill, please? River's sound asleep, so I'm hoping he'll stay that way. Oh, and that catch on his bedroom window is loose again. Can you remember to ask lovely Brandon to pop in to fix it? It's not safe, and we can't risk... well, you know. Look, take these glasses in and open some more wine. I think we're going to need it.'

'OK. Sure,' Eldon replies, wondering if he should comment on the fact that she's just referred to their, in his view far too attractive, handyman as 'lovely', then decides against it. He trusts Amy, and Brandon is a friend as well as an employee now, and if ever there was a time that friends were needed, it's now. He watches his wife for a moment, wondering what's changed. She looks almost… *What's the word? Serene? Composed?* The agitation, the extreme distress she's been displaying for the past few days seem to have melted away, to be replaced by brisk organisation. She's so… *calm*. She seems resigned, almost. Yes, resigned, that's the word. She seems resigned to what's going on, and to what's to come, and it worries him, this change, for some reason. But there's nothing he can do about it, and it's probably better that she's like this than the way she's been since Friday, and now the doorbell is ringing – *Reynold, finally?* – and Amy's shooing Eldon out of the kitchen, flapping a tea towel at him as if he's an annoying wasp at a picnic.

'Go! Answer that. I'll be right through.'

He goes, opening the door to Reynold and Petra and ushering them into the lounge where everyone else is waiting, some lined up on the two big sofas, others hovering by the fireplace, faces tense and anxious.

'I'm so sorry we're late,' Reynold says apologetically.

'It's OK. We were too,' says Ben, glancing at his wife.

For the next couple of minutes, Eldon and Amy pour drinks and offer round bowls of nuts and then, when everyone is holding a glass, Eldon clears his throat.

'OK, so… here we all are. It's been a horrible, horrible few days, hasn't it? Reynold, do you want to take the floor?'

Reynold, who's perching on the arm of the nearest sofa clutching a brandy glass, nods.

'Cheers, mate,' he says. 'Yep, absolutely dreadful few days. But it sounds at the moment as if the kids are OK, doesn't it? And so we just need to find a way of getting them home, as quickly as possible. Look, I know we probably shouldn't be meeting like this and going behind the police's back...'

'Exactly what I said to Clare on the way here,' mumbles Nick Tustain, who's leaning against the wall on the far side of the room, as his wife glares at him.

'I understand that some of you are going to feel like that,' Reynold says calmly. 'But we have to ask ourselves, how much longer? It's been five days now, and they still have no clue where the hostages are being held. It's all very well to tell us not to pay up, and to say they're going to do a TV appeal and ask the kidnappers to get in contact so they can try to negotiate, but what if that doesn't work? We need our children back home, *now*.'

'Hear, hear,' says Brett MacDonald-Cook.

'But how the hell do we raise £5 million by Friday? I mean, *you* might have a spare few million hanging around, Reynold, but most of us can only dream of that sort of money,' says Vanessa Carr, who's sitting on the arm of the sofa opposite Reynold. 'And actually, I think what we need to do first is to talk about *who* the messages are referring to. This thing about a secret? Because it's sure as hell not me, or Alex.'

She gestures at her husband who's sitting beside her, and he shakes his head.

'But clearly someone in this group knows what this is all about. So come on, spill. And while we're on the subject, why were you at the police station today, Reynold? You were seen leaving. What was that about?'

She's looking at Reynold with accusing eyes, and Eldon looks around the room and sees others looking at his friend in the same way.

Reynold was at the police station earlier? He didn't mention that… he thinks.

Reynold sighs and rubs his eyes.

'It was a huge misunderstanding,' he says firmly. 'Marc, our family liaison officer, was in my office and saw something on my computer. It was completely irrelevant… a proposal for a new game show which bore a passing resemblance to what has happened to the children, but only because it involved a group of people being taken off on a mystery trip in a coach. He felt he had to flag it and so I had to go in and explain myself to the detective superintendent. It's all been cleared up now. Something and nothing.'

There's a short silence in the room, and then Vanessa Carr speaks again.

'OK, well, fine. But we still need to narrow this down. Somebody here clearly has something to hide, and these people know about it. So who is it? Because I for one don't see why we should all pay for something someone else has done. Why are we all being made to suffer? *And* our children… They're the poor innocent ones in all this, and if anyone even lays a finger on my Luke, I swear to God…'

Her tone has become increasingly hysterical, and now she crumples, reaching for her husband for support and sliding off the arm of the sofa onto his lap, tears rolling down her cheeks.

'Well, I agree with Vanessa,' says Eugene Pearson loudly.

'Polly and I have talked about this until we're blue in the face, and we're damn sure it's nothing to do with us. We're the most boring people you could imagine. There's not a single thing in either of our pasts that that message could be referring to. And if one of you' – he swings an accusing finger around the room – 'if one of you is hiding something, and not telling us, and if that means our daughter's life is being put at risk, I'll kill you myself, and that's a promise.'

'I'll help you,' says Jon MacDonald-Cook. 'Because this can't be anything to do with me or Brett either. If it was some sort of homophobic thing, they would have been specific about it – those types always are. But we don't have any secrets. The police have checked out Oliver's birth family, just in case, but they don't think there's any connection. This is a living nightmare, not knowing where our son is or what's happening to him. He had a ruddy awful start in life and we promised that child we'd protect him and keep him safe forever, and now…'

He stops talking, clearly trying to compose himself. His husband slips an arm round his shoulders.

'So, who else?' he says. 'Because we seem to be eliminating ourselves from this thing pretty quickly.'

'I don't think it's anything to do with me,' says Rosie Duggan quietly. 'I don't have any secrets as such, but the police did wonder briefly if it might be something to do with an ex of mine. He was physically and mentally abusive when we were together, and I finally found the courage to leave, but then he started stalking me. I managed to get a restraining order and I haven't heard from him since, but when that message came the police did question if it might be him, some sort of revenge thing, even though quite honestly I couldn't see him having the brains to pull something like this off.' She rolls her eyes. 'Anyway, it's been followed up and apparently he's been in prison for the past eighteen months. Assault in a nightclub. I know how to pick 'em, don't I? So they've ruled him out. He's not Harper's dad, by the way, thank God.'

'I'm so sorry, Rosie. That must have been awful for you,' says Tasha Greer, and a few of the others murmur sympathetically.

'So I suppose I should lay our cards on the table too,' Tasha continues. 'Although most of our guilty past is no secret. Well, I should say *Spike's* guilty past, as I honestly can't think of anything I've ever done.'

Spike, sitting to her right, takes her hand in his, looking shamefaced.

'If you read the tabloids back in his playing days, you'll probably remember my husband being arrested a few times – for getting pissed up and punching a West Ham player, mainly.'

'Good man!' says Alex Carr, and then shuts up hastily as Vanessa elbows him sharply in the ribs.

'Sorry, inappropriate,' he mumbles.

Tasha gives him a small smile and continues.

'But all that was widely publicised at the time, so the police don't see the point in anyone blackmailing us about it so many years later. However, there is one more thing…'

She pauses, turning to look pointedly at Spike, who shrinks back in his seat, looking as if he's trying to disappear inside the sofa cushion.

'And this *was* before I met him, to be fair. But… well, Spike had a fling with the wife of one of his team-mates. This never made the papers, and the team-mate – I won't say who it was – never found out, and the wife was shagging around anyway, Spike wasn't the only one. He's happily re-married and living in America now. I never knew any of this until Spike told me yesterday…'

She turns to look at him again, and Eldon feels a tiny flicker of amusement at the stricken expression on the poor man's face.

'… but again, the police don't seem to think it's relevant. The man in question is a very wealthy guy now and they don't think he'd risk messing up his nice life by pulling a stunt like this, even if he did find out about Spike and his ex-missus. And Spike wasn't the only one, as I said. She had loads of affairs while they were married and it was so many years ago. If her husband was out for revenge on all of them, there'd be kids disappearing all over the country. So, you know… we can't entirely rule ourselves out, but we honestly don't think that message is aimed at us.'

There's another silence in the room as everyone digests this latest confession.

Then Tasha says, 'So, that leaves you and Petra, Reynold. Not your game show idea, but something else, maybe? Plus Ben and Monique…' She turns to look around at those sitting or standing behind her. 'And Clare and Nick. And, you and Amy, of course, Eldon.'

Eldon glances at Amy, who's on the other side of the room. Their eyes meet, and she shakes her head, just the tiniest little movement, but he knows exactly what she's trying to say.

No. Don't tell them.

For a moment, just one, he considers opening his mouth and lying. Saying he has no idea what the hostage takers' message means; saying that whatever it's about, it's nothing to do with him or with Amy; saying that their consciences are clear. But he can't, because suddenly all he can see is Noah's face. His first-born, one of the greatest loves of his life. His son, who's been taken and who he has to save. He *has* to, regardless of the personal cost. That simply doesn't matter anymore.

And so he looks at his wife, and he gives her the tiniest shake of the head back, and he can see that instantly she understands, her eyes filling with tears.

'Does anyone else want to rule themselves out?' he says quietly. 'Because this is getting very serious now. If we want our kids back, we have no choice. We have to be honest with each other, no matter how bad… no matter how shocking…'

He swallows hard. The room is so silent he can hear the hum of the big American-style refrigerator in the kitchen down the hall through the open door of the lounge.

'So what I propose is this,' he says, and now he can hear blood rushing in his ears and wonders if he might pass out. 'Anyone who genuinely does not believe that the message from the kidnappers is aimed at them, please leave now. Anyone who thinks otherwise, please stay. And we'll take it from there. There's no reason for those who are innocent parties here to pay any of the ransom demand. So – who's leaving, and who's staying?'

Heads turn, everyone looking at everyone else. Then, slowly, people begin to stand up and movetowards the door. Eugene and Polly Pearson, Spike and Tasha Greer, Vanessa and Alex Carr, Rosie Duggan, and Brett and Jon MacDonald-Cook all make their way silently out of the room, their footsteps echoing on the marble tiles of the hall floor, and moments later the front door closes. Eldon takes a deep breath and looks around the room again.

Who's left?

Nick Tustain is on his feet in the middle of the room, gesturing at his wife Clare, who's still seated.

'Come on,' he's hissing. 'What are you doing?'

But she's shaking her head, her face flushed.

'We have to stay, Nick. I'm so sorry,' she says, and he frowns and leans towards her, looking as if he's about to grab her arm and haul her to her feet.

'Nick!' She holds up a hand. 'Nick, please. We *have* to stay. I'll explain in a minute. *Please.*'

'But— Oh for Christ's sake. Fine. What the hell's going on?' he says, and sits down heavily, a look of pure bewilderment on his face.

So. Nick and Clare. Interesting, Eldon thinks. *Who else?*

Reynold Lyon. Still sitting there with Petra, who's pulling at the sleeve of his shirt, looking as confused as Nick is. Ben and Monique Townsend, sitting stiffly on two hard-backed chairs near the fireplace, Ben stony-faced, Monique glassy-eyed, as if she's not quite sure what's going on.

And me and Amy, of course, thinks Eldon, and he looks at his wife again, still on the other side of the room, still crying silently.

'And then there were eight,' he says.

Chapter Thirty-One

AMY

Day 5: Tuesday, 10.34 p.m.

For five seconds, ten, fifteen, there's silence in the room, everyone looking suspiciously at everyone else. Then Amy wipes her eyes with the backs of her hands and takes a deep breath.

'Reynold. Can I have a word? In private?' she says.

Reynold nods and stands up slowly.

'What's going on?' asks Petra. She sounds alarmed, eyes flitting from Amy and back to her husband, and Amy's stomach rolls. Petra is her *friend*, not a super-close friend but a friend nonetheless, and what she's about to find out is going to destroy her.

I'm a vile, horrible person, Amy thinks, and then looks at her husband, who's walking across the room towards her, confusion and concern etched on his face.

'Amy? What are you doing?' he asks, in a low, urgent voice,

and she reaches out and touches him on the arm, her heart beginning to race.

'I'm sorry,' she whispers. 'I just need a minute with Reynold. We'll be back… There's just something…'

Reynold is at her side now, taking her elbow and beginning to gently guide her out of the room.

'Eldon, mate…' He pauses. 'Please… we won't be long.'

Eldon is still staring at Amy, but she's heading for the door, and to her relief he doesn't try to stop her. Moments later, she and Reynold are out in the hallway, and she points to the kitchen.

'In there,' she says.

She closes the door behind them and leans against it, briefly closing her eyes. When she opens them again Reynold is reaching for her hand and pulling her into his arms.

'Christ, Amy,' he whispers, his lips close to her ear. 'What have we done?'

She rests her head on his shoulder, and feels her eyes filling with tears again as he runs a hand down her back, his touch simultaneously calming and, to her surprise at a moment like this, sparking the usual little fizz of excitement deep in her belly.

She'd never meant it to happen. The affair, with Reynold. But does anyone really set out to have an affair? Maybe some do, the people who use those websites to hook up with others looking for discreet extramarital fun. But *she* certainly hadn't planned it. It sounds so hypocritical, even to her, but she loves Eldon and their sons and their restaurants and their home and their *life*. She loves all of it, and for a long time putting it at any sort of risk would have been utterly unthinkable. But three years ago she'd been going through what she could only think of as an early midlife crisis. She'd just turned thirty-seven, and she had a four-year-old son and was trying to decide whether to acquiesce to Eldon's pleas to have another baby. But she was barely seeing Noah as it was, leaving him in the care of a nanny while she and Eldon worked long hours to get their latest restaurant, in a beautiful Art Deco-style building on the banks of the Thames in Berkshire, off the ground. Beckford Riverside was the latest in their growing chain, which had begun not long after they'd met, when Eldon opened his first small Caribbean cocktail bar and eatery in south London. Beckford Brixton quickly became a word-of-mouth success, with customers raving about its jerk chicken, conch ceviche and pineapple chow served tapas-style and its relaxed vibe. When a restaurant critic from a famous food magazine described Eldon as 'one of the most exciting new chefs working in London today', everything had exploded. Within a year, Beckford Brixton was booked up months in advance, and Amy had given up her job as an accountant in the City to help set up restaurant number two, Beckford on the Hill in Highgate, on the edge of Hampstead Heath. That was swiftly followed by Beckford Central in Soho, by which time Amy was pregnant with Noah. They waited a few years before deciding to expand further with their riverside restaurant, but by then Eldon had become a regular on the TV cookery shows as well as trying to oversee five kitchens, which meant Amy was having to work nearly as many hours as her husband. And then, Reynold and Petra had moved to Littleford.

She and Eldon had met them briefly several times before, when the famous chat show host and his beautiful model wife had dined at their restaurants, so when Reynold messaged Eldon to tell him they'd bought The Granary, just minutes away, Amy had been pleased. Reynold had seemed charming, and in Petra she'd felt she might have found a kindred spirit; a fellow mum who still had a busy working life outside the home and, even more importantly, understood the pressures of being in the public eye. But when they invited Reynold and Petra round for a 'welcome to Littleford' dinner, it was *Reynold* with whom she'd felt an instant connection. Petra was lovely, and clearly keen to strike up a friendship, and she and Amy soon fell into a regular routine of meeting for coffee and chats on their rare days off and texting each other if one of them spotted a pair of shoes or a dress that would be perfect for the other. But, Reynold... Reynold was something else entirely.

That first night, as they'd sat opposite each other across the table, their eyes had met and their gazes had lingered so frequently that Amy had finally had to escape to the kitchen to have a stern word with herself, thrilled and shocked in equal measure by a totally unexpected surge of longing.

She'd tried to resist him, but it had been impossible. Within weeks, they'd had their first kiss, a stolen moment in the garden when Amy and Eldon had been invited to The Granary for a small drinks party with some of Reynold's television friends. A month after that, when Eldon was staying overnight in London for work and Petra was away on a modelling job, they'd finally had sex, a passionate late-afternoon encounter on the small sofa upstairs in Reynold's office as Noah and the twins played downstairs. They'd only dared to leave the children alone for ten minutes, but those minutes changed everything. Neither of them could really explain it – both were, on the face of it, in happy, fulfilled marriages – but they *craved* each other. Maybe it was just that their lives had become a little too predictable, with the inevitable daily routines that accompany work and parenthood. Maybe it was just the thrill of it, the illicit nature of their hook-ups, that became addictive. Or maybe, for Amy, it was that the excitement of being with Reynold gave her respite from her own thoughts: helped her to forget, for a few hours now and again, the events of a dark night in her past, a night about which she never spoke but the horrors of which were always there, bubbling just under the surface. The memories had come surging back with a vengeance around that time, she didn't know why, and being with Reynold helped to suppress them, somehow. Whatever the reason, and despite both of them admitting the guilt was sometimes hard to bear, they couldn't seem to stop themselves.

Every now and again, they'd stay apart for a couple of weeks, even a month. But then they'd bump into each other in the school playground, or at the village shop, and off they'd go again. Having children of the same age who were friends made it so much easier; no casual onlooker or village busybody would ask questions about why Amy Beckford was seen coming out of The Granary with her son in the middle of the afternoon when Petra was away, or why Reynold and Amy were chatting earnestly outside the school gates. When Amy fell pregnant with River, they *did* stop seeing each other for a while; that had been a wake-up call. She had, of course, still been sleeping with her husband, as had Reynold with Petra, and she and Reynold had always been careful to use protection, but even so, terrified that River might not be Eldon's, Amy had organised a discreet DNA test days after the baby was born. It had all been fine, and a few months later – at River's christening party, to her shame – she'd dragged Reynold into the walk-in larder off the kitchen and they'd picked up where they'd left off. And so it had continued, on and off, ever since. Somehow – and they must both be terrible, terrible people, she frequently thought – she still managed to maintain her friendship with Petra, as did Reynold with Eldon. They still hung out together as couples too, still socialised and invited each other round for drinks and dinner. But whenever there was an opportunity, she and Reynold would take it, and after a while they'd almost stopped feeling guilty about it. They *needed* each other, and they no longer questioned it, became a little smug even, in retrospect, certain they'd never be caught, sure they'd made a fine art of all the sneaking around. They still tried, now and again, to cool things; they'd managed a whole month, recently. But the weekend before last (*Was it really so recently? It seems like forever ago, now,* Amy thinks), at the party, she'd seen the spark of lust in Reynold's eye again as she and Eldon had greeted him and Petra at the door, his fingers lingering on her bare shoulders as they'd exchanged chaste hugs. And at one in the morning, the music still booming and Eldon singing loudly and drunkenly along while Petra gyrated on the dance floor with a gaggle of others, they'd taken their chance and slipped out into the garden, closing the door of the summerhouse behind them and having fast, frenzied, incredible sex up against the wall, one of Amy's long legs hooked around Reynold's thighs, his hand over her mouth to muffle her moans of pleasure.

But that, she believed now, had been her biggest mistake. Well, *one* of her biggest mistakes, because there had been the other one of course, years ago, that had been even bigger – catastrophic, even. And now, she was utterly convinced that it was these, or *one* of these mistakes, that had led to all of this. The kidnap. The ransom demand. The *blackmail*. Someone knew. Someone knew about one, or both, of her secrets. Her worst nightmare, made real.

Now, she pulls away from Reynold, pushing her hair back off her face.

'What have we done?' he repeats. 'It's us this is aimed at, isn't it? It has to be. But how? How could anyone know about us? We've been so careful…'

He runs his hands through his thick hair, his cocoa-brown eyes looking deeply into hers, and despite herself, despite the horrific situation they're in, Amy feels a stirring in her groin. She ignores it, steeling herself. She has to tell him now, has to tell him all of it, she knows that, but how? *How?*

'OK, listen,' she says, then turns to look nervously at the kitchen door, checking it's firmly closed.

'I need to tell you two things, and I don't want you to interrupt.'

He frowns, and she takes a deep breath, unsure how to start.

'Sorry – this is so hard… Just give me a second…'

She turns away again briefly, trying to centre herself, but he takes her arm and twirls her back round to face him.

'What two things? What are you talking about, Amy? What's going on?'

He's managing to keep his voice low, but she can see the frustration in his eyes, and she takes another breath.

Just go for it. Just tell him. It's all going to come out anyway, now, isn't it? she thinks.

And so, she tells him the first thing. Tells him that at the party, when he was inside her in the summerhouse, his eyes closed, his body hot and hard against hers, a movement had caught her eye. Over his shoulder, she'd seen a silhouette at the window, a dark shape that at first had stayed completely still, and then had moved, drifting away down the garden, back towards the house, disappearing into the shadows. A person. Somebody outside the window, watching them, and then melting away. She'd tried to tell herself it had been a figment of her imagination, a physical embodiment of the renewed sense of guilt she felt about the affair, a result of the copious amount of champagne she'd drunk that evening. By the next morning, when she'd woken up with Eldon snoring beside her and her head pounding, her tongue like sandpaper in her mouth, she'd almost forgotten about it altogether. After all, if one of the remaining guests had seen her having sex with Reynold Lyon, surely there'd have been *some* reaction when they'd gone back into the house a few minutes later, a knowing glance or a sly wink? But there'd been nothing, and so she'd pushed it out of her mind, and had decided not to worry Reynold by mentioning it. The feelings of guilt had multiplied though, so much so that she shrank into herself in the days following the party, not wanting Eldon to touch her, feeling dirty. He clearly thought she was angry at *him*, for getting outrageously drunk and making a fool of himself on the dancefloor, things she couldn't care less about. But it was easier to let him think that, and so she did.

And then everything changed. With that first message from

the hostage takers her world, which had already fallen apart on Friday when Noah didn't come home, crumbled a little more. Because somebody *knew*, about this or, maybe, about her other secret, but either way that meant her life was pretty much over, didn't it? Her child was gone, and everything else she'd ever known and loved was about to be taken away too.

Now, she tells all this to Reynold, and when she's finished, his face somehow looks pale, despite his permanent tan.

'But who? Who was it?' he splutters. 'Who *could* it have been? You must know who was still at the party. I was so drunk, I didn't even look at who was still on the dance floor…'

'I don't know,' she whispers. 'It was just a shadow, but somebody was there, I'm sure of it. I mean, I think I'm sure. It was so dark, and we'd had so much booze… Oh God, I don't know, I just don't know. I can't think straight. I could be wrong, yes. But I still think that threat is aimed at me, even if it's not about us. Because of the second thing. There's something else I've never told you about. *We've* never told you about. This is Eldon's secret too, and we don't understand how anyone else could have found out about it, but maybe—'

'Christ, Amy. What the hell is it?' splutters Reynold. He grabs the tops of her arms and shakes her, ever so slightly, and she squirms.

'Sorry, I'm sorry,' he says, and immediately drops his hands. 'But please, put me out of my misery, for God's sake. What are you talking about?'

Amy feels tears pricking her eyes.

'It's something that happened years ago, before Noah was born,' she says. She's still whispering, and he frowns and leans closer.

'It was the worst day of my life.'

And so, slowly, haltingly, she tells him. Tells him about that cold December evening, when she and Eldon were driving home late from the Highgate restaurant. It was after 2 a.m., and Eldon had been exhausted after a long night plating up dishes and harshly rejecting anything not up to his exacting standards, so she'd offered to take the wheel, failing to tell him she'd had several glasses of wine during the evening as she'd greeted diners and chatted to them at their tables.

'I thought I'd be fine,' she says, and a tear rolls down her cheek. 'I'd only had a few, and the last one had been about an hour before we closed up, so…'

She runs a hand over her face and continues. She tells Reynold how they'd been living in a rented house near St Albans at the time; between properties, they'd wanted to try life outside central London, and the cathedral city, about twenty miles to the northwest, had seemed ideal. It was within easy commuting distance but, with its Roman ruins, street markets and the peaceful River Ver running through it, offered a still vibrant but slower-paced lifestyle for their rare days off. At that hour, it was just a forty-five-minute drive home from Beckford on the Hill, but that night Eldon could barely keep his eyes open, dozing in the passenger seat of their Range Rover as Amy sped along the M1 and then turned off to navigate the smaller roads that led to their detached house on a quiet street in Childwick Green, about four miles north of St Albans city centre. And that's when it happened. For Amy, it's still a blur now, remembered in flashes: an unlit empty road, high hedges on both sides; a figure, seemingly appearing out of nowhere; her foot, slamming on the brake; and then the noise, the sound she still hears in her nightmares, a sickening thud that seemed to reverberate through her very bones.

After that, more flashes: a slumped form on the tarmac, a dark, sticky pool spreading slowly from one end of it; Eldon, head in his hands, bellowing at her; Amy leaning on the bonnet of the car to vomit and, as she slowly straightened up again, seeing a clump of hair caught in the front grille; Amy beginning to scream, and Eldon clamping a hand over her mouth and dragging her around the vehicle, pushing her into the passenger seat; the drive home, Amy shaking so violently she could hear her teeth rattling.

Because yes, they drove home. They drove home, and they locked the Range Rover in the garage, and then they went inside and they made a plan. What else could they do? Call the police and tell them that Amy Beckford, one half of the power couple that was beginning to dominate London's trendy restaurant scene, had got behind the wheel of a powerful car with too much alcohol in her system and smashed into a pedestrian? It was unthinkable, for either of them. It would have ruined their lives. And so, instead, Eldon took buckets of water into the garage and cleaned every trace of hair and blood from the front of the Range Rover. And then, not long after dawn, at the time when he'd normally be leaving for another long day at one of the restaurants, he slipped behind the wheel and, very carefully and deliberately, drove the car straight into a big old fir tree on a country road a mile from the house. He'd gambled on the fact that, if he kept his speed low, this new accident would cover the damage from the first without causing him significant injury, and he was right; other than a vivid, diagonal bruise across his torso from the seat belt, and a black eye from the impact of the airbag as it deployed, Eldon was fine, and able to stagger from the car and call for help. He told anyone who asked what had happened that he'd had just a few hours of sleep the night before and had misjudged a bend in the road; the insurance company had paid for the car to be repaired without too many awkward questions, and that had been that.

Other than the dead body they'd left on the road a few miles away, of course.

The hit and run had featured prominently on the local news for days. Tim Wright, a local free-range turkey farmer with an eccentric habit of patrolling his land at night, obsessed with the idea that poachers might be after his birds, had been found by another motorist about half an hour after Amy had slammed the Range Rover into him. He was already dead, and there were no number-plate recognition cameras on the roads in that area, not back then and, on such a minor country road, probably not now either. An appeal had gone out to anyone who'd been in the vicinity that night to come forward, and after some more frightened discussion, and fearful that their vehicle may have been picked up by other cameras either side of the collision location, Amy and Eldon rang the police to tell them that they had indeed driven down that road that night, but had seen nothing.

'Shit. It could have happened just minutes after we were there. It doesn't bear thinking about,' Amy remembers Eldon saying to the officer who took their statement, and he'd nodded grimly.

'Horrific,' he'd agreed. 'What sort of person does something like that? Drives into a human being and leaves them there to die, eh?', and she and Eldon had both shaken their heads sadly, as if united in their disapproval of such an appalling act.

And, amazingly, that had been the end of it. The investigation into the death of poor Tim Wright had carried on for a few weeks and then quietly faded from the headlines, as these things are wont to do, and Eldon and Amy had carried on with their lives, expanding their business, winning accolades and awards, growing their family. They rarely spoke about what had happened, pushing it into the far recesses of their minds, only seeing it emerge occasionally in the form of flashbacks and nightmares. It had been a long time before Amy had felt able to drive a car again, and even now she's careful to the point of paranoia when she's behind the wheel. The whole business had left them both almost phobic of any dealings with the police too, the disappearance of the children taking on an even more nightmarish quality because the close proximity of police officers is now a daily occurrence. But even now, now they've been forced to talk about it to each other again, to make sure their stories about that night are identical, just in case, they can't understand how anyone can have discovered their secret. *Did* someone see their vehicle at the scene? But how? And why take so many years to let them know? It doesn't make sense, and yet...

One of you has a secret...

Could anyone else have a secret as monstrous as theirs? They couldn't. It's impossible. So is it that, or is it her affair with Reynold? Because all this is down to *one* of her secrets, Amy's convinced of that.

As she recounts this now, her voice is so quiet and so

broken with the pain of it that Reynold frequently has to stop her and ask her to repeat what she's just said. When she's finished, she dares to look in his eyes and sees exactly what she knew she would see: he is disgusted, nauseated, horrified.

'Christ,' he says, and he turns away, taking a few steps across the tiled floor of the kitchen before turning back to face her.

'So what am I supposed to do with that?' he says. 'Why have you even told me? Jesus, Amy.'

She says nothing. Instead, she turns and opens the door, and walks quickly back down the hallway.

'Amy? Where are you going?' she hears from behind her, but she ignores the question, and hears his growl of frustration and then his footsteps, mirroring hers. She pushes open the door to the living room and every head swivels.

'At last,' says Eldon, and she looks at her husband, his face crumpled with anxiety, and she feels a rush of sadness so intense she suddenly feels light-headed.

It's over, isn't it? she thinks. *My life is over. But if we can just get the children back, then at least one good thing will have come out of all of this. One good thing, out of the huge, stinking mess I've made of everything.*

She clears her throat, and turns to look briefly at Reynold, standing just behind her now, and she sees alarm in his eyes – a silent message, a desperate plea.

No, she can almost hear him saying. *Please, no.*

'I'm sorry,' she mouths. A strange calm has descended on her, and she has no idea why, but when she opens her mouth to speak her voice is steady, her breathing regular.

'Apologies for disappearing like that,' she says. 'There was something I needed to discuss with Reynold. And now, there's something I need to tell you all. Well, two things, actually.'

'Amy?'

Eldon is staring at her, and she can see the question and the worry in his eyes, but she shakes her head.

'It's OK, Eldon. Look, our children's *lives* are at stake here. And everyone in this room has stayed for a reason. Everyone here thinks something they're hiding might be behind this, right? And yet none of us have told the police our secrets, have we? So the time for silence is over. If we won't, if we *can't*, tell the police, then we're going to have to tell each other. This kidnap has clearly not been carried out by terrorists or people with a political agenda or anything like that. This is blackmail, and it's *personal*. So, this is where we talk. This is where we confess our deepest, darkest sins, right now. Because whoever is behind it, it's someone with a connection to one of us. And if we all know what we're dealing with, we might be able to work out who that is, and then we can decide on the best way forward. And maybe that *is* raising the money to get our children back, or maybe there'll be another way, who knows? But if we're all sneaking around, trying to hide whatever it is we're trying to hide, this is never going to work. The children are the only things that matter. They're our *lives*. So whatever it is that's caused them to be taken away from us, it's not important in the grand scheme of things. We can worry about all that later. So, let's make a pact. Whatever we hear in this room tonight, stays in this room. Whatever we hear, however awful it is, we keep between us, forever. We have each other's backs. We protect each other's secrets. Deal?'

She looks around the room, and she sees fear and

reluctance and confusion in the seven pairs of eyes looking back at her.

'Deal?' she asks again, louder this time. Then, to her surprise, Reynold, who's still standing behind her, takes a step forward.

'I'm in,' he says. 'Deal.'

'I have no secrets. But my husband clearly does. So, deal,' says Petra coldly.

'Deal,' says Clare Tustain quietly. Her husband spins around, and he stares at her pale, serious face for a moment, then he shrugs.

'I have no idea what's going on here. But fine, deal,' Nick says.

'Deal,' says Ben Townsend. His eyes are fixed on Clare's, for some reason, and Amy notices her give him an almost imperceptible nod, and wonders what that's about, and then realises they're probably all about to find out.

'I'm lost,' says Monique. 'I know what you all think…' She stands up unsteadily, then wags a finger, looking from face to face and swaying slightly on her high heels. 'I *know* some of you think I have something to do with all this, because the police pulled me in. But you're wrong, OK? I have nothing… I know *nothing*…' Her voice sounds slurred and there's an empty look in her eyes. 'But yeah, deal. Whatever.'

She flops back down into her seat, and Ben looks at her uneasily, then rubs a hand across his forehead and looks back at Amy.

She nods.

Only Eldon left now, she thinks, and she turns to her husband. He looks dazed.

'Eldon?

'Deal,' he says quietly.

Amy exhales slowly.

Is this a good idea? I have no clue, none. But it's the only one I've got, so…

'Good,' she says. 'So, here we go. Let's do this. Are you all sitting comfortably? Then let me begin.'

Chapter Thirty-Two

REYNOLD

Day 5: Tuesday, 11.06 p.m.

When Amy has finished speaking, there's a stunned silence in the room for several moments, and then Petra begins to cry.

Reynold starts to walk across the room towards her, but she hisses, 'Stay. Away. From. Me,' so furiously that he stops abruptly, sinking slowly onto the nearest chair instead. He feels sick, a hard knot of misery like a physical pain in his stomach. He had hoped that Petra would *never* discover what had been going on between him and Amy, and for her to find out like this, in a roomful of people, when she's already in such a dreadful state about the twins...

He's felt a little paranoid about it ever since the party; they'd never had sex in such close proximity to Petra and Eldon before, and he'd grown anxious that maybe Amy hadn't been in touch for a week because Eldon had suspected something. When he'd seen her in the school playground on

Friday, and she'd finally given him that small smile, he'd been deeply relieved. Even so, when the children vanished and Petra had wanted to call Amy, he'd felt he had to persuade her not to, scared that in her distressed state, Amy might blurt something out to his wife. And now, well... he certainly hadn't expected Petra to find out like *this*.

Christ. What's wrong with me? How could I do this to her? How could I risk everything for a few seedy shags? he thinks desperately, as Petra's sobs intensify, and Monique Townsend leaves her seat on the sofa opposite to sit next to his wife, slipping an arm around her shoulders and glaring at Reynold. He wonders if he might have a sex addiction. It's something he's wondered before, more than once over the years, when his urge to sleep with someone new became all-consuming, no matter how satisfying his current relationship was. When he'd met Petra, he'd thought that finally, *finally*, she might be the one who'd fix him, the one who'd stop him looking elsewhere, and for a while – *years* – she was. But then there was a brief dalliance with a pretty young runner at work, and then a tryst with a sexy barmaid in Budapest when he travelled to Hungary to shoot an interview with George Clooney on the set of his latest film. The two encounters, both just one-night stands, had happened in quick succession on booze-fuelled nights out in the space of a single week, and had, when he'd sobered up, rather freaked him out.

'If either of those women go to the press... Christ, Andrew, I'm finished,' he'd groaned, in a panicked phone call to his lawyer. But, miraculously, they hadn't. The barmaid, it emerged, regularly supplemented her income with escort work, and was happy to take a $2,000 tip to add Reynold to the long list of prominent men who were able to rely on her ability to keep her mouth shut about her client roster. The runner, meanwhile, was offered a junior producer role on double her then-salary, and seemed equally happy to consider her evening with Reynold as an enjoyable part of the recruitment process, even telling him she'd be more than happy to repeat the experience if it might help her to climb the career ladder. He'd politely declined and, counting his lucky stars that his week of madness hadn't had any major repercussions he had, as his lawyer had strongly advised, 'kept it in his pants' for quite a long time. But then, of course, Amy and Eldon Beckford had moved to Littleford and, well…

He's been scared to look in Eldon's direction, but now he dares to sneak a glance. To his relief the man is sitting with his eyes closed, a hand clamped to his forehead, as if it's simply too painful to look at anyone.

My friend. Can you ever forgive me? Reynold thinks, and the knot in his belly grows.

Amy, thankfully, hadn't gone into detail about the affair, simply telling the open-mouthed onlookers that she and Reynold had been sleeping together on and off for the past three years, and that she believed someone may have seen them during a recent hook-up, hence their fears that the hostage takers' note may have been aimed at them.

'Eldon… Petra… I am so, *so* sorry,' she'd said. 'And I know… *we* know…' – she'd gestured at Reynold – 'we know sorry isn't a big enough word. We'll regret this for the rest of our lives.'

Eldon had said nothing, simply turned away and stared for a long time through the glass of the bifold doors that run the length of the room, looking blankly into the darkness beyond, his reflection, grim-faced and almost frighteningly still, staring back at him. Then, as Amy had told a rapt audience that there was more, that she had yet another confession to make, and launched into the tale of the cover-up of the hit-and-run, he'd slowly returned to his chair, sinking his head into his hands. There'd been gasps of horror as his wife had recounted this new, even more appalling, potential reason for someone to choose to blackmail the Beckfords, and now that she's finished both stories the sense of shock in the room is almost palpable, the stunned silence broken only by Petra's sobs. Reynold wants desperately to go to her, to take Monique's place by her side, but he doesn't dare. She may never let him touch her again, and he wouldn't blame her.

'Holy shit,' says Nick Tustain. 'I mean, I have no idea what other dark secrets we're about to hear, but I'd be willing to put a lot of money on one of those bombshells being what's behind this. One of our biggest TV stars screwing the wife of one of our most famous chefs? *Jesus. And* the chef and his wife mowing someone down in a drink-driving accident and leaving him to die? I can't quite believe what I've just heard. Is this some sort of bad dream?'

Clare shifts uneasily in her seat next to him, opens her mouth as if she's about to speak, then clamps it shut again as Eldon stands up abruptly.

'We have no excuse for that accident and how we handled it, we know that,' he says sharply. 'And I know we've all agreed what's said in this room tonight stays in this room, but if we get Noah back safely – if we *all* get our children back safely – I wouldn't blame any of you for going to the police. It's been eating me up – eating both of us up – for years. And as for the... the *affair'* – he turns to look at Reynold as he says the word, snarling it at him, and Reynold feels himself shrink back in his seat – 'I'm very glad we were spared the details,' Eldon continues, a hard edge to his normally jovial tone. 'And Petra, I'm so sorry that my *wife'* – he turns to Petra, and Reynold sees the look of anguish in Amy's eyes, and his heart twists – 'that my *wife* has treated you like this,' Eldon says. 'But that's a discussion for another day.'

Petra sniffs, and very deliberately angles her body away from the spot where Amy is still standing, nodding to acknowledge Eldon's unnecessary apology.

'But what we *will* need to discuss now is who we think might know about either of these two things,' Eldon continues. 'First though, what else? Because we still need to hear from you, the Townsends and the Tustains. Why are you still here?'

'No idea,' says Monique angrily, and she stands up slowly, then makes her way back to sit down next to her husband again, stumbling slightly as she does so. 'Anyone care to enlighten me? Ben? Because, I'll say it again, this is nothing to do with me. I've got my problems, but there's no deep, dark confession coming from me, I promise you. So, Ben?'

Her husband opens his mouth and then, just as Clare did a few moments earlier, closes it again, and Nick Tustain gives an exasperated tut.

'I'm with you Monique,' he says. 'I can only assume my wife has something to contribute, but I've no idea what. Clare, why *are* we still here?'

Clare, who's now staring at the carpet, says nothing for a few moments, and Nick nudges her with his elbow.

'Clare? You're making me sweat here. What the hell's going on?' he says in a low voice, although the room is so quiet his words are clearly audible.

'I'm so sorry, Nick,' she whispers, and then she straightens up in her seat, and Reynold sees the glint of tears in her eyes.

'Sorry about what? What is this?' Nick replies, louder now, a hint of frustration and fear in his voice. But Clare isn't looking at him. Instead, her eyes are fixed on Ben, and he's returning her gaze, and suddenly Reynold thinks he knows exactly what this is all about.

Those two? Are they having an affair too? he thinks, and then instantly berates himself for the thought that follows: *Well, at least it's not just us, then.*

'Clare. I'll do this,' says Ben suddenly.

'No, I can—' says Clare, but he's shaking his head and standing up, making his way briskly towards the fireplace and turning to face them all, as if he's a university professor about to start a lecture.

'OK. I never dreamt this is how this would all come out, and I can't quite believe what I'm about to do but… well, these are extraordinary circumstances,' Ben says.

'What the actual…?' mutters Nick, and Clare gives him a stricken glance and then she stands up too, marching purposefully across the room and slipping her hand into Ben's.

Reynold hears Petra gasp. Nick's mouth has dropped open and, for the first time that evening, Monique suddenly looks a little more alert, her eyes focussed on her husband, her jaw clenched.

'Ben?' she says.

So I was right, Reynold thinks, and he realises that two more hearts in this room are about to be broken. For some reason that suddenly makes him feel even worse about what he and Amy have been doing, and not better at all.

'So, what we need to tell you is, well…'

Ben hesitates, then lifts up his right hand, the one Clare is still holding, their fingers tightly entwined.

'I suppose this is a bit of a giveaway. Monique… oh, God, this is not how I wanted you to find out.'

He gives his wife an anguished glance, and her mouth drops open.

'What? Seriously? With *her*? Oh, Ben…'

Monique reaches for the glass of whisky on the table in front of her – Reynold's pretty sure it's the glass Eldon was sipping from earlier – and downs the golden-hued liquid in one. She shudders, wipes her mouth with the back of her hand, and then shrugs.

'To be honest, I'm not even that surprised you've strayed,' she says. 'I mean, you and I haven't exactly been love's young dream for years, have we? But with *her*? I thought you had more taste…'

'WELL, *I'M* FUCKING SURPRISED!'

Monique is interrupted by a roar from Nick, and everyone in the room – all looking astounded by the latest turn of events – turns to gape at him.

'YOU'VE BEEN BANGING THAT LOSER?' he yells, and Clare shrinks back against the fireplace, looking terrified. Ben slips his hand from hers and puts his arm around her.

'Nick, I'm so sorry… Can we just—?' he stutters, and then stops talking as Eldon takes three strides across the room and takes Nick firmly by the shoulders.

'Mate, this isn't the time,' he says, quietly. 'We're all hearing unspeakable things in this room tonight, and life is never going to be the same again, for any of us. But you know why we're doing this, right? We need to get the kids back. So, please. Save it, OK? Sit down.'

For a moment, Nick looks as if he's about to swing a punch at Eldon, his fists curling into tight balls, his breath coming in angry gasps. Then, suddenly, he deflates like a popped balloon.

'Fine. Fine,' he mumbles. 'Fuck. What a night.'

'Not one any of us will forget,' says Eldon, giving Amy a sidelong glance. He releases Nick, who collapses back onto the sofa as if his legs have given way.

'Ben, Clare, carry on, please.' Eldon nods at the couple by the fireplace, and Ben nods back.

'Thanks,' he says. 'So, yes, fairly obviously, Clare and I have been... well, seeing each other. But...' – he looks from Monique to Nick and back again, and his cheeks, already flushed, deepen in colour to a dark red – 'I... I don't know how to say this. It's so difficult...'

'It's not just a recent thing,' Clare says quickly. 'It's not just a fling. It started a long time ago, and it's been on and off ever since, and... Look, we obviously never intended you to find out like this, Nick and Monique, but we want... we want a future together. We've been planning it for a long time, and we were just about to tell you, in the next couple of weeks, and then... well, all this happened. The timing, it's just horrendous, and we are so, *so* sorry...' She hesitates, and takes a deep, shuddering breath. 'And there's something even worse. Nick, I can hardly bear to tell you this, especially in front of everyone but...'

Her eyes have filled with tears while she's been talking, and now her voice cracks and she starts to sob. Ben pulls her closer.

'I'll finish,' he whispers, and takes a gulp of air.

'The thing is,' he says. 'The thing is, that… well, Clare's son Stanley, Clare and Nick's son. He's… he's actually mine. I'm his biological father.'

There are gasps from around the room, and a little yelp from Monique. Nick leans forward in his seat, the colour draining from his face.

'Wh–what?' he says.

'It's true,' says Clare, and her voice is thick with tears now. 'Stanley *is* Ben's child. And obviously, Willow is too.'

'So that means…' says Eldon. 'That means…'

'Yes,' says Clare. 'It means Reynold and Petra aren't the only ones with two kids who've been taken hostage. Ben does too.'

'Holy shit,' says Reynold.

Chapter Thirty-Three

CLARE

Day 6: Wednesday, 12.05 a.m.

'So. What now?' asks Eldon.

'I suppose we need to talk about *who*,' says Clare.

The past forty minutes or so have been a bit of a blur, but now things have calmed down a little, and she takes a long swig from the wineglass she's clutching in her still-clammy hands. The trembling in her limbs that began when she and Ben were standing in front of everyone, admitting their awful secret, has finally stopped, and she thinks that's probably partially down to the fact that Nick and Monique are no longer in the room, giving her a short reprieve from the storm she knows will be blowing up again within hours.

When they dropped the bombshell about Stanley's parentage, Nick jumped to his feet and launched himself at Ben, and Monique, a little less steadily, pushed herself up from her seat and ran at Clare, hands with long, beautifully manicured nails outstretched as if ready to claw her face off.

There were shrieks from Petra and Amy, and Reynold and Eldon yelled 'STOP!' simultaneously and joined the fray, pulling Nick and Monique away before any serious damage could be inflicted and dragging them out into the hall. There followed a few minutes of shouting, pleading and then some crying, but shortly afterwards Eldon returned to the lounge to say he'd called a taxi and that Nick and Monique were going home.

'They're both very upset, as you can imagine,' he said. 'This hasn't been an easy night for *any* of us.'

He gave Amy another cold glance.

'But they've accepted this isn't the time or the place. They've agreed to let us carry on with our discussions, and we can *all* deal with our marital issues once this is over. Everyone happy with that?'

There were murmurs of assent from around the room, and Reynold, who'd just walked in behind Eldon, nodded too and said softly, 'Mate, you have no idea how sorry I am, but—' only to be interrupted by a withering, 'Do *not* call me "mate",' from Eldon.

For a while, there was little conversation, as those remaining took bathroom breaks and refilled their glasses. Clare, suddenly feeling utterly exhausted, found her mind drifting as she sat curled up, feet under her, on one end of a sofa, her head on Ben's shoulder, his fingers gently caressing her hair.

It had all started on a balmy September evening some nine years ago, when Nick had been away at an IT conference and she'd popped into the village shop to buy a bottle of wine for a night alone in front of the TV. She'd seen Ben around Littleford from time to time, and had always thought him attractive from afar, with his tall, lean frame, sharp haircut and equally sharp suits. That evening in the shop though, when she'd *actually* bumped into him, stepping backwards from the wine shelf without checking to see if anyone was behind her, she'd looked up into amused hazel eyes and her stomach had done a little backflip.

'My favourite. Good choice,' he'd said with a cheeky grin, tapping the bottle in her hand.

They'd started chatting at the check-out and carried on out in the street, where Clare quickly discovered she wasn't the only one who was home alone that evening. Ben's wife, Monique, who was a retail manager back then, was away in Manchester overseeing the opening of a new store, and so it had seemed only polite to Clare to ask him if he wanted to pop in for a quick glass of wine on his way home, seeing as she'd bought his favourite. The quick glass had turned into three, at which point Ben had realised that the single-portion frozen lasagne he'd bought for dinner was now defrosting rapidly in the carrier bag he'd dumped in Clare's hallway and suggested that maybe they should order fish and chips and eat together instead. Two hours later they were both half-naked on the living room sofa, and that was that.

They'd been honest from the start about the fact that they both just needed a little amusement, a little excitement. Both were often lonely, their partners travelling frequently for work and often too tired to have much fun when they *were* at home. But soon real feelings began to develop. On paper, or to a casual onlooker, they were such a mismatched pair, Clare often thought. The handsome, clever architect with a first-class degree from Oxford and the dog kennel worker who'd failed most of her GCSEs. But when they were together, it just *worked*. With Clare, Ben could release his inner kid; he told her, often, that nobody had ever made him laugh like she did. And with Ben, Clare's ambitions for her future somehow began to change. Nick was completely *un*-ambitious; his IT job, while steady and secure, was at a low level and not massively well paid, and she knew he'd be happy to stay forever in their tired little terraced house, in the village where he was born and had lived for his entire life. He didn't even like going abroad for holidays, for God's sake. But with Ben, Clare suddenly saw a different future, one with a beautiful home and foreign travel and no more scrimping and saving and making do. It wasn't just about the money; Clare was a grafter, always had been. But life would be so much better with a partner she was genuinely in love with, but also one who had plans and dreams and who fully intended to turn them into reality. It made her dream big dreams too, like maybe opening her own animal sanctuary one day. She and Nick had been childhood sweethearts, meeting at fourteen and dating on and off for years until he finally proposed over a chicken balti at their favourite Indian restaurant in Cirencester. But while she still cared for him, there'd been many days when she'd wondered if they'd become more like housemates than life partners, even *before* she and Ben got together. Even so, for a long time the thought of leaving her husband, walking away from their long shared history, had seemed impossible. And Ben, apparently, had felt the same about Monique.

'She acts all tough and invincible, but she needs me, Clare,' he'd told her, on more than one occasion. 'I'm crazy about you, but I can't, I just can't, not yet...'

And then, a year or so into their clandestine relationship, Clare had found out she was pregnant. Weeks later Ben, white-faced, told her that Monique was pregnant too. And so, the waiting game had begun. There was a fifty-fifty chance that Ben was about to become father to two babies with two different mothers at pretty much the same time, and while Clare still hoped her baby would be Nick's – she still dutifully obliged him with his weekly Saturday night post-pub request for a quickie – there was a tiny part of her that wondered what would happen if it turned out to be Ben's. When Stanley was born, to her huge relief he looked just like *her*, but when she swabbed his tiny mouth and slipped the sample into an envelope alongside one from Ben to send off to the DNA Paternity Test laboratory, something inside her just *knew*. She was right. Days later, the email pinged into her inbox and everything changed. Except... it didn't, not really.

When Ben sneaked round to see his new son a few days later after Nick had gone back to work, tears in his eyes as he cradled the little boy in his arms and kissed his soft forehead, they'd talked and talked. They knew that, one day, they wanted to be together, but the arrival of the two new babies had made things overwhelmingly complicated, and so they'd agreed to wait. Wait for what, exactly, neither of them was quite sure; all they knew was that the time was not quite right, and that they'd both know when it was.

And so Clare and poor, clueless Nick had brought up Stanley, while Monique remained equally oblivious to the fact that her beautiful daughter, Willow, had a half-brother living just a mile away and, eventually, often sitting next to her in the classroom at Littleford Primary School. The two children became firm friends, which meant that Ben was able to see his son regularly, with no worry about anyone growing suspicious, but even so the fear that someone would find them out had been intense, at first. Clare had had nightmares and panic attacks and, unable to explain them to Nick, had had to feign mild post-natal depression. For a long time she and Ben had worried themselves stupid about Stanley having an accident, or needing a transplant of some sort, some kind of medical emergency that would require blood typing or tissue matching, and reveal that Nick was not his father. But as the years ticked by, the fears had faded and they'd begun to relax. The affair had carried on, and although it had been trickier since the children came along it was still possible; snatched moments here and there, the occasional night in a hotel when Ben had to travel for work and Clare told Nick she needed a break and was off to spend the evening with an old school friend. It was just in the past six months or so that things had really begun to progress, and they'd finally talked about being together properly. Monique's behaviour, always erratic, had become increasingly irrational, her drinking more and more problematic, and although Ben had tried to help her, he'd begun to struggle.

'At this point I'm just staying with her out of duty,' he told Clare. 'And life's so short. I just don't think I can do it anymore. It's time for us, isn't it?'

Clare too had been struggling. Nick, in her eyes, was becoming duller and grumpier by the year, the moodiness she'd found strangely sexy in him as a teenager becoming tedious, the loyalty she felt for the man she'd met as a child beginning to fade, and turning instead to resentment. And so she and Ben had at last begun to make firm plans. Plans to leave, to take Stanley and Willow with them if the courts allowed it, to start a new life away from Littleford. They'd been so close to pulling it all together, to setting a date to break the news to Nick and Monique, to that new, shiny future full of possibilities. And then, on Friday, the children got on a bus with their classmates and didn't come home, and everything imploded.

Now, in response to Clare's 'I suppose we need to talk about *who*', Eldon nods.

'Yes. *Who*,' he says. 'We need to talk about who the *hell* could know this stuff we've all just found out tonight. I mean, there *is* a chance they don't know anything at all, of course. They could just be bluffing. We're a big group of people, and they might just be hoping that at least one of us has something to hide, and be willing to pay good money to keep it hidden. But we can't risk it, can we?'

'I don't think we can,' says Ben.

'No,' says Eldon. 'OK, so let's think. For a start, who could know about the hit-and-run, all these years later? Amy and I both know we haven't told anyone about that, ever, so could someone really have found out about it? Did someone see us that night after all, and not say anything until now?'

He wags his head towards Amy, who's sitting alone in the big armchair to his right, and her face twitches but she says nothing.

She looks like the loneliest, saddest woman in the world, Clare thinks, and despite her own misery, she feels a wave of sympathy. Poor Amy. Her reputation, her marriage… everything, gone, in one evening.

A bit like mine, I suppose, she thinks ruefully, then drags her attention back to Eldon, who's still speaking. There are just the six of them in the room now: herself and Ben, plus Eldon and Amy and Reynold and Petra, all of them hurting and miserable, and the spacious room feels cold and cavernous, despite the colourful rugs scattered across the wooden floor and the flamboyant artworks that adorn the walls.

'Have any of you ever heard any rumours, anything like that?' Eldon asks, and there are shrugs and head shakes.

'Never,' says Ben. 'And it does seem weird that if someone saw you back then, they'd wait this long to do anything about it. Are you *sure* neither of you ever told anyone? Even in a drunken moment?'

'Well, I certainly didn't,' Eldon says firmly.

Ben turns to look at Amy.

'Absolutely, definitely not,' she says quietly.

'So it's probably not that, then, is it?' Ben says. 'How could it be?'

There's a brief silence, then Eldon says, 'OK, maybe not. So, the two affairs, then? Any thoughts on who might know about those? You'll forgive me if I don't lead the conversation on this bit. Ben, do you want to take over?'

Ben nods and lifts his arm from where it's been resting across Clare's shoulders, and she instantly misses the comforting warmth of it.

'Look, Clare and I aren't proud of what we've done, and how long it's gone on for,' he says. 'Especially, you know, Stanley… but I think we're pretty sure nobody ever knew we were seeing each other. I did worry about Monique – she's been a bit unstable recently, to say the least – but after seeing her reaction tonight, I'm almost certain she didn't know about it.'

He turns to Clare, and she nods vehemently.

'Definitely. And I'm equally certain Nick didn't know a thing until tonight either,' she says.

'Well, I've certainly never suspected you two, or heard anything to suggest you might be carrying on together,' says Petra, 'and I'm pretty much across all the gossip in this village. Shame I wasn't across the fact that my own husband has been sleeping around too, though, isn't it?'

'Petra, babe—' Reynold begins, then snaps his mouth shut again as his wife gives him a contemptuous look.

'It's us. I'm sure it is,' Amy says weakly. She looks completely drained, Clare thinks, her long black hair pulled back from her face into a tight little knot at the base of her neck and circles so dark they look like bruises under her eyes.

'I told you earlier I thought someone saw me and Reynold together recently. Well, it was actually here. Here at our house, I mean. At our party, last week. God, Eldon, I'm so sorry. Reynold and I met up outside, in the summer house…'

She gestures vaguely towards the window.

'Christ,' mutters Eldon, and Clare sees Reynold wince.

'I mean, I was pretty pissed – we all were – but I'm sure there was somebody…' Amy says. 'Outside the window, watching us. I just don't know who.'

'So, somebody who was at the party,' Ben says. 'Someone you know then. Someone we *all* know. Wow.'

'It could have been one of the caterers, or the fire-eaters or whatever,' Clare says. 'You did have quite a few people here that night, Amy.'

'Yes, but they'd all left by then,' replies Amy. 'Ages before that, in fact. The only outsider, as it were, was the DJ and he was in here, still playing. I don't know how many guests were still here, or who, that's the problem. I was drunk, and… well, you know, distracted…'

'Fuck's sake, Amy. We don't need the details,' says Eldon sharply, and she flinches.

'But even if someone at the party did see you, that doesn't really make sense,' Ben says quickly. 'It was less than a week before the kids were taken. That's not enough time, surely. If they wanted to blackmail you, I mean. I'd think it would take way longer than that to organise a kidnap, especially with so many people involved. It doesn't feel right to me.'

'Me neither,' says Reynold. 'This was all too professional. It doesn't look like something that was just thrown together in a few days. My fear is that someone's known about it for longer. I don't know how, though. Or who. It's hopeless.'

There's a long silence, then Petra says, 'So we basically have absolutely no idea whose secret they're talking about, or who might be behind this. Great. And if any of these things are made public… I mean, the whole *planet* is watching this story. *Everyone* is going to find out. Everyone is going to be judging… Can you imagine, being splashed across newspapers all over the world? Everyone knowing that what *you've* done is what caused all this?'

There's a note of hysteria in her voice, and she leans forward in her seat, eyes wide and frightened.

'The affairs are bad enough. But Eldon, you and Amy could

go to *prison*, if this *is* about your hit-and-run. And even though I now think that you, Amy, are a two-faced *bitch*...' – she pauses, giving Amy a filthy look, then takes a deep breath – 'we *can't* let any of this come out. We don't have a choice, do we? Because it's not just about keeping these secrets. I know they say the kids are all fine at the moment, but what if they're lying? They already killed Erica Lindsay. We have to get the children away from whoever's got them. We *have* to...'

She covers her face with her hands and lets out a strangled sob. Reynold half rises from his seat, then clearly thinks better of it and sits down again.

'Petra, babe...' he whispers, but she ignores him, still sobbing into her fingers.

Clare has an almost overwhelming urge to run from the room, to race all the way home and hide under her duvet and sleep for a long, long time, and then she remembers that Nick is probably going to be there and wonders where she's going to sleep tonight. She can't imagine her husband will be waiting for her with open arms.

'I think Petra's right,' she says. 'I don't think we have a choice either, whatever the police say about the rights and wrongs of paying ransoms, and trying an appeal to the kidnappers first. If we don't pay, we risk not only one or more of these secrets being exposed, but also, way more importantly, our children being hurt. We *can't* risk it, can we?'

'I agree,' Reynold says. 'But how do we raise the money? £5 million is a huge amount, and not everyone will be able to contribute much...'

Clare sees him glance at her, and she feels momentarily offended, then thinks: *To be fair, he's right. I've got about five hundred quid in my bank account. That's not going to get the children back, is it?*

'I can put in a bit,' says Ben. 'We've spent a lot of money doing up the house over the past few years but I've got forty, maybe fifty thousand at a push that I can get at fairly quickly. It was supposed to be for Willow and Stanley, for university, but...' He shrugs. 'It's not much. But in the time we have... Shit, how are we going to do this?' he asks, and Clare can hear the sudden note of desperation in his voice.

'Looks like it's down to you and me, Eldon,' Reynold says quietly. 'But I can't see how even between us we can come up with anything close to £5 million in the next couple of days. They must know nobody keeps money like that just sitting in a bank. They're probably just chancing their arm. They might accept less, if it's a decent amount. But we still need more *time*. We need to liquidate some assets, free up some cash... I suspect when they send payment instructions, it'll be an electronic transfer they want. We can add a message, can't we? I can't imagine it'll be a "Bring a bag of used tenners and put it behind this wall and come alone" scenario, not for such a large amount of money. We can tell them we'll send more, if they just give us a few more days?'

His tone is calm and measured, business-like even. Eldon doesn't look at Reynold, but he nods.

'We could try,' he says shortly.

'So... we do it then? Get as much money together as we can, and when they tell us how to pay, we pay? And we don't tell the police? We keep them out of *all* of this? What we've heard in this room tonight stays in this room, as we agreed?' asks Reynold.

'Fine by me,' says Ben, and Clare plants a kiss on his cheek.

'Yes,' she says simply.

'I just want the children home. I don't give a damn about anything else, so it's a yes from me too,' says Petra.

'And me,' says Amy.

'OK. Well, let's do it then. Whatever's gone on – and shit, it's a *lot* – we're just going to have to trust each other. I think everyone should go home now; try and get some sleep,' says Eldon. 'We can talk again tomorrow. I'll make a separate group on WhatsApp, just for us. I'll call it the Final Eight, OK? Jesus, it's after one o'clock. What a day.'

As they all stand up, gathering their things and saying muted goodbyes, Clare sees Reynold touching Amy briefly on the shoulder and then turning to Petra, who gives him a scornful look and hisses, 'Oh, come on then. Let's go home. But do *not* touch me.'

He holds his hands up in a placatory manner, and as they leave the room, Clare stares after them. She's always thought Reynold Lyon was OK, but he seems almost too calm, considering what's going on. *Is that just how he behaves in a crisis, or is it a bit weird?*

She turns to pick up her bag, thinking again about his visit to the police station for questioning. Then, as Ben takes her elbow and nods towards the door, asking her if she thinks she'll be OK to go home tonight, she finds herself wondering about Monique again too, and her visit to the wildlife park on Friday, as Eldon's words float into her weary mind.

We're just going to have to trust each other, OK?

Is she just so tired, scared and emotional now that she's

overthinking things? *Can* they trust each other, really? They have to, don't they...?

'Clare?'

Ben's voice brings her back, his hand warm on her arm.

'Sorry. Yes, it'll be fine. Don't worry,' she says. 'Nick will be asleep. I'll stay in the spare room tonight.'

They close the front door behind them, and head for Ben's car.

Chapter Thirty-Four

LITTLEFORD PRIMARY SCHOOL

Day 6: Wednesday, 10.57 a.m.

'Tea? Coffee? Mrs Chamberlain will be with you in a moment – she's on her way. Oh, and I think we have some chocolate biscuits too if you'd like some. Energy, you know. You must be exhausted with all... *this*.'

Richard Cunningham waves his hands vaguely and looks at Detective Superintendent Sadie Stewart and Detective Chief Inspector Daniel Sharma enquiringly.

'Tea, please. Black,' she replies.

'Coffee for me. And the biscuits would be great,' Daniel says, and Sadie gives him a sidelong glance as Richard gives them a thumbs-up sign and bustles out of the room.

'What? Don't tell me you won't have one too, when they're stuck under your nose!'

She shrugs.

'Yeah, you're probably right. But just for energy, as the man said. He's right. I'm bloody knackered.'

'You and me both.'

They're sitting side by side in comfortable upholstered armchairs in the headteacher's office at Littleford Primary, waiting for Olivia Chamberlain to join them. They haven't spoken to her personally for a couple of days, and having little else to do this morning except wait for more news, and for a decision from higher-ups about making a television appeal to the hostage takers, Sadie thought they might as well pop in. Olivia had been asked for her thoughts after the first message from the kidnappers arrived on Monday, and again after the second contact yesterday, but there was no harm in chatting to her again today.

'Heads know everyone and everything. Something might have occurred to her in the interim,' Sadie said to Daniel, as they headed towards Littleford, her behind the wheel as usual. It was a beautiful spring morning, and as they'd driven past a stretch of woodland a carpet of blue had caught her eye, the nodding heads of thousands of tiny flowers.

'Bluebells!' she'd said so loudly that Daniel had jumped and spilled his travel mug of coffee all down his pristine red tie. He's still dabbing ineffectually at the stain now.

'I'll have to get it dry cleaned,' he mutters.

'Sorry,' she says, for the fifth time.

'No biggie,' he replies.

Sadie gives him a little smile, but inside she's suddenly feeling utterly miserable.

Will this visit be a waste of time too, like pretty much everything else has been over the past few days?

The time spent questioning Monique Townsend about her strange behaviour on Friday. The time spent questioning

Reynold Lyon about his so-called game show. The time the teams on the ground are spending – relentlessly, day and night – trying to follow up on every single lead from the public, covertly searching every possible location that could be housing thirteen missing people. Everything they've been doing, every desperate moment of work that's being put into this, and so far, nothing, just *nothing*...

'Detective Superintendent Stewart! And Detective Chief Inspector Sharma. Is there news? Please, *please* tell me there's news. Good news?'

Oliva Chamberlain sweeps into the room in a cloud of floral perfume, wearing a flowing paisley-patterned maxi-dress, her hair loose around her face. She lowers herself into the high-backed leather chair behind her desk and looks at Sadie with a hopeful expression.

'No news, I'm afraid,' says Sadie. 'We were rather hoping you might have thought of something that could help us out. We're still no wiser about whose secret the kidnappers might be threatening to reveal. I know you're probably not party to any of the families' deep dark secrets, but is there anything, anything at all, that's struck you as odd or unusual about *anyone* recently?'

'No, I'm so sorry,' says Olivia, looking rather crestfallen. 'I've been racking my brains but I honestly can't think of anything that might be relevant. Although there is one *tiny* thing I was going to mention... but it's not about one of the families, so it may be nothing, of course. I've just been *so* distracted. We considered closing the school while this is all going on, but we thought it better for everyone to have some sort of routine, you know? It's been extremely difficult trying to keep a sense of normality, though. We're several members of staff down, obviously, and everyone's terribly upset about Mrs Lindsay, as you can imagine. We've tried to explain it to the children but they all have so many questions, and the parents are telling us many of the little ones have been having nightmares. Well, lots of us have, actually, not just the children. I'm barely sleeping, and— Oh, Richard, wonderful, thank you!'

Richard Cunningham has reappeared, bearing a large tray laden with white china mugs, coffee and tea pots, a milk jug, a small bowl of sugar lumps complete with silver tongs and a plate piled high not just with chocolate biscuits but with shortbread rounds and fig rolls too. Sadie, who can't even remember if she ate breakfast this morning but doesn't think so, suddenly feels ravenous.

'This is very kind, thank you,' she says, and Richard beams.

'Anything else you need, just shout,' he says, and heads off again, closing the door gently behind him.

'Do help yourself,' says Olivia, and Sadie is just reaching for a mug when her mobile beeps. She picks it up from the arm of her chair, reads the words on the screen and gasps.

'It's another message,' she says, thrusting it at Daniel, and then remembers where she is and turns to Olivia.

'It's a new contact from the kidnappers,' she says.

Olivia's eyes widen.

'Am I allowed to know what it says?' she asks.

'I'm sorry. I think we're going to have to go,' Sadie replies, ignoring the question, and she takes her phone back from Daniel, who's already standing up – and, she notes, quickly helping himself to a handful of biscuits from the plate – and reads the message again, forwarded from someone back at base who's clearly just been alerted to its arrival by one of the families.

> The £5 million must be deposited at 4pm on Friday.
> Account details will be sent at 3.55pm precisely. The
> hostages will be released at 4pm on Saturday, provided
> the money has cleared. We will send a message telling
> you where to find them. All safe and well. No further
> contact or negotiation.

Despite the fact that the room is warm, sunlight streaming through the windows, Sadie suddenly feels cold.

All safe and well.

God, I hope that's true. Do we do this TV appeal now? Is there any point, if they're still saying no further contact or negotiation? What do we do? What do we do?

She needs to get out of here, needs to process this as quickly as possible, but as she gets to her feet her head swims.

'Are you all right, Detective Superintendent? You look pale. Don't you even have time for a mouthful of coffee?' Olivia says, and Sadie hesitates just long enough for Daniel to answer for her.

'We do need to go, but actually yes, we can take two minutes. You *do* look pale – you need some sugar inside you, boss. Come on, sit down.'

'OK. You're probably right. Thanks,' Sadie says, and sinks gratefully back onto her chair, thoughts and questions leapfrogging each other in her mind.

Can we stop the parents paying the money? How, if we're still no closer to tracking these people down? Clever. Very clever, not giving the bank account details until five minutes before their deadline. No chance for us to trace it. And what if the parents do pay? Will they really release the hostages? And then run for it? Those bastards will be gone, won't they? They'll get away with it. We might never find them, never… And if they don't get their money, what then? They've killed once already… We know they're capable. Oh, shit…

'Here. Drink up. And have a biscuit.'

Daniel interrupts her stream of consciousness by thrusting a steaming mug into her hands.

'Good advice,' Olivia says solicitously, then leans forward on her desk and adds, 'I understand you can't share this new development with me. But as I said there's one tiny little thing I thought I should mention. The officer who contacted me yesterday read the latest message to me, and even though I don't know who it might be referring to in terms of the "secret", there was *something* about the wording. It niggled me at the time but I dismissed it because that wasn't really what I was being asked about. But… is there any way you could read it to me again? It might be nothing, as I say, but…'

Daniel looks questioningly at Sadie, who's just popped a piece of shortbread into her mouth, trying to force herself to calm down, to stay in the moment, to stop *panicking*. It's delicious, the sugary coating and crumbly, buttery biscuit strangely comforting, and she feels her heartbeat slowing. She nods.

'Fine,' she mumbles, her mouth still full, and he pulls his own phone out of his pocket.

'Here it is,' he says. '*£5 million. By Friday. Deposit instructions to follow. Pay = the hostages will be released unharmed and your secret stays safe forever. Don't pay = justice will be meted out.*'

When he reaches the final few words, Olivia nods slowly.

'Hang on,' she says.

She rises from her chair, marches across to a large filing cabinet in the corner of the room and begins rifling through it. Moments later, she pulls out a slim green file and returns to her desk, opening it and flipping through the pages within. Then she pauses, running her finger down one A4 sheet.

'There!' she says triumphantly. 'I knew it! I don't really understand though…'

'Understand what?' says Daniel. 'What is it?'

Olivia's face has clouded over, her smooth brow wrinkling.

'Well, it was that phrase, "justice will be meted out". It's rather unusual, you know? I mean, the word *meted*? Not many people use it. You'd be more likely to say "justice will be served", or "justice will prevail", maybe. And when I heard it, it rang a bell. I knew I'd seen it somewhere before, quite recently. Exactly the same phrase. And I was right. It's here, in a note I was sent when we had a minor theft at the school a few months back. We had a couple of lovely dwarf cherry trees in pots outside the front door and someone ran off with them. That was when we decided to put security cameras in, actually. We'd never felt the need before; crime rates are so low around here that it seemed like an unnecessary expense.'

Sadie swallows her mouthful of biscuit and wipes her mouth with the back of her hand.

'OK. And?'

'Well, the day the cameras were being fitted, I happened to be away – they did it on a Saturday morning, so I asked someone else to oversee the job. And afterwards, they left the invoice on my desk with a note, a sort of jokey one,' continues Olivia.

She looks down at the piece of paper in front of her.

'It says, "Cameras fitted, nice tidy job so all good. If those little buggers come back for round two, we'll be able to clearly ID them! Maybe justice can be meted out, eh?" I mean, it might be nothing, as I keep saying. Probably just a coincidence. But it's just a bit *unusual*...'

'It *is* unusual. I don't think I've *ever* used that word, or even heard it very often,' says Sadie. She looks at Daniel and sees the eagerness in his eyes as he nods his agreement, and even though she's still sitting down, she feels a little light-headed again. Coincidence? She doesn't believe in coincidences.

Olivia is staring at the page on her desk.

'No, me neither. So, I suppose, even if it doesn't really make sense to me...' She hesitates. 'I think I know. I think I know who wrote that message.'

Chapter Thirty-Five

LITTLEFORD

Day 6: Wednesday, 11.10 a.m.

Clare Tustain has never felt more wretched in her whole life. When Ben dropped her home just before one-thirty this morning, hugging her tightly and wishing her luck before she reluctantly left the safety of his car, she'd crept into the house desperately hoping that Nick would be asleep and that she could put off facing him until the morning. Instead, she found him in the living room, crying. She stood in the doorway watching him, feeling physically sick as she thought about how much she'd once loved him, and about how much she'd hurt him, and she'd found herself crying too, hot tears slipping silently down her cheeks.

He'd looked up then and seen her, and for a few moments they just stared at each other, both lost in their own worlds of pain. Then he'd cleared his throat and said, in a voice thick with emotion, 'We're over, obviously. But when we get Stanley back – *when* – I still want to see him. Full access. I may not be his biological father, but I'm still his *dad*.'

'Of course. Of *course*,' she'd spluttered, taking a few steps towards him. 'I would never, *ever* stop you seeing him. I don't even know how I'm going to tell him. I haven't thought that far—'

'Well, that's your problem. I'm going to bed,' he'd said coldly, and he'd stood up and marched past her, slamming the door as he left the room. Moments later she'd heard his footsteps on the stairs and then the sound of their bedroom door banging shut. She'd sunk onto the sofa then, feeling sadder than she'd imagined possible and, suddenly drained of the energy actually getting herself to bed would require, had sat there until her eyes closed and she'd fallen into a fitful sleep. She'd woken, shivering, just before six, her neck stiff and her limbs aching. A hot shower and two strong coffees have done little to make her feel better, but she knows she deserves to feel like this. She deserves everything she's got, and everything she'll no doubt continue to get over the coming days.

Maybe Stanley being taken away is part of my punishment, she thought, as she curled up in an armchair in the living room, trying to stay out of Nick's way as he crashed around in the kitchen, making himself some breakfast when he finally came downstairs just after nine.

Maybe this is the universe's way of making me pay for what I've done…

But does anyone else *really* know about the secret, other than, now, those in Eldon's living room last night? She's still thinking about that, going over and over it in her head. She and Ben had been so careful over the years, every meeting meticulously planned to avoid anyone they knew. But did they get a little less careful over time? Holding hands across the table in hotel restaurants, quick kisses in car parks as they parted... Did they *always* check that nobody they might know could have been watching? Probably not.

We got complacent, she thinks. *We thought nobody else would ever find out, until we were ready to tell them. But maybe they did...*

Or maybe they didn't. Since last night, since the astounding revelations about Eldon and Amy's hit-and-run and Reynold and Amy's affair, she's not so sure anymore that she and Ben are in the hostage takers' sights. They're nobodies, after all. Who would care if two nobodies had a long-term affair and a secret child together? It's a bit different to one of the country's most famous TV presenters having an affair with an equally famous TV chef's wife. And way, *way* less shocking than the same TV chef and his wife killing a man on a quiet country road. Those *are* secrets worth kidnapping and blackmailing over. Is hers, really? She's less scared of that now, and anyway, Nick and Monique know all about it after last night, so what does it matter if everyone does, as long as the children are OK?

£5 million though. £5 million...

And then the latest message from the hostage takers pings onto her phone.

'They want the money by four o'clock on Friday!' she says to Nick, her voice high-pitched with anxiety. They're the first words she's spoken to him today – he hasn't come near her – but he's the only one here and she can't deal with this by herself. She just can't.

'And if we do it, if we pay, we get the children back on

Saturday. Oh my *God*. Do you think we can trust them? And will we be able to get the cash together by then? Because we're going to do it, we decided last night. They've all said they don't care what the police say anymore. I know *we* have nothing to contribute, but Reynold and Eldon do... and Ben. Ben's putting some in too – not much but a bit. But it's so much money...'

She stops talking, aware that she's gabbling. Nick's been listening to her with a fixed, hard expression on his face, but now she sees a spark of hope in his eyes.

'Do you think it's the right thing to do?' she asks. 'I know you said we should take police advice, but—'

'I don't care anymore,' he says quietly. 'I don't care how we do it. I just want him home. And the police still have no idea where they are, or who's got them, do they? So, whatever.'

He looks sadly at her and leaves the room, but this time he closes the door gently behind him, and Clare wraps her arms around her knees and rocks slowly back and forth, the tears beginning to fall again, wishing that Ben was there to hold her.

***

Ben is making coffee and thinking about last night. He'd hoped that Monique might opt for the silent treatment when he'd got home, because he wasn't sure how much more drama he could handle after the past few days without his brain disintegrating. It wasn't to be; as he'd cautiously turned his key in the lock of the front door and pushed it open, a vase had whistled through the air and smashed into the wall beside him, and he'd yelped in shock.

'You *fucker*. You fucking *arsehole*.'

Monique, who was standing on the staircase, bending to pick up another vase in her right hand and holding a half-empty glass of red wine in her left, raised her arms and threw both items in his direction with surprising force and accuracy. He managed to move sharply to one side just in time, but the wine glass shattered on the wooden floor of the hall inches in front of him, spraying his jeans with deep-burgundy liquid.

'Mon, *please*. This isn't going to get us anywhere. I'm so sorry. Please, can we talk? Come on,' he'd begged, but she'd simply roared some more expletives at him and then turned and stumbled up the stairs, slamming the bedroom door and screaming at him to stay away from her when he timidly asked if he could come in so they could sort this out.

And how can I blame her? he'd thought, as he'd finally given up and trudged downstairs to spend the night wide awake in the lounge, sleep impossible to contemplate.

She's just found out that not only have I been unfaithful to her for years but that Willow has a brother. A brother she knows. I wouldn't let me in either.

When the message arrives, he reads it several times, his heart pounding, then races upstairs to see if Monique has seen it too, but when he taps on the bedroom door all he gets is a mumbled, 'Leave. Me. *Alone*,' so he does. A moment later, his phone buzzes again and this time it's a message from Eldon, on the new Final Eight group.

Assume you've all seen the latest message? We need to get this money together fast. Reynold, Ben – let's liaise again this afternoon. And remember, tell the police

nothing, OK? Let's let them think we're going along
with their advice not to pay up. For now anyway.

He replies with a thumbs-up emoji, then heads upstairs to
his home office and turns his laptop on. As he waits for it to
boot up, he realises Monique will have received Eldon's
message too, and that he needs to talk to her about the decision
to pay the ransom. He wonders how this is all going to pan out
financially, now that he's about to hand every penny of their
savings to a criminal and, presumably, has divorce proceedings
looming too. How will he make a future with Clare, with
nothing? And yet, he realises he doesn't even care. He doesn't
care whose secret the kidnappers are going to expose, and he
doesn't care how much it's going to take to stop them. What
does money matter? He just wants his child back. His *children*
back. Both of them. And if his relatively small contribution can
help, even if he ends up bankrupt, then so be it. Everything
else will just have to work itself out, when this is all over. Ben
swallows the lump in his throat, takes a deep breath, and logs
on to his online banking website.

———

Eldon Beckford is studying his accounts too, wondering how
much money he can free up in the next forty-eight hours.

£600,000, max, he thinks, and feels a tight knot of fear in his
stomach. *Will that be enough? How much will Reynold and Ben be
able to contribute? Maybe another million , if we're lucky?*

He wonders if that will be enough to persuade the
kidnappers to let the kids go; wonders if they'll understand the

impossibility of what they're asking; wonders if they'll be prepared to wait for the rest of the money; wonders what will happen if they refuse to wait. Will they *hurt* the children, or worse? At the thought of something terrible, something unthinkable, happening to Noah, his beloved son, Eldon springs from his chair and runs to the bathroom where he throws up, retching into the toilet until there's nothing but bitter-tasting bile trickling from his mouth. His stomach aches and his head pounds.

Last night, when everyone had finally gone home, he'd told Amy he didn't want to talk to her about any of it, and that he'd prefer it if she slept in another room. She'd nodded, her face a mask of anguish, and had muttered something about going up to check on River and seeing him in the morning. But half an hour later she'd crawled into bed beside him, sobbing, her arm snaking around him from behind, her face pressing into his shoulder, and to his own surprise he'd responded, twisting his body round to face her and pulling her into an embrace.

'I don't love Reynold. I promise I don't,' she'd whispered through her tears. 'It's just... sex. An escape or something. I love *you*. It's always been you. I'm so, *so* sorry and I'm so scared you won't forgive me and I'm so scared about what's going to happen now...'

'Shhh,' he'd said, fighting back tears himself. The thought of his wife shagging Reynold Lyon, shagging him for *years* on and off, was almost unbearable, but for some reason his anger was evaporating, the sense of betrayal and horror he'd felt when Amy had first confessed fading.

People get over affairs, don't they? he thought, as he stroked her hair, Amy's shoulders shaking with the ferocity of her

264

weeping. *We've got through worse. We can get through this. We can. We will. Just keep Lyon away from me, the duplicitous scumbag…*

'It's going to be OK,' he'd said softly. 'Let's just forget about it all for now, until Noah comes home. And then we'll talk. We'll decide what do about… about the other thing. *Both* things. We'll sort it out. It'll be all right, Amy.'

They'd slept wrapped in each other's arms, and this morning, although Amy was still red-eyed and more shamefaced than he'd ever seen her, they'd been able to make polite, if somewhat stilted conversation, trying to carry on as normal. Both of them were ignoring the large, adulterous TV-presenter-shaped elephant in the room, and the other, even bigger elephant – the fact that six other people now know they caused an innocent man's death.

When the new message arrived, Amy had been upstairs, about to show Brandon the handyman the broken catch on the baby's bedroom window. Eldon had yelled for her to come down, and when he showed her the words on his phone she screamed, almost dropping a surprised River who was draped over her shoulder.

'Oh my GOD! Oh my God, oh my God, oh my God!' she screeched, putting the little boy down on the living-room carpet. 'Eldon, we could get him back on Saturday! I don't care what the police say. I don't care about anything else. Please work out a way we can do this. *Please.*'

'We can do it,' he replied. 'We'll raise as much as we can, and hope it'll be enough. I'm on it.'

Amy had gone back upstairs to continue briefing Brandon about the window, and as he'd passed the room on his way to his office, Eldon had heard her excitedly telling the handyman there was now a chance the kids would be home by the weekend, and asking him to *please* not say anything to anyone about it. He'd started feeling nauseous then, wondering if what they were about to do would really work, or would turn out to be a massive mistake. How would Amy be able to carry on if Noah didn't come home? How would *he* survive it? He wasn't sure he would. The thought was utterly unbearable.

Now, still feeling sick, Eldon slowly picks himself up from the bathroom floor, splashes water on his face and walks slowly back to his desk. He takes a deep breath, and picks up his calculator.

———————

Reynold Lyon has already done his sums.

£1.3 million. And that's transferring every penny he can currently get his hands on, including the cash he's put away to pay his next tax bill. There's more money he can free up reasonably quickly, tied up in investment accounts, but most require at least fourteen days' notice to access, some thirty days. This will have to be enough, for now. But will it be? What if it's not? A chill runs through him, and he stands up, wanting to go and find Petra, to have her reassure him, and then he remembers and sinks back down onto his chair.

Petra hasn't spoken to him since they got home last night, when the last thing she said was, 'You're disgusting. You and Amy are *both* disgusting. And if what you've done is the cause of our children being taken away from us, I will never, *ever* forgive you. Never. I *hate* you. Just stay away from me. Go and sort your mess out, and leave me alone.'

And so he did, all night and until the message arrived this morning when he knocked quietly on the door of their bedroom and walked in to see Petra sitting cross-legged on the unmade bed, staring at her phone.

'I'm going to sort out the money,' he said softly. 'We're going to get them back. I promise.'

She'd looked at him blankly, nodded, then turned away, pulling the duvet over herself, not saying a word. He'd wanted so desperately to go to her, to try to ease her pain, but he knew that it was not the time. Marc Hackett, the bloody annoying family liaison officer – who seemed to spend far too much time in their house, in Reynold's view – had arrived shortly after that, checking in on them again. But at least that had meant that Petra had got up, showered and eaten some breakfast, putting on a brave face as usual, telling Marc that yes, they were following police advice, holding their nerve. Reynold had nodded along, but then he'd felt his phone vibrating in his pocket and excused himself. It was, as he'd suspected, a message on the Final Eight group, so he'd sneaked upstairs and done his calculations. He's messed up, big time – he knows that. But he's trying to fix it. He's *trying*. And Reynold Lyon rarely fails at anything he puts his mind to.

He doesn't want to think about what might happen if he fails now. If the children get hurt, or worse. And even if they get them back, and the kidnappers keep to their word and don't reveal whatever it is they know, if indeed they do know something… well, there are now *other* people who know, aren't there? They've all vowed not to tell, but can he trust them?

Monique, for instance, who seems to live her life in a booze-fuelled stupor? She could spill her guts at any second. Reynold can't stop thinking about it; about the impact the scandal of the affair with Amy Beckford would have not just on his marriage and his standing in this community, but on his career. It could all be over, just like that. And yet, TV careers survive infidelity, don't they? People might not understand why a man with a beautiful model wife like Petra might be tempted to stray – hell, he doesn't even understand that himself. And they might be horrified that the woman he's been straying with is the wife of a supposedly good friend of his. But it's not as if he's murdered anyone, is it? Or taken drugs, or raped someone? Nothing *that* bad. Nothing criminal. So, his career *might* survive. It might even make him *more* interesting, in some eyes, if it all comes out. His marriage is probably over now anyway. He can't see Petra forgiving him, not any time soon. And yet, he knows he's still going to pay the money, because he and Eldon – with a small contribution from Ben Townsend – are the only two who really can, and *somebody* has to. And if this works, and the children are released and come home safely, then maybe that will work in his favour, if the news does get out. Soften the blow. And God, he *needs* his children back. He can't bear this much longer.

If this doesn't work, I'll find another way, he thinks. *If it's the last thing I ever do as Petra's husband, I'm getting those kids back for her. For us. Hold on, guys. Just hold on.*

Chapter Thirty-Six

LITTLEFORD PRIMARY SCHOOL

Day 6: Wednesday, 11.15 a.m.

'I think I know who wrote that message.'

The headteacher's words hang in the air. Sadie and Daniel stare at her, Daniel frozen with a chocolate biscuit halfway to his mouth. He lowers his hand slowly.

'*Who?*' he asks.

Olivia hesitates, eyes darting from Sadie to Daniel, and Sadie wants to yell at her, to shout, *Tell us! TELL. US!*, but she can't seem to speak, and so she waits, for a second, two, three…

'I think it was Cally. Cally Norman. Miss Norman,' Olivia says slowly. 'Year 3. She wrote *this* note, so…'

She taps the piece of paper on her desk, and Sadie blinks.

'Cally Norman? The teacher who's one of the hostages?' she asks.

'Yes,' says Olivia. 'I mean, as I said, it's probably just a coincidence. But that word, that phrase…'

She clasps her hands in front of her, looking excited suddenly.

'Do you think the kidnappers *made* her write the message, and didn't tell her exactly what to say, maybe? So she used that phrase as a kind of secret code? Maybe she hoped I'd remember it was a phrase she'd used before?'

'A secret code to tell us what, though?' asks Daniel. 'She's not telling us anything, is she?'

'Oh. I... I don't know,' replies Olivia, and the eagerness in her expression fades. 'No. I suppose not.'

'Daniel. Outside, now,' says Sadie, and she stands up and marches from the room.

'B–but—' stutters Olivia, but Sadie ignores her, and moments later, Daniel is outside in the corridor with her, closing the door behind them.

'She thinks Cally Norman wrote that note? Dan, have we got this all wrong?' Sadie keeps her voice low, but even she can hear the trepidation in it. 'I mean, yes, there's a chance the hostage takers got *her* to send the messages to the families, I suppose. But what would be the point of her putting a phrase like that in? Just to reassure Olivia that she's alive?'

'Maybe,' replies Daniel doubtfully. 'But you'd think if she was going to try to get some sort of coded message out, she'd make it better than that. A clue to their location or something. But why else would she be writing the messages? Oh, Christ. You don't think...?'

Sadie leans her back against the magnolia-painted wall behind her, squeezes her eyes shut for a moment, then opens them again.

'I don't know. But let's just think about this. If *she's* behind it, if she organised all this… what if they're *all* in on it? All the teaching staff? I mean, I'm still not sure about Erica Lindsay, maybe something went wrong between them or something, I don't know. But maybe they all found out something about one of the parents, and cooked this kidnap and blackmail thing up between them? I don't know how much teachers earn, but I don't think it's vast amounts. £5 million split three ways, or four if Erica was supposed to be involved too? That's not bad for a few days' work, is it? Think about it, Daniel. Did Cally slip up when she used that phrase? What if we're not looking for anyone else at all? What if those adult kidnap victims *aren't* victims, but the *perpetrators*?'

Daniel is gaping at her, looking stunned.

'Holy crap. If you're right… That attack on Erica was *so* violent, though. It would mean they killed one of their colleagues, boss. They beat Erica Lindsay up and left her for dead. Do you really think one of those other three would do that?'

'I don't know. I just don't know. Erica mentioned a masked man before she died, didn't she, so maybe someone else was involved. The background checks didn't flag anything of concern, did they? But *maybe* there's some little detail we missed. We need to look at them again, *now*. And we need to… *Shit*. Who's that?'

Her phone is ringing, and she stabs at the screen.

'Hello, DSU Stewart.'

It's Eamonn Duffy, a member of the specialist anti-kidnap team, and she listens impatiently as he fills her in on their thoughts on the new message and the hostage takers' intention to provide bank details just five minutes before the money transfer deadline.

'I know we're still advising the parents not to pay. But in our experience, they don't always take our advice, so I just want us to be prepared,' he says. 'As for the bank account, we're expecting it to be offshore and, as you probably know, those places – you know, like the Bahamas or the Cayman Islands – they tend to have very strict privacy laws and usually won't cooperate with foreign law enforcement officers asking for info. And our government has no authority over foreign banks, of course.'

'OK, thanks. Look—' Sadie says, trying to end the call, but Eamonn is still talking.

'And what I suspect they'll do if any money is transferred is that they'll quickly move it through a number of different accounts; cycle it through the international payment system to obscure the trail, as it were, closing accounts behind them as they go. By the time we unravel it all they'll be long gone, and anyway, without cooperation from all the banks we can't trace where the money goes once it is transferred. Even in such a high-profile case as this, there are just so many hoops to jump through—'

'Well, thanks. But we're still advising the families not to pay any ransom money, and as yet we've got no reason to think they're planning to go against that advice,' Sadie says, finally interrupting him. 'And actually, Eamonn, we might have a new lead. We're heading back to base now, but Daniel is going to get on the phone and do a briefing as we drive, OK? Give us a few minutes. Thanks again.'

She ends the call, and looks at Daniel, who nods.

'I feel sick,' she says. 'What do you think? Could it really be something as wild as this? The *teachers*? Are we completely mad to even consider it? Do we even believe... *her*?'

She lowers her voice, gesturing towards Olivia Chamberlain's office door.

'I mean, call me paranoid, but what if *she's* involved somehow, and trying to steer us in the wrong direction? I've always said someone connected to the school could be helping with all this.'

'I don't know. I don't know anything right now. But we need to look into it, and fast,' Daniel says. 'Come on, let's get out of here.'

Chapter Thirty-Seven

CALLY

Day 6: Wednesday, 1.17 p.m.

*I*t's nearly over. Just a couple more days. We're nearly there…

Cally is marching up and down The Bunker, her head buzzing, unable to keep still.

'Just doing my exercise!' she said brightly, when a couple of the children asked her what she was doing, and they giggled and told her she looked like a horse.

'That's what we have to do in riding lessons. Up and down, up and down,' said Wanda Pearson with a chuckle, and Cally laughed too, but she carried on marching, nervous energy fizzing in her stomach. The children have got bored now and gone off to play a game, but still Cally walks, touching the wall at each end of the room with both hands before executing the turn, like a swimmer in a competition. She sees Dominic and Oscar eyeing her a little anxiously. She'll go and talk to them in a few minutes, she thinks; she'll reassure them that all is well, that she's fine. But for now, she needs to keep moving, and so she does.

As she strides back and forth, she thinks about how it all began, and about how remarkable it is that, after all her scheming and planning – *years* of it – now, somehow, the end is so close she can almost touch it, almost feel that money in her hands, feel the euphoria of finally getting the revenge she's craved for so long.

The actual nuts and bolts of it all – this hideout, the 'hijack' of the bus, the food and bedding and toys and all those other little details – didn't take years to plan, of course. That was all done in a matter of months. But the *idea*, that began to form a decade ago, and over the years it sprouted and grew from an indistinct, shadowy whisper into a fully-fledged, bright, technicolour dream that begged – no, shouted, *screamed* – to be brought to life. And so she did. She brought it to life, although not on her own of course. To pull this off, she needed help, and to her surprise, when she finally plucked up the courage to ask, that help was willingly offered. And of course, putting aside the delicious feeling of getting revenge on somebody who'd done something truly awful, the money definitely helped. You can persuade people to do an awful lot when a life-changing sum of money is on offer. So, they're all in it together now – Cally, Dominic, Oscar. And The Visitor of course.

It's tickled her, the fact that the children came up with that name.

The Visitor. It sounds so dark, so mysterious. But it's been so important, having The Visitor on the outside. Crucial. Before, driving around the Cotswolds with her to work out the best place to dump the bus, in those little-used woods. And over the past few days, being her eyes and ears in Littleford, telling her what's going on, what the police are up to, what the families are thinking. Playing such an excellent role as the bus hijacker too. So convincing, such good acting. What happened to Erica was a major blip, of course. That *hadn't* been in the plan, and Cally had flipped out when she'd heard about it. It had horrified all of them. Cally's been anxious throughout this extraordinary endeavour, but most of her tears have been for Erica. That *shouldn't* have happened. But otherwise… without The Visitor, the kids might not have believed they've all been in this together, children and teachers. They *will* find out eventually that it wasn't a big game after all, that they've actually been victims of a kidnap for ransom; that's inevitable – Cally's been kept up to date with how the story's hit the headlines all over the world. They'll realise their teachers were all lying to them, and she doesn't want to dwell on how that will make them feel. But it's been important to her that the kids felt they were all sharing the same experience while they were down here in The Bunker.

Plus, the fresh food deliveries, the sending of the messages she's composed – because of course there's no phone signal down here, no Wi-Fi, nothing like that – The Visitor did it all, and so will be compensated too, just like the rest of them. The children don't know who The Visitor is, which is a bonus. The roles of Cally and Oscar and Dominic will be exposed, when this thing reaches its culmination, but that's OK. By the time everyone knows, and knows *why* they did it, they should be far, far away.

It all depends on the money, of course, and that's what's

spiking her anxiety right now, the prospect of the money *not* being paid, because what then? And yet, she's almost certain it will be. It might not be the full £5 million – she took a chance, asking for that much. But she's fairly sure they'll pay a decent amount. There's just that tiny, *tiny* little worm of doubt wriggling around somewhere, very deep down.

She's trying to smother it though. At first, she'd just planned to target one person – the person who all this is really about. But when she took up the job at Littleford Primary, and realised how *many* insanely wealthy parents there were, well, what a chance. What an opportunity.

And so, after long discussions, she – *they* – decided to go for gold. To take *all* the kids. The whole damn class. There were regular school outings, each trip planned many months in advance, so they had a date to work towards, keeping their fingers crossed that the excursion wouldn't be postponed or cancelled for any reason, fearing an outbreak of sickness that would keep some of the children at home, which would have scuppered everything. They'd decided early on to keep the message to the families deliberately vague; to tell them that *somebody's* secret was about to be exposed, but not say *whose*. Because in a group like that, there's bound to be more than one dirty little secret, isn't there? So many people have done things they'd rather nobody knew about. It was another calculated risk, therefore, phrasing the message the way they did. They gambled on the fact that more than one of the parents might have something from their past they'd prefer to keep quiet. And if more than one thinks the message is aimed at them, more than one is likely to pay up, right?

OK, it's not perfect. Some will have no skeletons in their

closets; some will have no money to pay a ransom even if they do, and no doubt they'll all be under police orders not to hand over a penny. But it was worth a shot, and it looks like it's about to pay off. Some people, according to The Visitor, who's been watching everyone as closely as possible, are very rattled indeed. Erica's murder helped too, although the thought makes Cally shudder. But it made the parents *more* frightened, more likely to defy the police. And that, Cally hopes, means *kerching!* A nice, fat payday.

The kids are OK, she hopes. That's been one of her biggest worries, the thing that's kept her awake at night, gnawing at her. But they've all done so *well*. They've all kept smiling, kept busy. She doesn't know what the long-term effects of this incarceration will be, but she's hoping for minimum trauma. It's not their fault, and they're adorable, all of them. They've been as well looked after as humanly possible, under the circumstances. They just think this is a really rubbish game, which it truly would be, if it was one. And it's just for another couple of days now. They'll cope. Kids are tough – she knows that. She was a tough kid herself. She had to be.

Cally touches the wall of The Bunker one final time, takes a deep breath and walks over to where Dominic is lying on his front on his air bed, chin on his folded arms, keeping a watchful eye on half a dozen of the children who seem to be playing some sort of musical chairs game around the beanbags, although without any music of course.

'How does that work?' she asks him with a smile, gesturing at them, and Dominic's shoulders lift in a shrug.

'No clue, but they seem to be enjoying it,' he says. 'Are you OK? Burning off the nerves there?'

'Yep. Shit's getting real, now, eh?'

She sits down next to him, and lowers her head to drop a quick kiss onto the back of his neck, making sure that none of the children are looking in their direction before she does so.

'Getting real for them out there too,' replies Dominic, and he rolls onto his back and grins at her. 'Well, for one of them, anyway. Not that they know it, yet.'

She nods slowly.

'They have no idea what's about to hit them, do they?'

'I very much doubt it,' Dominic says.

Me too, she thinks. *Because there'll be no secret-keeping here, and they're all idiots if they believe that paying us off is going to make a blind bit of difference. And I can't wait to blow that nasty little life wide open. Soon, everyone will know what's been living amongst them.*

'Bring. It. On,' she says.

Chapter Thirty-Eight

Day 7: Thursday, 7.35 a.m.

'**D**o you *really* think they were considering paying the ransom? Are you sure they won't, now they know we might have a lead? Even if I'm still not a hundred per cent convinced about this Cally Norman theory…'

Sadie, tapping her pen irritably on her desk as she refreshes her emails, gets no reply. It's Thursday morning, and she and Daniel are in her small office on the floor above the incident room. There's a framed photo of Teddy on the bookshelf next to a drooping pot plant, the name of which has escaped Sadie but which looks seriously dehydrated, its leaves shrivelled and brown.

I really need to water that thing at some point, she thinks, then glances at the photograph, once again feeling extraordinarily grateful that her nephew is safe at home, surrounded by people who love him.

'Dan?' she says.

He gestures helplessly at his mouth, which is full of – judging by the half-eaten remains on the plate in front of him – a large bite of an enormous bacon roll. It looks revolting, cold and greasy and smothered in tomato ketchup, but Sadie knows Daniel must barely have had time to eat anything yesterday, spending all afternoon and evening personally calling in on every single family to tell them there may be a development in the case and to reassure them that everything possible was still being done to bring their children home. She averts her eyes from the plate and waits, trying to quell her impatience.

Finally, Daniel swallows and wipes his mouth with a paper napkin.

'Sorry, boss. I am *starving* this morning. Yes, when I told them we might be a bit closer to getting to the bottom of it, I definitely got the feeling there was something going on – there were some shifty looks, you know? And several of them quite openly told me they've somewhat lost faith in the police operation. I had a weird feeling they were closing ranks on me. I don't know. I could be wrong. And even if they *are* thinking of paying, the transfer can't be made until tomorrow anyway, can it? They haven't been told where to send it yet. I've told them we'll keep them posted as far as possible and stressed again that we strongly advise against paying ransom money, for all the reasons we've discussed before. And obviously, I didn't give them any details about our potential lead. Anything on that yet?'

'Not yet. I'm not holding my breath. It *could* be as simple as Cally Norman being forced to write that message and using her own words, who knows. And I don't think, deep down, that Olivia Chamberlain is dodgy and trying to give us a false lead, but you just can't assume anything, can you?'

She sighs.

'I wish they'd get a move on though. Oh, maybe this is it…'

Her desk phone is ringing, and she grabs the handset.

'DSU Stewart? Yes, hello Andy. Any news? What? Seriously?' She pauses, listening, then says, 'Hang on. Daniel's here; he needs to hear this. I'm putting you on speaker…'

Daniel has already pushed his breakfast aside, an expectant look on his face. Sadie hits the phone's loudspeaker button.

'Andy? OK, we can both hear you now. Go on, say that again.'

'Great. Mornin', Dan.'

The West Country burr of DS Andy Robins crackles from the speaker.

'Morning, mate. What have you got?'

'Right, well, we've bin lookin' into those three teachers again, as requested. As we already knew, none of 'em are known to the police – clean slates, all of 'em. That's still ongoing, but for now we've been specifically lookin' for locations, places, you know? Anything that stands out as a possible good spot to hide a group of kids. Somewhere one of 'em knows well. And this might be nothin', but there is one thing that's jumped out at us, when we had a closer look at Cally Norman's activities over the past few years.'

'OK. Shoot,' says Dan.

'Right, well, she studied 'istory at the University of Westminster. And her dissertation was somethin' about 'istorical buildings and the ethics of reconstructin' 'em when they fall into disrepair. Anyway, she featured one such place quite prominently. It's a stately 'ome called Morcombe Manor. It's Elizabethan, so built in the fifteen 'undreds, and until about ten years ago it was owned by a Lady somethin' or other, but when she passed away it was just closed up and left to rot. It's been empty for years. And, wait for it, it's about five miles from the village of Lower Lockton. You know, where the school minibus was dumped?'

Daniel lets out a low whistle, and Sadie feels her scalp start to prickle, as if insects are crawling in her hair.

'The thing is that we've searched it already,' Andy says. 'Right back on day two or whenever it was, and we didn't find a thing. The place is pretty secure, by all accounts, all the windows well boarded up and no sign of squatters or anythin', just a big old pile slowly fallin' apart. The search team did break their way in and had a good look around and then moved on. But now someone's managed to pull up some old floor plans of the place, and there's a cellar. A big one. And we've checked the records and there's no note of a cellar bein' searched the other day. Maybe the entrance was well 'idden, and they just didn't realise it was there. So, you know, maybe? Maybe we need to go back.'

It's ringing a bell for Sadie now too, a briefing that feels like months in the past but was, in fact, actually just a few days ago, a list of buildings that had been searched.

Abandoned farm buildings, an airport hangar that's rarely used, a derelict manor house…

'Bloody hell, Andy.'

Could we really have done that? Searched the building they're being held in and missed them? Oh my God… she thinks.

She turns to Daniel.

'That would mean Cally Norman really does have something to do with all this. *Why?* Why on earth? But it fits, doesn't it?' she says.

He nods, his eyes shining. 'It's so close to the bus dumping site. They'd be there in minutes, wouldn't they? Which would mean a much lower risk of anyone spotting them en route. And a *cellar*. Very little noise comes up from an old cellar, and in an abandoned building… It sounds good to me, boss.'

'Me too,' she says and turns back to address Andy on the other end of the phone.

'Andy, we absolutely need to go back. But we need to move very, very carefully, just in case. The whole world is watching us and we can't afford to screw this up. Stand by. I'll get back to you.'

Chapter Thirty-Nine

LUCA

Day 7: Thursday, 1.33 p.m.

There's something going on in The Bunker. Luca doesn't know what it is yet, but it's *something*. He's seen Miss Norman and Mr Jones whispering together more than once today, then calling Mr Moore over and whispering to him too. They all look like they're kind of excited but kind of worried too. Miss Norman keeps running her hands through her hair, so it's all sticking up, and she keeps walking up and down The Bunker, as if she can't keep still.

'Ants in her pants,' Noah Beckford said quietly to Luca earlier, and they both snorted with laughter. Luca felt a little guilty about that afterwards though, because he wasn't sure it was a good thing to be doing, talking about your teacher's pants, and also if she *did* have ants in her pants that wouldn't be very nice at all, because ants bite, don't they? Imagine ants biting your bottom! He's not the only one to have noticed something's going on though; he thinks everyone's noticed now.

'Do you think the game is nearly over? Has someone's mum or dad worked out where we are?' Lola asked him earlier. 'Willow thinks so.'

'Maybe,' Luca said.

'Will you go and ask?' his sister replied.

So he went to ask Miss Norman, and she patted his arm and said, 'I'm not a hundred per cent sure, sweetie. But I really hope so. I think we might be on our way home by Saturday. I'll let you know as soon as we know, OK?'

It's Thursday today. So that really does mean just two more sleeps now, and when Luca spread the news, there were happy faces and claps all round, and Gresham Greer made them all laugh by running round and round in big circles about ten times, like a dog doing zoomies, before collapsing in a heap on the nearest bean bag.

Luca's spent the past hour reading on his bed, and also doing some more thinking. And one thing he's thought of is puzzling him. It's about The Visitor. When the usual rattle at the door came earlier today, the familiar noise which always makes everyone smile because it means lunch or dinner has arrived, he waited until Miss Norman went up the stairs to take delivery, checked to see where Mr Jones and Mr Moore were (both at the far end of The Bunker, playing a board game with Stanley and Willow) and then sidled as close as he dared to the bottom of the stairs. He flattened his back against the wall, in the shadows at the side of the stairwell, and he listened hard. He did this today because he also did it yesterday, and that was when he heard The Visitor laugh, and something sparked in his head.

Is that really who I think it is?

But he wasn't sure, so this morning he tried to get even closer, and listen even harder. And he heard a tiny snippet of conversation – just a few words, nothing that meant anything really – but the voice wasn't as quiet as it normally was. *Maybe The Visitor was excited too, that this stupid game is nearly over,* he'd thought. The spark in Luca's head had suddenly got bigger and brighter, and then he knew. He just *knew*.

Now, sitting on his slowly deflating air bed, he puts his book down and thinks about The Visitor. He definitely knows who it is now. He's kind of *surprised* about who it is, and he wonders if he should tell anyone, and then he wonders if maybe this is part of the game too, and when it's over he might get extra points or a bonus prize or something, for guessing who kept them all fed during this long week underground.

Best not to tell anyone then, he thinks. *Not even Lola, or Noah.*

No. He won't say a word.

He smiles with secret satisfaction, and picks up his book again.

Chapter Forty

REYNOLD

Day 7: Thursday, 1.45 p.m.

'Everyone's here. I think the police are about to start. Are you OK?'

Reynold reaches out a hand to touch Petra on the arm, but she moves away, out of his reach.

'I'm fine. Just grab those pains au chocolat, will you? I found them in the freezer and stuck them in the oven, just in case anyone's hungry. It's hardly lunch, but I wasn't exactly expecting to be entertaining half the village today, so it's better than nothing.'

She points at a plate piled high with pastries, and Reynold nods, picks it up and follows her into the lounge. Last night was another long, tortuous, sleepless one, but at least she's speaking to him today, which is progress, even if it's just to snap at him. When the police called an hour ago, saying they needed to hold an urgent briefing and wondering if they could possibly direct everyone to gather at The Granary, because of its privacy, space and central village location, Petra had rolled her eyes and grunted, 'I suppose so, if they have to.'

She'd then proceeded to hightail it round the house, changing her clothes, straightening cushions, laying out mugs and napkins and largely ignoring Reynold when he offered to help.

'Just keep out of my way, and show everyone in when they arrive,' she'd muttered, and he'd meekly obeyed.

He'd noted though that she'd been more than happy to let Marc Hackett move some extra chairs into the lounge for her. Reynold's dislike of the FLO is growing by the minute.

'Why is he here so early?' he'd muttered, when the doorbell had rung not long after nine.

'To *support* us,' Petra had replied, glaring at him. 'And I'm very grateful. You're still angry because he looked at your computer, aren't you? Get over it, Reynold.'

Now, Marc is standing alongside Detective Superintendent Sadie Stewart and her DCI Daniel Sharma by the fireplace in the lounge, all of them looking serious. Everyone else is sitting or standing around the room, seventeen adults whose lives have changed beyond recognition in the past week. Some are red-eyed and exhausted-looking, others twitchy and fidgety; all are eyeing the police party anxiously. Reynold puts the pastry plate down on the nearest table and looks around, noticing that Monique Townsend is sitting as far away as possible from her husband, Ben, but that Clare and Nick Tustain are standing together by the window, although without any body contact, both looking stiff and uncomfortable. Eldon and Amy are sitting together too, on one of the sofas, and

Reynold meets Amy's eye briefly then both of them look away.

I'll have to talk to her eventually, he thinks. *But not today.*

He wonders where Petra's going to sit, then sees her lowering herself onto the arm of the easy chair occupied by Rosie Duggan. She doesn't meet his eye, patting Rosie's hand and saying something to her in a low voice. Reynold watches her for a few seconds, feeling an ache somewhere deep inside, then hears Sadie Stewart clearing her throat, all heads turning towards her.

'Right, thank you all for getting here at such short notice, and to Reynold and Petra for hosting,' she begins, and gives Petra a little smile.

'As Daniel here told you all yesterday, we have a possible development in the case, and things are now moving quite rapidly. We'd like to stress again that there should be no question of any ransom money being paid, particularly in light of what's happened in the past few hours. I can't give you much more information, I'm so sorry. And I'm not going to ask you now if paying the ransom is something you've been considering, but if it is, *please* hold off for now, OK? I know you can't pay until you're sent bank account details anyway, but even if those come early, please don't. It could scupper things at what might be a very delicate stage, if we get lucky.'

There's a short silence, as eyes meet and meaningful glances are exchanged, and then a few of the parents murmur their assent, the rest nodding in agreement.

'Good. Now, I'm sure you're all keen to know what's going on. All I can tell you is that we now have a theory about who's behind the kidnapping. We're working to establish a motive, but without further details regarding the "secret" referred to in the message, this is proving to be very difficult.'

She looks meaningfully around the room, and a few people shift uncomfortably in their seats. Reynold redirects his gaze to Daniel, and then to the floor for a moment, before forcing himself to look back at the Detective Superintendent.

'So,' she continues, 'it *is* just a theory at the moment. But it's led us to a possible location that we need to search thoroughly...'

'A location? *What?* You mean you think you might know where they're being held?' says Eldon, leaping to his feet, as several of the others gasp, and Monique Townsend lets out a little cry and begins to weep. Sadie holds up a hand.

'Hang on, hang on. It's just a *possible* lead we're investigating but the location sounds as if it might fit – it's not far from where the bus was dumped, so the hostage takers would have been able to get everyone there pretty quickly after the ambush. I'm sorry, that's all I can tell you right now...'

She carries on talking, but Reynold, who's standing near the door, is distracted by a sudden movement in the hall outside. He turns to see Brandon peering in at him. The man was doing something out in the garden earlier, and had popped into the kitchen briefly for a catch-up with Petra. Reynold had walked in to find the two of them and Marc Hackett looking very cosy over cups of tea, and had felt quite irrationally upset that nobody had bothered to offer him one. But Brandon's not supposed to be working *inside* the house today.

'Brandon? What's up?' Reynold hisses.

'Sorry, the front door was open,' Brandon stutters, looking

embarrassed. 'I needed to speak to you... I didn't realise everyone was here... I'm really sorry. I'll go...'

He starts to back away, but Reynold, hearing Sadie continuing to tell the group there's little more she can say and to try to stay positive, steps out of the room and pulls the door shut behind him.

'It's OK. What did you want?'

Brandon hesitates for a moment, then turns to Reynold. He looks flushed and a little agitated, bouncing from foot to foot as if he's desperate to get out of there. Reynold frowns and says, 'Is everything OK?'

'Yes. Yes. Fine,' says Brandon hurriedly. 'It's just, well, I wanted to let you know I won't be able to work here anymore. I'm sorry. I know this is a bad time and all that, with everything that's going on...'

He gestures towards the living room.

'It's just that I'm moving away from Littleford. Life's short, you know? And with all this stuff that's happened, well...'

He shrugs, and Reynold suddenly wonders if Petra's told him about his affair with Amy. Maybe she told Marc too. Maybe that's what they were all chatting about earlier in the kitchen...

God. She wouldn't, would she?

He feels heat rising up his neck, a combination of shame and anger, but Brandon is still talking, so he blinks and tries to focus.

'... anyway, I hope everything works out OK, you know, with Luca and Lola. They're great kids, and I'm so sorry for what you've been going through. I'm sure you'll get them back any day now. Good luck.'

'Ermm… OK. Well, thanks…'

Reynold holds out a hand, but Brandon is already walking away, heading for the front door.

'Bye, then…' Reynold calls after him, but there's no reply, and moments later he hears the front door closing. He stares down the hallway for a moment, unsure of what to make of what's just happened, then feels a wave of annoyance.

The guy could have waited to let us know he's buggering off, he thinks, as he slips back into the lounge. *As if the local handyman matters, at a time like this?*

'Sorry,' he says, as Sadie looks at him quizzically, clearly wondering where he's been.

'We had a visitor – nothing important. What have I missed?'

'I think you heard most of it. Just the fact that, as I said, there's a location we want to search,' she replies. 'We're working on a plan for that now and we'll keep you posted.'

'And what if you're wrong?' Reynold asks. The words come out more angrily than he intended them to, and he wonders why he feels so rattled.

'What if there's nothing at this mystery location?' he continues. 'What then? *Then* will you let us pay the ransom money tomorrow, and try and get our children back?'

Sadie's brow crinkles.

'Let's just wait and see how today goes, sir,' she says politely.

And giving him a final cool stare, she marches from the room, her colleagues following close behind her. Marc gives him a stern look as he passes him, and Reynold takes a deep breath, then crosses the room to where Petra is saying goodbye to the other parents.

'I need to get out for a bit. I'm going for a drive,' he says, and she nods, not looking at him. By the time he's found his car keys and grabbed a jacket, the large driveway is emptying of vehicles. Reynold joins the back of the queue for the gateway, watching impatiently as some cars turn right, some left. He watches the two senior police officers drive off together, and then Marc, alone in his car and heading off in the opposite direction. Then Reynold pulls out too, and puts his foot down.

Chapter Forty-One

THE BUNKER

Day 7: Thursday, 2.47 p.m.

The Visitor is anxious. *Very* anxious. The drive from Littleford isn't long, but it feels as if it's lasting forever, every traffic light on red and queues at every roundabout, as if the universe is conspiring to slow the vehicle down, to stop it getting to The Bunker.

What the police have just announced, about a location they're about to search... Could they have worked it out?

It seems unlikely, especially as The Visitor knows the building has been searched before, days ago, and the idiots found nothing. But it's a risk they can't take, and not for the first time The Visitor, finally getting up some speed on a relatively empty stretch of road, curses the fact they chose an underground room to hold the hostages in. No damn phone signal, no way of contacting anyone down there without actually making the journey.

The Visitor has no idea what the others will make of this

piece of news, but it needs to be relayed *now* – that's pretty obvious. They've come too far, taken too many risks, to let it all fall apart right at the last minute. They'll work something out, won't they? Move the kids, quickly. Cally must have a back-up plan, right? One she hasn't shared yet, but kept on the back burner, just in case? That's what she's done throughout, through all the long months of planning. She's told them everything on a 'need to know' basis. Even so, as The Visitor leaps from the car and fumbles in a pocket for the keys to The Bunker, that deep-in-the-stomach ball of stress is growing bigger with each passing second.

The key sticks in the lock of the front door of the building, but with a sharp tug it's released and the door creaks open. Long, dark corridors, so familiar now; feet pounding on cracked tiles and ancient floorboards. Then the pantry, dank and chilly, and the innocent-looking wall cupboard that hides another heavy wooden door, centuries old. The locks aren't old though; they're brand new, shiny and smooth, and in those the keys move easily, soundlessly. The Visitor taps on the door, once, twice, waits for twenty seconds, and then, heart pounding, heaves at the door, which swings open on well-oiled hinges.

'Cally,' The Visitor says quietly.

She's standing on the stairs with a puzzled expression. This visit was not expected, not at this time, and The Visitor is empty-handed – no bags of food or fresh supplies of towels or toilet paper – and she's clearly confused, the questioning look in her eyes turning rapidly to fear.

'What? What is it? Has something happened?' she

whispers. Down below, The Visitor can hear children's laughter, a raucous game of some sort being played.

'The police. I think they might have worked out where you are. They've told everyone they have a new lead, and a location not far from where the bus was dumped. They're planning a search. I'm not sure if they mean here, but they *might* have the right spot. We can't risk it, Cally. We need to move everyone out of here, fast.'

She takes a deep breath and blows the air back out again.

'Do they know *we're* behind it? Have they worked that out?' she says, and glances over her shoulder, obviously checking that nobody in The Bunker is within earshot.

'I don't know. They haven't said.'

'Right. Well, thanks. I'll tell the others and we'll work out what to do. Stay out there for a bit, can you, until we've decided?'

'Sure. I'll be right here. Don't be long though, OK?'

She nods, and turns away, disappearing into the darkness of the stairwell. The Visitor closes the door gently, then sits down on the cold stone floor and waits.

Chapter Forty-Two

CALLY

Day 7: Thursday, 3.15 p.m.

Half an hour later, Cally has decided. She's discussed it with Oscar and Dominic, and they've all agreed. It's a gamble, but they're going to hold their nerve. Cally's original Plan B was piling the children and themselves into the vehicles they used to travel from the bus site – the vehicles currently hidden in outbuildings at the rear of this house – and moving location. Location B is a large mobile home, a holiday let in an isolated spot in the New Forest, the rent already paid for a month. Cally told the owners it was for a long Easter break and that various family members would be coming to join her there at various times, and they hadn't asked any questions at all. She'd used a false name for the booking of course; over the past few years, living frugally and using every spare penny to pay for it, she's gradually been gathering everything she needs for the new life she's going to lead after this: a forged passport, a credit card in her new name, all the other documents she'll need. But now, Plan B doesn't seem like a good idea. If the police really are on their way, and soon, they may already be closing off roads, sealing off the exits from the estate. They'd be trapped, sitting ducks, and then it will all have been for nothing, all the scheming, all the risks.

The police could still have it wrong, of course; they could be heading to another location entirely. But they've all agreed that even if they're about to be surrounded, staying put is probably actually safer. Their escape plan from this place should still work, and the kids will be fine down here on their own for a short while, until the cops realise the adults have vanished and come in and rescue the children. And then... a new life, for all of them. Oscar and The Visitor have been on board for a while; Dominic is the latest recruit and Cally was able to speed things up for him when she decided she could trust him to get involved. She's become a bit of an expert now in the dark web and the right places to go, the right questions to ask. He's assembled everything he needs in just a few months. It cost a lot – if these things are good, they're expensive – but Dominic had been lucky enough to inherit some cash from a deceased uncle, and anyway, they'll have more money than they ever dreamed of soon, won't they, so what does a few thousand here or there matter? They'll always be on the run, of course, the three of them, the three whose names are known. For the rest of their lives, probably. Not just the kidnap, but murder too – they'll be on the Most Wanted lists across the world – but their escape plans are solid, and they really believe they can pull this off. The Visitor will have an easier time of it, of course, anonymity preserved, but they're all going away together anyway. They're a team now, bonded for life, and for what they hope will be a good life, and a life where they *do* good too, once they've put all this behind them. They're not bad people, not really. They're just doing what needed to be done.

And so, Plan A is to carry on, but they're just going to speed things up a little bit. Cally is currently typing another message into a burner phone, ready for The Visitor to send from upstairs, but this time the message is to just one person. The person all of this has been about, right from the beginning. She's telling them who she is, and why she's doing this. She's saying she believes the police may be on their way, and that because of that the ransom payment deadline is being moved to today. To *now*, in fact, as soon as possible after the message is received. She's giving the details of the bank account to pay the money into, and she's saying that once that's been done, she and the other adults are going to leave immediately, and three hours later she's going to confirm the location where the children can be found.

Then she adds the warning. She says that if anything goes wrong, if the police are told about this message, if they attempt to *stop* any of the adults leaving, if they attempt any sort of rescue operation, then what will happen is this.

Cally pauses, her fingers trembling a little. She doesn't want to write this bit, even though she knows she must. She doesn't want to carry out this threat either – the very thought of it horrifies her. But that will be Oscar's role. That's always been the plan. He doesn't want to do it either, but she knows he will, if he really has to. They've come too far to give up now.

And the parents will pay, won't they? Of course they will, when they read this. Nobody will get hurt. It's going to be fine.

Cally steels herself, and taps the final words into the phone.

What will happen is this:
The children will be sent out one by one.
But they won't be walking out.
They won't be able to walk.
Their lives are in your hands now.
Pay up, or your children will die.

Chapter Forty-Three

REYNOLD

Day 7: Thursday, 3.25 p.m.

Reynold is back home and in the garden when the latest message arrives. His short car drive after the police briefing did little to clear his head, and when he got back he could tell that Petra wasn't happy about his early return, glaring at him as he walked into the house. And so Reynold crept outside, like a dog that's soiled its bedding and is in disgrace, and has been wandering up and down the lawn, looking without much interest at the plants in the neat borders and adding 'find new gardener/handyman' to his mental to-do list. It's a bright, warm day, the sky duck-egg blue and almost cloudless. The pacing is becoming strangely soothing, almost meditative, and when his phone beeps in his pocket he jumps violently. And then he reads the message, and he stops walking. He almost stops breathing.

What? Oh, Jesus. Holy shit. Oh no. No, no, no…

There's a wooden bench halfway down the lawn, under the

shade of the big oak tree, and Reynold collapses onto it. His whole body is shaking, and there's a chill spreading from somewhere deep in his belly, little shivers running up his spine. He reads the message again, and then a third time, trying to make sense of it. What it's saying, what it's accusing him of, is rapidly taking him back a quarter of a century, as if someone's just pressed rewind in his memory bank. He remembers it, of course, but it was *so* long ago, and he'd pushed it out of his head and moved on; tried to forget it. That hadn't worked, not completely; now and again, over the years, in quiet moments, he'd wondered about it, wondered if he'd done the right thing, a whisper of unease in the far, dark recesses of his mind telling him that maybe he hadn't. But he'd always ignored it, and now – *twenty-five, twenty-six years later?* – it seems almost unimportant. Something lost in the past. But it wasn't lost, at all, was it? And the fact that what he did had so many consequences, so many repercussions...

How? How did he not know any of this, until now?

He groans out loud.

Is this real? Is it some sort of scam?

And yet, there are enough facts in here for it to be entirely believable. Nobody else knew about it, at the time, just him and... her. Well, *one* other person knew, but they died a long time ago. And yet this message contains a name, and dates, and details. It *is* real, it must be. And the implications are *huge*. For him, for his family, for his career. The affair with Amy may not, in the end, decimate his livelihood, but this could. This *will*, if anyone finds out about it.

And then, there's this last bit. The terrifying end to this awful, awful message.

Pay up, or your children will die.

Oh. My. God.

Reynold is shivering violently now, despite the mild weather. He could take this to the police; he *should* take this to the police. But can he take the risk? What if they're wrong about this location they suspect the children are being held in? What if these people – this *woman* who's written this message, the children's teacher, for God's sake, not a hostage at all but the hostage *taker* – what if she really does carry out her hideous threat? His children could die. *All* the children could die.

He wants to sit here and think some more about this; think about pretty, young Cally Norman, who he's spoken to so many times in the playground, and at parent–teacher meetings, and who always seemed so pleasant, so complimentary about his beautiful twins. He wants to think about who she *really* is, and about what it all means. He wants to think about how the hell she's pulled off something of this magnitude, and why she's gone to such lengths. Why she's involved so many other parents and children in all of this, when *he's* the one she really wants to punish. He wants to think about the other teachers and how they might be involved, and about the fact that one teacher, Erica Lindsay, didn't even make it out of this alive. And about how, if this money isn't paid, what he did so long ago will be revealed to the world. Can he really trust her, to keep his secret now, if he pays her? How long has she known? She's kept quiet so far, hasn't she? So maybe all she wants is the money. Maybe that's enough for her. But what if it's not?

Reynold's head is spinning, but there isn't time to sit and think about any of this, not now. Instead, with trembling hands, he opens the Final Eight group and composes a new message. He tells them he's had a private communication from the hostage takers. He tells them that somehow they know the police may be on to them, and because of that they want their money *now*. He tells them he's been told, in no uncertain terms, that if this payment is *not* made, and made immediately, there will be dire consequences for the children; that he now has the details of the account to pay the money into. And he tells them they cannot, *must* not share this information with the police. He gives no further information; he doesn't mention Cally Norman, and the fact that she's not just an innocent victim but the woman behind everything. And he doesn't mention the fact that this is, after all, down to him, but not for the reason he'd feared. Nothing to do with him and Amy and their affair, and all to do with something atrocious he did many, many years ago, something he thought would never trouble him again.

He presses send, and then he waits. It doesn't take long. Within a minute, the door from the kitchen opens and Petra is striding down the garden towards him, white-faced. Seconds later, the replies from the others begin to ping onto his phone.

This is it. The end game has begun, he thinks. *God help us.*

Chapter Forty-Four

CALLY

Day 7: Thursday, 4.10 p.m.

Halfway up the stairs to the door of The Bunker, Cally sits and waits. The children are scattered around the room in little groups, some at the table, playing a card game with Oscar. The two packs of playing cards were sitting at the bottom of the bag of food The Visitor delivered yesterday, and they've been a welcome new distraction, yells of 'SNAP!' followed by peals of laughter echoing around The Bunker. In the opposite corner, the never-ending remote-controlled car wars continue, the obstacles becoming more and more elaborate with each passing day. Dominic is over there now, apparently competing for the title of supreme champion with Luca, Gresham and Wanda. He keeps glancing Cally's way though, and she keeps shaking her head.

Nothing yet.

She wonders how much money the parents will manage to get together, especially with a day less to do it now. She's assuming that, even though this is all about one person, the gathering of the money will be a joint effort, but she still doesn't think they'll pay the full £5 million – that was definitely a long shot. Even a couple of million would be enough, though. She'd deliberately waited a few days before issuing the first ransom demand; it had been Dominic, the psychology graduate, who'd suggested making everyone wait.

'The longer they wait, the more frightened they'll be,' he said. 'And the more frightened, the more willing they'll be to do anything to get their kids back.'

They might even cobble together a bit *more* now, now that Cally's made that awful, unthinkable threat to the children's lives. The very thought of it being carried out makes her want to throw up, but she's assuming, hoping, it won't come to that. Instead, she's trying to think about the nice, fat sum they'll all have in their bank accounts soon, and about their escape plan, the flights, the destination, the new life that beckons.

She shifts restlessly on the cold step. She's waiting anxiously for The Bunker's door to open again, and for The Visitor, who's still out there, eyes glued to their new banking app, to tell her that the notification has come through, that the payment has been made.

Hurry up, she thinks. *Please, please, hurry.*

It *will* come though. She knows it will. Because he is *not* going to let his kids die and she's pretty damn sure he won't want his story coming out either. She's going to tell it anyway, when this is all over. But he doesn't know that, does he? So he'll pay, she's sure of that.

She wonders what he's doing now, how scared he is, how much in shock. Reynold Lyon. The man all this is about. The man she's dreamt about for years, but not because he's a famous, handsome TV star. She's followed his career with great interest, yes. But not because she likes him. Because she *hates* him. And because she always knew that one day, she was going to bring him down, just like he brought someone else down, way back when.

Her name was Julie, and back in the mid-90s, when she was just twenty years old and working as a runner for a TV company, she met Reynold Lyon and fell head over heels. Eight years her senior, he'd been on his way up as a presenter, his face already all over the tabloids, his champagne habit legendary. At the time, he was seeing an equally high-profile woman, a newsreader called Linda Arlingham, so quite what possessed him to decide to also date Julie on the side, Cally has no idea, but that was what happened. Julie was young and beautiful and besotted with him, and Reynold took her out after work a few times and then booked a hotel room. Weeks later, Julie discovered she was pregnant. For a few brief days she had fantasised about a glittering future, about Reynold leaving Linda for her, about being married to a television star and living in a stunning home and showing off their gorgeous children in the pages of the glossy magazines. And then she told Reynold about the pregnancy, and all her dreams died in an instant. He didn't want to leave his famous girlfriend, and he didn't want a child, not then. He wanted the glamorous life and the high-flying career, and a baby simply didn't figure in his plans. Maybe one day, far into the future, but not then, and certainly not with her.

And so, he took charge.

First, he demanded she have an abortion, offering her a

large sum of money to pay for both the procedure and her silence. Then when, horrified, she refused, he sent a friend round. The friend was a boxer – huge and terrifying – and he told Julie that if she opened her mouth about any of it, *ever*, then she and her child would pay the price. And so Julie kept her mouth firmly shut. She had no siblings, and her parents had both died young, so she was pretty much alone in the world. She'd had such high hopes for her own career, but she'd already fallen deeply in love with the new life growing inside her, and there was no way, no *way*, she was going to let it down. Unable to face seeing Reynold again, she left her television runner's job the same day and took a job in a café instead, the only thing she could find where she could start immediately and carry on paying her rent. And eventually she gave birth, and did the best she could as a mother. She thought about Reynold Lyon every single day, but she never said a word, not to anyone. Not even when the boxer died in the ring five years later, after a punch to the head caused a blood clot in his brain. Julie had a quiet celebration that day, but she still kept her mouth shut, for Reynold could easily find a new thug to do his dirty work, couldn't he? She did think about going to the police, now and again. She *almost* did it, twice getting as far as the door to the local station before, trembling like a leaf, turning away again. She had no proof, after all; the threats against her had all been verbal ones, and there was no easy way of even doing a DNA test to prove that Reynold was her child's father, not without his cooperation. Reporting him was too risky, too dangerous. That threat had been a lifelong one, she had no doubt about that. He'd find a way of getting to her, somehow.

Julie died eighteen years later, a frightened shell of the vibrant young woman she had once been. By then she had three children, but had always remained a single mother, scared to trust another man with news of a pregnancy, just in case. The children had not always lived with her over the years; from time to time, she'd turned to drugs to escape the ever-present sense of fear and foreboding, and more than once this had led to incidents which had meant that social services had to step in, taking the children into temporary foster care until she got back on track again. But her final year had been one of the better ones. She'd been working as an office cleaner, the latest in a string of low-paid jobs she'd taken over the years to keep her little family going, but it had been a steady job with colleagues she liked. A bout of flu had been going around the building, which she caught and which then developed into bacterial pneumonia. She'd waited until she was gasping for breath before staggering into the accident and emergency department of Charing Cross Hospital. They did their best, but it was too late. The infection had spread, the air sacs in her lungs filling with fluid. She died two days later, but before she did, she finally gasped out her story, to her daughter.

To Cally. Barely eighteen, and about to lose the mother who meant everything to her. That story – of why her mother had lived her life as she had – changed everything, and when Cally walked out of the hospital that night, tears streaming down her face and her heart breaking in her chest, a fire began to burn somewhere deep inside her.

Revenge. That was what she wanted. For her mother, and for herself and her brothers. She didn't care how long it took, and Cally was smart enough, even then, to know it would take time, maybe a long time, to do it properly. Years, in the end, as it turned out. A lot of things had needed to fall into place first and others had to be recruited to help. But finally, she'd done it, and it had been worth the wait.

Because now, he's finally going to pay, isn't he? Not just financially, but in every possible way.

Cally wants him to lose everything, just as her mother did.

She could have just blackmailed him, of course, simply by threatening to reveal the story to the world. But she wanted to cause him *real* pain, and to do that she'd needed to get close to him, to find out what makes him tick.

The research hadn't been difficult; his whole life was right there online, documented on Wikipedia and in endless magazine articles. He'd only stayed with Linda, his newsreader girlfriend, for a year or so after he'd done what he did to Julie; a string of beautiful women had followed her, and then he'd met Petra Sanderson, and finally married. It hadn't been hard to discover where their kids went to school either; a *Hello!* magazine spread featuring Reynold and Petra taking the twins to Littleford Primary on their first day had made that bit very easy. And Cally was, by then, already a qualified teacher; it was just a matter of waiting for a job vacancy, and when one was finally advertised she jumped on it. When she arrived in Littleford and met him for the first time – *what a day that was!* – she could see immediately how much he loved Luca and Lola. And that's when it all clicked into place.

Steal his children.

And so the plan progressed, and grew, until they decided to take *all* the children, not just for the money but for the global news coverage that inevitably would follow, and the total humiliation that would result for Reynold when his dark secret was finally revealed. And maybe, just maybe, he'd feel terrible guilt too when he discovered that his actions had ended up causing so much pain to so many families, families who'd become his friends; pain like he'd caused his own first unwanted family, all those years ago. *That would be a bonus,* Cally thought, *if the man was even capable of feeling guilt.*

Now she looks down to where Luca and Lola are sitting on Lola's bed, heads close together, giggling at something in a book that's open on their knees, and her heart twists.

He's my father. Reynold Lyon is my father. And Luca and Lola are my little brother and sister, she thinks, and feels a rush of love and hate and sadness, all mixed up together. Despite what she said in her message to Reynold, she won't let them get hurt, not those two. She envies them, in a way; they have the childhood she never had – the stability, the love from their father. But it's not their fault. She doesn't want to see *any* of the children get hurt, although that might be inevitable if things don't go her way. But she'd stand in front of a gun for the twins, she's certain of that.

Lola looks up suddenly, as if she can sense she's being watched. She catches Cally's eye and smiles. Cally smiles back, and wonders what Petra, the exquisite model who bore these children for Reynold, will make of all this. Petra is lovely, Cally has always thought when she's met her at the school gates and at parents' evenings; as beautiful on the inside as she is on the outside. What will she think, when she hears that her husband once told a young woman to kill her baby – to kill *his* baby – and threatened her life too? What will Petra think when she finds out that Luca and Lola are not her husband's only offspring?

Well, we're all about to find out, Cally thinks, and as she does so she hears a quiet tap on the door above her, and her breath catches in her chest.

She jumps to her feet, and clambers unsteadily up the steps, the door opening as she does so. The Visitor is standing there, smiling, holding the phone out for her to see the notification on the screen.

It's in. They've paid. Oh my God. This is really happening, she thinks.

It's not the full amount, but it's nearly £2 million. There's a note attached to the payment too – an apology and a promise of more funds as soon as possible. It's enough, more than enough, for now. She gives The Visitor a thumbs up sign, and heads back down the stairs, seeing Oscar and Dominic's heads turn. She nods and takes a deep breath, trying to centre herself. It's nearly over, but this is the most dangerous part now, because finally Reynold knows who she is and why she's doing this, and she knows what he's capable of. He's ruthless, but she can be just as ruthless. Maybe she got that from him.

Don't underestimate me, she thinks, as she watches Oscar and Dominic making their way across the room towards her, delight and fear mingled in the expressions on their faces.

Don't underestimate me, daddy dearest. Because I'm a Lyon too. You never mess with a Lyon, human or animal, do you? And you're about to get your head bitten off.

Chapter Forty-Five

COTSWOLDS POLICE HEADQUARTERS

Day 7: Thursday, 4.30 p.m.

Sadie is coming back from the canteen, balancing a mug of tea and a plate bearing a late lunch consisting of a cheese and pickle sandwich curling at the edges, when she hears the shout.

'NO! They've paid the frigging money! The ransom. Shit. SHIT!'

It's Daniel, standing at a desk on the other side of the room and gesticulating wildly at her.

'What?'

Sadie dumps her mug and plate on the nearest flat surface and jogs over to him, as some of the other officers leap to their feet and others sink their heads into their hands and groan.

'What did you say? Who's that on the phone?'

Daniel holds out the handset, his expression a mix of fury and hopelessness.

'It's Eldon Beckford. They paid the money ten minutes ago. Here, you speak to him. I think I'm too angry to be civil.'

Sadie grabs it.

'Mr Beckford? It's Detective Superintendent Stewart. What's going on?'

'Hi. Yes, we've paid. I wasn't supposed to say anything, but… I thought you needed to know.'

The man sounds beaten, exhausted, but Sadie is, like Daniel, suddenly too furious to be kind.

'What the hell? After everything we talked about earlier? *Why?* You do realise this could scupper everything?'

'I know, I know… I'm so sorry, but look, when I tell you what happened…'

He pauses, and Sadie hits the loudspeaker button on the phone, aware that there are now a dozen people hovering around her, clearly desperate to find out what's going on.

'Please do. And *quickly*,' she says.

'OK.'

She hears Eldon clearing his throat.

'So, earlier, Reynold Lyon received a private message direct from the hostage takers. They told him they think the police – you – might know where they are, and so they'd decided to speed everything up, and they wanted the money straight away. They said if we didn't pay up, they'd kill the children. *Kill* them. And they said we couldn't tell you what we were doing. We got scared, you know? So me and Ben Townsend forwarded our share of the money to Reynold and he paid it. The three of us are covering the ransom, you see. We cobbled together just under £2 million in total. We're hoping it'll be enough. We should get a message telling us where the kids are in three hours' time, so not long after seven this evening. But…' Another pause. 'I'm not sure I trust Reynold. We've had a bit of a… well, a bit of a falling out. I mean, I don't think he'd mess with the kids' lives, but even so… I don't know why they'd send him a *private* message. It's a bit weird, you know? So I thought we *should* tell you. I want the kids back safe, but I don't want these shits to get away with it. And if you think you might know where they are… Anyway, that's it. I've told you. I haven't told anyone else I'm speaking to you, not even my wife…'

His voice tails off.

'Did Mr Lyon get any clue as to the identity of the hostage takers, or where they are right now, in this message he received?' Sadie snaps.

'No. Well, at least, if he did, he didn't say,' replies Eldon.

'OK. Well, thanks for letting us know. We'll get back to you. Stay at home, please. And if you hear anything else, call me immediately, do you understand?'

'Yes. Sorry, again.'

Sadie ends the call, and looks at the stunned faces all around her.

'How the hell do they know we might be on to them?' asks Daniel. 'Do we have a mole somewhere?'

'I don't know,' replies Sadie. 'And we might not even have the right location, remember? But wherever they are, right now they'll be transferring that money to some other account and if it's enough for them, if they think it's all they're going to get, they're going to be starting to move. If we have the right place, if it *is* Morcombe Manor – and I know it's a big if – then we have *one* chance to grab them before they make their getaway and it all gets way more complicated. We need to get up there, *now*. Shit, who's that?'

Her mobile phone is buzzing in her jacket pocket, and she pulls it out and looks at the display.

'Interesting,' she says. Then, 'Hello, Mr Lyon. Have you got news for me? Because a little bird has told me you've just handed over a rather large sum of money.'

'*What?* Who the—!'

She hears Reynold Lyon give a heavy sigh.

'Oh. Eldon Beckford, I presume. I suppose I don't blame him, after— Anyway, yes, I admit it. We've paid. Fine. I suppose you know about the threat to the children, too. Look, what I was calling about was to tell you that, well, I think I know what this is all about now. And I believe it's to do with me, nobody else. So I was wondering… If you're planning to head to a suspected location, is there any chance I could come along? I think if maybe I could speak to… to whoever is behind it, then I might be able to persuade them to… well, not to hurt anyone, for a start…'

'Do you *know* who's behind this, Mr Lyon?' Sadie says sharply.

'No… Look, we don't have any time to waste. Can I come, or not? I'm actually driving in your direction right now. I could meet you somewhere?'

'Oh, for God's sake. Fine. I'll message you the location.'

Sadie ends the call, and Daniel, who's been edging closer and closer to her as she's been talking to Reynold, gapes at her.

'*What* did you just do? Was that Reynold Lyon?'

'Yes. And he's coming with us. Yes, I *know*. I know that sounds ridiculous, but I'll explain on the way. Come on. We need to get out of here.'

Chapter Forty-Six

REYNOLD

Day 7: Thursday, 5.36 p.m.

Reynold drives, as instructed, through tall, rusty gates and round the first bend of a winding driveway and then turns left, bumping across the grass towards a densely wooded area. As he reaches it, he sees three marked police vehicles parked among the trees, and Detective Superintendent Sadie Stewart walking towards him, her face unsmiling, her mouth a tight line.

'Mr Lyon,' she says. 'Can you park there, please, next to that car? We need to stay out of sight of the entrance driveway. There are no signs of life up at the house right now but we have officers stationed discreetly all around it in case anyone who *might* be in there decides to make an exit. We're waiting for armed back-up and kidnap negotiators to arrive before we attempt to go inside. It shouldn't be more than half an hour.'

'What is this place?'

She doesn't reply, so Reynold parks where she's indicated

and gets out of his car. He can just see Morcombe Manor in the distance, a huge L-shaped Elizabethan mansion, its windows boarded up. Are his children really in there? Are they all right? He didn't tell anyone where he was going, not even Petra; he simply walked out of the house and drove off. They'll have to wait, all of them. He has no idea what's going to unfold here, and his stomach is churning, especially as now he's undoubtedly about to have to deal with a host of unwanted and very awkward questions. The police superintendent is looking at him curiously, eyes like lasers, and he has the most uncomfortable feeling that maybe she can see right into his head and knows exactly what he's thinking. Then he tells himself not to be so ridiculous, and looks away from her for a moment, trying to compose himself. DCI Daniel Sharma is a few paces away, tapping on his mobile phone, and he glances at Reynold and nods, then carries on with whatever he's doing.

'So. While we wait, would you like to tell me a little bit more about why you're here?' Sadie says. 'And why you now say this kidnap situation is in some way connected to *you*? Why were you sent a *private* message?'

She's still making him nervous, but she looks exhausted, Reynold thinks, as he tries to work out what to say in reply. She's an attractive woman, the dark hair and green eyes a striking combination, but her eyes look hooded and puffy today, the fine lines around them deeper.

'I'd rather not say, not in detail, not right now,' he says finally. 'But it's related to something that happened a really long time ago. Something I... well, something I did. I'm talking more than twenty-five years ago, and to be honest, I'd almost forgotten about it, which is why I never mentioned it before, but clearly... well, clearly, someone else hasn't.'

Sadie is staring intently at him now, and Daniel has moved closer too, his phone back in his pocket. There's a scuffling sound coming from somewhere nearby, a rabbit maybe, and although the day is warm, a breeze meanders between the trees heralding a colder evening to come. Reynold shivers.

'Something you did? And what was that, Mr Lyon? And who did you do it *to*? Who's behind this? We have a suspicion, but I want *you* to tell me. What's this about?' the policewoman asks.

Reynold swallows. His mouth feels dry.

'Oh, nothing illegal. What I did, I mean. Unethical, maybe, but not criminal. And I can't... I can't tell you who's involved. They've told me not to say. The children could get hurt if I do. Look, can we leave this for now?'

As he speaks, he's suddenly realising, maybe for the first time, that what he did probably *was* illegal. Of *course* it was illegal. Not asking the girl to have a termination, or even offering her cash to keep quiet about it and their affair – a bit dodgy, certainly, but not *criminal*. But what he did afterwards. Sending Jimmy, his boxer friend, to threaten her. To threaten her life, and that of her child, bullying her into what must have been, in retrospect, a petrified silence. A silence that lasted for *years*.

Christ.

At the time, he'd been dating the gorgeous Linda Arlingham, a move which had definitely catapulted him to even dizzier heights on the ladder to fame and fortune. As always, though, for some reason one woman hadn't been enough, and so he'd made what he now knew to be a hideous mistake. At the time, though, it had simply seemed like a bit of harmless fun: a few dates on the side with the pretty little runner who'd been flirting with him as they'd worked together on his latest show. What it had resulted in had horrified him, the very idea of fatherhood appalling. Threatening Julie had been a knee-jerk reaction, a way to protect himself, his high-profile relationship and his burgeoning career from what felt then like an impossible burden: a pregnant girlfriend, one he had no interest in a future with, and a child he had no desire to have in his life. But the *consequences*…

Had he really been *that* selfish back then? Obviously, he had. He'd never seen or heard from her again, but it *had* taught him a lesson: no more unprotected sex, no matter how drunk he was. No more unwanted babies. He'd never made *that* mistake again. He'd been well into his forties by the time he'd met Petra, the thought of finally settling down no longer so scary, and the thought of children to carry on the Lyon name had brought, to his astonishment, a frisson of joy for the first time instead of a shiver of distaste. When the twins had been born, they'd brought such happiness that he did wonder, briefly, about the other child, but he'd pushed the thought from his mind. It had been so long ago, and it was the future that mattered, not the past. Only now, that child – Cally Norman, his *daughter*! – has tracked him down and *taken* his other children, and he only has himself to blame. That was why as soon as he'd paid the ransom, he realised he couldn't just sit at home and wait. It would drive him insane. He needed to *do* something, needed to try to speak to her, to explain, to apologise, to do whatever it took to stop her hurting

Luca and Lola and the other kids. But how can he explain all that now, to the police? He can't; he *won't*. He still has a chance of keeping this secret, and so he doesn't care how many times he is asked about it. He's keeping his mouth shut.

'I'm not happy about this,' Sadie says, glaring at him. 'Why do you think you coming here can make a difference? It's such a risk, and we might not even have the right place, remember? And by paying that money, you've—'

The radio clipped to her jacket crackles suddenly, interrupting her, and she quickly takes a few steps away, listening, then whirls around.

'There's a van leaving the back of the property and heading down the driveway,' she says urgently. 'It was hidden inside an outbuilding – a man's just emerged from the house and got into it. He's on his way. Quick!'

'Keep back please, Mr Lyon,' says Daniel. They can hear the sound of an approaching engine now, and suddenly two of the parked police cars are on the move, backing out of the wooded area and turning sharply to face the driveway. Seconds later, a rusty-looking white van appears around the bend, moving quickly. It is, to Reynold's surprise, instantly familiar, but before he has time to process that thought and work out why he recognises it, everything seems to happen at once in a squeal of brakes and a cloud of gravel dust: the police cars pulling out into the path of the van in one smooth, co-coordinated movement, the van skidding to a halt, the driver's door opening and a man with a shocked expression on his face leaping out, three other officers jumping on him and wrestling him to the ground.

'Brandon? *Brandon?* What the hell?'

Reynold stares at the man wriggling on the driveway, one officer holding his legs, another pinning him down with a firm hand on his back.

'You *know* this man?' Sadie says.

'Yes. Yes, it's… it's Brandon. Brandon Simpson. He's the local handyman,' says Reynold, still staring, utterly confused. 'Well, ex-handyman now. He told me he was leaving earlier today. But I don't understand…'

'Ohh-kay,' says Sadie slowly.

She walks over and says something to the officers holding Brandon, and they nod and pull him roughly to his feet, two of them still keeping a firm grip on his arms.

'Over here,' Sadie says, and points to the wooded area. They all walk across, Brandon stumbling and swearing as he's dragged along with them, and when they're amongst the trees again Sadie says, 'So, Brandon Simpson, I believe? Can you tell me what you're doing here, Mr Simpson? And don't tell me you're here to do a few home repair jobs, please.'

Brandon scowls at her, his boyish, handsome face slick with sweat. Then he meets Reynold's eye for a long moment, before turning back to Sadie.

'Ah, sod it,' he says. '*He* knows what it's all about, and everyone will soon. The game is up. And the others have got the money now. I'll take what's coming to me. It's worth it to see him suffer.'

There's real venom in his voice, and Reynold feels a chill rippling down his back, as if someone's running a cold finger along his spine.

'OK, so you *both* know what's going on here, then? Can one of you please enlighten the rest of us?' says Sadie, her frustration clear, but Reynold ignores her, locking eyes with Brandon.

'We are in the right place then?' he asks quietly. 'The children are inside? Are they OK?'

Brandon hesitates for a few seconds, then nods.

'Yes, you're in the right place. I don't know how you figured it out. Very smart. And yes, they're fine,' he says, and Reynold hears Sadie give a small gasp. 'They won't be hurt unless it's really necessary... which it might be, now...'

He pauses again, the threat hanging in the air, and Reynold's stomach rolls.

'We've paid,' he says. 'Please, let them go.'

Brandon smiles, then his mouth twists into a mocking sneer.

'Yeah, but not really enough, you know? £2 million is a good start, but hey...'

'You *bastard*!'

Reynold can't help himself. He lunges at Brandon, aiming a punch at his face, but the two police officers react quickly, pulling the man out of his reach, and at the same time Daniel grabs Reynold from behind, bear-hugging him.

'Mr Lyon, please. We understand this is difficult, but that's not going to help,' he says. Reynold is breathing heavily, rage coursing through him, but he nods.

'OK. Sorry,' he mutters. Daniel releases him, then turns to Sadie.

'Shall we...?' he begins, but Reynold has taken a step towards Brandon again. He can't get his head around this. Fine, so Cally Norman is inside with his kids, with all the kids, and she's clearly the mastermind behind it all. But what of the other teachers? And why on earth is *Brandon* here?

'You. Why are *you* involved? Why are you helping her?' he says. 'How do you even *know* each other, for God's sake?'

Brandon glances in the direction of the mansion, then rolls his head from side to side slowly, as if his neck is stiff.

'Because she's my sister,' he says.

Chapter Forty-Seven

REYNOLD

Day 7: Thursday, 5.40 p.m.

There's a stunned silence.

'Your… your sister?' whispers Reynold. Suddenly, it all feels too much. His knees are beginning to quiver, a similar sensation to the one he gets when he's overdone leg day in the gym, and he wishes he could sit down, but there's nowhere to sit and anyway he can't take his eyes off Brandon, can't take this *in*.

'Can one of you confirm that it's Cally Norman, the Year 3 teacher, who's behind this?' asks Sadie, sounding exasperated. 'Is she who you're both talking about, or have we got this entirely wrong? Can someone *please* explain what's going on here?'

Reynold and Brandon both ignore her.

'But you have different surnames,' Reynold mutters feebly, realising even as the words leave his lips that it's a stupid thing to say. A name is the easiest thing in the world to fake, or to change by deed poll.

Brandon smiles his sneering smile again.

'Yeah, Simpson isn't my real name,' he says. 'But as you were all paying me cash in hand, it didn't really matter, did it? All declared to the tax man, obviously.'

He winks in Sadie's direction and Reynold sees her raise an eyebrow, but she says nothing.

'And as for your question about why I helped her, well, yes, because she's my big sister, and I love her, obviously. But also because you didn't just make *her* life shit, and our *mum's* life shit, with what you did. You made *my* life shit too. I never knew *my* dad either, because Mum was too scared to tell him she was pregnant, after what you did when *you* got her pregnant. She was terrified to trust another man for the rest of her life. And while you were living it up with all your money and your flash job, she never had the confidence to go back to working in TV. She was too scared of bumping into *you* again, so she ended up in a string of crappy jobs with crappy pay, and then she got into drugs, and we were in and out of foster homes, and it was *horrible*. She did her best. She was a brilliant mum on a good day. But then she got sick. She died when I was just sixteen – did Cally tell you that in her message? *Sixteen*. No dad, and then no mum. And that's your fault, you wanker.'

'I'm sorry. I'm so sorry,' whispers Reynold.

'Hang on – have I got this right?' Sadie says. She sounds bemused.

'Mr Lyon, you got his mother pregnant? And the child was Cally Norman?'

'That's what it sounds like to me,' says Daniel.

'Me too,' says one of the two officers holding Brandon's arms. They're both looking from him to Reynold and back again, seemingly transfixed.

'Yes,' says Reynold quietly.

'And so… so she's your daughter. And your twins are her half-brother and half-sister? And you really didn't know this until now? Wow.'

Sadie is shaking her head. She runs a hand through her hair and exchanges looks with Daniel, who's looking equally baffled, then says, 'So is that what this is about? To punish you for abandoning her mother? That seems extraordinary. What else did you do? There must be more to it, surely? I just don't get it. Why take *all* the kids? And are the other teachers involved too? Oscar Jones and Dominic Moore? Why would *they* help her?'

'I'm sure Reynold here will explain why he's being punished,' says Brandon. 'And Cally's dating Dominic. Has been for a while. He loves her. As for Oscar – well, you'd have to ask *him* why he got involved. Not my place to say.'

He shrugs, and Reynold risks a glance at Sadie, who's looking at him expectantly, but before he can say anything Brandon speaks again.

'You know what though? Let me just tell you something. I came to Littleford at Cally's request, to act as the guy on the outside, kinda thing, when all this kicked off. She recommended me to the MacDonald-Cooks when she heard they were looking for a handyman, and they recommended me to the Pearsons, and then I started doing the Beckfords. It tends to work like that in my job, which is useful when you're using a false name. You don't want too many background checks, you know? And then, finally, you needed some work doing too, and your lovely wife took me on. And when I say your lovely wife... Petra *is* lovely, by the way. Far too good for you. Your kids are lovely too. And actually, for a while I thought *you* were OK. Not as bad as Cally thought you were, anyway. I thought maybe you'd changed. You were always friendly, always nice to me, bit extra in my pay packet here and there. And, you know what? Only a couple of weeks ago I suddenly started to wonder if we were doing the right thing after all, even asked Cally if she was sure, you know? If maybe doing all this to you was going too far. I said maybe she should just come and talk to you, tell you who she is. But then you screwed up. You screwed up big time.'

'How? What do you mean?'

Reynold's voice emerges as a hoarse croak, and he swallows, then wishes he hadn't asked the question. He's already dreading the answer. Brandon stares at him, and for a few moments there's almost complete silence, the only sound the rustling of leaves overhead. Everyone is standing stock still, eyes glued to the drama unfolding so unexpectedly in this little clump of trees.

'The Beckfords's party,' says Brandon.

Oh bugger. Bugger, thinks Reynold, and suddenly there's a heaviness in his chest, as if someone's dropped a weight into his breast pocket.

'It was really nice of them to invite me, and it was a great night, wasn't it? Well, you certainly enjoyed it. I saw you together, you see. You and Amy Beckford, out in the summer house,' Brandon continues. 'It was pretty obvious it wasn't the first time that had happened.'

'Whaaaaat?' Reynold hears Daniel murmur, but he doesn't look at him. He doesn't want to look at *anyone*.

'And I just thought, well, he *hasn't* changed, has he? Beautiful wife and kids at home, and screwing his mate's wife. Still a selfish pig. And so I told Cally I was definitely in. And here we are.'

Reynold wipes a hand across his damp forehead. He has no idea what to say or do, and he can feel his cheeks burning. He opens his mouth and closes it again, and then, to his relief, Sadie takes a step forward.

'Well, this is all very interesting,' she says. 'Fascinating, in fact. But I think the chat can wait for now. Where were you going when we caught you leaving, Brandon? What's going on in there right now? And can you tell me exactly what your role has been in all of this? You said you've been "the guy on the outside"? What does that mean?'

Brandon shakes his head, clamping his lips tightly together in an exaggerated fashion for a moment, then says, 'I can't tell you what's going on in there. I'm sorry. But there is one thing I want to talk about: Erica Lindsay.'

'It was *you*?' asks Sadie.

He nods, and his shoulders sag.

'Yes. I was the one who hijacked the bus,' he says, his eyes downcast, his voice much quieter suddenly. 'It was all planned for so long. Dominic messed with the real school bus the night before, so they'd have to rent a replacement without a tracker, to buy us more time. He'd been keeping an eye on Arnie's fleet of minibuses, and he knew there was usually one free, so we should be able to get one fairly quickly. Then he put on a show for Erica when she noticed the warning light on the Mercedes. She was the only one not in on it; Cally tried to persuade her not to go on that trip, but she insisted, and Cally thought she'd think it was weird if she kept telling her she wasn't needed, so she gave up. In the end we thought actually it might be more believable anyway, if one person was left behind and could tell everyone it was a real kidnap. Anyway, Erica was driving, so Cally suggested she turn off the main road on the way back because they were running late – she persuaded Erica it was a shortcut that would help them avoid rush-hour traffic. Then I leapt out of a hedge waving a gun – it was a fake one, I bought it online – and they all screamed at Erica to pull over, and… Anyway, we'd bought three cheap cars, little runarounds we got with false ID documents, and between us we'd parked them in the layby next to the field the day before. We got the kids off the bus and into the cars and all that pretty easily. They all thought it was a game, you know? I'd tied Erica up in the bus while the others did that, and the plan was that I was supposed to just rough her up a little bit before I left. Nothing major, just enough to make the cops – you guys – believe it was a real attack. And then… I don't know what happened…'

His head is drooping now, as if he can no longer hold it up, his voice low and hesitant.

'Go on,' says Sadie quietly.

'I don't know if it was adrenalin, or the fear that someone might come along any minute and catch me, or… or what. But once I started hitting her… I couldn't stop. It was like… a *frenzy* or something. I hit her and then I hit her again and I kicked her and… *Jesus.* It was awful. I've never done anything like that, *ever*. A minute later I sort of came to my senses and stopped, but... it was too late. I knew she was really badly injured. I drove away and I felt the worst I've ever felt in my life. And then we heard she'd died, and... oh, Christ. I was devastated. We all were. She didn't deserve that. So, yeah. Lock me up. But you can take some of the blame for that too, Lyon. It wouldn't have happened if it wasn't for you. None of this would. You think about that.'

He's looking Reynold straight in the eye again, and Reynold remembers Petra telling him how Brandon had tears in his eyes when he came in from the garden for a chat on Monday and heard that Erica had died in hospital. He feels his throat constricting.

He's right. This is all on me. Dear God, what have I done?

'Thank you for being so frank,' Sadie says suddenly, all business-like again. 'We'll obviously have to take a proper statement later, and I'm hoping for your full cooperation?'

Brandon nods, and Sadie turns to Daniel.

'How far away are the firearms officers? We need to get in there, quickly.'

'Still about twenty minutes,' says Daniel. 'They're moving as quickly as they can, but it was such short notice. There's one helicopter coming, but the rest are on the road.'

'Damn,' she says, then turns to Brandon again.

'They're still there, right? Cally and the others? And the children?'

He nods.

'They won't be able to get away now. I was going out to stock up on some supplies for them before they leave. The cars we used to get here are stashed in outbuildings at the back, but if you have the place surrounded and block off the exits, there's no way they can get out. I'm just worried… I'm just scared that if Cally realises you're here already, she might… well, something bad might happen. And you won't be able to talk her out of it, trust me. She won't speak to you, or to any negotiators or whoever you're waiting for. I know Cally. This is a bad situation now, and I don't want anyone else to get hurt. I couldn't bear it…'

His voice tails off, and Reynold, who's been listening with a growing feeling of suspicion, looks at Sadie and wonders if she's feeling as sceptical as he is.

This sudden confession… why is Brandon telling them all this?

Reynold thinks he's quite good at reading people; years of interviewing everyone from politicians to career criminals on television has given him a sixth sense about when someone isn't being entirely genuine, and that sense is flashing him a warning right now. But at the same time, what if the man is right? What if, when Cally realises the police are outside, she does the unthinkable?

'Look, let me go in there,' he says.

He can feel his heart starting to pound.

'Let me talk to Cally. That's why I came. Let me try to explain, try to apologise to her, whatever she wants. We can't wait for your back-up to arrive. It's too risky. *Please.* Isn't it worth a try?'

'I think he's right,' says Brandon. 'It might work. Look, what have you got to lose? I've been straight with you, I've told you everything, and I'm willing to take my punishment for what I did. I'm not going to go in there and top myself or anything. I'll bring him in. Just give us ten minutes, if you like. Leave your guys at all the exits. If any of them come in with us, she'll freak, I'm telling you now. Those kids will not be safe. I know it's hard, after what I've just told you, but if you could just trust me on this? Take a chance? Because it might be our only hope of getting them all out alive.'

Sadie and Daniel exchange glances.

'We could ask…?' Daniel says hesitantly, but Brandon shakes his head.

'Don't. You know what they'll say. They'll tell you not to let us do it. And this is worth trying. It *is*. I know her better than anyone.'

There's a long pause, Sadie looking from Reynold to Brandon and back again, indecision written all over her face. Then she takes a deep breath.

'OK. I must be insane, but maybe it'll buy us some time, at least. Let's do it.'

Chapter Forty-Eight

CALLY

Day 7: Thursday, 5.55 p.m.

If seeing The Visitor – her little brother, Brandon – back at the door to The Bunker so soon is a surprise, it's nothing compared to the shock of seeing who's standing there with him. At first, Cally thinks the extreme stress of this last risk-filled day has finally taken its toll and she's beginning to hallucinate. When she sees the sheepish, apologetic look on Brandon's face though, and tries to focus on what he's saying instead of gaping at Reynold Lyon, she quickly realises that this is all too real. Something has gone horribly wrong. She stares at them both for a moment, then bounds up the top few steps of the stairs and out of The Bunker.

It doesn't even matter if the kids see me walking out now, she thinks. *This is nearly over anyway.*

'The police are here, Cally. They caught me driving out,' her brother is saying. 'I have no idea how they worked out you're

336

here, but he was here too, and they've let me come back in with him' – he jerks a thumb in Reynold's direction – 'because he wanted to talk to you, face to face. Look, there are cops on all the exits. Not many, yet, but there are more on their way. There's no way out now. I had to tell them everything. I'm so sorry. They know you're planning to use the cars to get away, and they're going to block your path. I've warned them you'll... well, you know, if they try to stop you, and that's why they agreed to let me come back inside, but we don't have long. So we're both here to say, please don't do anything stupid. You don't want anyone else to die, do you? One was enough, Cally. Please, just give it up now. There's no way out of this. It's over. It's done.'

He sounds desperate, on the verge of tears, but as he speaks Cally is beginning to understand what's going on here, and when he gives her the tiniest of winks, her panic begins to subside.

Ohhhh. You're clever. Clever, clever, clever. Well done, little brother.

She buries her face in her hands for a few moments, buying herself some time, working out how to play this. Then she looks up, and gives a little groan.

'I can't believe this... right at the last minute...' she stutters. 'But... OK. You're right. I don't want anyone else to get hurt. I give up. Look, you go down and tell Oscar and Dom what's happening. It doesn't matter if the children see you now, does it, if the police already know you're involved? Go. I'll be all right.'

Brandon hesitates for a moment, looking from her to

Reynold and back again, then nods and slips through the door to The Bunker. Cally watches him go, then takes a deep breath and turns to Reynold. The man looks rough, his usually neatly styled hair unbrushed and greasy-looking, his eyes bloodshot.

He's suffering, she thinks. *Good.*

'What do you want? And be quick, please.'

She knows her voice sounds cold and hard, and she sees him flinch.

'Are they OK?' he asks, his voice rasping as if his throat is raw. 'Luca and Lola? You haven't hurt them?'

'No, I haven't hurt them. They're my half-siblings, for God's sake. And if that's all you've come to ask me, you can fuck off right now. You're a disgusting human being, and I'm ashamed that I share any DNA with you at all. But an apology might be nice right now. It's too late for you to say sorry to my mother for the nightmare you put her through. But you could at least say sorry to *me*…'

She pauses. Reynold is holding out his hands, reaching for her, and she backs away, suddenly wondering if she's gone too far, if maybe he's about to *attack* her, not apologise to her. She gropes behind her, trying to locate the door, ready to run through it and slam it in his face, but then she hears a whimper and realises with a shock that he's crying, fat tears rolling down his tanned cheeks.

'I'm sorry. I am so, so sorry, Cally,' he whispers, and he drops his hands to his sides, his shoulders slumping. 'If I could turn back the clock…'

'Well, you can't,' she snaps. She has a sudden strange urge to take his hand, to try to stop his tears, but she can't – she knows that. She has to stay strong, stay angry.

'Do you have any idea how hard it was, growing up with no father and with a mother who was scared of her own shadow? You destroyed her. She had so little confidence... She could have had a great career, if it wasn't for you. Instead she took drugs and got herself in trouble over and over again and then she died. I was eighteen. *Eighteen*. And there was you, with all your money and fame, not giving a damn. I'm your *daughter*. You *knew* she wasn't going to have a termination. And yet you never tried to find me, did you? You're *scum*.'

'I'm sorry. I don't know what else to say,' he whispers weakly, and wipes his eyes with the backs of his hands. 'But this... why all this? Why not just come and find *me*? It's not like I'd have been hard to track down. I would have helped you out; I would have given you money. You didn't need to do all this.'

'Really? Seriously? After what you did to Mum, you think I'd trust you? You could have done the same thing to me, sent some thug after me, had me killed to keep your sordid little secret, couldn't you?'

He's shaking his head, mumbling, 'I wouldn't. I'm different now...' but she ignores him.

'And as for money – just under £2 million? Is that all I'm worth? Is that all protecting yourself from everyone knowing what you really are is worth? Because this has made headlines everywhere, I know that. Do you really want the whole world knowing what you did? I'll take the two-ish million, for now. But I want the rest. You have two weeks from today. I'll send you new bank details as soon as I can, once we're out of here safely. Because we *will* still be getting out of here safely, by the way. You're as stupid as the police clearly are. Brandon did very well, out there, telling them a crock of lies about our exit plans. So, is that clear? Two weeks, or I spill.'

Reynold's mouth has fallen open, and there's a dazed look in his eyes, but he sniffs and nods.

'OK,' he says. 'I can do that. There just wasn't time. But please, please don't hurt the children. Any of them. *Please*.'

'Oh, stop whining,' she says. 'I won't hurt anyone. You just need to stay here now and shut up, OK? Until we're out of here.'

'But… but the police have only given us ten minutes,' Reynold says falteringly. 'We need to go back out. Brandon needs to come with me, or—'

'No, he'll be coming with us,' Cally replies sharply. 'Please, just shut up for a minute. I need to *think*.'

She leans against the wall behind her, closing her eyes briefly, a wave of exhaustion washing over her.

It's still going to work. It will still be OK. The money's been transferred to a safe account. We just need to move, and quickly…

She opens her eyes. Reynold is leaning against the wall opposite, eyes fixed on his shoes, and even though the urge to flee is now all-consuming, Cally suddenly has the most peculiar desire to rush over to him, to shake him, to tell him how hard this past week has been, to tell him how long she's been planning all this and how difficult it was.

Why do I feel like this? she wonders. *Do I want praise for what I've done, like a small child? Praise from my daddy? What's wrong with me?*

She shudders. But she's still fighting the compulsion to tell him; to tell him how she first came up with the idea for this particular location when she was writing her thesis and decided to ask the elderly owner, Lady Frazer, if she could possibly have a tour of the property. How Lady Frazer – Eleanora – a sweet, lonely woman of eighty, had seemed to take an immediate shine to her, and was delighted to share some of the secrets of her once so grand home; how, when she heard several years later that Eleanora had died, and then discovered that Morcombe Manor had been left empty and falling into disrepair, her mind had begun to whirr. She wants to tell Reynold how one middle-of-the-night, very careful break-in later, with the help of Brandon, the cellar door and one exterior door had new secure locks. And she wants to tell him how they prepared for months, the four of them. So many shopping trips to different stores in different towns, gathering everything they needed: air beds, blankets, clothes, toys. The stash of cheap burner phones, so she could write messages, Brandon destroying and disposing of each phone on his way back to Littleford each day. So much *stuff*, and so many clandestine trips to the manor house under cover of darkness to clean the cellar and prepare it for its visitors.

She looks over at Reynold again, but he's still avoiding her gaze. She wonders what he'd think if she told him how she felt last Friday, the day her plans finally, *finally*, came to fruition; the excitement combined with gut-wrenching fear when they rounded the bend in the road and saw Brandon, unrecognisable in a black hat and ski-mask, and heard poor Erica slamming her foot on the brakes of the minibus and screaming in terror; the horror they all felt when Brandon confessed he'd taken his planned assault on Erica too far, and the devastation when he brought the news that she'd died; his terror that the police would find some of his DNA on her body and somehow track him down, although it seemed he'd got lucky there. Cally, in her meticulous planning, had thought she'd considered every eventuality, but an accidental murder hadn't even entered her head. Fortunately, the prospect of the police searching this house when they were inside had; that was why she'd decided that, unpleasant and claustrophobic as it might be for an entire week, being locked inside the cellar was the safest place to be. When, on day two, she'd heard footsteps overhead, the faint shouts of the search team, she'd held her breath, but nobody had rattled the hidden door inside the pantry cupboard, and she'd laughed out loud with relief when, half an hour later, all was silent again.

But now, of course, somehow the police have worked out where they are. She really hadn't thought that would happen, for some reason. She wants to ask Reynold if he knows how they did it, but she can hear footsteps, someone climbing back up the stairs of The Bunker – more than one set of footsteps, which means it's nearly time. Time to make use of something else Eleanora told her about, all those years ago. A secret about Morcombe Manor that she's pretty sure nobody else knows, and one that certainly doesn't show up on any of the building's floor plans or documents. A secret that Eleanora gleefully shared with Cally, the eager young history student she spent such a pleasant afternoon with, talking about her beloved home. A secret that's going to save them, and get them out of here, undetected.

I'm going to leave you now, Daddy dearest, Cally thinks, as she sees Reynold lifting his head and meeting her eye for a second, then shifting his gaze to the cellar door. *And the police won't be able to stop me, however many armed officers they have out there, because there's no plan whatsoever to leave by car, of course. That would have been REALLY stupid.*

She turns as Brandon appears, closely followed by Oscar and Dominic. They're both carrying small rucksacks; Dominic has two and holds one out to Cally.

'This is yours,' he says, and she smiles and takes it.

'Thank you. Are you ready? The kids are OK? You've told them someone will be coming for them soon?'

'Yep,' he says. 'All done and I'm ready to rock. But I'm not sure Oscar and Brandon are. There's something they want to do first.'

'What?' Cally says. She turns to look at the two men, and sees that they're both staring at Reynold, who's still standing against the wall opposite, an uneasy expression on his face now.

'What's going on?' he asks.

Oscar gives him a withering glance, then turns back to Cally.

'You go, with Dom,' he says. 'We'll be right behind you. We just want to have a little word with *Daddy* here first. Give him something to remember us by.'

He sounds so calm, his tone so measured, but Cally instantly understands what he means, and her jaw clenches.

Is that what I want? Isn't what we've done to him enough? And there's still more to come, when we tell the world what he's really like. Do we need to do this, as well?

The thoughts race around her brain, but then she looks at

Reynold and the doubts vanish as quickly as they came. Why should she show him any mercy, after what he did?

'Do what you have to do,' she says. 'But be quick. We don't have long. Come on, Dom.'

She gives Reynold one final scornful look, and then walks out of the room, not looking back.

Chapter Forty-Nine

SADIE

Day 7: Thursday, 6.05 p.m.

Outside, Sadie is getting twitchy. It's been just over ten minutes since Brandon led Reynold into the manor house – ten minutes and forty-five seconds, to be precise – and while she's very aware that not everyone is as obsessive about timekeeping as she is, she was very much hoping that this time, ten minutes would *mean* ten minutes. She's pretty sure that Brandon will bring Reynold out again – the man spilled his guts, after all, told them everything, and seemed so keen to make amends. But what if she's misjudged this? What if Brandon is attacking Reynold in there right now, or hurting *himself* in some way, despite what he said? He must know he's facing a long prison sentence for what he did to Erica, as well as for his role in the kidnap. Maybe he's decided he can't handle that after all, and has chosen a different way to end this?

Have I made a huge mistake? Where ARE they? Sadie thinks desperately. Her eyes are fixed so firmly on the door through which Brandon and Reynold disappeared that they've started to hurt. She blinks a few times, and looks for a moment instead at the probably once beautiful formal garden at the front of the house, now grossly overgrown, filled with towering weeds and brambles. Then she turns back to the door, which is flanked by two officers, and resumes the staring.

But what else could she do, if it was true that Cally had plans to start killing the children? Reynold *might* be able to get through to her. He *might* be able to persuade her to let them go, and if Sadie *had* told the kidnap negotiators they *would* have said no, so what then? The loss of a chance to resolve this quickly, with no more bloodshed. She feels a little sick though, about what they're going to say when they arrive – any minute now, according to Daniel – and they find out what she's done; when they hear about the risk she's taken. She feels a little sick about a lot of things right now. About the fact she didn't take the idea of any of the teachers being involved in this seriously enough, and focussed so much attention on the parents: Monique Townsend and her peculiar behaviour, following the children to the wildlife park; Reynold Lyon and his new game show that *coincidentally* opened with a load of people on a bus. It *was* just a coincidence, wasn't it? And Monique's odd behaviour was just that – the odd behaviour of a clearly unwell woman.

She still doesn't understand all of it. OK, so Cally is Reynold's daughter, and out for revenge for whatever reason, and Brandon is involved because he's her brother, and

346

Dominic because he's her boyfriend. But why is Oscar Jones part of this? They're probably all friends, as people of a similar age who work together often are. But to join in with something as huge as this, as *criminal* as this? *Is* it just for the money? The chance to make many times a teacher's annual salary for a single week's work?

Maybe, but it still doesn't really add up, Sadie thinks.

Cally and Oscar can't even have known each other that long; as far as she can recall, they both joined Littleford Primary last year, a few months apart. Why would he help her with something like this? She thinks about Brandon's vague answer when *he* was asked about Oscar – *You'd have to ask him why he got involved. Not my place to say* – then pushes the questions from her mind. She can worry about it later, and she knows there will be a *lot* to worry about later. The press, for a start; they're going to have a field day when they find out that the 'kidnapped' teachers are actually the hostage takers. What a story. What a *shambles*.

'One minute, boss. They're nearly here. And I'm not liking this situation now. How long has it been?'

Sadie looks at her watch.

'Thirteen minutes. No, I'm not liking it either. I can hardly bear to say this, Dan, but I think something's going on in there. I think I made the wrong call.'

She swallows hard, feeling suddenly, humiliatingly, as if she might burst into tears. Daniel puts a hand on her sleeve.

'It was an impossible call to judge,' he says softly. 'Damned if you do and damned if you don't. It was worth a gamble.'

She nods, not trusting herself to speak. Seconds later she

hears sirens, distant at first, then growing louder, and Daniel looks over his shoulder towards the driveway, then back at her, sliding his fingers down her arm to squeeze her hand.

'Here comes the cavalry,' he says.

Chapter Fifty

REYNOLD

Day 7: Thursday, 6.08 p.m.

Oscar lands the first punch. His fist connects with Reynold's jaw, and Reynold staggers backwards, a white-hot starburst of pain making him gasp.

'Please…' he stutters, but Oscar is coming towards him again, and this time it's a blow to the stomach, and now Brandon is there too, kicking him behind the knees. He groans, clutching his belly, then crumples to the ground, moving one hand to his head, instinctively trying to protect his skull. A foot swings into his ribs, then another makes contact with his nose, and Reynold hears a crunch and feels a gush of blood.

'You've broken my nose!' he screams, and he rolls over on the cold, hard floor, trying to get away from the stabbing feet, the pain exploding in his head. He finds the wall and pushes his legs under him, and suddenly, somehow, he's upright again, whirling around to face his two attackers, his breathing ragged, blood sticky on his lips.

'Ready for round two?' says Oscar nastily, and Reynold holds up his fists, but his arms are shaking, his legs wobbly, and he knows that if they start hitting him again he's not going to last long. He's fit and strong, but he's fifty-five and there's only one of him; these two are half his age, and he's feeling dizzy now, black spots dancing in front of his eyes. He wonders if he might black out, and what they'll do if he does.

They'll kill me, he finds himself thinking. *I came here to try to make things better, and instead I'm actually going to die. God, the irony...*

'Why, Oscar?'

He barely recognises the husky, guttural noise as his own voice, but at the sound of his name Oscar, who's been moving slowly towards Reynold again, stops.

'Why?' Reynold repeats, then coughs as blood slides down his throat. 'Why are *you* doing this? I don't understand...'

Oscar takes a breath, as if he's about to reply, and then he spins around, as they all hear the sound at the same time. Sirens. Police sirens, growing louder by the second. Brandon and Oscar lock eyes.

'We've got to get out of here,' says Brandon urgently. 'Now. Leave him. He's not worth it.'

Oscar hesitates.

'OK. I'm coming. Just one more...'

He marches back across the small space, and Reynold sees pure, cold hatred in his eyes, and his throat constricts with fear. Why is this man looking at him like this? But now there's no time to wonder anymore, because Oscar is swinging his arm back, the fist clenched, ready to smash it into some part of Reynold again, and he's suddenly not sure if his body can take another assault, and so he does the only thing he can think of to do. He ducks and, to his amazement, Oscar, seemingly not expecting that, slams his fist into the wall instead and then, off balance, tilts forward slightly at the same time as Reynold rushes him, using all his body weight to push the younger man backwards. Oscar crashes to the ground like a felled tree, the back of his head hitting the floor with a sickening crack.

Breathing heavily, Reynold straightens up slowly and, his vision still blurred, tries to focus on Brandon, who's crouching down next to Oscar, a horrified look on his face.

'Oscar. *Oscar*. Jesus Christ, this can't be happening. OSCAR!'

He's shaking the other man, grabbing his shoulders and shouting his name, but Oscar, even though his eyes are wide open, looks limp, and his head lolls to one side. Brandon bellows his name once more, then moans, like an animal in pain, and stands up, still watching the motionless figure on the ground as he backs towards the door.

'You've killed him,' he whispers, and Reynold realises he's crying, his voice thick with emotion. 'You've *killed* him.'

'I–I didn't…' he stutters, but Brandon is gone, the doorway empty; the sound of running footsteps echoes down the corridor and then fades to nothing. Reynold swipes a hand across his face and feels the bones in his nose moving, blood still dripping down his chin. The pain is almost unbearable, shooting through his skull like a burning arrow, and he crumples to his knees and whimpers, but he knows he has to check, has to find out, so he crawls, hands slippery with sweat, towards the body on the ground, the body that's still silent and unmoving.

'Oscar? Oscar?' he whispers.

Nothing. He moves a few inches closer, trying to see a twitch, an eyelid flicker, *anything*.

Can this be real? Is he dead? But he can't be... I just pushed him. He banged his head. It was nothing. I didn't mean to hurt him, I was just trying to protect myself...

Reynold groans, then crawls closer still, his whole body shaking, and leans over Oscar. He smells stale, the odour a combination of unwashed clothing and sweat, and his T-shirt is stained with spilled food maybe. Reynold stares at the man's chest, but there's no movement, no sign that he's breathing.

'Oscar! Oscar, *please...*'

In desperation, Reynold pokes the teacher viciously in the side, in the soft space under his ribs, but there's no reaction, no flinch or grunt of pain, and suddenly there's no doubt.

He's dead. He's really dead. I've actually killed somebody. Oh my God, oh my God...

And then he hears a noise and jumps violently. It's not a sound being emitted by the now very obviously dead body in front of him though; it's coming from behind him, from the door to the cellar, and he turns slowly, his heart suddenly beating so hard he can hear it pounding in his ears. The door is opening, inch by inch, creaking gently as it does so. And then there's a face, the eyes blinking, the expression confused, and a voice so familiar, so loved, that Reynold feels his heart racing even faster, until he thinks his chest might actually burst, but from joy now, not fear.

'Daddy?' says the voice. 'Is that you? Did you win the game, Daddy? Can we go home now?'

Chapter Fifty-One

REYNOLD

Day 10: Sunday, 3.10 p.m.

'**D**addy! Can we go out in the garden? All of us?'

Luca tugs at Reynold's sleeve, and Reynold touches his son's cheek, smiling down at him. He still can't quite believe the twins are home again, and that everything feels so… *normal*. OK, maybe normal isn't quite the right word. So much has changed in the past ten days, as if the world has tilted on its axis, and all the pieces of Littleford life have been shuffled around and put back together again in slightly different places. But even so, compared to the days that immediately followed the disappearance of Class 3B, this is bliss. This is *heaven*.

'Of course. Shoo!' he says.

Luca grins and shouts, 'Come on! Let's go!'

There's a mad exodus through the open French windows, Noah Beckford and Luca leading the stampede, Lola linking arms with Luke Carr and Harper Duggan and skipping out behind them. Next comes Gresham Greer, Oliver MacDonald-Cook and Wanda Pearson, tussling over a football, and then, bringing up the rear, Stanley Tustain and Willow Townsend, hand in hand, heads close together, chatting earnestly.

Reynold watches them all spilling out into the sunny garden where earlier he'd arranged an Easter Egg hunt, for today, of course, is Easter Sunday. It's why he suggested inviting everyone round, just to mark the occasion, now they've all had some time to reacclimatise, to hold the children close and assess the astonishing amount of damage the past days have wrought; to regroup, and try to move forward.

'Look at them. They can't get enough of each other,' says a voice beside him, and Reynold turns to see Clare Tustain watching Stanley and Willow with a smile on her face. 'They'd always been pally,' she'd told the group earlier, as they updated each other on how things had been since the families were reunited. 'But now they know they're siblings – well, half-siblings – they're obsessed. They had so many questions, mind you. Some uncomfortable ones, as you can imagine.'

She'd looked guiltily at her husband, Nick, and he had rolled his eyes.

They're splitting up, but it seems to be amicable enough, considering what's happened, Reynold had thought while watching the exchange.

'They also wanted to know why their skin colour is different, if they're sister and brother, so we had to give them a bit of a genetics lesson,' Ben said. 'We had to try to explain that Monique is a black mummy and I'm a white daddy so Willow's skin is a bit darker than Stan's, because Clare and I are both white. And then they decided they weren't interested anyway, because it's so nice to have a sibling, apparently.'

He had smiled affectionately at Clare, who had smiled back, and Reynold then looked across to where Monique was sitting next to Vanessa Carr, sipping tea for once instead of wine. Her face was expressionless, but she looked calm; content almost.

Maybe getting her daughter back is enough to make up for losing her husband, Reynold had thought. *I hope she'll be OK. I hope we all will.*

Now, he watches the children haring around the garden for another minute, then picks up a champagne bottle and tours the kitchen, refilling glasses. It's been amazing, how well the kids seem to be recovering, astounding their traumatised parents with their cheerful acceptance of what's happened, even when it was carefully explained to them that their week in 'The Bunker', as they apparently christened it, wasn't a big game at all, which is what they'd been told, but something orchestrated by their teachers in order to blackmail their parents into parting with a large sum of money. They had been, it seemed, extremely well looked after during their week underground, and although they emerged grubby and very keen to get back to their own bedrooms, pets and parents, they had slipped seamlessly back into their normal lives. They've even rather enjoyed seeing their faces in the newspapers and all over the TV news as the world celebrates their safe return, although a child psychologist working with the police has warned the families that things could change, and to be aware of any symptoms of post-traumatic stress disorder further down the line. But for the moment, the children seem relatively unscathed; it's the parents who are still finding themselves unable to sleep, repeatedly waking and rushing into their offspring's rooms, checking that they're still there, safe and peaceful in their beds.

Reynold has had constant nightmares, a bloody scene replaying over and over in his dreams. The body, still and lifeless, on the cold stone floor; and Luca's face, peering around the cellar door, full of delight to see his father, then his eyes widening in horror as he sees the blood, and the slumped form of his teacher on the ground.

Reynold had yelled at him to go back inside, just for a few minutes, telling him that everything was fine, and Luca had obeyed, pulling the door shut behind him. Reynold had staggered out of the pantry then, somehow retracing his steps to the door to the outside world and stumbling into the arms of a shocked-looking Detective Superintendent Stewart. After that, everything had been a bit of a blur: a stampede of armed officers, a flashing blue light, an ambulance, the antiseptic smell of a too-bright hospital room. And then the police, and the questions about why there was a dead man lying outside the cellar door.

Reynold touches his nose gingerly as he heads back to the fridge to retrieve another bottle. The broken bone will, he's been told, heal naturally in a few weeks, although it will never look quite the same.

'I think it will suit you, actually,' the young doctor who treated him said. 'It gives you a bit of a rugged look. But you can always have a nose job later on, if you don't like it.'

Reynold, to his surprise, has realised he doesn't remotely care what his nose looks like. Initially, he was more concerned about Luca and his reaction to seeing his father's bloody injuries and his teacher's fatal ones. But again, the little boy has amazed him, simply saying in an extraordinarily grown-up fashion, 'If he was hurting you, Daddy, you *had* to fight him, didn't you? It wasn't your fault he banged his head. It was an accident, like the time I accidentally kicked Noah in the stomach when he got too close to me when I was on the swing. Don't worry about it.'

To Reynold's immense relief, the police seem to have taken a similar stance, putting the death of Oscar Jones down as manslaughter carried out in self-defence; they've told him he's unlikely to be charged. The only people they do hope to charge one day, if they can find them, are Cally Norman, Brandon Simpson – not Simpson at all, in fact – and Dominic Moore. There's an international manhunt going on for the trio, but they seem to have vanished without trace. Nobody has yet managed to work out how they escaped from the manor house undetected, with so many people surrounding the place, although Reynold knows that this weekend a team of police officers has been searching the building, inch by inch, trying to find out how they did it.

Oh, she's a clever one, my daughter, Cally, he thinks, as he pops the cork from the fresh bottle, and feels a peculiar rush of something resembling pride. He's thought, briefly, of demanding a DNA test when he next hears from her, for he only has her word that she's his. She doesn't look like him at all, but maybe she resembles her mother; to his shame, Reynold struggles to remember what Julie even looked like. But if she's not his, how else would she know everything she knows about what happened back then? She *is* his daughter. He has little doubt about that.

If only things had been different. If only she'd talked to him, instead of doing what she did. Maybe they could have actually got on. Maybe she could have become part of his family. Maybe he could have made amends, and maybe she could have forgiven him, one day.

But it's too late now, and it's Petra he needs to focus on. She's softened since the twins returned, even, just briefly, hugging Reynold hard when he returned from the hospital.

'Thank you, for getting them back,' she whispered. The hug had squished his broken nose, but he'd suppressed his groan of agony. He deserves to feel pain – he knows that. He's told her everything now, about Cally and her mother and what he did, and she's still here, which gives him hope. Luca and Lola don't know, though. Both Reynold and Petra feel it's too much to explain right now. Too complicated. Possibly one day, when they're older. The police know the full story, but Reynold hasn't had the courage to tell the other parents, not yet. For now, he's simply said that the kidnapping happened because of him after all, and that it was due to something he did a very, very long time ago. He's promised to tell them all about it very soon, when he's had a chance to process what's happened, and he knows many of them are frustrated by this, but they've agreed to wait until he's ready to talk. They're so happy to have their children back and they know he played a small part in that and that's buying him some time, although he's sure the gossip and speculation are rife.

He's planning to transfer the rest of the ransom money to Cally as soon as he can, although he's still waiting for her to send him her new account details. He's not telling the police that bit. He's letting them think that what's been paid already was enough. He's told Eldon and Ben he'll repay them too, as this, in the end, had nothing to do with them. They've accepted the offer, and it will mean cleaning out a big chunk of his and Petra's savings and investments, but he knows it's worth it. Cally hasn't gone to the press with her story, and she could have by now, so he's hoping that means she won't. And if she comes back looking for more money in the future, well, he'll deal with it. One day at a time. In the meantime, maybe he can fix his marriage, somehow. He's certainly going to give it his best shot, and he crosses the room now to top up Petra's glass, risking leaning in to peck her on the cheek as he does so. She smells of vanilla, her skin peachy-soft against his lips. She raises her eyebrows at the kiss, but doesn't pull away, glancing at him and then turning back to the conversation she's having with Rosie Duggan.

That'll do, for now, Reynold thinks.

On the other side of the kitchen, leaning against the worktop, are Eldon and Amy Beckford. He thinks they might be OK too. The affair between him and Amy is definitely over, and she and Eldon look almost happy, chatting to Brett and Jon MacDonald-Cook about some new restaurant they all want to visit. He'd heard Amy talking to Clare earlier, the two women recounting to some of the others how they'd both coped with the stress of the abduction by driving aimlessly around the area, frequently at the same time, nodding as their cars passed one another on the road.

'We were both going through pretty much the same thing without even knowing it,' Amy said. 'Both having an affair, both so scared that we were to blame for the kids being taken. Crazy…'

They'd hugged each other then, and even laughed a little, and Reynold had thought about how good it was to hear Amy laugh. He hopes she'll carry on being happy, and that her secret hit-and-run will remain a secret. The Final Eight agreed, before closing down their message group yesterday, that what they all vowed on Tuesday night still stands: nobody will ever talk about what happened in Eldon's living room, even though the two affairs are public knowledge now. Even the police know about them. But the hit-and-run will never be spoken about again, unless the Beckfords one day decide to confess, which seems unlikely. They all know how dreadful this decision is, and what a horrific secret they'll all now carry with them for the rest of their lives, but none of them are exactly saints, are they? They've all done terrible things. They can live with another one.

Reynold hears a yell and looks outside. Luca is racing down the garden, waving a large twig at Noah, who's laughing and swerving in big, dramatic arcs across the lawn to avoid his friend's swipes. Reynold catches his son's eye and raises a hand, and Luca waves the twig at him, then doubles back to chase a rapidly escaping Noah.

Reynold's been so impressed with the way Luca, in particular, has helped the police in the past few days. He had, it seemed, been a little sceptical about their incarceration being part of an elaborate game, and he'd somehow also worked out that the person who came to the door daily with food and other essentials was actually Brandon, the man he loved to follow around the garden at home, talking about birds.

'I didn't know for ages, but then I worked it out,' he told Reynold smugly. 'I didn't say anything to anyone, because I thought I might get a bonus prize. Can you get me one anyway? I'd love a driving game for my PlayStation.'

Reynold had promised him anything he wanted, pulling him close and telling him he was 'so, so proud' of him. But Luca wasn't able to tell the police what they really wanted to know: where the three missing teaching staff have gone. They've spoken to Dominic's parents, and told the families that both are horrified at their son's involvement. And during their continued deep dive into the teachers' backgrounds, they've also discovered, a little too late to be terribly helpful, that Cally changed her name by deed poll some years back – she was born Caroline Jones. Reynold had completely forgotten that Julie, his long-ago ex-fling, had been a Jones; to his shame, he's not sure he ever even *knew* her surname.

'Her brother, Brandon, who called himself Simpson in Littleford, is also really a Jones, of course, so all three of them, Oscar included, have the same last name,' Sadie told the families. 'Which was a surprise. We're thinking now that Oscar may be a relation too, which is probably why he was helping them. Maybe a cousin? Although, of course, Jones is a very common surname, so it could just be a coincidence. We just don't know, and we've been having trouble tracking down next of kin for any of those three. Turns out the names Cally and Oscar gave in their employment records as their next of kin are probably fake – we simply can't find them. They've covered their pasts up very well. We're working on it though. And we'll release all this to the press this coming week too. It might help find them, who knows.'

An entire family, hating me enough to do what they did, Reynold thought when he heard. It explained a lot though, in particular why Oscar had taken it on himself to attack Reynold so viciously. Reynold very much hopes the man was a *distant* relative; if Cally hates him already, she'll hate him even more now, knowing that Oscar died at his hands, albeit accidentally. The four of them were clearly all very close, regardless of family relationships, and finding out that three of them share a name has rattled Reynold. He's thinking about it again now, as he walks towards Olivia Chamberlain, who's chatting animatedly to Tasha Greer.

'Top up, Mrs Chamberlain?' he asks, and she smiles and holds out her glass.

'I'd love one,' she says. 'And call me Olivia, *please*!'

It was Olivia, it has emerged, who put the police on the path that led them to Morcombe Manor; an unusual expression used in one of Cally's messages, which rang a bell for the headteacher. In retrospect, though, it seems doubtful how helpful this actually was. The families would probably still have paid the ransom and, with no police or Reynold turning up at the mansion, the hostage takers would have simply slipped away without any fuss and Oscar would still be alive. Olivia is aware of this and, apparently, has been upset by it, and by the global attention on her little school; she plans to take early retirement and move to Cornwall, she informed them all when she arrived earlier.

The attention from the media has been stressful for all of them over the past few days. The initial jubilant headlines about the safe return of all the vanished children were quickly replaced by those questioning why the police let the hostage takers escape, and why a group of teaching staff would do such a dreadful thing to the children in their care. None of the parents have, as yet, given interviews, other than appearing at a press conference on Friday to thank the public for their support and allow photos of their reunited families. Littleford is still crawling with reporters, but right now nobody's engaging with them; they just want to forget and move on. Erica Lindsay's funeral has been arranged for two weeks' time, and that will be a terribly sad day, but once they get through that, the rebuilding of lives can commence.

We'll be OK, Reynold thinks now, as he refills the final glass, picks up his own and joins Petra and Rosie who are still deep in conversation – something about the girls starting dance classes together next term. As he listens idly, he realises he feels relaxed for the first time in weeks. He's even allowing himself to feel optimistic about the future. Maybe Petra will forgive him; maybe his new game show will get the green light, although he may tweak it a little now, maybe open with the contestants on a plane and not a bus.

Clare Tustain had pulled him aside earlier to admit she'd had her doubts about him when he'd been questioned by the police, and doubts about Monique's involvement too.

'I was wrong, about both of you. I hope your game show is a smash hit. And thank you, Reynold, for what you did,' she said, and squeezed his arm, and he'd felt a warm glow.

He takes another sip of champagne, then sighs as his mobile phone vibrates in his pocket. Half expecting it to be yet another request for a press interview, he pulls the phone out and glances at the screen, and then freezes.

What? What the hell is this?

He reads the message again, and his vision blurs.

'Reynold? Reynold, you've gone white as a ghost. What's wrong?'

Reynold hears Petra's voice, but he can't look at her, can't respond, and then he hears a crash, and realises his champagne glass has slipped from his other hand, and that the room has fallen silent suddenly, heads turning to see where the noise has come from. He carries on staring at the phone as his world begins to fall apart all over again.

Chapter Fifty-Two

CALLY

Day 10: Sunday, 9.10 a.m.

Cally Norman throws the cheap mobile phone into the fire and, her face expressionless, watches as the flames begin to lick around it. It's morning in Honduras, just after breakfast, but she's still jetlagged and has been up for hours, lighting the firepit in the garden of their rented bungalow just after six and sitting there staring into its flickering depths. And now it's done, the final message sent. The last communication she ever intends to have with Reynold Lyon. With her *father*. She's not planning to send him any new bank account details; she's decided she doesn't want any more of his money after all. She doesn't want anything from him now. She just wants to watch from a distance as his life disintegrates, because the pleasure she'll take from that will be worth more than any money.

Cally stands up slowly, raising her arms over her head and stretching her back, then checks that the mobile phone is quickly turning into an unrecognisable lump of molten plastic. She picks up her coffee cup and moves away from the fire, sitting down instead on a little bench on the terrace. It's already warming up, another hot blue-sky day ahead, and she kicks off her flip-flops and tucks her feet up under her, wishing she'd brought her sunglasses outside. Brandon and Dominic are still asleep and no sound comes through the open door of the small two-bedroomed villa. Cally takes a sip of coffee and savours the silence, which is broken only by the unfamiliar trilling of a tropical bird, perched on the branch of a scrubby shrub at the end of the lawn. She's looking forward to learning a bit more about Honduran wildlife, once they have their new business up and running. It'll be a water sports company, Brandon and Dominic fronting it while she, wanting to keep a low profile for the first few years at least, takes a behind-the-scenes role. It was the obvious choice here in the beautiful Bay Islands, which have the second largest barrier reef in world. They took their time, deciding where to run to, but they think they've chosen well; it has no extradition treaty with the UK, most importantly, of course. And the cost of living is low, which means their nearly £2 million will go a very long way, and last a very long time. Especially, Cally thinks, with a pang of grief, as there are only three of them now, and not four.

English isn't widely spoken, which is one small drawback, but they've all been learning Spanish for a while now, even practising it in The Bunker with the children under the guise of language lessons, and they're managing well so far. Getting residency wasn't hard either, and they really think they can be happy here. Happy eventually, anyway. Right now, everything is still a little raw, a little too painful. But they'll get there. They have no choice. There's no going back, after all.

Cally closes her eyes and breathes deeply, letting the warm rays soak into her skin. She'll check the news websites again shortly. She wonders if there'll be anything new today on the hunt for the 'Kidnappers of Class 3B'. She wonders if the police have found the tunnel yet. It was the very best secret that Eleanora shared with her about Morcombe Manor, like a scene from the adventure stories she'd read as a child: an underground tunnel. A tunnel that leaves the corridor just outside the pantry, via *another* hidden door, beautifully concealed behind a false section of wall and then, quite remarkably, wends its way under the house and the kitchen garden, crosses a field and then leads under the boundary wall of the estate, emerging via a metal ladder in another cupboard in a tumbledown cottage at the side of a quiet country road. It's the most extraordinary feat of engineering, and its endpoint is where Brandon was actually heading when the police jumped him in the driveway. He'd intended one final check that the tunnel exit was unobstructed, so the three cellar-dwellers could make their escape and meet him there. The tunnel had been built by Eleanora's great-grandfather, Lord George, clearly a very paranoid man, who had lived his life believing that military big-wigs were after him, and had therefore wanted a way of escaping the manor house grounds without detection, should the worst happen. Not even the servants, when the house was grand enough to *have* a staff, ever knew about George's underground escape route; the existence of the tunnel was a closely guarded secret, passed down in whispers from family member to family member. It was a secret which surely would have died with the passing of Eleanora, had she not shared it with Cally.

The escape had worked beautifully; they already had their false documents and, after donning disguises waiting for them in the cottage, they were on the road within minutes, splitting up and using different modes of public transport to make their way to Birmingham airport, where they boarded separate flights and took circuitous routes to their destination, more than five thousand miles away. Once back together again in the prearranged rental, they dyed and cut their hair, fake-tanned their skin, and inserted coloured contact lenses; they look so different that even they, to their amusement, don't recognise each other sometimes when they bump into each other unexpectedly. Brandon will get his own place soon too, further blurring the public links between the three of them.

So yes, all has gone well, although to say it had all gone to plan isn't strictly true, of course. Because they left one of them behind, dead on the pantry floor in Morcombe Manor. Dead at the hands of Reynold Lyon. The fact that Oscar isn't here with them, starting *his* new life, hurts so much that sometimes Cally isn't sure she can bear it. Brandon and Dominic are grieving too, but it's different for them. For Cally, losing Oscar is like losing part of herself.

It's like that with twins, isn't it? she thinks.

They'd started planning all this together, so long ago. They'd started when their mum had died, haltingly telling her story to her two older children while they sat by her hospital bed, clinging onto her hands until her grip slowly loosened and her fingers grew cold. Her final breath had been a tiny puff that had propelled them into a frightening, lonely new world.

They'd kept their scheming to themselves at first, not bringing Brandon into it until he was a little older; they'd made sure they attended different universities, both changing their appearance as much as possible, taking all the steps required to erase all visible links between them. They had no other relatives that they knew of, but they wanted to ensure that *nobody* who knew the twins in their youth would come forward to tell police they were brother and sister when, inevitably, their photos were published in the newspapers later on.

'Nobody must know we're related,' Cally had stressed to Oscar, and so they had told university friends they had just one younger brother, no mention of a twin. They deliberately lost contact with anyone they'd known as children, and all lived separately in grotty bedsits, paid for by Oscar and Cally working long shifts in bars and restaurants after lectures, Brandon joining in with the money earning as soon as he left school. After uni, the twins had both chosen to do postgraduate teacher training, and then the waiting game began. When one job became available at Littleford Primary School, Cally couldn't believe their luck; when a second job was advertised for the following term, it was as if fate was on their side at last. And so the twins were reunited, working side by side, plotting the downfall of the famous TV star they now saw in the flesh on a regular basis. Neither of them looked anything like him, both very much taking after their mother, which was a blessing; they knew he had absolutely no idea that the two pleasant, friendly teachers he passed the time of day with were his own grown-up children, or that they were nursing a fierce burning hatred.

Cally opens her eyes. The sun is getting hotter now, and she puts her empty coffee cup down on the arm of the bench. She wonders if the police know that she, Oscar and Brandon are siblings yet, and whether Reynold will tell them today, now that *he* knows. Will he call them, and tell them the content of the message he's just received? She wonders too if her 'father' remembers the words Oscar used when he emerged from The Bunker, before he and Brandon decided to rough him up a little.

We just want to have a little word with Daddy here first…

The news bulletins had reported that one of the kidnappers, Oscar Jones, died in a struggle as attempts were made to free the hostages. No further details have been released as to who killed him, or how, and the reason for the kidnap hasn't been revealed either. The papers have been running headlines that assume it was all about the money, an attempt to extort £5 million from a group of wealthy parents. All about greed.

Well, they'll soon know the truth, won't they? Cally thinks and, despite her aching sense of loss, she allows herself a small, satisfied smile. Today, Reynold Lyon knows the full truth too.

And I hope it's agony.

Now, she has one final task. She has one more burner phone and a list of television, radio and newspaper contacts, and she's about to send them all the same devastating document, the one she's spent months writing, with just that one, tragic amendment, added last night. The story was always going to be told, but revenge will be even sweeter now.

Cally uncurls her legs and stands up, watching as the colourful bird on the bush spreads its wings and swoops upwards, hovering over the house for a moment and then soaring even higher, a flash of green and red in the azure sky. Then she walks across to the firepit, staring down at the deformed black blob that was, minutes earlier, a mobile phone, transmitting that final message. The message that told Reynold he didn't father just *one* set of twins in his life, but two, the first a very long time ago. It was a little nugget of information they'd always planned to keep from him until the end, just for fun. But now Cally has had to tell him all by herself, and soon the whole world will know exactly what sort of man Reynold Lyon really is. Everyone is going to learn about Julie, and what he did to her.

They're going to hear about how, many years later, Cally and her two brothers finally got their revenge, via the kidnapping of Class 3B.

They're going to learn that it was Reynold who killed one of the hostage takers.

And they're going to learn that, as he's just discovered in the last message Cally will ever send him, the TV star didn't just kill a random man who'd played a part in stealing his children.

He killed his own son.

Cally raises her eyes to the cloudless sky.

'Love you, Oscar. Always and forever,' she whispers.

Then she turns away from the fire, walks back into the house and opens her laptop.

Acknowledgments

Book eight, and my fifth psychological thriller – how did that happen? This one has my biggest cast of characters to date, and I hope you enjoyed getting to know them as much as I enjoyed creating them. The villages of Littleford and Lower Lockton, and the Cotswold Wilderness Park, are fictional, although these 'may' be loosely based on places I know, as a Gloucestershire resident; I have also played around a little with the geography of the Cotswolds for the purposes of this story. My police force, Cotswolds Police, is imaginary too, but huge thanks go as always to former senior police detective Stuart Gibbon, who gives me such invaluable advice on real-life policing – any irregularities or errors (accidental or deliberate) in this fictional investigation are mine.

Enormous thanks also to friends and former headteachers Catherine and Peter Fenton for steering this childfree writer through some of the mysteries of a rural primary school; I am so grateful to you, Catherine, in particular, for your patience and for your thoughtful, detailed answers to my *very* basic questions!

It has now reached the stage of my writing career where friends are asking for their names to be used in my books, and once again I have been happy to oblige. So, take a bow Clare Tustain, Nicki Mitchinson and your gorgeous dog Stanley, who became Clare and Nick Tustain and their son in this novel. I hope you enjoy your brief foray into being a man, Nicki, and that Stanley enjoys being human for a while. And Clare, I'm so proud of you and the journey you've been on; I hope you like starring in this book (this Clare swears a *lot* less than you do, though).

Clare is one of my producers in my television day job, and others from that world also feature in this book: my gorgeous makeup artist friend, the wonderfully named Krystal Bell, plus camera operator Marc Hackett and another producer, Nikki Lemon. Marc and Nikki, thank you so much for your enthusiastic support, and for accosting complete strangers on sunbeds and at airports while on holiday and forcing copies of my books into their hands. You are now police officers in this one – I appreciate you both so much.

Also big thanks to lovely colleague Shanie Ryan, whose adorable son, River, provided the inspiration for the name of little River Beckford. Mummy has a signed copy for you, River – I hope you enjoy reading the book one day!

And, just for fun, Peanut, the toy dog who lives backstage at work and sometimes appears on air, has been brought to life in this book too, as the dog accompanying the man who finds the missing minibus.

And now to the publishing world, where there are so many people who play such a vital role in every book. My amazing literary agent, Clare Hulton – thank you for everything, always. The incredible, small but MIGHTY team at HarperCollins One More Chapter – you absolutely *rock*. My editor for my first four thrillers, the wonderful Kathryn Cheshire, who gave the idea for this book the go-ahead before heading off on maternity leave (congratulations, again!) and the fabulous Jennie Rothwell, who took over and helped me make this book the very best it could be – thank you so much. My copy editor, Lydia Mason, for your eagle eyes and insightful comments; I promise I will try very hard to stop accidentally giving completely unrelated people the same surname in my books, and hence stop giving you headaches from trying to work out who's who! And my proofreader, Simon Fox, for the final polish – thank you very much too.

Lucy Bennett, who designs my covers – you are so talented, and I love this one just as much as all the others. The HarperCollins teams in the USA, Canada and Australia, and the brilliant team at ILA who handle my other foreign rights; I am now published in eight languages, and it will *never* stop being the most enormous thrill to see those translations and hear from readers around the world who have been able to access my books in their own languages.

Speaking of readers – thank you so much! I have been overwhelmed by your support, and for the lovely messages I get on an almost daily basis. I am so grateful that you read and listen to my books – you make me so happy.

And, of course, the biggest of thank-yous and the hugest of hugs to my husband, JJ, and to my family and friends, for all the untiring support.

You are my biggest cheerleaders and I love you all so much.

The Jackie Kabler Thriller Collection

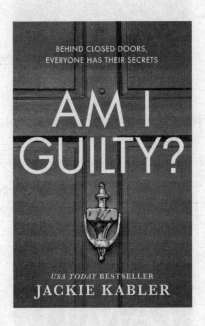

BEHIND CLOSED DOORS,
EVERYONE HAS THEIR SECRETS

AM I
GUILTY?

USA TODAY BESTSELLER
JACKIE KABLER

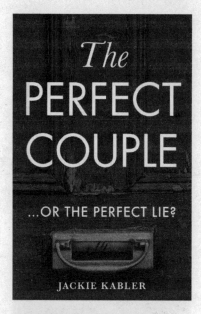

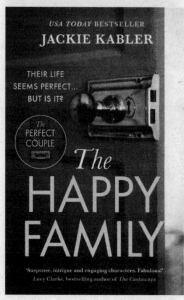

One More Chapter is an award-winning global division of HarperCollins.

Subscribe to our newsletter to get our latest eBook deals and stay up to date with all our new releases!

signup.harpercollins.co.uk/
join/signup-omc

Meet the team at
www.onemorechapter.com

Follow us!

@OneMoreChapter_
@OneMoreChapter
@onemorechapterhc

Do you write unputdownable fiction?
We love to hear from new voices.
Find out how to submit your novel at
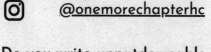
www.onemorechapter.com/submissions